Berkley Prime Crime titles by Cleo Coyle

Coffeehouse Mysteries

ON WHAT GROUNDS
THROUGH THE GRINDER
LATTE TROUBLE
MURDER MOST FROTHY
DECAFFEINATED CORPSE
FRENCH PRESSED
ESPRESSO SHOT
HOLIDAY GRIND
ROAST MORTEM

Haunted Bookshop Mysteries
writing as Alice Kimberly

THE GHOST AND MRS. MCCLURE
THE GHOST AND THE DEAD DEB
THE GHOST AND THE DEAD MAN'S LIBRARY
THE GHOST AND THE FEMME FATALE
THE GHOST AND THE HAUNTED MANSION

Roast Mortem

Roast Mortem

Cleo Coyle

BERKLEY PRIME CRIME, NEW YORK

THE BERKLEY PUBLISHING GROUP
Published by the Penguin Group
Penguin Group (USA) Inc.
375 Hudson Street, New York, New York 10014, USA
Penguin Group (Canada), 90 Eglinton Avenue East, Suite 700, Toronto, Ontario M4P 2Y3, Canada
(a division of Pearson Penguin Canada Inc.)
Penguin Books Ltd., 80 Strand, London WC2R 0RL, England
Penguin Group Ireland, 25 St. Stephen's Green, Dublin 2, Ireland (a division of Penguin Books Ltd.)
Penguin Group (Australia), 250 Camberwell Road, Camberwell, Victoria 3124, Australia
(a division of Pearson Australia Group Pty. Ltd.)
Penguin Books India Pvt. Ltd., 11 Community Centre, Panchsheel Park, New Delhi—110 017, India
Penguin Group (NZ), 67 Apollo Drive, Rosedale, North Shore 0632, New Zealand
(a division of Pearson New Zealand Ltd.)
Penguin Books (South Africa) (Pty.) Ltd., 24 Sturdee Avenue, Rosebank, Johannesburg 2196,
South Africa

Penguin Books Ltd., Registered Offices: 80 Strand, London WC2R 0RL, England

This book is an original publication of The Berkley Publishing Group.

FIRST EDITION: August 2010

Library of Congress Cataloging-in-Publication Data

Coyle, Cleo.
   Roast mortem : a coffeehouse mystery / Cleo Coyle.—1st ed.
      p.   cm.
   ISBN 978-0-425-23459-4
   1. Cosi, Clare (Fictitious character)—Fiction. 2. Arson investigation—Fiction. 3. Coffeehouses—Fiction. 4. New York (N.Y.)—Fiction. I. Title.
   PS3603.O94R63   2010
   813'.6—dc22   2010014028

PRINTED IN THE UNITED STATES OF AMERICA

10 9 8 7 6 5 4 3 2 1

Hero *is not a word one hears in the course of a typical workweek. When it's used at all these days, it generally involves magic wands and superpowers. But if you're a New Yorker who witnessed the events on September 11, 2001, then you know what a hero is. As the FDNY writes in its official description of its symbol, the Maltese Cross: Every firefighter works in courage, a ladder rung away from death, willing to lay down his life for you. This book is dedicated to the firefighters, paramedics, and police officers who lost their lives on 9/11. We will never forget you.*

The Terry Farrell Firefighters Fund was formed in honor of Terry Farrell, a decorated firefighter who perished on September 11, 2001. To find out more, visit the fund's Web site at www.terryfarrellfund.org.

ACKNOWLEDGMENTS

While the characters and events of this book are complete fiction, part of the plotline was initially inspired by a real incident. (More on this in the afterword.) For now, I would like to thank several members of the FDNY who answered my questions (off the record) for background. I would also like to thank author Tom Downey for his excellent insider's look at the New York City Fire Department—*The Last Men Out: Life on the Edge at Rescue 2 Firehouse,* a work I highly recommend to anyone whose interest in New York's Bravest is sparked by this tale. Please note, however, that because this is a light work of amateur sleuth fiction, liberties are sometimes taken with procedure. In the Coffeehouse Mysteries the rules occasionally get bent.

Once again, I thank the excellent Joe the Art of Coffee of New York City (www.JoetheArtofCoffee.com), including its co-owners, Jonathan Rubinstein and his sister Gabrielle Rubinstein. I also owe a big thank-you to their manager and coffee director Amanda Byron, who shared insights into the world behind her espresso machine, including her recommendation of a true barista bible, *Espresso Coffee* by David C. Schomer.

My second java shout-out goes to the amazing Gimme! Coffee (www.GimmeCoffee.com) as well as its founder and CEO, Kenneth Cuddeback, for taking the time to speak with me about our favorite subject. I must also thank Gimme! for its inspiring handling of the Ethiopian Amaro Gayo, a unique and exotic coffee that also happens to be sold by Asnakech Thomas, the only female coffee miller and exporter in all of Ethiopia. Additional caffeinated hugs to Mary Tracy, a dedicated Coffeehouse Mystery reader, who recommended Gimme! to me.

With epic gratitude, I would like to recognize the intrepid

posse of publishing professionals at Berkley Prime Crime who shepherded this book from manuscript to printed page. Enormous thanks especially to executive editor Wendy McCurdy for her great goodwill as well as her ingenuity and insight. Props and snaps must also be given to Katherine Pelz for her hard work and gusto.

As always, I thank my husband, Marc, who is my partner in writing not only this Coffeehouse Mystery series but also our Haunted Bookshop Mystery series. (A better partner a girl couldn't ask for.)

Last but far from least, a heartfelt thank you to our friends and family for their support as well as to our literary agent John Talbot, a premium professional and a darn good joe.

Yours sincerely,
Cleo Coyle

www.CoffeehouseMystery.com
Where coffee and crime are always brewing.

Love is a fire. But whether it is going to warm your hearth or burn down your house, you can never tell.

—Joan Crawford

ROAST MORTEM

PROLOGUE

~~~~~~

COLD here in the alley, but things will get hotter soon . . .

The Arsonist moved deeper into the shadows, orange shopping bag in hand. Back on the busy Queens sidewalk, the day felt bright and balmy. Just a few steps away from humanity, all warmth fled and nearly all light.

Weak shafts of sun barely penetrated the crisscrossing maze of phone wires and fire escapes, coaxial cables and clothing lines. With certain strides, the Arsonist bypassed iron grates and grimy windows, broken crates and dented trash cans. Finally the destination—one particular back door.

Down went the glossy tangerine sack, squatting on the cold concrete. Cloying scents of soy and garlic still haunted its boxy interior, ghosts of last night's Korean takeout. The reinforced bottom and laminated sides made it sturdy enough to carry the necessary items.

Feeling sweaty despite the chill, the Arsonist bent over the shopping bag, grasped two wires from the battery, and fixed them to circuits on the bleach bottle with no bleach inside.

Now it's ready . . .

The Arsonist rose, lifting the bag's handles of nylon rope.

Heavier now, or my imagination?

Nervous fingers tested the shiny brass knob. Unlocked, as promised, the back door swung open on a small utility room. A sink, shelves, supplies neatly stacked.

Male laughter seeped through the brocade curtain. The Arsonist crossed the tight space, teased apart the muffling fabric. An archway framed the caffè's main room. Up front, the elderly owner gabbed with a customer about the rush hour pedestrian parade, mostly about the women.

Stepping back, the Arsonist quickly searched out a spot for the bag. Under the shelf, behind the cleaning products . . .

Perfect.

A stifled sneeze, a few more steps, and the Arsonist was back on the sidewalk. Warmth, pedestrians, unobstructed light. It felt as if nothing had happened—or more like something good had happened.

At 9:25 PM, the caffè would be closed, the old Italian off playing bocce in the park. No one would be in the building. No one would be hurt.

Unless something goes wrong . . .

That prick of a thought had vexed the Arsonist multiple times. This would be the last.

After all, *thought the Arsonist,* it's out of my hands now. The schedule was set for me, and I held up my end. Tonight Caffè Lucia will burn. If people get in the way, it's their own stupid fault.

One

"**Boss,** I hate to leave you like this, but I have *got* to go."

"Go," I told Esther. "We'll be okay . . ."

At least I hoped we would. I was standing behind my espresso machine, facing a line out my door. The usual Village Blend regulars were here along with a swell of caffeine-deprived commuters grabbing a java hit before heading home. Nothing out of the ordinary, really, and in most respects the day felt like any other. Except it wasn't. This was the day the fires began. When the smoke finally cleared, the fatalities would number two, and they would not be accidents. The deaths would turn out to be murders and I, Clare Cosi, would be the one to prove it.

At this particular moment, however, I wasn't thinking about killers or arsonists, lovesick Italian women or blustery FDNY captains, and I certainly wasn't thinking about a bomb. Mostly what I was thinking about was traffic.

Tucker Burton, my lanky, floppy-haired assistant manager, had arrived on time for his shift and was just tying on his Village Blend apron. A part-time actor-playwright and occasional cabaret director, Tuck loved being a barista in the Italian tradition, which (like a good bartender) had as much to do with convivial customer interaction as it did with temperature and pressure.

"Excuse me, Clare," he said, "but where is Gardner again?"

"Trapped in his car," I replied, "on the New Jersey side of the Holland Tunnel."

Tuck pointed to Esther. "And why can't our resident slam poetess stay and work another hour until he shows? I'll bet my Actors' Equity card she's been late to more than a few of her classes."

Esther's wine-dark fingertips went to her Botticelli waist. "Excuse me, Broadway Boy, but I am not simply taking this class. I am a TA and need to be there on time."

"For what? Introduction to Baggy Pants and Bling 101?"

"Urban Rap's Influence on Mainstream America!"

"Who's the professor? Eminem?"

Esther smirked. "The man has a PhD from Brown in linguistics and is heading my program in the semiotics of urban expression."

"Yeah? And I know what seat he holds: the Snoop Dog Chair."

"Okay, you two, enough!" I turned to Tucker. "Let her off the hook."

"But it's not very fair to you, Clare. You've been here since eight AM."

"And I can't leave you here alone, can I? Traffic is traffic and Esther is a teaching assistant now. Her shift's over and she has to go."

"Thank you!" she said.

I caught her eye. "Just call Vicki Glockner, okay? Tell her I'll give her double time until Gardner can get through that tunnel."

"Will do, boss," Esther promised, and she was gone.

Now my focus was back on that customer line. As Tuck

manned the register and the single-cup Clover machine, I turned out the espresso drink orders: one Skinny Lat (latte with skim milk); one Breve Cap (cappuccino with half-and-half); 3 *doppios* (double espressos); one Cortado (a single shot caressed with steamed milk); two Flat Whites (cappuccinos without foam); one Americano (espresso diluted with hot water); two Thunder Thighs (double-tall mocha lattes with whole milk and extra whipped cream); and a Why Bother (decaf espresso).

When the crush finally eased, I turned to the octogenarian sitting on the other side of my counter. Madame Dreyfus Allegro Dubois was looking as stylish as ever in a springy apricot pantsuit, her silver-gray hair coiffed into a supernaturally smooth twist.

"I'm so sorry," I told her, sliding a *crema*-rich espresso across the blueberry marble.

"Why should you be sorry, dear?"

"Because we're going to be *very* late."

"*C'est dommage,*" Madame said, lifting the demitasse to her peach-glossed lips. "But Enzo will understand. Managerial setbacks are an inescapable aspect of New York's mise-en-scène."

"You mean like bureaucratic bribes and obscene levels of sales tax?"

Madame's reply was an amused little shrug. The woman's Gallic aplomb was admirable, I had to admit, but then what was a minor traffic delay to someone who'd seen Nazi tanks roll down the Champs-Élysées?

Given that I was half her age—with duskier skin, Italian hips, and a preference for discount store jeans—Madame and I made an incongruous pair. At our core, however, we weren't so different, which was why our relationship had survived my late-teen pregnancy and hasty marriage to her wayward son, his drug addiction and recovery, our rocky divorce, and my decade spent in New Jersey exile before returning to Manhattan to run her beloved coffeehouse again.

The latter development was the reason I'd agreed to drive

Madame to Queens today. A valuable piece of Village Blend history was waiting for us at Astoria's Caffè Lucia, and we were both determined to reclaim it.

Just then my thigh vibrated—actually the cell phone in my pocket next to my thigh. I answered without checking the screen.

"Gardner?" I asked, hoping my jazz-musician barista was calling to say he'd finally blown through the Holland Tunnel.

"It's Mike."

As in Mike Quinn, my boyfriend (for lack of a better word). He certainly wasn't a *boy* and he was much more than a *friend*, although that's the way we'd started out. The phrase "Mike is my lover" would have been accurate, but it sounded absurdly decadent to the ears of a girl who was raised by a strict Italian grandmother.

"I'm sorry, Mike, I can't talk—"

"Yes, you can, dear." A hand touched my shoulder. I turned to find Madame behind me, tying on a Blend apron. "Take a break, Clare."

"But—"

"No buts. My hands are clean." With a wink, Madame showed me. "And as you know, I've done this a few times before."

I would have argued, but I really did need to take five, so I pulled off my apron and grabbed her seat on the customer side of the bar.

"Are you still driving to Queens?" Mike asked.

"Slight delay but yes," I said. "Why?"

"I've got another meeting on the undercover operation," he said. "It may run late, but I was still hoping to see you tonight."

"Just come by the duplex," I said, happily accepting the freshly pulled double from my employer. "Use your key. You still have it, right?"

"I still have it." He paused. "So how's your head?"

"Better," I lied, and took a reviving sip of the *doppio*.

In fact, I was still recovering from the Quinn family's St. Patrick's Day bash the night before—"*The* annual event," or so I was told by Mike's clan. He was the only cop among a family of firefighters so he didn't always attend (cops had their own gatherings), but this year Mike wanted to introduce me around.

While the beer flowed like Trevi, I was regaled with heroic stories about the "Mighty Quinn," Mike's late father, a fire captain. Then Mike's mother asked me if I'd be willing to contribute some coffeehouse specialties to the FDNY's upcoming Five-Borough Bake Sale, and she promptly introduced me to the head of the coordinating committee—a lovely (and very sharp) woman named Valerie Noonan.

"And have you made your decision yet?" Mike asked.

I could almost hear him smiling over the cellular line, but I couldn't blame him. I'd called the man three times today, obsessing over what would impress his family more: my cinnamon-sugar doughnut muffins; blueberries 'n' cream coffee cake pie; or honey-glazed peach crostata with fresh ginger-infused whipped cream. There were always my pastry case standbys: caramelized banana bread; almond-roca scones; and mini Italian coffeehouse cakes. (Ricotta cheese was my secret ingredient to making those tasty little loaves tender and delicious.) They were absolutely perfect with coffee, and I topped each with a different glaze inspired by the gourmet syrups of my coffeehouse: chocolate-hazelnut; buttery toffee; candied orange-cinnamon; raspberry–white chocolate; and sugar-kissed lemon, the flavor found in my Romano "sweet," an espresso served in a cup with its rim rubbed by a lemon twist, then dipped in granulated cane— the way the old-timers drank it in the Pennsylvania factory town where I'd grown up.

"I think I should make them all," I said.

"All?"

Am I trying too hard? I thought. *Probably.* Then I remembered tomorrow was March 19, the feast day of St. Joseph (patron saint of pastry chefs). Every year my *nonna* would fry up crunchy sweet bow tie cookies and set them out with hot, fresh, doughy zeppolinis in her little Italian grocery. *That's it!*

"I'll make champagne cream puffs!"

"Champagne cream puffs?"

"Zeppole dough baked in the oven and filled with Asti Spumante–based zabaglione!"

"It's a bake sale, sweetheart, not a four-star dessert cart."

Just then our shop bell rang and a young woman with fluffy, crumpet-colored curls walked across our main floor. "Hey, everyone!" Vicki Glockner waved at me.

"Mike, I've got to go. My relief is here."

"Okay," he said, "but that's why I called. It's my turn to relieve you. Don't worry about cooking tonight. I'll get us takeout."

By the time I drove down the Queensboro Bridge ramp, dusk had fully descended, and streetlights were flickering on, their halogen bulbs pouring pools of blue-tinged light into an ocean of deepening darkness. Madame and I had been late getting started. Then a pileup on the bridge left me inching and lurching my way across the mile-long span. Now we were more than an hour behind schedule.

"Do you want to try calling again?" I asked, swinging my old Honda beneath the subway's elevated tracks.

"It's all right, dear," Madame replied. "I left a message apologizing for our tardiness. Let's hope Enzo picks it up."

Enzo was "Lorenzo" Testa, the owner of Caffè Lucia. He'd called Madame that morning, telling her he'd been cleaning out his basement and came across an old Blend roaster and a photo album with pictures of Madame and her late first husband, Antonio Allegro. While Madame was thrilled about the photos, I was itching to get my paws on the old Probat, a small-batch German coffee roaster, circa 1921. Enzo had bought it used from the Blend in the sixties.

"So this man worked for you and Matt's father," I asked.

Madame nodded. "He came to us fresh off the boat from Italy. An eager aspiring artist."

"Marlon Brando–ish? Isn't that how you described him?"

"More Victor Mature, dear. The young female customers absolutely swooned when they saw him in our shop or Washington Square Park—that's where he liked to set up his painter's easel."

"So he was hot stuff?"

"Oh, yes. Smoldering male charisma, liquid bedroom gaze . . . *Oo-la-la* . . ."

Oo-la-la? I suppressed a smile. "Is that why I'm the one driving you to Astoria to meet with him instead of Otto?"

"My. Don't *you* have a suspicious mind?"

"I think we've already established that."

"Well, the answer to your question is *no*. My Otto would have taken me, but he has a very important business dinner lined up this evening so I'm a free agent."

"Uh-huh." The last time Madame characterized herself as a "free agent" she was in East Hampton, enjoying a fling with a septuagenarian expert on Jackson Pollock.

"And, besides," she added. "I've wanted you to meet Enzo for ages. Given your background, I thought it was about time."

"Whatever became of Enzo's art career, anyway?" (Myself an art school dropout, I couldn't help wondering.) "Did his work ever sell?"

"Oh, yes. Enzo's female admirers bought many of his paintings. Restaurants and caffès hired him, too. At one time, you could see his trompe l'oeil frescos in dozens of pizzerias around town. But most of them are gone now. Irreplaceable because Enzo stopped selling his work."

"Why? What happened?"

Madame shrugged. "Life."

"Life?"

"His lover became pregnant," she said, glancing at the fast-passing rows of storefronts. "The same year her father died. Angela asked Enzo to marry her and take over her family's caffè in Queens, save them from financial ruin." Madame shrugged. "Enzo adored her . . ."

I nodded at Enzo's story (half of it, anyway) because I knew just how many hours it took to run a successful business, and just how much love it took to give up on a dream. Suddenly, without having ever met the man, I liked him, very much.

"Caffè Lucia is a pretty name," I said.

"He renamed the place for his daughter. A lively, outspoken child, as I recall; all grown up by now. And sadly, last year, Angela passed away during their annual visit to Italy . . ."

As I turned onto Steinway Street, I noticed Madame glancing at her watch.

"This trip isn't over yet," I warned.

"I know, dear. I'm looking."

Parking is what we were looking for, and I didn't see a single open spot. Eyeing the crowded curbs, I rolled by cell phone shops, clothing stores, and restaurants with Greek, Italian, Cyrillic, and Naskh signage. Finally I turned onto the tree-lined block where Caffè Lucia was located, and Madame began waving frantically (because attempting to find parking in this town could turn even the most urbane cosmopolitan into a raving maniac).

"There! There! A spot on the right! Get it! Get it!"

"Fire hydrant," I said. "I'll circle again—"

"Look! Look! That car is leaving! Go! Go!"

I zoomed into the spot, right behind a mammoth SUV. As I climbed out from behind the wheel, I could almost feel the adrenaline ebbing from my bloodstream. (Not quite as stressful as driving a golf cart through a war zone, but close.) Unfortunately, I wasn't off the battlefield yet. More trouble was heading our way—in size-twelve Air Jordans.

"Hey, lady!" (The greeting was quintessential Jerry Lewis but the accent was definitely foreign.) "You can't park here!"

A scowling man barreled toward us, gesturing wildly.

"Excuse me?" I said.

"You have to move your car!"

Stone black eyes under tight curls the color of Sicilian licorice; a slate gray leisure suit (sans tie) over incongruous white tube socks. I couldn't place the guy's accent, but that was no surprise. While this area used to be primarily Greek and Italian, more recent arrivals included Brazilians, Bosnians, and natives of Egypt, Yemen, and Morocco.

The guy stopped right in front of us, hands outstretched to keep us from moving down the sidewalk. For a moment, I stared at his day-old jaw stubble. *Another blind follower of Hollywood's derelict chic trend? Or simply a misplaced razor?*

"You have to move that junk heap! I can't have it in front of my club!"

Junk heap? I frowned, scanning the area around my admittedly *non*-late-model Honda. I saw no fire hydrant, construction cones, or city signage.

Madame glanced at me, then back at our human road block. "I don't understand, young man. Are you saying this isn't a legal parking spot?"

"I'm saying you can't park here unless you're going to my club."

"Your club?" I said.

He jerked his head at the shadowy doorway behind him. Under a scarlet neon *Red Mirage* banner, a sign announced: *Happy Hour 5–8 PM. Monday thru Thursday.*

Madame's large, expressive eyes—so intensely blue that tricks of light turned them lavender—displayed gentle crow's feet when she smiled. She wasn't smiling now.

"Listen up, friend—" (Her voice dropped to a serious octave.) "Our parking spot is legal. Your attempt at extortion is not."

Given the level of society to which Madame's late second husband (a French importer) had elevated her, not to mention her Fifth Avenue address, even I sometimes failed to remember that the doyenne of polite society was no cream-filled profiterole. The woman had come to this country as a motherless, penniless refugee. Not long after, she'd found herself alone, a widow in her prime, with a boy to raise and a coffeehouse to run—no mean feat in a city that challenged its shop owners with difficult regulations, sky-high overhead, and a demanding (and occasionally dangerous) customer base.

Of course, Club Guy here didn't know any of that. And when Madame actually took a step *closer*, he froze. A moment later, he began muttering in another language, obviously befuddled by a dignified older lady's willingness to go toe-to-toe with him. Finally, he waved his arms and cried, "I'm a businessman, lady! I'm just trying to keep this spot open for taxis to drop off paying customers!"

Score one for Madame. He was on the defensive. But his Air Jordans had yet to budge. That's when I noticed a flash of headlights. The driver in that mammoth SUV had started his engine.

"There," I said, "why don't you keep *that* spot open for your customers!"

Our human road block instantly raced off to reserve the vacated space.

Madame tapped my shoulder. "Shall we, dear?"

"We shall."

Then I looped my arm through hers, and together we started down the sidewalk toward our hard won destination: Caffè Lucia.

Two

LIKE the accident on the bridge, I approached Enzo Testa's caffè without knowing exactly what lay ahead, although I should have had a clue—not because of the smell of accelerants or the sound of cartoonishly loud ticking, but because of the woman who unlocked the door.

In her early forties, Enzo's daughter Lucia seemed almost storklike in her fashionable gangliness. Her nose was long, her squinting eyes the flat color of sour pickles. Her sleek, short, slicked down hair, which should have echoed the same dark hue as her salon-shaped brows, was striated instead with the sort of shades you'd find in a jar of whole-grain Dijon (or the bottles of an uptown colorist).

Hugging her slim figure was a black designer frock with a high hemline and low neckline, the better to show off the heavy gold bling around her neck and chic gladiator sandals (also gilded) with four-inch heels that added dauntingly unnecessary height to her already lengthy legs. All of this seemed a bit much for shift work in a neighborhood coffeehouse, and I assumed she was dressed for a hot dinner date.

"We're closed," she said, her plum-glossed lips forming a bad-luck horseshoe.

"We have an appointment," I began, all business.

"With Enzo, your father." Madame stepped up, her tone of voice much more placating than mine.

"You're *late*."

"And we do apologize," Madame told the woman. "I did call—"

"It's my fault," I cut in. "I'm very sorry, but I run a coffeehouse, too, and I had trouble getting away. Then we got stuck on the bridge. There was an accident . . ."

Lucia propped a narrow hip, more bling clattering on her narrow wrist. "When isn't there?"

"You're right," I said, biting back a less civil response. "But won't you at least tell your father we made it?"

Lucia's reply was to make a show of looking me up and down. I hadn't changed from my Blend shift so my Italian roast hair was still pulled back in a barista-ready (and now supremely messy) ponytail. My makeup had sweated off in traffic, and my simple cotton Henley was tragically wrinkled.

She squinted with open disgust at my scuffed black boots and economically priced jeans, and in case I missed the squint, she threw in a smirk to go with it.

I was about to say something I'd probably regret when a deep voice boomed from inside the caffè: "Lucia, *che cosa*? Is that Blanche?"

Lucia stepped back—with obvious annoyance—and opened the door all the way. A gentleman in shirtsleeves strode across the spotlessly clean mosaic tile floor. Tall, like his daughter, Enzo was not at all gangly. On the contrary, he appeared especially robust for a man in his seventies. The line of his chin and jaw were giving way, like the inevitable decline of a classic old foundation, but his head was still thick with hair, albeit receding in front, the black pepper copiously sprinkled with gray salt.

When the Italian flung out his arms, Madame stepped

into them, and the man's wide smile tightened the skin at his jaw, restoring for a flickering moment the hallmarks of those Victor Mature looks. Instantly I knew that I was glimpsing a vision of Enzo's earlier self, a long-gone ghost of youth. Like a dying ember, the apparition faded, yet the man continued to give off a color of energy I more commonly saw in the budding green of youth (or diehard romantics)—a color Madame had always embraced.

"*Bella!* Blanche, you are ravishing still. *Bella! Bella!*"

The shop was small, half the size of my Village Blend, with a marble counter the shade of mature avocado, a restored tin ceiling, and a pair of hanging fans with wooden paddles lazily stirring the air. Large and small tables of sturdy, polished, marble-topped oak crowded the floor. Behind the bar sat a modern, low-slung espresso machine, typical of a New York café.

Not at all typical, however, was the sweeping mural on the opposite wall, which stretched the length of the building. The artwork itself contained multiple images, each rendered in a different artistic style.

Is it all Enzo's? I was unable to look away as every thoughtful section of the work evoked either meaningful recognition or absolute astonishment.

Enzo stepped back from hugging Madame, one arm continuing to claim her waist. His free hand reached into a pocket for a large pair of steel-framed glasses.

"Glasses? Oh, no!" Madame laughed. "I doubt I'll look as 'ravishing' now!"

"These old eyes just need a little help for a better view of your beauty." He slipped them on and grinned again. "You haven't aged a day."

Madame glanced back at me and mouthed, *Didn't I tell you? Such a charmer!*

"And *you*, Enzo!" she said. "You're as dashing as the day we first met!"

After more cooing and multiple cheek kisses, Madame stepped away. "There, now that all of those whopping lies are out of the way, we can talk honestly, just like old friends should."

She gestured in my direction. "This is my manager, Clare."

Forcing myself to stop gawking at the finely wrought fresco, I smiled. "So nice to meet you, Signore Testa."

He shook my hand, his grip warm, firm, a little stiff (the beginnings of arthritis?). "At last we meet. I've heard so much about you over the years . . ."

Enzo's stare was as penetrating as his offspring's but held no scorn. I sensed only the painter inside him, evaluating my colors and contours, contemplating depths with his eyes.

"*Bellissima*," he whispered, lifting the back of my hand to his lips. As he held my gaze, he spoke softly to Madame: "Such a jewel, Blanche. Eyes like emeralds set afire. Lady Apples for cheeks, lips full and pillowy, yet the girlish face sits upon a ripened figure. So lush!"

Oh, good God.

"She is another Claudia Cardinale!"

"I always thought so," Madame said.

Lucia made a noise behind me. It sounded like a snort. I didn't blame her. A Fellini leading lady I wasn't. Clearly, the prescription on the man's glasses had expired.

"And you have given Blanche a granddaughter as beautiful?"

"I, uh . . ." The man's aura was so hypnotic I had a hard time finding my tongue. Madame really wasn't kidding about this guy's mojo. "Yes, I have a daughter." I finally replied. "Her name is Joy, and she's—"

"A chef! That's right! Blanche told me this morning in our phone call. She is at work in Paris."

"Not a chef yet. Just a line cook. Of course, in my mind she's still twelve years old, inventing cake-mix biscotti in our New Jersey kitchen."

Enzo's eyes smiled. "Where does the time go, eh?" Then he looked away in what appeared to be a pointedly unhappy frown for his daughter.

"Speaking of *time*," Lucia interrupted. "It's Thursday, and your bocce game is starting *very* soon." She glared at us. "They're expecting my father at the park."

Enzo waved his hand. "Luigi and Thomas can wait."

"But what about *Mrs. Quadrelli*." Lucia's gaze stabbed Madame on that one. "You know she'll be disappointed if you're late."

Enzo folded his arms. "Rita Quadrelli will find some other man's ear to talk off until I get there."

"We always close early on Thursday, just so you can play your weekly game. I don't see why you should let their lateness change your plans."

"That's no way to treat guests!" Enzo replied in Italian. "Show some respect—"

A hesitant knock interrupted. "Yo, Lucy! You in there? I'm double-parked."

A wiry, gum-chewing male about ten years Lucia's junior emerged from the shadows of the sidewalk. His cuffed gabardine slacks, two-toned bowling shirt, and black-and-brown saddle shoes looked like a tribute to the *Happy Days* wardrobe department. Platinum pompadour cocked, he moved to join us.

"Sorry, Glenn," Lucia folded her arms. "I was going to meet you outside, but these *people* came."

Madame shot me a glance.

There's an old Italian saying: "With a contented stomach, your heart is forgiving; with an empty stomach, you forgive nothing." Madame had to be thinking the same thing I was: *Lucia Testa is in sore need of a decent meal.*

Glenn didn't answer his girlfriend. Instead, he put on a warm smile and approached her father, extending a sinewy arm. "Mr. T, how you doin' tonight, sir?"

Enzo shook the man's hand and then gestured toward me and Madame. "This is Glenn Duffy, Lucia's boyfriend—"

"*Fiancé*, Papa, Lucia corrected.

"Yes, yes," Enzo said, but under his breath I heard him mutter. "Who ever heard of an engagement with no ring?"

To this, Glenn made no reply—maybe he hadn't heard Enzo's low remark or maybe he was smart enough to pretend he hadn't. Either way, he turned his full attention to greeting us. As he happily chewed his gum, dimples appeared in his lean cheeks. A bleach-blond Elvis.

"I hope I didn't interrupt anything here," Glenn said.

"You are always welcome," Enzo replied. "How about an espresso?"

"Sure." Glenn shrugged, taking out his gum. "Maybe a few cookies, too?" He smiled a little sheepishly, "I really liked those Italian ones—"

Enzo snorted. "They're all Italian."

Lucia tapped her watch. "No coffee tonight, Glenn! We have to *go*."

"Why?" he asked. "What's the hurry?"

"You said it yourself. You're double-parked! You didn't work for a solid year to restore that car of yours just so some jerk can sideswipe you!"

Glenn put the gum back in his mouth. "The New Jersey Custom Car Show's this weekend," he informed us, jerking his thumb toward the door. "I'm showing my '68 Mustang."

Madame and I moved to the caffè's picture window. The restored coup sported a chassis that gleamed redder than strawberries in a newly glazed tart. The convertible top and leather interior were whiter than castor sugar. Racing stripes ran like Christmas ribbons from bumper to fender, a retro bonnet scoop topped the hood, and the chrome grill was so highly polished it could have been cut from a mirror.

Note to self: Do not, under any circumstances, let Lucia Testa see my *car!*

As Madame and I gushed compliments to Glenn, Enzo turned to his daughter and spoke in Italian. "What's one espresso? What would your mama say about your rude behavior?"

"Well, I don't want *you* to be rude to *Mrs. Quadrelli*," Lucia replied in English.

"*Basta*, child! Blanche and Clare do not have all night to sit here with me! We will drink our coffee, and I will be on the bocce court in less than an hour. Okay? Happy?"

"Okay! That's all I wanted to hear!" Lucia finally looked relieved. "I'll see you on Sunday, Papa. C'mon, Glenn. Don't forget my bag." She pointed to a Pullman in the corner as her gilded gladiators clicked toward the front door.

"Sorry, Mr. T," Glenn shrugged again, grabbed the Pullman's handle. "Maybe next time. Nice to meet you, ladies."

A moment later the door shut, and we heard Lucia struggling to throw the old lock. Silence hovered. Finally, Madame cleared her throat.

"Mr. Duffy seems like a nice young man . . ."

Enzo let out a breath. "He's nice enough, *sì*. And he has a good job working on cars. That is how he met my daughter. Car trouble. Mr. Fix-it comes to the rescue, but Lucia, she is pushing too hard . . ."

He shook his head with that exasperated parent shake (one I knew *oh* so well). "For years, she had offers to marry—plenty. None of them were good enough. Now she is finally feeling the hands of life's clock spinning faster. But Glenn is still a boy. Time passes slower for the young. He is in no hurry. That's why there is no ring!"

Madame and I exchanged glances. *What do you say to that?*

"Well," Madame finally replied, "Lucia wasn't wrong about our tardiness. If you have someplace else to go, perhaps we can reschedule—"

"Nonsense! Sit down!"

We did, taking seats at one of the marble-topped caffè tables.

"I have no intention of playing bocce tonight," he said as he slipped behind the counter and prepared our espressos. "I fibbed to my daughter to send her on her way. Meeting up with that *donna pazzesca*, Mrs. Quadrelli? That's Lucia's idea, not mine."

Donna pazzesca? My eyebrows rose. *Crazy woman?* I mouthed to Madame.

"She's trying to fix you up?" Madame asked, obviously curious.

"I take her to dinner a few times. Nothing special. A movie once or twice. Now the woman stalks me at my game every Thursday, and how she talks my ear off! *Madonna mia!*"

Madame sent me an amused look.

"Knows all the gossip in the neighborhood, that one! And she's always complaining—the daughter-in-law, the store clerk, the upstairs neighbor, eh! Enough already! I told her last week, as clear as I could, that my business was taking too much of my time so she should leave me *alone*."

Enzo crossed the room with a small tray, set the espressos in front of us. "I don't want to hear complaining tonight." He lifted his demitasse and made a toast. "Tonight I am visiting with my ravishing Blanche and her Clare . . ."

TWO hours later, Enzo and Madame were reliving their past via an illustrated narrative of old photo albums. They'd continued toasting, too, only now they'd moved on to grappa.

"It's so quiet down here," Madame declared (because we'd also moved on to the caffè's basement). She proffered her drained glass for a refill.

"I'll put on some records," Enzo said. "Good stuff, too. Not that crap kids listen to today."

He rose, a little wobbly, and crossed to an ancient machine with an actual diamond needle. I checked my watch. Being the designated driver, I'd declined the Italian brandy—no big sacrifice since I was still drying out from last night's green beer—and I was beginning to wonder when this visit was going to end.

As Madame and Enzo fox-trotted around stacks of clutter, I felt my jeans vibrating. Assuming a certain NYPD detective was the reason once more, I dug into my pocket with relish. (Watching these two old friends reflame their affections had me aching for my own man.) But it wasn't

Mike on the line. The cell call came from Dante Silva, one of my baristas.

"Hey, boss. Did you get it? The Blend's old roaster?"

In fact, the vintage German Probat was standing right in front of me. It was about the girth of a small washing machine (only taller) and tarnished with age and neglect—nothing I couldn't remedy with a lot of polish and elbow grease. (Seeing Glenn's restoration job was sufficiently inspiring.)

Of course, I wasn't enough of a mechanic to get the thing up and running again, but that was never my intention. I wanted the antique for display purposes.

"How did you know about the Probat?" I asked Dante, raising my voice over Tony Bennett's dulcet crooning. "You didn't have a shift today."

"I called in to check my schedule and Tuck told me about it. And since I was here in Queens anyway, I thought I'd snap a few pics."

"You're in Queens now? Where?"

"Here. On the sidewalk out in front of Caffè Lucia," he said. "Unless I'm at the wrong Caffè Lucia. The lights are off and the place looks closed."

"We're in the basement. I'll be right up to let you in."

Topside, I spotted Dante's form hovering near the picture window, his trendy chin stubble a textural contrast to the clean geometry of his shaved head. A distressed leather jacket covered the self-designed tattoos on his ropy arms, and around his neck hung a digital camera, which he used for artistic studies, capturing the play of light on urban images from dawn till dusk.

He waved at me as I emerged from the back of the shop. The door's old lock was gluey as Marshmallow Fluff, but I managed to throw the bolt. Then my young, talented barista breezed in, full of beer and good cheer.

"Is that knockwurst on your breath?"

"And sauerkraut. But mostly hops, boss. Lots of hops."

"Where were you, anyway?"

Dante grinned, glassy-eyed. "I helped a buddy install his exhibit at the Socrates Sculpture Park; then I hung at the Bohemian Hall Beer Garden with a bunch of aspiring Jasper Johns."

I almost laughed. Not so long ago someone as terminally hip as Dante Silva wouldn't have been caught dead at an outer-borough beer hall. But that was before the Great Recession completely flipped New York's social scene. These days, slick neon bars with velvet ropes were out. Keggers and kielbasa were in.

Then again, every few years I'd notice my collegiate coffeehouse customers celebrating some kind of music, clothing, food, or art form that had become so outdated and square it went all the way around the wheel to come up hip again: bowling, bacon, sliders, cupcakes, hip-hugger jeans, Tom Jones, Neil Diamond . . . I dreaded the day preground coffee in a can made a comeback.

"So where's this roaster?" Dante asked.

"Let me lock this door and I'll show you."

"Whoa, boss," Dante murmured.

He'd stopped in the middle of the room to stare at Enzo's mural. I walked up to join him. "What do you think?"

"Freakin' awesome."

"That's what I thought."

In a phrase, looking at Enzo's mural was like taking a visual journey through the movements of modern art. The narrative began with impressionism, moved to expressionism, fauvism, cubism, Dadaism, surrealism, and abstract expressionism. Layered in among it all were touches of Iberian art, as well as Japonism and primitivism—all of which influenced twentieth-century artistic developments.

Paul Gauguin's fascination with Polynesian culture and Oceanic art was represented, as well as Parisian fascination with African fetish sculptures. The postmodern movement was explored, with its blurring of high and low cultural lines; the vibrant pop images of spoof and irony were also here, along with the (often misunderstood) reframing of common objects by those visual poets who helped us see with new eyes our cans of soup and boxes of Brillo pads.

Enzo's work served it all up in one continuous masterpiece that felt (like Pollack's best) as if it would go on and on, and yet, this fresco was more than a succession of finely wrought forgeries. He'd stirred the ingredients into an epic stew of modernism, simmering iconic ideas to form a wholly new dish, and while some areas of the mural were no more than well-executed servings of familiar flavors, other sections displayed expressions of color, texture, and imagery that I'd never seen before.

"I've got to get some snaps of this."

"Take your time."

I turned on the lights and Dante clicked away, capturing every foot of the expansive wall art. Then I returned to secure the front door. Unfortunately, the lock started giving me real agita. I jiggled the key several times. No luck. I half opened the door and knelt down to see if I could fix the thing.

"You need help, boss?" Dante turned, took a few steps toward me.

That's when the bomb went off.

THREE

FIRST came the sound, a monumental *whoosh* followed by a hissing roar. Then the white-hot concussion rippled through the air, the caffè's front window exploded outward and the blast washed over me.

My eyes were at keyhole level while I worked the stupid, stubborn lock, and the force of the firebomb knocked me right through the doorway.

Sprawled on my back on the debris-strewn sidewalk, I turned my head, stared at the carpet of glass shards. Blood started pumping through my system so fast I could barely recognize voices yelling, a car horn beeping. I was unhurt. Small scratches maybe, a few bruises, a little bleeding—*big deal*—I was okay otherwise, and I focused on throwing off the shock.

Smoke rolled out of the caffè, the noxious fog billowing upward in a succession of black, misshapen balloons. Wheezing and coughing, I got back on my feet and scanned the sidewalk for my beer-filled barista.

"Dante!" I shouted, rushing to the caffè entrance. "Dante!"

Flames were repainting the caffè's walls, spilling their

colors onto its tables. The searing light in the urban night would have been beautiful if it weren't so deadly.

"Dante! *Answer* me!"

Smoke stung my eyes. I gritted my teeth, swiped at my cheeks, peered harder into the chaos.

Up front, the heavy marble espresso-bar counter appeared undamaged. But in the rear of the shop, the embroidered fabric that had masked the utility room was a raging curtain of flame. There was no other way out of the cellar. Madame and Enzo were trapped.

I opened my mouth to call out to them but hesitated. The fire door blocking the stairs was so heavy I doubted they could hear me through it. *But will that door be strong enough to keep them safe with an inferno raging above their heads?*

Shoving away the unthinkable, I refocused on Dante and finally spotted him—or, rather, his big black Diesel boots—sticking out amid a cluster of overturned tables. Their heavy marble tops had formed a kind of fortress, shielding him from the dragon, but I knew the protection was only temporary.

Taking a deep breath (and praying to God it wouldn't be my last), I went in. Choking smoke hovered between floor and ceiling, so I dropped to all fours. The bumpy mosaic tiles bruised my hands and knees; the smoke and heat stung my eyes, but I kept on crawling, half feeling, half guessing my way over to Dante's inert form.

I tried to revive him by shaking his shoulders; then I saw the bloody gouge in his head and realized he'd been knocked unconscious by flying debris.

Oh, God . . .

Was he breathing? I couldn't tell. The fire was sucking the oxygen out of the room, replacing it with toxic gasses, and the heat was unbearable. If we didn't get out of this oven, we were going to be baked alive.

I couldn't lift my barista, so I grabbed both of his wrists under his scorched leather jacket and dragged his limp form across the floor. I don't even know where I found the strength, but I was soon hauling him through the narrow doorway and spilling him out onto the sidewalk.

The cold concrete and fresh night air felt like a sweet arctic kiss, but I couldn't enjoy it. I knelt beside Dante, preparing to give him CPR—and saw that I didn't need to. He was breathing on his own.

Thank you, God!

I noticed the sparse crowd then, gathering a few feet away: younger versions of Lucia Testa wearing micro miniskirts, older males behind them with more of that ubiquitous chin scruff, their expressions ranging from blank confusion to morbid excitement—yet no one lifted a spiked heel or over-priced basketball shoe to help!

They're from the Red Mirage, I realized, but I didn't see the owner among them. *Where is that club jerk now? Mr. Guardian of Happy Hour Parking? Isn't he at least worried about his club burning, too? It's right next door!*

Two minutes, maybe three, had passed since the initial blast. It felt like hours. I fumbled for my cell, impatient with my shaking hands and pressed a nine, a one—screaming sirens interrupted me. Flashing lights, nearly the same hues as the caffè's inferno illuminated the shadowy street. The lead fire truck was massive, like a rolling T. rex. One basso blast from its reverberating horn sent tricked-out vans and giant SUVs scampering for the curb.

Seconds later the cavalry pulled up, men bailing out before their ride even stopped. This was an engine, the kind of truck that carried endless canvas hoses folded in its rear. Behind it was a ladder truck, just as big with men leaping off just as quickly. Three police cars and an ambulance rounded out the first responder parade.

With the FDNY here, there was nothing else to do but turn my focus back on the fire and literally begin to pray.

Behind me I was vaguely aware of boots hitting the ground, doors slamming, men yelling, police pushing back onlookers. I stayed on the hard concrete, cradling Dante's head, my eyes fixed on blazing agony.

"Ma'am, are you all right?" (The first person to ask.)

"My friends are trapped!" I pointed, my focus still on those flames. I was shaking pretty badly now and I couldn't keep the hysteria out of my voice—

"My friends! They're in there! I don't know what to do!"

A steady hand squeezed my shoulder. "Slow down, ma'am. Who's trapped? Talk to me."

I glanced up. Under a bulky fire helmet, intelligent eyes were leveled on mine. Wisps of wiry blond hair peeked out from under that Darth Vader headgear. The man's pale skin was smooth. He was on the young side, late twenties maybe, but his voice and expression were cool and composed, his translucent blue eyes like clear beacons in the middle of this searing, dark fog.

"My friend . . . an elderly lady," I said, feeling steadier in the presence of this man's calm. "She's in the basement with the owner of the shop. They're both trapped. There are no windows down there, and the sidewalk chute was bricked up long ago. The only way into or out of that basement is *on fire*. Do you understand what I'm saying?"

"Yes. Anyone else in the upper floors?"

I blanked for a second. "No. There shouldn't be. Enzo—the building's owner—lives alone on the third floor, but he's in the basement now. He mentioned the second floor was being rented, but the business went under a month ago and the space is still vacant."

The fireman nodded, spoke evenly into a radio attached to his coat. "We have two civilians in the basement. The only means of egress is blocked. Fire is doubtful at this time. Repeat. Fire is doubtful at this time—"

"Doubtful!" I cried. "You *doubt* you can save my friends?"

"Easy, ma'am. We'll get 'em out. Try to calm down."

While we spoke, three firemen reached the building, a length of hose unfurling behind them. Another man raised an odd-looking tool—like the long, skinny offspring of a crowbar and a claw hammer. Wielding the thing as confidently as a Yankee all-star, he tore the caffè's front door off its hinges and swept away the jagged remnants of the plate glass window, deftly avoiding the spilling of razor-sharp shards onto the sidewalk's already twinkling concrete.

"Ma'am?"

My fireman again—the one with the reassuring voice. I turned to find he'd waved over a pair of FDNY paramedics.

Two women in dark blue uniforms lifted Dante out of my arms and onto a stretcher. I rose and followed them to the back of their ambulance, watched them take vital signs, cover his mouth with an oxygen mask.

"Will he be okay?"

"He's coming around," one replied. "His vitals are strong, but he'll need a CAT scan . . ."

A paramedic tried to take my pulse, but I waved him off. Knowing Dante was in good hands, I returned to the sidewalk to see if there was anything else I could do for Madame and Enzo.

What else can I tell these people to help them?

Another stocky, older fireman approached me. Like the rest, he wore thick, fire-resistant pants under a long, charcoal-colored duster with horizontal stripes of neon yellow, "a turnout coat," that's what the firefighters in Mike's family had called it. *Bunker gear* was the more common term because they once literally stored it beside their bunks.

"We have a three-story attached commercial building," the stocky man recited into a radio, "the fire began on the first floor and is going vertical—"

"Yeah and fast," my fireman added. He must have seen the shock and alarm on my face because he put a hand on my shoulder once more. "Take it easy, okay? The fire is moving up and away from your friends. Right, Lieutenant?"

The lieutenant threw a deadpan glance at my guy, and I finally saw his face full on. The shape, beneath that large helmet, was more oval than square—as if it had once been chiseled quite sharply, but time had added weight, rounding off the angled landscape. His skin texture was craggy, and he had one of those big, red drinker's noses, the kind I'd seen among the crowd in my late father's bookie days. But his celery green eyes were not cloudy or dulled like my dad's old gambling customers. They were as sharp as his voice.

"Two victims are out, two more are trapped behind a fire door to the basement. The fire is confined to the single structure, and there's no shared cockloft with the adjacent building . . ."

After completing his radio report, the lieutenant turned to my fireman. "What the *hell* were those people doing in that basement past Enzo's Thursday night closing time?"

"You know Enzo?" I asked, surprised.

The lieutenant ignored my question. "Is this lady a victim?"

"Yeah, Loo. She got herself and another person out. Shaved-headed guy twice her size. That makes her civilian of the week, right?"

The lieutenant barely glanced my way. "Where's her rescue?"

"He's with the paramedics!" I shouted at the man, barely able to stay sane. "What about my friends? They're trapped in there!"

"We know," my fireman assured me. He was now strapping a bulky oxygen tank onto his back. "But they're safe behind the fire door for the moment. Right now we've got guys on the fire escape. Look—" He pointed. "And they're on the roof doing their thing, too. Right, Loo?"

But the lieutenant was already heading for the caffè's front doorway. I noticed the name *Crowley* printed in yellow across the bottom backside of his turnout coat.

"Okay, get ready with that hose," Lieutenant Crowley bellowed at the nozzle team.

A loud crash sounded over our heads. A spectator cried out as black smoke began to pour off the top of the building's roof.

I pointed. "Is that supposed to happen?"

"They're venting the fire," my guy replied. "That's how we begin to control it, release the heat and smoke, direct it up and out—and away from your friends."

Away from Madame and Enzo, I silently repeated, clinging to that thought.

"Okay," Crowley yelled. "Let's knock this monster down!"

The flat hose swelled like an overstuffed sausage. The men clutching the nozzle released the explosive water stream. Gripping the engorged hose, they moved closer to the blazing shop while more firemen scurried up ladders braced against the walls of the second and third floor. The sound of splintering glass filled the night as they broke windows and climbed through.

"Go, boys!" Crowley cried.

The men gripping the hose advanced through the doorway and vanished into the haze. As the first blast of cold water hit the broiling blaze, a sustained hiss filled the air, and the thick smoke pouring out of the caffè's broken windows quickly faded from black to gray.

The firefighters moved even deeper, directing the stream of water toward the blazing ceiling as they advanced. Smoke billowed, obscuring everything for a minute. Just as the veil lifted, a hanging fan came crashing down, narrowly missing one of them. The firefighters didn't appear to care—they just kept pressing farther into the conflagration.

"What's happening?" I asked my fireman.

"The nozzle team is using the water to cool the combustible gasses at ceiling level. They're cutting a path through the fire to the basement door, then Dino Elfante and Ronny Shaw—that's the man you saw pull the front door off its hinges—those two will get that basement door down and bring your friends out."

But a moment later, one of those firefighter's emerged from the oily smoke with his arms wrapped around the other. Paramedics rushed to the pair.

"Put him in a Stokes basket and strap him down tight! It might be snapneck," Lieutenant Crowley barked to the EMT team. Then he signaled my fireman. "Ronny got clobbered by a chunk of ceiling. We need someone else to go in and make the grab."

"I'm on it," my fireman said. Grinning as if he lived for this, he lowered his Plexiglas face shield.

"Not alone, James—" Crowley warned.

James, I repeated to myself, finally knowing my guy's name.

"Remember: two in, two out," Crowley added then spoke into his radio. "Bigsby, you reading me? You're up."

James ran toward the burning building and another fireman, with *Brewer* stenciled across the back of his coat, paired up with him. Bigsby Brewer was a real colossus, more than a full head taller than my guy, who wasn't exactly a midget. Side by side, the two vanished into the smoke.

As I watched them go, I felt my fragile steadiness going with it. James, like every other firefighter here, seemed almost gleeful about risking his life. But after his kindness toward me I couldn't help feeling I had a third friend in harm's way.

I kept my eyes focused on the building's front door, waiting, hoping, *praying* that those men would emerge with Madame and Enzo safe, ready for more grappa, and foxtrotting.

It was about then I sensed a large presence just behind me. In a deep, vaguely familiar voice, the hovering form spoke—

"Let's have an update, Lieutenant."

"Fire is contained to the single building," Crowley replied. "The adjacent structure has been evacuated as a precaution, but there's no sign of any spread. Right now, the nozzle team's pushing back . . ."

"Anyone hurt?" asked the male voice.

"The lady here says two civilians are trapped in the basement. Ronny Shaw's skull got harassed by a nasty chunk of ceiling and is on his way to the docs. Jim and Bigsie are doin' the snatch and grab on the vics. They should be out any second now."

"It's not like you to miss a rescue, Oat."

Oat Crowley shrugged. "I'm going to Lake George in June, Cap. No time to attend Medal Day."

The man behind me chuckled and I finally glanced over my shoulder. One look at his face confirmed what I'd suspected: the captain and I had met before. In the reflected shadows of the nighttime inferno, his fair complexion had an almost burnt orange cast. Legs braced, one balled hand propped on a hip, Michael Quinn stood like a municipal tower, a full head taller than his lieutenant and most of the men under his command. His substantial chin sported a prominent cleft, and above his upper lip he wore a trimmed handlebar right out of nineteenth-century New York (or a *Lonesome Dove* casting call).

Needless to say, this man was not *my* Mike Quinn. This fire-haired giant was Captain Michael Joseph Quinn of the FDNY—Mike's first cousin. Both were born in the same month and year, and both shared their paternal grandfather's first name, but that's where the solidarity ended.

The captain caught my eye. "You went to an awful lot of trouble to get my attention again, Clare, darlin'. You could have just rung me up for a nice romantic dinner. No need for this elaborate production."

When I didn't immediately reply to the man's stunningly out-of-place innuendo, his hint of a smile blew up into a grin wide enough for his gold tooth to wink at me in the firelight.

"So are you here all alone, then? Where's my cousin Mikey? Spending too much time shaking down parking violators, is he?"

I just kept staring. The last time I saw this character was aboard a fire-rescue boat that had pulled me out of New York Harbor. Even then, surrounded by the men of the marine squad, he was throwing thinly veiled insults at his cop cousin.

The captain grinned wider at my silence, then used a thumb and forefinger to smooth his mustache, more vivid than his flame-colored roof. "Well, the Quinn family black sheep never did know how to treat a lady."

Before my fried brain could even *begin* to formulate a response to that charge, the radio clipped to the man's coat came to life. As if in stereo, the transmission also echoed through Lieutenant Crowley's receiver.

"This is Brewer," the voice said.

"Go ahead, Bigs," Crowley answered.

"Ten forty-five. Repeat. Ten forty-five. Both victims—"

Victims? "What's a ten forty-five?" I shouted. "What's he saying?"

"Take it easy, honey," the captain replied, his monotone maddeningly casual. "They're bringing your friends out right now. Alive and well."

Donning his white helmet, the captain pushed toward the smoldering building. A whoop went up from the firefighters around me as James emerged from the smoking caffè, cradling Madame.

Pristine peach pantsuit blackened, silver hair a sooty tangle, cheeks and chin smudged with grime, my former mother-in-law looked like an elegant, antique doll that some careless child had badly mistreated. One thin arm held on to her rescuer's strong neck, while the other hugged the old photo album from Enzo's basement.

The enormous firefighter named Bigsby appeared next, toting Enzo Testa. As he gently laid the elderly man out on a stretcher, I could see Enzo was in bad shape—conscious but gasping, a long string of dark phlegm under his nose.

In no time, Madame was ringed by a concerned circle of bunker coats. I had to push through the wall of muscle just to get to her.

"Clare!" Tears were in her eyes and mine, too. I moved to hug her, but a female paramedic jumped in first, trying to place an oxygen mask over her mouth. Madame pushed it away.

"Are you insane?" I told her. With her cheeks flushed, I wasn't sure what had affected her more—the ordeal of the fire or all the grappa she'd drunk. "You need oxygen after the smoke you've inhaled!"

"Yes, but"—the octogenarian coughed once then gestured to the army of strapping young firemen surrounding her—"I'd really prefer mouth to mouth."

Four

⬖ ⬖ ⬖ ⬖ ⬖ ⬖ ⬖ ⬖ ⬖ ⬖ ⬖ ⬖ ⬖ ⬖ ⬖ ⬖ ⬖ ⬖ ⬖

THE puddle-strewn pavement gleamed like black onyx. The street was so drenched in places you'd think a cleansing storm had passed. But there was no rain-swept freshness in the evening's air, just a miasma of smoke, creosote, and scorched wood.

Next door, the Red Mirage was vacated and closed. But the continued glow of its neon sign, along with the flashing lights of the emergency vehicles, made the scattered puddles flicker with an almost demonic hue.

Around me, the men of Engine Company 335 were going through the painstaking process of draining and rewrapping the infinite hose. A rookie fireman swept glass off the sidewalk. Others tossed metal tools back into the truck. I'd watched them use those same tools to tear apart the caffè's walls and ceiling.

I would have gone with Madame to Elmhurst Hospital, but she asked me to remain behind and retrieve her handbag from the basement. Because the keys to my car, my apartment, and every single lock in the Village Blend were in my own bag (also in the basement) I decided she was right and I'd better stick around.

Shivering in the cold March night, I peered once more into Enzo's place. The flames were gone now, but his beautiful interior looked like a rest stop on the road to hell. Water had replaced the element of fire, and it was just as damaging.

Though the hydrants were turned off, torrents of gray sludge still poured from the building's upper levels, staining walls and soiling the colorfully tiled floor. The highly polished wooden tables looked like charred kindling. Broken lumber and bent panels of tin dangled from the ceiling like ragged fangs inside the mouth of a dead monster.

Flashlight beams from the fire marshals played across the blackened walls and sodden plaster. Though the stainless steel espresso machine appeared intact behind the thick marble counter, Enzo's breathtaking mural had been burned beyond recognition.

A building could always be restored, new furniture purchased, but that astonishing fresco, completed over decades, could never be replaced. As I surveyed the devastation, tears filled my eyes for the man's lost art.

Something inside the shop crashed to the floor and I started. A moment later, I felt a large body step up behind me and place a blanket over my shoulders.

"You're shiverin', dove."

Captain Michael Quinn turned me around to face him. Hot tears had slipped down my chilled cheeks. I swiped at them.

"I heard you made a save tonight," he said. "The men told me you pulled out a kid twice your size."

"Dante is one of my baristas. I wasn't about to let him burn alive."

"But you could have burned alive tryin' to save him."

"Anyone would have done what I did."

"Oh, sure, any firefighter with a cast-iron pair." He gave me a little smile.

For the first time, I noticed an old burn scar, just under the man's left ear, a patch of flesh blanched pinkish white. His bulky white helmet was tucked under one arm, baring his sweat-slickened hair. The change in light had altered the shade, I realized. At the height of the blaze, it looked fiery orange. Now it seemed more subdued, a deep, muted burgundy, like brandy-soaked cherries.

The man's bunker coat was open and flapped a bit in a sudden March gust. Ignoring his own fluttering clothing, he tucked the blanket more tightly around me.

"I'm surprised you're still here," he said. "Unless you lingered for a reason? To catch a ride home with me, maybe?"

Is he kidding? Laugh lines creased the edges of his smoke-gray eyes, but I wasn't entirely sure he was joking.

"I can't go anywhere, not at the moment. My car keys are in my handbag in the basement, so I'm waiting on a couple of your guys. They volunteered to search for it . . ."

"Then take a load off while you're waiting. After what you went through, you shouldn't be on your feet."

My mouth was dry, my skin was clammy, and my legs were beginning to feel like underchilled aspic. "I'm fine."

"You're *fine*? Right. Sure you are." The captain shook his head. "Come *on* . . ."

His big hand went to my lower back. Too weak to fight the current, I flowed along, letting him propel me toward the back of one of the fire trucks.

He plunked down his helmet on the truck's wide running board, unwrapped another blanket, and placed it on the cold metal. With two heavy hands, he pressed my shoulders until I was sitting on it. Then he grabbed a paper cup and decanted something from a canary yellow barrel strapped to the vehicle's side.

"Drink."

I took the cup, sniffed. It smelled citrusy. *Gatorade*, I realized, and took a sip, followed by a big swallow.

Oh my God . . .

I hadn't realized I was so thirsty, but now my body seemed

to be absorbing the liquid's electrolytes before they even hit my stomach. As I drained the first cup, I realized the captain was already offering me a second. I drained that, too.

"Good girl."

I threw him a look.

"What?"

"I'm not a girl."

"What should I be sayin', then? *Good boy?*" He folded his arms. "Too late, darlin'. I've already glimpsed what's under that blanket and unless I need eye surgery"—he winked— "it's all female."

I exhaled. Dealing with this guy was going to be a challenge, but I shouldn't have been surprised, given our previous meeting . . .

Last December, a not-so-nice person helped me off the Staten Island Ferry (in the middle of New York Bay). Amid my shivering rants to the FDNY marine squad who rescued me was a request that someone contact Mike Quinn. How could I know there was more than one?

The men called the Quinn they knew, this larger-than-life creature of the FDNY. From his blustery entrance on that rescue boat and the flirtation that followed, I got the impression that battling blazes was only one of the captain's burning interests. As usual, the man's suggestive stare was making me feel less than fully dressed (even with this first-responder blanket swathed around me like I'd just taken a seat at his personal powwow).

"Listen, Chief, considering your men just saved my friends' lives, I'm going to cut you some slack—"

"Well, isn't that big of you."

"But I'm not in the mood for games. So would you please drop the retro macho condescension and just call me *Clare?*"

"Whatever you say . . . *darlin'*."

I exhaled. "At least you're true to form."

"How's that?"

"Your attitude comes from the same era as you preferred style of facial hair."

The captain proudly smoothed his trimmed handlebar. "Can't resist the old soot filter, can you?"

"Actually, I can. On the other hand, I wouldn't mind another one of these." I held out my empty cup.

"Women," he grunted, shaking his head. But he refilled it. Then he grabbed a plastic water bottle, chugged half the contents, and gazed at the fire-ravaged coffee shop.

"Hell of a blaze," he said. "Wonder what set it off?"

"What did the fire marshals say?"

"Nothing. They keep their theories to themselves, those boys."

"What do you think happened?"

"When I first rolled up to the scene, I assumed Enzo's espresso machine was the cause—"

"You know Lorenzo Testa?"

"I know every shop owner in this neighborhood. Old Enzo's got the best coffee around. A lot of my men come here for it and his pastries, too."

"What made you think the espresso machine was the cause?"

"The steam pressure, the gas lines, any number of things could go wrong with a mechanism like that. It seemed the most likely culprit for the intensity of the blaze—"

"But that's not what happened. The start of the fire was farther back in the store, near the utility room—"

"That's right, honey. You didn't let me finish. When I saw the actual burn pattern, it was clear the espresso machine wasn't the cause. The mechanism was intact. And the gas line didn't break, even after the fire started—"

"That's because the bomb went off in the back of the store—"

"Whoa there." The captain raised a calloused hand. "Don't be usin' a word like *bomb* so freely."

"I was an eyewitness. I know what I saw."

"And what did you hear then? A loud explosion?"

"No . . ." That made me pause. "There wasn't a loud

noise. No boom; it was more like the sound I hear when the pilot light on my stove is out and I relight it after running the gas."

"So you think the cause was a gas leak?"

"I think it was *arson*, some kind of device rigged to go off at a certain time—"

"Stop. You're back to describing a bomb."

I crossed my arms and met his eyes. "It *was* a bomb. The only questions those fire marshals should be asking now is who set it off and why."

The captain held my eyes a long moment but this time it wasn't a leer. The man was staring into me like a mentalist studying an audience volunteer.

"Oh, no," he finally said, as if he'd just rifled every thought in my brain pan. "No, no, *no* you don't."

"No I don't *what*?"

The captain bent down, moved his face two inches from mine. "I heard about your games, dove—"

"Games?"

"You like to play detective. A bad habit you no doubt picked up from my black sheep cousin. But listen to me now: You're not a fire marshal, and you're not trained to recognize the cause of a fire—"

"But—"

"The real marshals are inside that building." He extended his long arm for a sustained point. "They're taking pictures, evaluating burn patterns, looking for traces of chemical accelerants or electrical damage. They're going to determine how and where the blaze started, and document how my smoke-eaters knocked the monster down, too. They don't need help from an *amateur*."

I met the man's stare. "I may be an amateur, but I'm also an *eyewitness*."

The captain straightened up, moved his hands to his hips. "Now why would you want to worry that lovely head of yours about this, anyway? The marshals will make the final determination on what caused the fire, and they'll do it based on proven investigative techniques, not some womanly hunch."

"I never said anything about a hunch, womanly or otherwise. And this head was there, in that café, when the fire started, remember? I only told you what I saw and what I heard."

"What you saw and heard is all you should be telling anyone—without speculation."

"Why?"

"Why . . ." The captain rubbed his eyes, loudly exhaled. Finally, he sat down beside me. When he spoke again, his tone was no longer combative. "Do you know what a fire triangle is, Clare?"

"No."

"Fire is a chemical reaction that occurs when three elements are present: oxygen for the fire to breathe, fuel for it to consume, and heat to ignite the other two in a chain reaction." He ticked off the three points on his fingers. "You followin' me?"

"Three elements. Combustibility."

"Any time these elements are combined, the fire can occur—whether intentionally or accidentally."

"But I witnessed more than the fire itself. I heard a *whoosh,* saw the initial blast. It must have been arson."

"You're so sure, eh? Well, factor this in, darlin'. Of the hundreds of fires I put out last year, there were two that were practically identical. Both started in the kitchen trash can of a row house on a quiet street. In the first fire, a woman lit the end of a cigarette and intentionally tossed it into the can. She was broke, couldn't make the mortgage payment, and needed an insurance pay out to stay afloat."

He paused, met my eyes. "That's arson."

"Yes, obviously."

"In the second fire a man emptied a cigarette ashtray into a closed metal can, not realizing there were still burning ashes. The ashes ignited tissues stuffed into the can.

The fire smoldered, contained and unnoticed, until it reached critical mass and burst out of the metal can, immediately setting the walls and ceiling ablaze. And because an unchallenged fire doubles in size every thirty seconds, the fire spread throughout the house in minutes, destroying everything. You see?"

"No. I'm sorry but you lost me. What's your point?"

"The first fire was arson—obviously, as you say, once the facts were discovered. The second was accidental, but not so obvious. If a witness had been present to hear and see that second fire break loose, he might have sworn that exploding trash can was a bomb, too."

I thought about that. "Okay. I understand. I do. And nothing against your fire triangle, but have you ever heard of the blink theory of trusting your first impressions? As a detective, Mike believes—"

"*Mike?*"

"Yes," I said. "Mike. Your cousin. He believes—"

"To *hell* with what my cousin believes! He's not a fire investigator and neither are you. Stick to the facts, Clare, not what anyone *believes*."

I sat very still for a moment, letting the man's anger dissipate like those black balloons of smoke released by the burning caffè. Then calmly and quietly I asked—

"Why do you care what I think, anyway?"

"Because Enzo's a good man, and I won't have him accused of arson. He's the last person who'd put his own life at risk, or anyone else's, for some lousy insurance money."

"I'm sure Enzo is a good man. My friend Madame has known him for years, decades—"

"But if you start shouting *bomb*, the press may get wind of it, and the marshals will be forced to start treating Enzo as a suspect before they even finish with the forensics."

"Wait a second! I was with Enzo in that basement minutes before the fire started. He could have found an excuse to get out, but he didn't. He was trapped down there, in harm's way. Surely that exonerates him."

"It does not. He may have played a part in the event to throw off suspicion."

"So now you're saying Enzo could be guilty?"

"No! I am not saying that. Listen, Clare, you and I know Enzo's a stand-up guy. To these marshals, Mr. Testa is just another victim, but if this fire is found suspicious and he's the beneficiary of an insurance payout, he'll be their number one suspect. Then they'll tear his life apart looking for evidence of guilt."

I lowered my voice to a whisper. "But what if someone else had a motive to burn Enzo's shop?"

The captain studied me again. He bent his head closer. "Like who? And why?"

Before I could reply, a voice called out: "Ma'am? Are you still here? Ma'am?"

It was my fireman, the one who'd been so kind to me earlier, the one who'd risked his life to rescue Madame and Enzo. He was wandering along the sidewalk, searching for me.

"I'm here, James!" I called. "In back of the fire truck!"

With perceptible reluctance, the captain put distance between his head and mine. A moment later, my young hero firefighter appeared wearing a grin and two handbags.

FIVE

ҩ҂ҩ҂ҩ҂ҩ҂ҩ҂ҩ҂ҩ҂ҩ҂ҩ҂ҩ҂ҩ҂ҩ҂ҩ

"Yo, ma'am, check it out!" James made a show of pointing to the women's purses dangling off his broad shoulder. "Can you ID these so I can turn them over to you?"

"Of course. That one's mine and the other is my employers. They're the bags I asked you to look for."

Bigsby Brewer strolled up behind James. His shoulders were so wide, I couldn't imagine the guy going through an average doorway without tilting to one side. Massive muscles notwithstanding, Bigsby was far from intimidating. His manner was so happy-go-lucky, his spirit so energetic, he came off about as threatening as an excited puppy.

"So, how do I look, Bigs?" James said, showing off the women's handbags to his friend. "Too last season?"

Shaking his head, Bigsby tugged the bags off James's arm and thrust them into my hands. They reeked of smoke.

"You better take these back, ma'am." Bigs jerked his thumb in James's direction. "Noonan is too dumb to see they clash with his bunker gear!"

The two men laughed.

"Sorry it took so long," James said. "The fire marshals

had to inspect them before we could take them out. They wanted to make sure we weren't removing evidence."

"It's okay. I'm just grateful you located them." I regarded James again. "Did I hear your friend right? Is your last name Noonan?"

James nodded.

"You aren't by any chance related to Valerie Noonan, the banquet manager at Union Square West Hotel?"

James opened his mouth to answer but Bigsby interrupted: "Oh, no, ma'am, you've got that wrong."

"I do?"

"James isn't *related* to Val. It's much worse than that—" As if someone had died, Bigsby took off his helmet and placed it over his heart. "He's *married* to her."

With one sharp, hard thrust, James shot his elbow into his partner's gut. It was a real blow, and Bigs doubled over, gasping and cussing.

"So, you know Val?" James said, ignoring Bigsby's groans while calmly extending his hand. "I'm her husband. Very nice to meet you—"

I stared in horror for a second until Bigs came up again, red-faced but laughing. Apparently, this was business as usual between the two men because James's affecting smile never wavered—as if he hadn't just sucker punched his best buddy right in front of me.

"I, uh . . . I'm Clare Cosi, manager of the Village Blend, and I love Val. I mean, I just met her last night, at the Quinn's St. Patrick's Day party—"

I paused to glance at the captain, wondering why he hadn't shown at the biggest family gathering of the year. He looked away.

"Anyway," I continued, "Val and I are both in the same general trade, so we shared a nice conversation. My boyfriend's mother asked me to help with the Five-Borough Bake Sale, so we had even more to talk over. I understand Val's on the coordinating committee?"

At the mention of the bake sale, the corners of James's

mouth turned down. "If you ask me, she *is* the coordinating committee. Or at least it seems that way from all the hours she's been working on it."

Woops. Obviously a touchy subject. "Well, the sale is for a good cause, right? Scholarships for children of fallen firefighters—and it will all be over in a week or so."

"Just take my wife in stride," James said. "She can turn into a little dictator when it comes to organizing public events."

Bigsby, still nursing his bruised torso, risked a snicker. "Not just public events, brother. From what I've seen, Val is no slouch at ordering you around, either."

Still sitting next to me, the captain finally made a comment: "Women."

It was the second time tonight he'd grunted the single word. I turned on the man. "What is that supposed to mean exactly?"

"You don't know?" he said.

"If I knew, why would I ask?"

The captain glanced at Bigsby. "You want to tell her?"

"Hell no!"

James winked at me. "Don't let them jerk your chain, Ms. Cosi. Two confirmed bachelors—what do they know about women, anyway?"

Bigsby snorted. "We know enough not to hitch our horse to one post, right, Captain?"

"Listen, bro," James replied, "I saw your last one-night stand. She was about as dumb as a post."

"And that would be a problem because . . . ?"

"You guys are terrible," I said.

"They are, aren't they?" James gave an exaggerated nod. "They're really a sad pair. They *wish* they had a beautiful woman in their lives, telling them what she wants."

"On the contrary," the captain replied. "Beautiful women tell me what they want all the time." He threw a suggestive gaze my way. "Even if it's not in so many words . . ."

"Ho!" Bigs nudged James. "Looks like the cap'n's workin' here."

James's brow furrowed. "Working on what?"

"You've been married too long, brother. Four's a crowd." Pulling on James's collar, Bigs headed back to the sidewalk.

"See you at the bake sale, Ms. Cosi," James called as Bigsby dragged him away.

I cleared my throat. Bigsby's joking implication might not have bothered me if the captain's proximity hadn't changed. He was still sitting next to me on the running board, but he'd gradually eased his body closer to mine, so close I could feel the heat from his thigh against my leg.

"You know, darlin', my tour's nearly over." His voice had gone sweeter than maple tree sap. "How 'bout I take you home, make sure you get there safe . . ."

And there's the pitch. "Thanks, Captain, but you know very well I have someone to do that for me. Someone I care for very much."

The captain's little smile twisted into a smirk. "So it's official, then? You're still wasting your time with Mikey—"

"*Mike* is a good guy."

Captain Quinn looked at me as if I'd just declared Adolf Hitler a great humanitarian.

"What's the beef between you two, anyway?"

He folded his arms. "Better you find out from my cousin."

"I asked Mike twice. Both times his answers were so vague I didn't bother asking a third."

"Then do yourself a favor and take the hint."

Touchy, touchy. I studied the man, wondering if I could needle it out of him. "You know what? . . . I'm betting the reason neither of you will answer that question is because neither of you can even remember how the whole thing started. No doubt it was some childish, testosterone-fueled competition back on your parochial school playground."

The captain glared.

"Why two supposedly intelligent men can't work out their differences is beyond me."

"Yeah, honey, it is beyond you. So take my advice and keep it that way."

"Men," I muttered, getting a clue what the captain's single-word epithet was all about. "Well, Michael, it's been a barrel of fun, but now that I have our fire-roasted handbags back, I better get going."

I began to rise, but the captain took hold of my upper arm, pulled me back down. "You're not going anywhere."

"I told you already, I'm not interested—"

"You're not going anywhere until you *give your statement.*"

"My statement?"

"Wait here," the captain said. "I'll be back with one of the marshals."

True to his word, the captain returned with one of the FDNY's fire marshals, clipboard in hand. By the newcomer's size, I judged him to be a former firefighter, but there was evidence of more than that here. His nose was mashed a bit, his ears crooked. One was larger than the other, the lobe puffy and swollen into a permanent cauliflower—clearly he'd done some serious boxing. His mind didn't appear to be addled from it, however, because there was astuteness in his gaze; and in the few seconds before he spoke, I could see he was looking me over with a practiced eye, absorbing, evaluating, just like my Mike. Before he even asked a question, this FDNY detective was beginning his interview.

"Are you Miss Cody?"

"*Cosi,*" I corrected. "*Ms.* Clare Cosi."

"Spell it for me, please."

I did. Then I smiled and offered him my hand. He shook it but didn't smile back. With every movement his nylon jacket swished, and the array of tech devices on his belt clanked. He flashed the badge clipped onto his jacket.

"I'm a fire marshal, Ms. Cosi; my name is Stuart Rossi. Captain Quinn here tells me you were on premises when the event began?"

"That's right." I felt Captain Michael's intense gaze on us as the marshal asked me a series of standard questions. How did I know they were standard? Because the man made continuous checkmarks on a standardized form.

About five minutes into the interview, Crowley appeared. He signaled the captain, who took a few steps away to speak with his lieutenant. With the man's attention diverted, I lowered my voice to tell Marshal Rossi what I felt in my gut was true.

"I also want to add that I believe this was arson."

"Excuse me?"

I explained how I saw and heard the fire start—with an explosion that I'd witnessed and that felt extremely suspicious. I led the man to the remains of Caffè Lucia. Rossi wouldn't allow me to cross the threshold, so I pointed out the area near the curtain and basement door, where I thought the blaze might have begun. Then I directed his attention to the intact espresso bar and the machines behind it.

"Minimal damage there," I said. "So with the espresso machine and the gas line ruled out as possible culprits, what else could it have been but a bomb?"

"Ms. Cosi, were you a witness to any threats or discussions that involved perpetrating arson on this or any other premises?"

"No. I didn't overhear anything or witness any threats or confessions *directly*, but—"

"So your arson charge is based solely on—"

"What I saw and heard. What I witnessed at the start of the fire."

I left out the part about my gut feelings. Captain Michael made it abundantly clear that these guys wanted hard proof, not guesses, theories, or (God forbid) womanly hunches.

Marshal Rossi went silent as he finished scribbling notes. Finally he slipped the pen into his pocket, tucked the clipboard under his arm, and looked up.

"I want to thank you for your cooperation, Ms. Cosi."

"You're welcome, but won't you tell me what you think about all of this? From what you've seen, what do you think happened here?"

"Thank you again," he said politely. "We have your address and phone number, so if we need to get in touch with you for any reason—"

"Aren't you going to answer my questions?"

"No, Ms. Cosi, I'm not."

"Why?"

"Because it's too early in the investigation to come to any conclusions. Arson is a serious charge with serious consequences. There are tests that have to be done before we'd even consider launching a criminal investigation."

"When will you know?"

"Here's my card. If you think of any other information that you believe is pertinent, give me a call. If I'm not at my desk, leave a message."

The fire marshal gave a polite but final little nod; then, with the swish of his dark blue nylon jacket and the clanking of his gear, he reentered the ruined caffè.

And I thought cops in this town were closemouthed. Compared to New York's Bravest, New York's Finest are downright chatty.

I let the card dangle between my fingertips for a moment and realized my hand was now shaking. My heart was racing, too, and breathing was no picnic. I didn't know if this was some sort of posttraumatic aftershock, exhaustion, hunger, or all three. Maybe it was just plain old ordinary frustration with the bureaucratic wall of silence.

I stuffed the card into my jeans pocket then dug into my bag for my car keys.

"Going somewhere?"

The captain's voice startled me. "Yes. I'm headed for Elmhurst's ER. Now that I have my keys back, I can drive myself. Mike should be at the hospital by now and I've got to meet him—"

"My cousin's meeting you, is he?"

"Yes"—*Didn't I just say that?*—"I called him right after they took my friends to the hospital."

"Good, because a hospital is where you *should* be going, too, and not under your own power."

"I'm fine—"

"Your hands are trembling and you're whiter than a jug of Clorox. Have you eaten anything lately?"

"Uh . . ." Enzo had shared some biscotti and pizzelles with us, but other than the Gatorade, that was it for nutrition. I hadn't had a proper meal since brunch nearly twelve hours earlier.

"Okay," I confessed, "I'm a little shaky and I could use a bite to eat. But I'm certainly capable of driving myself a few miles."

Unfortunately, stating something firmly doesn't make it so. When I took a few steps, my knees refused to go with me.

"Easy, darlin'," the captain said, taking my arm. "An adrenaline crash is catching up to you and your blood sugar's bottoming out."

"I'm fine."

"You should not be driving, and I won't let you." Slipping the keys from my fingers, the captain bellowed to Lieutenant Crowley.

"Oat! Drive Ms. Cosi's car to Elmhurst's ER and park it!"

Crowley frowned. "And how is she getting there?"

"In the captain's car. She's too queasy to drive herself."

"Okay. I'll get Sergeant Ennis—"

"No, Oat, I won't be needin' my driver. I'll be takin' her myself. Sergeant Ennis can hitch a ride home on the engine."

I tensed, not relishing the idea of getting into a car alone with Michael Quinn. Still, he wasn't wrong to take my keys. I was depleted, my brain fuzzy. Driving a car in New York City was no mean feat; doing it at night, in my current condition, approached genuine stupidity.

For some reason Crowley didn't agree. First his gaze ping-ponged back and forth between me and his superior. Then he came right out and said, "Uh, Cap. Not a good idea."

"Why?" the captain replied. "Someone's got to drop by the ER, look in on Ronny Shaw. The poor man may have snapneck."

"Sure," said Crowley, "and that's where I was headed after

we pack up here. Tell you what? Why don't I save you the trouble and drive Ms. Cosi to Elmhurst myself?"

"And why don't you follow orders?"

Silence ensued for a good five seconds. Crowley's cheeks turned the color of pink peppercorns. Then he spoke through a pair of calcified jaws.

"Yes, sir. Meet you at the hospital."

Six

⁓⁓⁓⁓⁓⁓⁓⁓⁓⁓⁓⁓⁓⁓⁓⁓⁓⁓⁓⁓⁓⁓

AFTER pointing out my car to the lieutenant, Michael Quinn led me to his official vehicle and helped me into the passenger seat. The Chevy Suburban might have been roomy if all kinds of extra gear hadn't been jammed into the compartment—a computer and GPS unit, a radio that constantly crackled with chatter from all over the borough, and a rack between the passenger and driver to hold a shorter version of the claw-topped shaft every fireman seemed to carry.

"It's called a Halligan tool," the captain replied when I asked.

"I see. Why were the firemen tearing out the café walls with it, after the flames were out?"

"You mean after the flames *appeared* to be out." The captain tossed his helmet into the backseat. "Fire's a canny beast. She can hide in the walls, the ceilings, the floorboards."

She, I noted. *He thinks of the fire-beast as a she. There must be a story behind that . . .*

The captain leaned over, opened the glove compartment. "Here," he said, handing me a plastic packet of some kind of snack food. "Eat."

I didn't argue—or care, frankly, what the heck it was. There were carbs here and I was light-headed. I ripped it open.

"So what else is the Halligan tool used for? I mean, besides breaking things?" (I said this around a less-than-ladylike mouthful of what tasted like cheddar cheese filled pretzel bites. If it had been royal beluga on a half baguette, I couldn't have shoveled it in any faster.)

"Let me put it to you this way," the captain said, swinging the Suburban around to get clear of the trucks. "King Arthur civilized the British Isles with Excaliber. Babe Ruth broke every record with his Louisville Slugger. And every man jack of us in the FDNY tames the beast with his Halligan tool."

The she-beast? Hmm . . . "I think I'm getting it," I said. *And, brother, does it sound Freudian.*

The captain peered through the windshield. "Now where the hell is Oat and that car of yours?"

My mouth full again, I pointed then swallowed. "Up the block. He's driving the red Honda."

"If that's your clunker, then you *really* shouldn't be behind the wheel right now—or ever."

"You're the second man to insult my car tonight. Not everyone can afford the latest model, you know? It might not look like much, but my Honda's got pep. And it still gets good gas mileage."

"So does a horse. Really, honey. I'm worried about Oat's safety. Running into a fire is one thing, driving that death-trap is another."

"Why do you call Lieutenant Crowley 'Oat'?"

"You haven't seen him without his bottle top—"

"His what?

"His soup bucket, his umbrella."

"English?"

"His *fire helmet*. You haven't seen him without his head gear."

"Oh."

"He's prematurely gray," the captain explained. "When Crowley was still a probie, someone at breakfast noticed his hair was the same color as the milky oatmeal being served and the name stuck."

"He's named after oatmeal? I'm sure he hates that moniker."

"Trust me, it could have been worse."

As we came to a red light, the Number 7 train rumbled loudly along the elevated train tracks over our heads. When it finally passed, the captain turned toward me.

"Clare . . ." His tone was different, no longer playful. "Earlier you said someone else might have a motive to torch old man Enzo's shop."

"Yes."

"Who exactly were you thinking of accusing?"

I may have been tired and feeling a little weak, but a part of me came alert with that question. Maybe it was the way the man asked—as if he were afraid of knowing the person. Maybe it was something else. But I went with my gut and held my tongue.

"You were right, Michael," I replied carefully. "It's not my line of work. Forget I said anything."

ELMHURST Hospital was an incongruous sight: a shiny, ultramodern facility planted in the middle of a hardscrabble neighborhood of worn-out storefronts and rundown row houses, most of them packed with recent immigrants from Ecuador, India, Colombia, and Pakistan. By the time we turned onto the hospital's drive, I'd decided that I would put some questions to Enzo Testa. I didn't believe the old coffeehouse owner was responsible for torching his own business. But I was far from convinced that the fire was accidental.

Fire Marshal Rossi had given me his card and told me I could contact him with any further information that I believed was pertinent. As far as I was concerned, that was an invitation to find some.

As I checked my watch again, Captain Michael swung his official vehicle up to the ER entrance and cut the engine.

"You know, darlin'," he said, "it's not too late to forgo the hospital's oxygen for a little mouth to mouth at my place."

Give it up, man. "I don't think so."

"You sure? It's late and you're taking your chances in there. The ER will be packed. You could be here for a long time, only to be seen by an exhausted intern with a funny-sounding name on the unlucky thirteenth hour of a fourteen-hour shift."

I popped the door. "Thanks—but I'll take my chances with the exhausted intern."

My knees nearly gave out as I jumped down from the high vehicle, but I felt a whole lot better a moment later, when Mike Quinn, *my* Mike Quinn, pushed through the ER's exterior doors, his ruddy complexion looking pale in the halogen-flooded entryway.

"You okay, sweetheart?"

I nodded.

Mike's arms went around me. The embrace was much needed, but it came with the slight, familiar stab from the handle of his service weapon, tucked into the holster beneath his sport coat and trench. The momentary prod perfectly summed up our relationship—extraordinarily affectionate, punctuated with the occasional, unexpected jab (metaphorically speaking).

My ex-husband once called the man Dudley Do-Right, but Mike wasn't perfect or even above using a dodgy ploy to get the job done. He hadn't started out as a suit-wearing detective, either. He'd earned his gold shield by coming up in the ranks, which included decorated undercover work as an anticrime street cop, so he was far from naïve or a guy you'd want to cross.

Still my ex was right about one thing: Crime solving wasn't a game to Mike Quinn. It was the fulfillment of what he saw as an almost sacred obligation to remove murderers, rapists, drug dealers, and predators from the rest of the population, which was why I didn't mind the familiar little butt from his weapon. I liked the momentary reminder of my man's place in the world, his dedication to a job that protected the weak, the innocent, the naively trustworthy—which occasionally included yours truly.

When we parted, he held me at arm's length for a cool Mike-like once-over, from the top of my smoke-scented hair to the tips of my soiled, ruined boots.

"I'm fine, Mike, really. How is Madame? And Dante?"

"They're both doing well."

"Thank goodness."

"They'll probably release Mrs. Dubois in the next hour," Mike said. "Dante Silva is awake, with a mighty big headache. He may have a concussion so they're waiting for the results of his tests before they'll release him. And Mr. Testa isn't doing so well . . ."

I tensed. "What's wrong with Enzo?"

"It's his heart they're worried about, but he's in good hands. They're monitoring every beat in the ICU—"

And that's when it came: the *slam*. Like a gunshot, the driver's side door on the Suburban opened and closed with explosive force.

"Hi there, *Mikey.*"

Arms folded, Captain Michael Quinn regarded his cousin across the vehicle's hood then flashed him what might have been a grin if it hadn't look more like the baring of gritted teeth.

Crap. I'd held out hope that we'd dodged this bullet, but it came all the same.

"Tore yourself away from doling out traffic tickets to check up on the little lady, eh?"

Mike's eyes went dead cold. "Excuse me a minute, sweetheart," he said with disturbing calm. In a few smooth strides he'd circumvented the front of the Suburban to confront his cousin.

The two were pretty evenly matched, which is to say both were over six feet with wide shoulders, long legs, and prize-fighter reaches. Captain Michael may have been a bit taller, but I'd seen Mike power-cuff suspects with the kind of fluid force that I doubted the fireman could counter.

The conversation began with the captain folding his arms and muttering something. Mike's eyes narrowed, and he shoved his finger into the breast of his cousin's bunker coat. His other hand reached backward, toward his belt, as if he were going for his handcuffs. Now the captain's eyes blazed, and I feared a shouting match—or worse—was about to explode.

"Guys, don't fight!" I called.

Without even glancing in my direction, the men stepped farther away, locking themselves in a furious, whispered exchange.

I strained my ears to hear what the two were saying, but the noise of traffic and hospital workers was too loud. Finally, when it looked like fisticuffs were about to break out, a third figure in fireman's gear thrust himself between the men.

"Knock it off!" Oat Crowley barked.

That I heard.

Crowley reached into his pocket and shoved a set of keys into Mike's hand. "Your girlfriend's car is parked down that block." He pointed then shot a naked glare my way before pushing against his boss with both arms. "C'mon, Cap, I'm going inside to check on Ronny Shaw, and you need to go back to the firehouse. There's paperwork waiting."

Captain Michael looked pleased with the scene he'd created, even threw a final, cheeky wink in my direction before turning back to continue arguing with Oat.

My Mike didn't miss the devil's wink. He came back to me in body after that but not in spirit. "Let's go inside," he said, taking my elbow a little too roughly.

"No! What was that all about?"

"Forget it happened," he said with a brusque finality that I rarely heard from him. The retrograde attitude sounded more like his cousin's.

"Sorry. No sale." I planted myself.

"This is not the time or place, Clare." His expression was still rigid, but when he spoke once more, his tone was softer.

"Please." He stepped close, put his hands on my shoulders. "Let's not do this. Let's go check on your friends."

I didn't argue. Not then. Mike wasn't wrong about the timing. So I shelved my questions (for the moment) and let him guide me through the doors of the emergency room.

Seven

"**Osso** buco is another example," Madame was saying.

"Is that beef? Like the bourguignon?" The voice was gruffly male, its pitch low enough to dub James Earl Jones.

"Veal, dear. The veal hind shank, to be precise, sawed into three-inch-thick pieces . . ."

As I came around the white partitioning curtain in the busy ER, I found Madame regally propped on the pristine sheets of a narrow hospital stretcher. Her silk pantsuit was still smoke stained and wrinkled, but her face was freshly washed, her hair brushed into a sleek silver pageboy.

Relief washed over me—along with fear, anger, gratefulness—the internal emotional swell was nearly as powerful as the moment I'd seen her carried out of that charred caffè.

She hadn't yet noticed me. Her focus was on the man occupying the next stretcher, and I was glad of that. It gave me a few moments to swallow back tears, compose myself.

"So how hard is to make?" asked Madame's ER neighbor.

The bare-chested guy wore black leather pants and a Vandyke beard long enough to braid. Every inch of skin art along his muscled arms had something to do with Harley Davidson, and if that weren't enough of a giveaway, the flaming hog across his chest released scripted exhaust that plainly read *Hells Angels.*

"Osso buco? It's a snap!" Madame chirped. "Salt and pepper the shanks, dredge them in flour, and brown them in a skillet with a bit of olive oil. Then just cover with a mixture of chicken or veal stock, sautéed onions, carrots, and celery and dry white wine—or French vermouth, whichever you prefer."

"I like bourbon. Can I use bourbon?"

"I wouldn't."

"So why put flour on the shanks if you're covering 'em with stock, anyways?"

"As the shanks are braising, flour will thicken the sauce for you. Then there's no need for more difficult measures."

"I get it. Cooking time?"

"Two hours or so. Finish with a sprinkle of gremolata to add a sprightly flavor note."

"Gremo-what-a?"

"It's just a bit of minced garlic with chopped parsley and zest from a lemon."

"Oh, *zest!* I know zest! I seen them make zest on the Food Channel. You grate it off citrus skins with a metal file, right?"

"Almost, dear. That zesting tool is called a Microplane—"

I cleared my throat. Madame turned. "Clare!"

I stepped into her open arms, and the festive aroma of grappa on her breath lifted my spirits. The clashing acridness of smoke in her hair, however, ignited other feelings—ugly ones. I wanted to know who was responsible for putting her here, and I wanted them to pay.

"How are you, Madame?"

"Fit as a Stradivarius."

"Did you call Otto?"

Otto Visser was the "younger man" in Madame's life. (He was only pushing seventy.) The dignified, European-born gallery owner had become smitten with my former mother-in-law after they'd eye-flirted across a semicrowded Manhattan dining room. The two had been a couple ever since.

"I'm not troubling Otto with this," Madame stated.

"That's crazy." I pulled out my cell. "I'll call him."

"Please don't."

"For heaven's sake, why not?"

"Otto's hosting an important dinner between a promising young painter and a very serious Japanese collector. I wouldn't dream of doing anything to hurt the artist's prospects."

Considering what the woman had just gone through, I found that reply frustrating, although I knew where it came from. For decades, Madame had run our Village Blend as a second home for poets, writers, dramatists, and yes—as cliché as it sounded—struggling fine artists.

Actors, dancers, singers, writers, visual artists, and students burning to prove themselves worthy of said identifiers still frequented our Village coffeehouse. But the neighborhood's skyrocketing real estate values had driven the majority of them to more affordable neighborhoods in Brooklyn, here in Queens, and (in the case of many jazz musicians) North Jersey.

Back in Madame's prime, however, when Greenwich Village was still a "cheap" place to live on Manhattan island, she'd befriended some true legends of the art world (before they'd become legends): Hopper, Pollock, de Kooning, Rauschenberg, Warhol, Lichtenstein, even the graffiti prodigy Jean-Michel Basquiat.

She'd also known artists, just as talented, who'd failed. Not in their art but in their ability to make a passable living at it. What the bottle and needle didn't claim, the demands of day jobs or young families did. So it was no mystery to me why Madame didn't want to feel responsible for interfering with even one aspiring artist's sale.

Still, I had to point out: "When Otto finds out, he'll be extremely upset that you didn't call."

Madame waved her hand. "To tell you the truth, dear, the last time I was in harm's way—you recall, don't you? At Matteo's wedding last year?"

"The shooting?"

"Yes, for weeks after that little incident, Otto was solicitous to the point of annoyance. I'd rather not go through that again. I do adore the man, but a woman needs her space."

Madame glanced up then, beyond me, into the vast fluorescent bustle of the ER's central area. "And where is your knightly young officer?"

Knightly? That's a first. I pointed. "Waiting room."

"I must tell you, Clare, he took excellent care of me, found me a sparkling water, brought me a hairbrush and mirror. Oh!" She pointed to my shoulder. "I see you have my bag. At last, I can do my makeup."

I handed over the recovered booty. As Madame pulled out her compact and lipstick, I heard male laughter and hearty greetings coming through the closed curtain to her right. That patient, whoever he was, had just gotten a visitor. At the same moment, I realized the Biker Guy on the stretcher to the left of Madame was watching us with interest—easy enough to do because the partitioning curtain on his side was pulled completely open.

"Howyadoin'?" he called when he noticed me noticing him.

"Fine," I replied, then gestured to the plastic brace around his neck (the one beneath his narrow version of a ZZ Top beard). "What happened? Traffic accident? Spin out?"

"Slipped in the shower."

"Oh . . ."

"Clare, this is Diggy-Dog Dare." Madame turned to the biker. "Diggy, this is Clare Cosi, my daughter-in-law—"

"Ex," I corrected, and not for the first time.

"Charmed, I'm sure," Diggy replied in basso profundo.

"Before you arrived, we were exchanging recipes," Madame explained. "Diggy gave me his favorite: tequila chicken."

"With tomatillo sauce," Diggy noted.

"And I gave him my bourguignon-style short ribs and—"

"Osso buco," I interjected with a nod. "I overheard."

Madame tapped her chin. "Now that I think of it, dear, didn't you used to make a steak with bourbon sauce? I recall Matt raving about it and Diggy has a proclivity for bourbon. Don't you, Diggy?"

"A proclivity? No. But I do like it a lot."

"Of course, Matt always raved about your cooking," Madame went on. She turned back to Diggy. "Matt's my son. He and Clare have the most beautiful daughter together."

"Is that right?" Diggy scratched the roots of his beard. "I have two myself. Wife number three's got custody of the first. Wife number four's bringing up the second."

"Excuse me, Mr. Dare," I said, moving to the partitioning curtain. "Would you mind very much if I had a private word with my ex-mother-in-law?"

"Naw, no problem. Pull it."

I did, hoping the wall of white on both sides of her would help Madame's grappa-happy mind to focus—on something other than alcohol-soaked meat, anyway.

"What is it, dear? What's wrong?"

"Don't forget!" Diggy-Dog's voice boomed through the drapery. "I sure would like that recipe for bourbon steak!"

"Okay!" I called, then took a breath and approached Madame with my serious face. "Enzo's in the ICU."

"What? Why didn't your young man tell me?"

"For the same reason you didn't call Otto. Mike didn't want to upset you. Enzo's stable now, but they're monitoring him. It's his heart . . ."

Madame closed her eyes. "If anything happens to him, I'll never forgive myself."

"That's absurd. Why would you say that?

"We arrived at the caffè an hour late, Clare. If we'd been on time, we all might have been out of harm's way before the fire started." In a rare show of naked anxiety, Madame wrung her hands. "If only we'd gotten there earlier—"

"Listen to me—" I took hold of her shoulders. "If Enzo dies, the person that killed him is the arsonist who set that blaze."

Madame's hand-wringing stopped. "Arsonist?"

I nodded.

"What are you saying, Clare? Did you see someone set the fire?"

"No. But I witnessed the start. I think someone set off a bomb in Enzo's shop."

"A bomb in Enzo's shop!"

Crap. The laughing voices beyond the curtain fell silent. I waited a few seconds, until the muffled sound of men chatting drifted back through the thin material again. Then I turned back to Madame.

"Try to keep your voice down, okay? Tell me what you remember about the fire."

"There was a *whoosh* at first, that's what I recall, a very loud *whoosh*. Enzo went up the stairs, felt the door, and knew there was a terrible blaze on the other side. Smoke began seeping through the floor." Madame shook her head. "Enzo kept us alive, Clare."

"He did?"

"Yes. He was a rock. We couldn't get out of that basement. But Enzo kept assuring me the basement's metal door was a fire door and we'd be all right as long as we could get fresh air. The man didn't show one moment of panic. I can't say the same for myself."

"Given what was happening, Madame, panic would have been normal." And that thought made me pause . . .

Had Enzo planned, all along, to end up trapped in the building, behind a fire door, to make himself appear innocent?

"And then smoke began to fill the room, and he used all his strength to move some heavy crates. He helped me down onto the floor and made me move my head all the way into an old air vent. The smoke in the room became unbearable. There was only room for one of us to get fresh air. I wanted us to switch off, but he refused. He physically forced me to lie with my face in that vent for fresh outside air . . ."

Madame's voice trailed off as her eyes filled with tears. "And now he's in the ICU . . . he's in there for one reason, Clare, because he did everything he could to make sure I wouldn't be . . ."

I fell silent as Madame composed herself. I grabbed some tissues, handed them to her, one after another. Finally, she wiped her cheeks.

"Thank God those two young men came down when they did to carry us out . . . When they told me you were all right, I nearly fainted. I was so worried about you, Clare . . . You'd gone up there to the caffè to let Dante in, and we didn't know what had happened . . ."

We hugged again and I sat down on the edge of her stretcher. Madame grasped my arm, looked into my eyes. "Who do you think set that bomb? An enemy of Enzo's? Someone with a vendetta?"

"I think it was someone who had something to gain."

"Gain?" Madame frowned. "You're not suggesting Enzo did this?"

"No," I said, thinking *not anymore.* "Enzo put himself in the ICU to save you. That doesn't add up to a snake-blooded arsonist."

"Then who?"

Madame's big, blue-violet eyes were fixed on me. She wasn't making the leap. *Because she doesn't want to . . .*

"I need to speak to Enzo," I said carefully. "I need to find out more about . . ."

"About?" she prompted.

"I just need to speak with him."

"We'll do it together!" Madame announced so loudly the men next to us quieted again.

"Madame, please—"

"If someone deliberately set fire to that beautiful caffè and put all of our lives in danger, we are not going to let that bastard get away with it! Are we, Clare?"

"No, of course not, but please calm down . . ." Not only wasn't the woman calming down, she wasn't staying down. "*Please*. Don't tax your system—"

"What's going on here?" A middle-aged nurse with iron-gray hair instantly materialized. "Where are you going, Mrs. Dubois? You haven't been released yet."

"But I need to speak with my friend—"

"What you *need* to do is get your *butt* back on that stretcher—"

Madame shook her head.

I took firm hold of her upper arms. "Madame, *think*. Enzo is in the ICU. They're not going to let us both in there at the same time, and they're certainly not going to let in another patient."

I felt her muscles relax under my hands. She stopped fighting

"Yes. Of course, of course . . . you're right, dear."

"It's okay," I told the nurse. "She's not going anywhere."

The nurse nodded and hustled away.

"Now rest, okay?" I kept my voice pleasant as I helped Madame return to her hospital sheets, but I really wanted to kick myself. I'd brought up the arsonist to relieve the woman's guilt, not give her a heart attack, too. "Why don't you pass the time by talking to Mr. Dog Dare again?"

I pulled back the curtain to her left.

"Bourbon steak?" Diggy sang in greeting.

"When I come back," I promised.

"Clare," Madame called as I turned to go. "Tell me. Who do you think set that bomb?"

Enzo's bratty little witch of a daughter, who else? And I didn't think she did it alone. But was Glenn her accomplice? Or someone else? How many other lapdog beaus did that woman have on a leash?

I wanted to tell Madame what I thought and what I was beginning to fear—if Lucia had been ruthless enough to torch her father's caffè, what other crimes would she be capable of committing? Would she harm her own father to get her hands on her inheritance faster? Was she capable of setting him up for an "accident"? Poisoning him?

I needed to know more before I started accusing anyone, even through speculation, and as Mike had warned me outside, this was not the time or the place. So my reply to Madame was—

"I have a few people in mind."

"Who?"

"I'll let you know."

I took off fast after that, to avoid any further questions. But after just three steps, I stopped dead.

On the other side of the partitioning curtain, a big man stood, ear cocked against the snowy fabric.

"Oat?"

Lieutenant Oat Crowley had been listening to every word we'd said. Propped up on the stretcher next to him was Ronny Shaw, the firefighter who'd landed in here thanks to a chunk of ceiling.

Crowley and I stood staring at each other. His craggy, roundish face betrayed a mix of embarrassment and annoyance. Finally, beneath the slightly shaggy crown of his oatmeal-colored hair, the man's features hardened into an iron mask. His eyes narrowed like a shooter's gun sight, and I was in his crosshairs.

Crowley opened his mouth to address me, but considering our surroundings and the amount of ears and eyes so close, he appeared to be hamstrung.

Now what?

The lieutenant had shot me some pretty nasty looks outside, as if I'd been the sole cause of the animosity between the Quinn cousins, which was patently ridiculous. Their feud had been going on for years before I'd known either one of them. Still, showing weakness to Crowley would be a mistake (I'd learned a thing or two from Madame by now), and I boldly stepped up to the man.

"Hello," I said.

"Ms. Cosi." The words were more statement than greeting.

"How is your friend doing?"

"Who's this?" Ronny asked from his stretcher, looking a little dazed.

"Nobody," Crowley answered, then stepped toward me—and kept on stepping. He danced me backward, right out of Ronny's designated ER rectangle. "He's going to be fine, Ms. Cosi. How's your old lady?"

"My *employer* is doing all right, *considering . . .*"

"Considering what?"

"Considering someone tried to murder her."

Crowley stopped dancing me backward. "You ought to be careful what you say in a public place."

"Maybe." I folded my arms, finally standing my ground. "But what do you care? You must put out dozens of fires in any given year—"

"*Hundreds.*"

"Exactly. You'll have another fire tomorrow, maybe two. More next week. So what do you care what anyone says about any one of them?"

"I don't."

I studied the man's eyes. *You do. You do care. Why?* I opened my mouth to ask, but Crowley spoke first, his voice so low even I could barely hear him.

"Steer clear of this, missy. For your own good."

"Why? What do you know?"

"I don't know a thing," Crowley said. Then he spun around, walked back to his buddy's bedside, and closed the curtain on our conversation.

EIGHT

~~~~~~

SEEING Enzo was more difficult than I'd anticipated. For one thing I was tired—emotionally drained over my worries about Madame and Dante, and mentally strained by the absurd scene between Mike and his cousin. The cryptic threat from Oat hadn't helped, and the hospital's critical care facility wasn't exactly a laugh a minute, either.

Laid out like the ER downstairs, the ICU consisted of beds lined up in tidy partitioned rows, but that's where the similarity ended. There was a hypersterile scent to the ICU; no sharp, astringent sting of ER alcohol or bright, clean bleach. There were no grounding smells at all, which only increased the surreal feeling of disconnection, and where the ER was filled with bustle and noise, this unit exhibited the chilling reverence of a funeral home's viewing room.

Male and female nurses in scrubs went about their duties like polite androids, fully aware yet completely detached from ongoing human dramas around them: a young Filipino woman sobbing at the bedside of a comatose grandfather; a Hispanic man mumbling Hail Marys next to a youth swathed in bandages . . .

An RN escorted me through it all, to the bedside of Madame's friend. Enzo's skin appeared fragile as rice paper, his cheeks sunken, his surfaces painted paler than a winter moon. This robust older gentleman, so full of burning energy, now had all the life of one of Mike's postmortems.

I took a breath and closed my eyes, willing myself to toughen up. It wasn't easy. Feelings were washing over me, images from half a lifetime ago: that phone call in the dark morning hours; my frightened little girl crying in her bed; the summons to an ICU like this one to find my dynamic, young husband laid out like a corpse, clinging to life, his strong body brought down by a little white powder.

I thought I'd frozen those memories, left them far away, like ancient snow on a mountain top, but the smells and sounds flash-melted it all, raining it down in a sudden, unavoidable flood.

"Mr. Testa?" The nurse's voice. "Your daughter is here to see you."

"Daughter?" he repeated, voice weak. "Lucia?"

For a few seconds, the steadfast beeping of Enzo's cardiac monitor was the only sound on the planet. Then I silently wished myself luck and stepped up to the bedrail.

"How are you, *Papa*?" I said in clear English, then quickly switched to quiet Italian: "I said you were my father so they would let me in here. Is that all right with you, sir?"

The corners of Enzo's mouth lifted. "Hello, *daughter*," he croaked in English, strong enough for the nurse to hear. Like me (and more than a few Italians) the man obviously believed that rules were made to be broken.

With relief I leaned over the rail and kissed his colorless cheek. Despite the oxygen tube taped under his nose and the IV snaking into the bulging blue vein in his hand, Enzo's eyes appeared clear, a miracle considering everything he'd been through.

He patted me on the cheek, and the nurse walked away. She'd already explained that his lungs were strained from the toxic fumes he'd inhaled, and his heartbeat had become erratic. Further tests were needed to pinpoint the problem.

I knew how important this interview was. None of the fire marshals had come around yet to question Enzo. If he died before they spoke with him, they might just pin the arson on him, which meant the real perpetrator would get away with murder.

"I'm glad you're safe, Clare," Enzo rasped. "When everything went boom, Blanche was worried only about you and your friend. How are they doing?"

"The ER is getting ready to release Madame. How are you feeling?"

"Me? I'm about ready to run the New York City Marathon." Enzo laughed, but it quickly degenerated into a weak cough. "How is your artist friend?"

"Dante was hit on the head, so they're holding him overnight for observation." I summoned a tight smile, still worried about my *artista* barista. "You know, before the fire, he was admiring your mural . . ."

Enzo nodded, eyes glistening as my voice trailed off. "I'm afraid he was the last to admire it . . ." He coughed again. "I still want to meet your friend, see his work maybe?"

"You will, I promise." I touched the man's hand. His graciousness, despite his condition, was moving—and made me all the more determined to nail the monster who'd put him here, destroying his art in the process.

"Has anyone called your daughter yet?"

Enzo shook his head. "No. I don't want that. What happened at the shop is enough of a shock without this, too . . ." He touched the IV tube in his arm. "I feel like a slab of veal."

"Let me call Lucia," I replied, reaching for my cell. "I can do it right now—"

"*No*," Enzo said. "She looked forward to this weekend for a month. I might be out of here by tomorrow; then *nobody* has to call."

I wasn't comfortable with Enzo's choice, but when I checked my cell phone's screen, I saw there was no reception in the ICU.

"I hate being in this place," Enzo said, eyes spearing the IV bag above. "I want to retire, go back to Italy to be with my two sisters . . . visit my Angela's grave every Sunday . . ."

Retire to Italy? Back at the caffè, Enzo hadn't once mentioned retirement. But then I considered the timing of his call to Madame, unearthing that photo album and wanting to give the Blend back its old roaster. Was that the reason he'd been cleaning out his basement? Had he been planning on moving back to the old country? If Enzo innocently revealed his plans to the fire marshals, what were they going to think?

I leaned closer. "What about the caffè, *signore?* Who is going to run your business?"

"Lucia," Enzo replied. "When I leave this country, I'm signing it all over to my daughter. That was always the plan. Now my daughter's going to have to rebuild . . . if she wants to."

"You sound doubtful. Why is that? Don't you think she'll have the funds to give it a go?"

"It's not the money. There's plenty of insurance coverage on the building—"

(*Exactly what I suspected.*) "So what's the problem, then?"

Enzo sighed, stared off into space. "My Angela . . . she was such a beauty . . ."

"Your *wife*, Angela?"

"We met in the park, in the spring . . ."

Enzo smiled weakly, turned his gaze back to me. "You are like her, Clare . . . like Blanche, too . . . such fire in your spirits yet still so good-natured . . ." He reached out to touch my cheek. "My Angelina came to my loft many times . . . I painted her . . . We made love . . . many times . . . so sweet . . . My best work, those portraits . . . I could not bear to sell them . . ."

Uh-oh, I'm losing him. I tried switching to Italian. "About the caffè, *signore* . . ."

"Angela indulged her, you understand?" he said in English. "Treated her like a baby doll, dressed her up, took her shopping, wherever she wanted to go . . ."

"Lucia? Your daughter? Is that who you mean?"

"If she wanted to stay home from school, she stayed—no questions. Never had to work. Just lessons—dancing, singing, whatever she desired. And then the boys started coming around." He shook his head. "When she was young, Lucia had my Angela's beauty, but not her heart. Her mother could not see it . . . back then, neither could I . . ."

"But now you can?"

"I looked at my daughter through my wife's eyes. Now that Angela is gone, I see with my own eyes: Lucia is not like her mother . . ."

"You don't think Lucia will rebuild the caffè?"

"She talks about marrying Glenn."

The tone was disdainful. "What's the matter with Glenn? You don't approve?"

"What's to approve? Lucia is a grown woman. She can make up her own mind about her life, about this . . . this *boy* . . ."

"A boy? Not a man?"

"You saw how she treats him?"

I nodded.

"Why do you think he puts up with it? He is still a boy. Lucia says they're engaged. *Eh.* She won't go through with it."

"Because?"

"Because there is a man from my daughter's past who still comes sniffing around . . . a real man, a grown one. Lucia has a special smile for this one. Glenn doesn't know it, but she does. Love is a game to my daughter . . . she is not like her mother . . . to Lucia men are playthings . . ."

"And who is this man? The one from her past who still comes around to play with her?"

Enzo shrugged once more. "You don't know him . . ." He looked away again, into space.

"Glenn rebuilds cars, right?" I prodded, trying to keep

the man focused. "With his skills, maybe he can help Lucia rebuild the caffe."

"Glenn Duffy is a *mechanic*, not a carpenter. He has no interest in running a caffè . . ." Enzo paused to cough. "I've heard him talk. He wants to open his own car shop in North Jersey, where he has family."

"It takes money to start your own business," I said. And I was willing to bet ten kilos of Kona Peaberry that a competent car mechanic would possess enough skill to rig a basic incendiary device with a timer.

"Enzo, where do you think Glenn Duffy is going to get the money to—"

"Excuse me." The RN appeared again, a tall, slender woman of East Indian heritage. "How are you feeling?" she asked Enzo, her voice a sweet singsong.

Taking in the nurse's dark, cat-shaped eyes and flawless dusky-skinned face, Enzo immediately perked up. "I died and went to heaven, that's how I feel. Only this can explain the angel I see before me."

The nurse laughed. "You're still here on Earth, I'm glad to say, Mr. Testa."

"You call me Enzo, okay? No more of that Mr. Testa stuff. Mr. Testa was my father."

She arched a pretty eyebrow then turned to face me. "I'm afraid you'll have to wrap up your visit. Mr. Testa has another family member waiting. As soon as you come out, I'll show his sister in . . ."

"Sister?" Enzo and I blurted out at the same time.

"Yes, Mr. Testa, your sister Mrs. Rita Quadrelli."

As the nurse turned and strode away, Enzo's eyes widened in obvious panic. "Clare! A favor, *please*! I beg you."

I already guessed.

"The widow Quadrelli is not my sister. She must have fibbed like you to get in here—"

"And you don't want to see her?"

"When God made that woman, he left out the quiet! Five

minutes with her babbling in my ear, and I'll be pulling these tubes out to get away, even if it means certain death!"

I considered going to the nurse, but that had the potential to turn ugly, especially if Mrs. Quadrelli were confronted. After all, how could I accuse her of not being his sister when I wasn't his daughter?

"I'd better deal with Mrs. Quadrelli directly," I said. "What do you want me to tell her?"

"Tell her I'm sleeping. Tell her I'm drugged. Tell her I'm in a coma!"

I touched his shoulder. "I'll think of something. And I'll keep checking in with your nurse to see how you're doing."

Moments later, I spotted Mrs. Quadrelli just outside the critical-care unit. She was waiting in a small seating area, but the woman wasn't sitting, she was frantically pacing next to the sliding glass doors. And when she saw me walking away from Enzo's station, her expression morphed from impatience to outrage.

"What's this? I was told Enzo was visiting with his daughter. But you're not Enzo's daughter!"

Okay, Clare, come up with something—fast.

NINE

〰〰〰〰〰〰〰〰〰〰〰〰〰〰〰〰〰〰

ENZO had described Mrs. Quadrelli as a *donna pazzesca*, which is why I'd mentally cast her as a bug-eyed Phyllis Diller with a wild gray 'fro and a voice like Alvin the singing chipmunk.

Way off.

Impeccably tailored in a sleek black pantsuit, Enzo's wannabe love interest was a handsome, slender lady in her midsixties. Her dark hair was cropped short like Lucia's, dead straight, and shiny as a beetle shell with enough shimmering red highlights to have been recently salon-glossed. A cloying cloud of flowery cologne floated around her. Like Lucia, she sported plenty of gold jewelry, which jangled with every fidget, and although she appeared upset to see me, she was far from what I would have described as a *crazy woman*.

"Let me introduce myself," I began, trying to ignore the increasing itch in my nose. *Lord, that cologne. She must have just doused herself!* "My name is—"

"You're not Lucia."

No kidding. "My name is Clare Cosi and—"

"I don't understand! The nurse told me Enzo was visiting with his daughter!"

"And she told me his *sister* was waiting to see him. We both know you're not his sister."

The woman's squinting eyes collapsed another millimeter. "Who *are* you?"

"I told you, my name is Clare—"

"Who are you to *Enzo*?"

"A friend in the coffee business. I went by his place this evening with my employer to look over an antique roaster. We were all caught in the fire."

Mrs. Quadrelli fell silent. Her red lipstick was so boldly applied that when she twisted her mouth into a scowl, I flashed on my years taking Joy to the Big Apple Circus.

Finally she said, "You people shouldn't have been there at all."

"Excuse me?"

"Enzo closes early on Thursdays to play bocce. Everyone knows that." She looked away then, as if a poster on flu prevention were in immediate need of study.

"I don't understand. What does that have to do with—"

She whipped her head back around. "If not for *you* and your *employer*, he'd have been in that park with me. It's *your* fault Enzo is in this hospital."

I studied the woman. "What do you know about the fire, anyway?"

"Me? Nothing! Not a thing!" She threw up her hands. "I wasn't even near Enzo's caffè. It was Mrs. Mercer who told me about it. Mary saw the whole thing, and she came to the park with her dog, Pinto. Little Pinto is famous in the neighborhood. Do you know about him?"

"No, but if you—"

"He's the dog who rides around in the red wagon. Pinto was featured in the *Daily News* last year. He has cerebral palsy or something and can't walk. Or is Pinto a she? I forget. Anyway, Pinto's vet is that new fellow on Steinway Street—"

"Sorry to interrupt," I said, beginning to get a clue why Enzo was willing to choose a coma over *this* conversation, "but I think we should head downstairs."

The glass ICU doors slid wide just then, and I noticed Enzo's pretty nurse glancing curiously our way.

"Enzo can't see you tonight," I quietly told Mrs. Q.

"And why would that be? He saw *you,* didn't he?"

"The doctors just ordered more tests, so no more visitors, not even family—"

"Tests!" Mrs. Q snorted. "I know all about doctors and their tests! Maria Tobinski, on Thirty-ninth Avenue, she has a husband who's a conductor on the MTA. Works the F train—anyway, Maria went to her gynecologist for a routine checkup and they found—"

"You know what?" I said, cutting her off before I heard every private detail about poor Maria Tobinski's medical history. "Let's you and I go downstairs together—"

I was forming the plan as I said the words. Mrs. Q appeared to know every little happening in Enzo's neighborhood, and Mike's stories of his fieldwork hadn't been lost on me. A source like this one was too good to pass up.

"I need coffee," I said. "Let me buy you a cup . . ." (I had no idea where I'd get one at this late hour, but this was a hospital; they had to have at least four things: doctors, nurses, stethoscopes, and java juice.)

Mrs. Quadrelli frowned at my offer. "Maybe I should double-check with the nurse."

"Don't do that!"

"Why not?"

Why not? "Because, well . . . it's a *secret.*" I motioned her closer. "I didn't want to say anything, but . . ."

"What? What?"

The woman's entire body came awake. Her head cocked, even her pupils dilated. *A gossip addict, for sure.*

"The truth is," I continued, snaking my arm around hers, "it's not pretty. Are you sure you want to hear?"

"What? Tell me!"

"Enzo is in trouble," I whispered, guiding her away from the ICU doors, down the hallway, toward the elevators.

"What kind of trouble?"

"Officials are investigating whether or not the fire was deliberately set." *Not a lie!*

Mrs. Quadrelli looked sufficiently horrified. "What makes them think that?"

"I don't know. But Enzo will be their prime suspect."

"Why!"

"Because he's the owner, of course, and the beneficiary of the fire insurance payoff. Did you know he was planning to move back to Italy? It sounds incriminating."

"That's just talk! His daughter will tell you. He's been saying that for years, but he never goes through with it!"

We actually made it to the elevators. I pushed the *down* button. "So you're saying Enzo had no concrete plans to leave the country?"

"None. Not before the fire, at least. Now things have changed though, haven't they? I mean, with the caffè up in smoke."

"I see. So you think he'll bank the insurance money and finally retire to Italy?"

"I certainly hope so because I intend to go with him."

I gaped at her. "You plan to move to Italy? With Enzo?" *This has to be news to him.*

"Don't look so surprised, Miss Cosi, my husband was born in Italy, so I've been there quite a few times already. I just wish it had been more. For years, you see, we ran a restaurant together on Thirtieth Avenue—"

"You're divorced?"

"Bite your tongue! I'm a widow. The restaurant business killed my husband! Put him into an early grave . . . But that's behind me now. And the fire can be behind Enzo soon, too."

She exhaled, gaze turning glassy. "It's been years since I've toured Italy, but it is a beautiful place, and I know I'd love to retire there. Enzo and I could set up a very nice little home near his two sisters."

"You don't sound very broken up about the fire."

"After Enzo gets out of this wretched place and we're all settled in Italy, he'll see it's really a good thing his business went up in flames . . ."

I blinked, recalling the masterpiece of a mural the man had spent half a lifetime creating—not to mention his spotless floor, polished tables, meticulously maintained espresso machine—and wanted to punch this *donna pazzesca* right in the nose.

"Now, Mrs. Quadrelli," I managed through gritted teeth, "why would you say such a thing?"

"The man is over seventy! He should retire already, enjoy his life, not spend every waking hour making silly coffee drinks!"

Bing! Bing! I had two words for this woman: "Elevator's here!" *Those weren't it.*

Four endless stories of pointless babble later, we reached the hospital's ground floor.

"Come with me to the waiting room," I said, deciding something that very second. "I'll get us coffee and you can talk to the police officer."

"Police officer!"

"Shhhh . . ."

"What's a police officer doing here?"

"That's what I was trying to tell you. I went up to warn Enzo that the officials were looking into the fire being suspicious, so he shouldn't say anything to incriminate himself."

"Oh! I see!"

"And you can help, too."

"How?"

"Well, to start with, you can back me up when I tell this officer that Enzo can't see any more visitors this evening."

Mrs. Quadrelli's head bobbed like an eager parrot. Inside of ten minutes, I'd transformed the woman from suspicious shrew to co-conspirator. Even Mike would be impressed, of that I was certain—what I wasn't so certain about was his reaction to the way I was about to use him.

Ten

~~~~~~~~~~~~~~~~~~~~~~~~~~~~~~~

"**EXCUSE** me, *Officer?*"

Amused blue eyes peeked over newsprint.

I never called Mike *officer.* I sometimes addressed him as detective in a teasing way, which was why I wasn't surprised to see the beginnings of a smile behind the man's *New York Times*.

"This is Mrs. Quadrelli," I quickly added in serious staccato. "I brought her down from the ICU to verify that Enzo is not available for an official interview at this time."

"That's right! Ms. Cosi is right!" Mrs. Quadrelli's beetle-brown head began bobbing again. "Lorenzo is undergoing tests. He can have no visitors. None at all, certainly not *you.*"

Mike shifted in his yellow plastic waiting room chair, set the newspaper down, and regarded us, his amused expression fading into one of guarded confusion.

Mrs. Quadrelli frowned at Mike's off-track expression. "You *are* a police officer, aren't you?" She turned to me. "Did he ever show you his identification, Miss Cosi? You can't be too careful these days."

I met Mike's eyes. "Officer, let me explain: This woman is

a friend of Enzo's. As I told you earlier, I don't live in Queens, but Mrs. Quadrelli here might have some ideas about who set that fire because I'm sure it wasn't Enzo."

"That's right," she said. "Enzo would never set fire to that caffè. He was attached to it. *Too* attached if you really want to know."

I cleared my throat. "So, *Officer*, if you'd like to *ask questions* about who might have had a motive to burn the place down, Mrs. Quadrelli here might be able to offer you some leads." *Please follow me, Mike. Please!*

A nano-flash of annoyance crossed Mike's rugged features. It was instantly replaced with his still-as-stone cop mask. Slowly, deliberately, he unfolded his endless form to its full height. With his gaze holding mine, he said, "Have a seat, Mrs. Quadrelli. And talk to me . . ."

Oh, Mike, thank you . . .

"Tell me what you think is relevant," Mike began. "Talk about anything you can think of—"

Anything other than Maria Tobinski's medical history, and the saga of Pinto, the dog who rides around in a little red wagon.

I touched the woman's arm. "Try to stay on the subject of Enzo and his caffè. Police officers don't have a lot of patience." I shot Mike an apologetic look. In my experience, patience was Mike Quinn's defining characteristic—although with Chatty Cathy here, who knew?

Mrs. Quadrelli settled into the plastic chair and looked up (way up) at the broad-shouldered cop now towering over her. Finally, she turned to me.

"He showed you his ID, right, Miss Cosi? You never said."

With a barely perceptible sigh, Mike reached inside his sport coat, pulled out the well-worn leather wallet and flashed his shield.

"That's a *gold* badge!" A scolding finger appeared in my face. "This man's not just an *officer*, Miss Cosi. He's a *detective*."

"Oh?" I said, exchanging another look with Mike. "I'm so sorry, *Detective*. I didn't mean to demote you."

Mike's lips twitched. "No problem." He turned his attention to Mrs. Quadrelli. "Now why don't you start at the beginning . . ."

Contrary to my advice, Mrs. Q began filling Mike in on her relationship with Enzo, starting with their first passing conversation, the weather that day, and what clothes they were wearing.

I am going to need caffeine, I realized, *as soon as possible.*

The only visible source was a bank of machines on the other side of the waiting room.

Vending machine coffee. God help me . . .

Cringing, I crossed over. My handbag smelled of smoke as I opened it and gathered enough change to satisfy the DelishiCo Individual Brew coffee machine twice. *Oh, sure, each cup was "individually brewed," as promised, but that didn't matter much when the water bin hadn't been flushed in months, and coffee oils had built up along the internal spout.*

I loaded up on the powdered cream, poured in a stack of sugar packets, and returned to Mrs. Quadrelli's side, handing over the cup of coffee I'd promised her.

About then, Mrs. Q's eyes went teary. "And I think maybe it was those men who did it, who set the fire . . ."

"Men?" I echoed. "What men?"

"Theo, the Greek boy, and the other one, Kareem—he's from Morocco or Egypt or something. They run that night-club next to Caffè Lucia—"

"The Red Mirage?" I asked, recalling the scruffy-chinned guy with the foreign accent who'd called my car a junk heap.

"That's the one. Those are the two fellows who manage the place. Theo's been here for years. His family lives by the park. But Kareem is a new émigré, a real shady type."

"What do you mean by shady?" Mike asked. His deep voice remained measured, but his eyes betrayed the tiniest flicker of newly awakened interest.

"Just . . . *shady.*"

"You mean criminal shady?" I pressed.

The woman shrugged. "I wouldn't be surprised."

Mike glanced at me a moment then focused back on Mrs. Quadrelli. "And why do you think these men would want to burn down Enzo's shop?"

"They wanted to buy his place," she explained. "Maybe two months after they opened the club, they began making offers. They were *very* insistent, if you know what I mean—*threatening*, that's what Enzo said. You can ask him; he'll tell you. They kept it up, too, even after Enzo dug in his heels and told them absolutely not."

Mike leaned in a bit. "Why did they want him out so badly?"

"So they could double the size of that nightclub of theirs. When Enzo wouldn't give in, they expanded in the other direction, after Mr. Ganzano moved his real estate office to that new building on Broadway. I think they forced him out. Did you know he left his wife after thirty-one years of marriage? I hear he has a Dominican floozy stashed in an apartment near LaGuardia Airport—"

"But they stopped bothering Enzo, right?" I said. "It sounds like these men got what they wanted. They were able to expand in the other direction?"

"Yes—and then the club doubled in size. Oh, the noise! My goodness the noise on that block was terrible! They kept the music blaring until three, sometimes four, in the morning. There were people crowding the sidewalk, fights every night! And the street was always jammed with cars!"

"Did Enzo complain?" I asked. "Get them into trouble?"

"Oh, no. After a time, there was no need to. All that noise and trouble went away."

"Why is that?" Mike asked. "The club's still there, isn't it?"

"Yes, but the crowds aren't. The place used to have lines around the block. But then the economy took a nosedive and a lot of the young people lost their jobs, thank goodness! Now very few of them have money for overpriced night-clubs, so it's a quiet street again."

A dying business, in other words. Mike raised an eyebrow at me. He was thinking the same thing. Here was the perfect motive for a torch job—and what better way to make yourself look innocent than to start the blaze in the business next door?

Mrs. Quadrelli kept talking, but nothing else seemed as promising a lead as these Red Mirage guys. As she chattered on, I continued forcing myself to drink the vending machine coffee.

About a hundred years ago cowboys used to heat ground coffee in a sock placed in a pot of simmering water. When their campfire coffee was ready, they'd pour it into a tin cup. I'd never tasted boiled cowboy sock coffee, but I was absolutely sure it tasted better than *this*.

"So I told him he should call our city councilmen and complain. Those children of hers make such a racket; they should be made to play someplace else, not to mention that barking dog. Don't you agree it's a public nuisance? And what do you think about the lack of response from 311? Isn't that a disgrace, Detective?"

Mike's cop-neutral expression remained as firmly fixed as ever, but I could tell—from the deepening grooves around his eyes and mouth—that even the most patient detective in the NYPD was becoming exasperated.

"I think I got what I need for now, Mrs. Quadrelli . . ." He glanced at me, a trace of pleading on the edge of it. *Are we done now, Detective Cosi?*

With a twinge of guilt, I said. "Just one more thing, Officer—"

"Not officer!" Mrs. Q reminded me with a correcting *tsk-tsk*. "This man is a detective, remember?"

"Yes, of course." I cleared my throat. "*Detective*, weren't you asking me earlier about Lucia? Maybe Mrs. Quadrelli here can help." I turned to her. "How well do you know Enzo's daughter?"

"Oh, very! She and I have so much in common. We just love to shop! She has such a good eye for shoes and jewelry, that one. We also have the same hairdresser—Gustave Flaubert—"

"Flaubert?" I said. "The nineteenth-century novelist?"

"You know him?" She asked. "He works on Fifth at Jean Michel Dubonnet—"

Mike caught my eye. *Dubonnet on the rocks,* he mouthed, and I nearly choked on the last dregs of my coffee (which would have been appropriate since I'd been gagging the stuff down for the past fifteen minutes).

"That's where we met," the woman continued. "It was Lucia who introduced me to her father, said it was time he started dating again—"

"Oh, I almost forgot," I interrupted as I shot Mike a hang-in-there-partner look. "The detective asked me about Lucia's boyfriends. He might want to follow up with them, see if they have anything to add." I lowered my voice. "Their statements could also help clear Enzo of suspicion."

"Of course! She's seeing a younger man now. His name is Glenn Duffy . . . I'll spell it." She stared at Mike. "Aren't you going to write it down?"

Mike gave a little sigh, pulled out his notebook. "Go ahead . . ."

After Mrs. Q gave the background on Duffy, I waited for another name. There was none. Once again, I pressed—

"Enzo mentioned there was another man from Lucia's past who's been coming around lately. Do you know about him?"

"Oh, you mean the fireman?"

Fireman? I glanced at Mike. Even he seemed surprised.

"What fireman would that be?" Mike asked, his pen poised over his notebook with much more readiness.

"I don't know," Mrs. Quadrelli said.

"You don't know?" I couldn't believe it.

She threw up her hands. "I asked, believe me! Enzo mentioned 'the fireman' was back. He said it once, but then he dropped it, refused to say more. And Lucia insists that Glenn is the only man in her life. That's all I know."

She shrugged. "You want more? Go ask Lucia."

Eleven

~~~~~~

"CLARE? You okay?"

Two hours after our unorthodox interview with the widow Quadrelli, I was back home in my West Village duplex with a still-empty stomach and a head full of questions.

After we'd dropped Madame off at her Fifth Avenue digs, I ran down my theories with Mike. He agreed with my observations, encouraged me to contact Stuart Rossi, and reminded me that FDNY marshals assigned to a fire were like NYPD detectives working a crime scene.

Fire marshals weren't "just like" law enforcement officers, they *were* officers. They carried guns, interviewed witnesses, and (if warranted) made arrests.

"Just treat the man like a police detective," Mike told me. "Call him first thing in the morning, give him everything you dug up, he'll take it from there."

Now I was descending my apartment's staircase, dragging and tired, until a whiff of smoke hit me. Adrenaline instantly juiced my system.

"Clare? You okay?" Mike was gawking at me. I must have looked ill or gone pale or something until I realized the offending agent was safely contained in my living room fireplace.

"Did you hear me, sweetheart? You okay?"

"I'm okay."

I wasn't. Not really. But I didn't want Mike feeling bad about his cozy fire-building gesture. The lengthening flames would warm the chilly room. Even the disturbing shadows flickering across the polished antiques made me conclude (in a whole new way) how lucky I was to reside in this place.

While this entire Federal-era townhouse was still technically my ex-mother-in-law's, she'd made clear to me that she was legally willing its ownership to me as well as her son, so I felt like a caretaker now as much as a resident—an invaluable bonus that came with managing her coffeehouse two floors below.

As my sock-covered feet slipped across the chilly parquet floor, I noticed Mike's gaze tracking me with unabashed interest. For a second, I couldn't imagine why.

Sexy was not a word I'd use to describe me at the moment. Postshower, I'd dressed for sloppy comfort in a pair of black bike shorts and an oversized T-shirt that warned: *Do Not Give This Woman Decaf!*

The tee—along with an apron that said *I Serve It Up Hot!*—had been a gag gift from my staff last Christmas. But Mike had seen this shirt before. On the other hand, it was the first time I'd gone braless wearing it. (My street clothes, down to my underwear, had reeked of char, and my other bras were still damp from a morning's hand-washing.)

Whatever the reason for the man's open scrutiny, I was happy to return the gesture. With his sport coat tossed off, Mike's muscular shoulders were nicely defined by his dress shirt—spotlessly white yet noticeably wrinkled from hours of wearing his leather holster. Tie well loosened, long, strong form folded into a relaxed crouch, he looked comfortably assured, entrenched in a zone of cool-blue control that was quintessentially Mike.

From our very first meeting, I'd been impressed by the

man's natural confidence, mainly because—unlike my ex-husband—it lacked arrogance. Mike was often wary and sometimes skeptical, but he was never cynical, not in the way some people were, using it as an excuse for complacency or indifference. What attracted me most, I think, was his equilibrium. Mike was as hardened as any cop from the New York streets, yet he'd refused to let the job or the city kill his compassion.

Like a buttoned-down Ivanhoe, he now picked up the black iron poker and stabbed at the heart of the fire he'd built, not to kill the thing but to give it more air. And that's when it hit me just how much Mike Quinn enjoyed igniting blazes in my hearth.

Hmmm . . .

Considering the occupation of the man's cousin and younger brothers, I figured the desire to play with fire was probably a Quinn thing. Or maybe it was just some gene buried deep in the alpha-male string, a primal urge leftover from the DNA of grunting cavemen.

As I settled into the carved rosewood sofa, my gaze caught on his well-worn shoulder holster now hanging off the delicate lyre back of one of Madame's heirloom chairs. Tucked inside the leather was his rather large handgun. *Yet another kind of fire stick . . . ?*

"You look a little funny, sweetheart. Do you need a drink?"

"I need to eat."

I would have chowed down sooner, but I hadn't been able to stand those reeking clothes another minute; so while Mike had taken care of parking my old Honda, I'd headed upstairs for a hot, soapy shower.

I could see from the shopping bag now sitting on the coffee table—not to mention the aromas of cooked meat assaulting my sensory receptors—that Mike had taken care of food, too. But what was it exactly?

The large, glossy bag didn't look like your typical brown paper take-out sack. Vivid orange with a laminated exterior and nylon rope handles, it looked self-consciously hip, which was hardly ever a good thing when it came to authentically tasty takeout.

"UFC?" I said, reading the logo. "KFC I've heard of, but UFC?"

"It's Korean-style fried chicken," Mike said, putting down the poker.

I looked closer at the small print under the large UFC logo. "Unidentified Flying Chickens? I never heard of them."

"There are only three stores in the metro area," Mike said, rising to his full height, "one in Elmhurst, one in Brooklyn, and one in North Jersey. Sully swears by them, says he's addicted. He just dropped it off."

"Sully was here?"

Finbar "Sully" Sullivan worked closely with Mike on the OD Squad, a special task force Mike supervised out of the Sixth Precinct here in Greenwich Village. Sully was one of the nicest men I knew—an openly cheerful forty-something guy with ready quips delivered in a native Queens accent.

"I left my car back in Elmhurst," Mike explained. "I asked Sully and Franco to swing by, bring it back to Manhattan."

"Wait, back up. Did you just say Sully and *Franco*? As in Sergeant Emmanuel Franco?"

Mike nodded and I tensed. Detective Sergeant Franco was the complete opposite of Finbar Sullivan. Edgy and volatile, the man was about as subtle as a ball-peen hammer to the forehead (something I had learned over this past holiday season).

Where Mike and Sully wore suits, ties, and their methodical patience on their sleeves, the younger Franco displayed cocky confidence and a street-tough attitude, with a wardrobe to match: a Yankee jacket, cowboy boots, and an in-your-face red, white, and, blue 'do rag.

Despite the guy's bulldog approach to law enforcement, however, I did not *dislike* him. What concerned me was Franco's interest in my daughter. He'd taken Joy out a number of times while she was visiting me on her last holiday break. But, *thank goodness,* my girl was back in Paris.

I didn't relish the idea of Joy meeting and falling for another French line cook, which could sway her to remain in Europe indefinitely, but I was even less happy with her developing an attachment to a detective whose persona seemed to fall somewhere between Dirty Harry and Rambo.

"I can't believe you're working with Franco," I said.

"Why not?" He crossed his arm. "I needed the manpower."

"The construction site investigation?"

Mike nodded. Over the past two weeks, he'd been following up on recent OD cases, one of which had ended in death. Working closely with the DEA, he and Sully had supervised a covert investigation of a popular nightclub on the Lower East Side, near the Williamsburg Bridge, where both victims had ingested the drugs.

Unfortunately, the place came up clean. No dealing had been uncovered on the premises. Now a source claimed the selling was being done at an adjacent construction site, where someone working on the site itself was dealing recreational drugs like ecstasy and Liquid E to club-goers.

"Well . . ." I tried to focus on the positive. (After all, I could see where a rough-edged guy like Franco would be an asset in working an undercover operation on a construction crew. And when it came to Mike's choice of police personnel, who was I to argue?) "I suppose it was nice of the two of them to bring over dinner, along with your car . . ."

"Yes, it was."

"Unidentified Flying Chickens . . ." I shook my head. "A Queens restaurant with an ironic name."

"Yeah . . ." Mike sat down next to me. "It's way too Manhattan hipster for the geography."

"Have you tried it? What do you think of it?"

Mike arched an eyebrow. "You really care?"

He was right. I didn't. The enticing aromas were making my stomach growl and my mouth salivate. I dug into the bag. The first box I opened was stuffed with warm chicken wings. A second later, my teeth were tearing into skin crispier than a newly fried kettle chip. The caramelized taste of slow-roasted garlic hit my palate first, next came a play of sweet brown sugar, slightly tingly ginger, and under it all, a low, meaty *umami* base note of soy.

"Oh my God," I garbled as I masticated.

"Good?"

"Mm, mm . . . mmmmm . . ."

Mike joined me, opening another box, which was stuffed with fried drumsticks, glistening with a sweet-and-sour glaze. A third held containers of tangy cold slaw with a hint of Chinese mustard; cubes of cold, crunchy Korean radish; and sweet potato matchsticks.

"You know, I could duplicate this," I managed to boast around a mouthful of soy-garlic wing.

"I don't doubt it," Mike said, who'd swooned over my cooking more times than I could count.

"They must fry their chicken twice to get it this crispy . . ." I munched some more, gathering flavor and textural clues, deducing the culinary technique. "Then after they fry it, they must roll it in the sticky glaze and dry it out in a warm oven . . ."

"Sounds like your famous Buffalo wings."

"Except I don't deep-fry those, just crisp them up in a cast-iron skillet. A tempura batter might be interesting to try . . ." I couldn't help channeling one of my old In the Kitchen with Clare columns. "Home cooks tend to use all-purpose flour because it's always in the pantry, but cake flour is the best way to go for frying batters, even for beer-battered onion rings, because it's lower in gluten."

"Well, sweetheart, the day you want to experiment, give me a call. I'll be happy to help with the taste testing."

"I've noticed you're always available for that."

"I'm always available for a lot of things." He threw me his best leering wink. I laughed and leaned back on the sofa, grateful my bike pants had an expanding waistband. "Man, I really needed that . . ."

Mike reached out with a paper napkin, gently wiped at a ruby smear along my cheek. "I'm guessing you liked it . . ."

I did the same for him, rubbing at a smudge on his chin. "I'd say your man Sully's a good guy to trust."

"So am I," Mike said. Then he leaned in and moved his mouth over mine.

That tasted even better.

Mike's mouth was sweet and slightly sticky from the chicken glaze, and (frankly) I would have been happy to gorge myself on nothing but him for the rest of the night. But, after a few blissful minutes, I was the one who broke contact.

"I'm sorry, Mike . . ." I softly pushed on his hard chest. "I'd like to talk a little more . . ."

TWELVE

〜〜〜〜〜〜〜〜〜〜〜〜〜〜〜〜〜〜〜〜

As we broke contact, I saw the disappointment in Mike's eyes. I didn't blame him. I needed to talk, and that's not what he needed.

"Everything you did tonight was wonderful," I quickly reassured him, "coming to the hospital, helping with Mrs. Quadrelli, driving us home, arranging the food . . ."

But I wanted one more thing from Mike Quinn: answers about his cousin. And if the lip-lock went on any longer, I wouldn't care about getting them—or anything else apart from the two of us upstairs on my mahogany four-poster.

Mike studied my face. "It's okay," he finally said. "I'm always glad to help . . ."

He leaned back on the sofa, stretched an arm across the back, gestured for me to move closer. I did, leaning into him.

"I have to admit," he said, gazing at the crackling hearth, "it was nice seeing you with a satisfied expression again. The way you were choking down that vending machine coffee back at the hospital . . ." He shook his head. "I had to bite my tongue to keep from cracking up."

"You had to bite *your* tongue? I thought I was going to

lose it when Mrs. Quadrelli went on about Gustave Flaubert styling her hair."

"Yeah, old Gustave's probably some poor kid from Brooklyn named Gus Flabberson."

"Par for the course on the hustle-a-buck schemes that go on in this town."

"I thought I'd heard every alias in the book," Mike said. "Jacking the name of *Madame Bovary*'s author is more creative than some."

"I'm betting Gustave's boss has an entire list of famous French author names ready to go."

"So you think he's got Stendhal doing the shampooing and Balzac on the register?"

"No," I said. "If the man knows his French writers, Dumas is on the register and Stendhal's in charge of color. Balzac belongs with the stylists."

Mike laughed. "I actually do follow you, you know?"

"Oh? You mean not all cops are jarheads?"

"Naw. We only *look* like a paramilitary organization."

I smiled. "Well, I'm not in a position to throw stones. I used a false identity to get in to see Enzo."

"And you got some good information, too."

"You think so?"

"Like I told you earlier," he said, "call that fire marshal first thing in the morning. Tell him everything . . ."

The list of suspects wasn't small, but I'd gathered good leads. Only one thing still troubled me: "I can't stop wondering who that fireman is, the mysterious one who's secretly seeing Lucia."

"Me, too," Mike said. "If that woman was looking for expertise in torching her dad's caffè, she couldn't do any better than a fireman."

"You're speaking from experience?"

Mike didn't answer directly. What he said was, "Firefighters are experts in the methods of starting blazes, not just stopping them. It's part of their training . . ."

And there's my opening . . .

"So tell me, Detective, why didn't you ever go through the training? I mean, given your hero father and your younger brothers . . ." *Not to mention your evil twin of a cousin.* "Why aren't you a fireman, too?"

I'd kept the tone light, but my question failed to amuse. Mike's body tensed beside mine; his prolonged silence felt heavy. So I took a guess—and not a very wild one: "Is that the reason why you and your cousin don't get along? Because you didn't follow family tradition and join the FDNY?"

He exhaled. "That's part of it."

I shifted on the sofa, getting some distance so I could see his eyes. This was a situation I'd faced before with this man—*How do you interrogate a trained interrogator?*

Not with tricks. When I wanted answers from Mike, I asked him straight. "I'd like to know what started the beef between you two."

"What *started* it . . ." He let out another audible breath. "I guess you could say it *started* a long time ago . . . when we were in the academy together."

"Police academy?" I assumed.

"Fire academy."

"Fire academy? You went to the fire academy with your cousin?"

Mike nodded.

"What about that story you told me? About always wanting to be a cop? That schoolyard epiphany thing . . ."

Just like me, Mike had gone to Catholic school, where the priests and nuns were big on the idea of vocation. At some point in our lives, they told us, God was supposed to reveal our life's calling.

I'd gotten the cosmic message with the birth of my daughter. According to Mike, he'd picked up the Almighty's voicemail at the age of thirteen during a vicious fight that had broken out between two boys in the school courtyard.

Instead of standing on the sidelines with the others, Mike jumped in to stop it and got a beating for his trouble—from both boys. The Jesuit who finally broke it up told Mike that with his zealousness to leap into human matters and make things right, he was destined to become a priest or a cop.

"I probably could have been a priest," he'd told me when we first started seeing each other. "I just couldn't hack the chastity."

"So how did you end up in the fire academy?"

"My dad wanted it. I respected the man, so I gave it a shot . . ." He shrugged. "It just wasn't for me. After a few weeks, I quit."

"And your cousin Michael couldn't understand?"

Again, Mike shrugged. "He thought we were in it together . . ."

"So he turned on you?"

"Like I said, that's how it *started*. Trust me when I say that my cousin has no love for me, and I'd like you to stay away from him. Can you do that for me, Clare?"

"Yes, of course."

"Thank you."

As we sat gazing at the hearth, I felt Mike's hand brush aside my hair, begin to caress my shoulder. His heavy body leaned into me, and I felt his lips at my nape, applying little kisses.

I knew what the man wanted. (I wanted it, too.) But I couldn't let go. An idea kept banging around my brain, a pithy piece of police wisdom Mike once shared: *If a smart perp wants to dodge an interview, he doesn't clam up or even argue. He keeps feeding the interviewer information—just not any key information . . .*

And that's what Mike had done with me. I was sure of it. Considering the Quinn clan's history with the FDNY, I figured there had to be more to his story. Not that I was some expert on familial expectation.

After my mother left us, my father expressed zero thoughts about my future apart from *I just want you to be happy, cupcake . . .* The equivalent of a "Good girl, Lassie" pat on the head. My old-world grandmother, who'd primarily raised me, never pushed me to be anything—beyond a well-behaved young lady.

It wasn't until college that I realized not everyone was

like me. A number of my classmates were pressured children, saddled with the baggage of parental aspirations. When the stars aligned, they had few issues: *I always wanted to study contract law . . . Electrical engineering works for me . . . Sure, I'm going for the PhD . . .*

But when one future had two different maps, kids got lost.

The strong ones waged external rebellion, raising shields against arrows as they followed the sound of Henry David's drummer. The pragmatic ones chose deafness—*screw the different drummer, he's suspect*—and locked down their spirits to the road often taken.

The ones I worried about lived in the gray purgatory of indecision, giving their families the appearance of going along while quietly burning for another life. These kids saw the lights of an inspiring new highway yet continued to plod along the deadening old one, nurturing quiet resentment with every step. (And I knew from my own lousy marriage that a pretense like that was about as healthy as feeding a piranha in your stomach. Inevitably the thing grew bigger and bigger, gnawing at your insides until it completely hollowed you out.)

Given the Quinn legacy, Mike's father must have been devastated when his eldest quit the fire academy. It couldn't have been the casual decision Mike was now making it out to be.

I cleared my throat: "I noticed you like sharing that story about the schoolyard fight, but there's something more, isn't there? Something you don't want people to know about why you became a cop."

The kisses stopped. The magic fingers quit moving. Mike leaned back, taking his hand and lips with him.

"Mike?"

"It's not a pretty story, Clare."

"I don't care. I'd like to hear it . . ."

For a full minute, he stayed silent, shifting a few times on the sofa. Then just when I thought he would clam up for good, he rubbed his jaw, took a breath, and said—

"When I hit high school, I started dating a classmate.

Leta was her name, Leta Diaz. Bright girl, beautiful smile. She was my lab partner in chemistry, a class we both enjoyed, so we hit it off . . ."

He paused to glance over at me. I nodded. "Go on."

"Leta's family came here from the Dominican Republic. They ran their own little convenience store just off the Brooklyn-Queens Expressway. One afternoon, Leta's dad was robbed at the store. He resisted and was shot to death."

"Oh God, that's awful. Your poor girlfriend."

"Yeah, she took it extremely hard. I tried to be there for her. But I wanted to do more than just hold her hand and watch her cry her heart out, you know? I wanted to do something. So I did."

"What do you mean? You were just a high school kid."

"I had a gut feeling. The week before, at one of the school's basketball games, I noticed the father of a classmate talking to Leta's father. There was something about the way he was chatting up the man—it seemed odd, like a hustle."

"So?"

"So this robbery that happened—it was during a very narrow window of time when Leta's father had a great deal of cash on hand at the store to pay their packaged-food distributor. Once a week they got that delivery, once a week on a certain day, between certain hours."

"And you thought this man, this father of your classmate at school, was the stick-up guy?"

"I knew he'd already done time for mail fraud. My classmate—Pete Hogarth was his name—he'd been complaining that his old man couldn't get any work, also hinted that he had a worsening cocaine habit. So I took matters into my own hands."

"What did you do?"

"I buddied up to Pete, went back to his apartment to hang out. The place was small, no privacy, but when I heard his dad kept pigeons on the roof, I knew that's where I'd find evidence—and I did. The gun and the cash were buried in one of the coops. I called the detectives assigned to the case.

They arrested Pete's father. The ballistics matched up. He was the shooter."

"Leta must have been grateful."

"Honestly, she was too numb to fully understand what I did. Less than a month later, her family was back living in the Dominican Republic."

"So much for young love."

"Don't sweat it, Cosi. My heart survived."

"Those detectives handling the case must have been impressed."

"They were. They checked in on me after that, encouraged me to go to the police academy."

"But your father wanted you to join the FDNY?"

"I was the oldest. Like I said, I respected my dad, wanted to make him proud. But . . ."

"But . . . ?"

Mike turned on the sofa to fully face me. "As it came down, two of the guys in my class at the fire academy—they were relatives of Pete Hogarth's. These guys didn't care that Pete's father was a scumbag killer. They just figured me for a narc, a rat, a guy you could never trust, and they made it a point of spreading the story of what I'd done."

"Is that how your cousin felt about you?"

"No. Michael defended me. But it wasn't enough, and after a few weeks, my reality check kicked in. I knew what I wanted to be doing for the next four decades of my life, and it wasn't fighting fires. I wanted to be hunting down predators, Clare, getting them the hell off the street. Hogarth shot Leta's father in cold blood, and I made sure he couldn't kill again. I *liked* how it felt when I took him down."

My mind flashed on Enzo, pale as a cadaver in the ICU; Madame weak and teary on that stretcher; Dante unconscious on the glass-strewn concrete . . .

I closed my eyes. "Does it always feel good to take them down?"

"For me it does. But you don't always get them, Clare."

I realized something then, something Mike had known all along . . .

"That's why you've never discouraged me, isn't it?" I met his gaze. "You solved your first homicide as a kid, without a badge or a gun. You know what someone like me can do."

"Information and evidence, sweetheart. That's what clears cases. I can flash my shield all day long, but without information and evidence, I can't do my job. That's why we work to develop informants on the street, interview witnesses, run background checks. If you can get those things for an investigator, then you can help him—or her."

I exhaled. Given the fire marshal's brush off earlier in the evening, not to mention Captain Michael's oh-so-subtle warning not to get involved, I hadn't realized how much I needed to hear some encouraging words. Well, I was happy to return the favor.

"I can see why you don't like retelling that story. But it's really something what you did. It took guts . . ."

"Thanks." Mike smiled, but only a little, as if he were flattered by my words but embarrassed, too. Pointing to the take-out bag, he changed the subject. "You want more?"

"Not of that."

"Something else, then?"

I nodded. The flames in the fireplace were at their peak. I could feel their heat against my skin, hear their teasing pops and sparks. Leaning over, I pulled Mike's mouth back onto mine.

He was pleased I'd started the kiss. I could feel it in his tightening arms, his widening smile against my mouth. He tugged me closer, used his tongue to part my lips, deepen our connection. Then his hands slipped under my oversized tee, and his slightly calloused fingers generated something with a whole lot more intensity than what he'd started in my living room hearth.

"C'mon," he whispered, finally breaking away. "Let's go upstairs . . ."

I wasn't about to argue.

Thirteen

∽∾∽∾∽∾∽∾∽∾∽∾∽∾∽∾∽∾∽∾∽∾∽∾

I woke the next morning to a pair of cat paws kneading my shoulder. I instinctively reached out for Mike. With a stab of disappointment, I realized the pillow next to mine was empty. That's when I remembered dozing off in his arms. He'd kissed my forehead and whispered something about an early meeting with prosecutors ahead of a grand jury appearance.

Suddenly I felt another kind of stab, a prickly one to my right foot. Java and Frothy were circling me like a pair of miniature *Jurassic Park* raptors.

"Okay, I'm up!"

I threw off the covers. "Happy now?"

Tails raised in feline triumph, the girls bounded off the bed and waited for me at the door. With another yawn, I tied on a robe, thrust my feet into slippers, and followed their proud little forms—one coffee-bean brown, the other latte-foam white—to the kitchen.

Despite that long, steamy shower the night before, I still had a thickness in my throat, a funky odor in my sinuses, and notwithstanding the many splendored moments of

Mike's lovemaking, my subsequent dreams had been filled with images of billowing black smoke, flashing red lights, and glinting razors of splintered glass.

Tucker, my assistant manager, was scheduled to open today, which meant I still had a little time to pull myself together. Thankfully, I felt more human after I fed my tiny, furry raptors a can of furry raptor food and mainlined a Moka-brewed *doppio* espresso.

Next I phoned Dante at Elmhurst Hospital. He was in good spirits this AM, announcing he was "ready to roll!" His release paperwork was already being prepared, and two friends were waiting in his room to take him home—Kiki and Bahni, the two young women who also shared his apartment.

One for each of his tattooed arms, I thought, relieved to hear some good news.

Next I called Madame, surprised to find her already dressed and on her way out the door. A driver was waiting downstairs, she explained, ready to return her to Queens and the bedside of her old friend.

"You'll need to say you're a family member if you want to see him," I warned.

"Yes, dear, I've already thought of that."

"Well, don't say you're his sister, okay? He may think you're Rita Quadrelli!"

"I plan to inform the nurses that I am his *sister-in-law*. I will be sure to give my name so Enzo knows my true identity."

"Great. Please let me know how he's doing, okay?"

"Of course."

"And there's one more thing . . . Last night, while I was questioning Enzo, he mentioned to me that Lucia was still seeing a fireman."

"Old flame?"

"Very funny."

"Yes, dear, well, it would have to be an old flame, wouldn't it? She described herself as engaged to that other boy, Glenn, didn't she?"

"See if you can get Enzo to tell you who this fireman is. Get a name."

After a pause, Madame said, "Did this fireman have something to do with setting the firebomb, dear?"

"You've certainly had your coffee this morning."

"With or without the java, I'm a lot sharper than you think."

"I think you're *plenty* sharp."

"Don't worry. I'll speak to Enzo."

"Thank you . . ."

By the time I hung up, it was after nine—late for me, but just about the perfect time to contact my favorite FDNY fire marshal. I dug his card out of my charcoal-scented handbag and dialed.

"Rossi."

"Hello," I said, envisioning the big man's slightly mashed nose, blue nylon jacket, and clanking tool belt. "This is the woman you spoke to last night at the Astoria fire. My name is Cla—"

"Clare Cosi. Yes, Ms. Cosi? What can I do for you?"

The speed and clarity of Rossi's response caught me by surprise. Obviously, the man had mainlined his morning joe. "Last night I spoke to the man who owns Caffè Lucia—"

"Lorenzo Testa? You went to the ICU?"

"I did, and I have some information for you. I spoke at length to a friend and neighbor of his, a Rita Quadrelli?"

"Yes."

I took a deep breath, feeling as righteous as Don Quixote—which was apropos. Five minutes from now, Rossi would probably dismiss me as tilting at windmills. But the stakes were too high to be indulging my pride. If I looked like an ass, so be it.

"Let me just say, Marshal, that when you find the evidence that the fire was intentionally set, as I know you will, I'm aware you'll be looking at Enzo as your prime suspect because he's the sole beneficiary of the fire insurance policy. But there are a number of much more viable suspects around Mr. Testa with very strong motives to torch his caffè."

I paused, waited.

"Go on."

"Mr. Testa's adult daughter, Lucia, has no interest in running the business, yet she's set to inherit the store and building when her father finally decides to retire. I think she may have hastened that retirement by having that fire set.

"Then there's the widow Quadrelli. That woman clearly views the caffè as the only thing standing between her and Enzo having some sort of 'happily ever after' scenario.

"And I also think you should look at the two men who run the Red Mirage nightclub: Theo and Kareem. These guys have been losing business since the economy tanked and may have tried to get a fire insurance payout by starting a suspicious fire next door, in Enzo's caffè, hoping it would spread to their property."

I listened for a reaction. But there was none. The line went silent. "Marshal Rossi?"

"Hold on, Ms. Cosi—"

Damn. "I really do think this is *important* information."

"So do I, ma'am. I'm taking notes . . ."

I blinked. *He's actually listening to me?* "So you'll follow up then?"

"That's my job."

"I'm very glad to hear you say that."

"Do you have anything else to add, Ms. Cosi?"

"I do. If Lucia Testa is responsible for setting that blaze— or even if she conspired to do it with Rita Quadrelli—I doubt very much she would have created the actual firebomb herself."

"Why is that?"

"She's a fastidious fashionista, that's why. Building a firebomb set on a timer might ruin her manicure. Ditto for the widow."

"So what's your theory?"

"I think it's possible that Lucia hired an accomplice or persuaded one to help her, either for personal reasons or a monetary payoff."

"And . . . ? Do you have any thoughts on who Ms. Testa or Mrs. Quadrelli may have worked with on that?"

"Yes. I believe there are two strong suspects. The first man is Lucia's boyfriend Glenn Duffy . . ." I told the marshal all I knew about Duffy, including his expertise as a mechanic. "And the second man is . . . actually, I don't have a name, but I know for certain he's a fireman."

"Excuse me?"

"Mr. Testa told me that a fireman's been sniffing around after Lucia. It sounds like a sexual relationship. I would have tried questioning Lucia herself, but she's not in town right now. She went away for the weekend, just a few hours before the bomb went off, which is highly suspicious timing, don't you think? I mean, getting out of town certainly helps her look completely detached from what happened . . ."

Rossi said nothing.

"Anyway," I added. "I think she may have used this fireman and his knowledge to help set off a firebomb and burn down the caffè."

"And you don't have any other information on this man's identity?"

"The only thing I can tell you concerns the firefighters who responded—"

"You're talking about Ladder 189 and Engine 335?"

"If that's who responded."

"It is."

"Well, Enzo confessed to me that his daughter liked to play with men. And the captain of the firehouse that responded told me that a lot of his guys liked to frequent Enzo's caffè, so . . ."

"So you think a member of the FDNY from Ladder 189 or Engine 335 helped Lucia Testa set the fire?"

"It's one theory, but yes, I do . . ."

After another moment of silence, Rossi asked, "Are you sure you can't *get* me a name, Ms. Cosi?"

The question confused me. It took me a moment to process it. "Marshal Rossi, are you saying that you'd like me to investigate further?"

"No comment."

I took a breath. "You can't officially ask me to investigate, can you?"

Rossi didn't answer directly. What he said was: "Like I told you before, Ms. Cosi, if you have *any new information* for me, just give me a call." He lowered his voice. "Call me anytime, okay?"

"I'll see what I can do . . ."

I hung up and stood staring for a moment.

Given Mike's talk with me last night, I shouldn't have been so astonished by Rossi's reaction. The man was a detective, after all, and I was an informant bringing him leads. It was no different from a street cop using snitches. Sure Rossi might have gotten the same leads once he started questioning Enzo, but I'd given him a head start and he knew it.

Obviously, the fire company was another matter. Those guys were tighter than family. James Noonan and Bigsby Brewer even referred to each other as brothers. The second an investigator like Rossi started asking questions, they'd stonewall him, especially if it meant protecting a man in their own firehouse.

And if Lucia has a history of sleeping with more than one of those men, that was just another reason for the entire company to make like irritated oysters and clam up . . .

I dug into the pocket of my robe for an elastic band, scraped my sleep-mussed hair into a taut, work-ready ponytail, and considered my options.

Enzo had been reluctant to give me the name of Lucia's secret fireman lover. Would he give it to Madame? I wasn't so sure.

The strongest connection I had to Ladder 189 and Engine 335 was Captain Michael Quinn. I could talk to him. But Mike specifically asked me to stay away from his cousin.

Just wait, Clare. Calm down and wait . . .

Madame would get a name. That was the easiest solution. And if that failed, there was always next week's Five-Borough Bake Sale to benefit the NYC Fallen Firefighters Fund. I'd have a chance to question some of the guys there, though I had to admit the idea of pressing those men to betray one of their own made me a little queasy.

Now I know how Mike must have felt turning in his classmate's father . . .

Feeling the acute need for some reassuring warmth, I went to the stove, poured filtered water into the lower half of my three-cup Moka Express. I ground the beans fine, piled them into the little filter basket, screwed the two pieces together, and placed them over medium heat.

The shimmering blue flame of the gas burner reminded me of Mike's eyes in the firelight. I chewed my lower lip, still a little swollen from his kisses, and in the quiet of the kitchen, I felt the faintest echoes of his lovemaking still singing through my body—so sweet and slow at first then breathtaking in its intensity. I ached for him now, sorry he'd had to leave so early.

As the express water came to a boil, however, my thoughts began to turn . . .

"Captain Michael," I whispered to the empty air. He truly was my best bet for a source inside that firehouse, which made me reconsider Mike's request to stay away from the man.

Given Mike's fire-academy story, I didn't doubt that things had gone down badly between the two cousins. *But didn't all of that stuff happen more than twenty years ago?*

Last night's Quinn vs. Quinn standoff came to mind—Captain Michael smirking at his cousin in the hospital drive; Mike doing a reach around for his handcuffs.

There must be more to the story. I moved to sit down at the kitchen table and that's when I realized . . .

There is.

A powerful, roasted scent suddenly suffused the air. My espresso was done. I moved to the stove, sloshed the steaming liquor into a demitasse, and sipped it so quickly it burned my tongue. I didn't care.

Quinn was one of the best interrogator's in the NYPD. He could effortlessly manipulate any information exchange. I thought I was hot stuff, getting him to spill, but the reverse was true: Mike Quinn had manipulated me.

My fist hit the kitchen table so hard it sent the cats scurrying into the next room.

When I'd asked Mike what had started the beef between him and his cousin, he'd treated the phrasing literally: "What started it," he'd said, emphasizing the *started*. "I guess you could say it started a long time ago . . ."

Then why is it still going on? That's what I should have asked the man!

After downing the hot coffee, I banged open my cupboards and made a hasty breakfast—a giant popover pancake (aka Dutch Baby, Bismarck, poor girl's soufflé): flour, eggs, milk, salt, all whisked up with more fury than Dorothy's tornado.

I poured the batter into a preheated pan and flung it into a blistering oven where it quickly inflated like the puffy exterior of a Navajo bread; but instead of honey, I finished the whole thing in the bracing-sweet style of an espresso Romano, with a quick, tart squeeze from a lemon wedge and a generous dusting of powdered sugar.

My breakfast eaten, I went back to my cupboards and pulled out more ingredients: flour, baking soda, salt . . . I began throwing things together: brown sugar, cocoa powder, leftover espresso . . .

A few minutes later I had a batter for my Magnificent Melt-in-Your-Mouth Mocha Brownies. The manic activity made me feel less like an ineffectual sap, but only a little, so I poured the dark elixir into a square pan, set it aside, and went to the fridge once more . . .

Milk, eggs, butter, and a treasure from the spice rack. Nutmeg? Piquant yet soothing; exotic yet wistfully familiar. The Elizabethans believed it could ward off the plague;

Charlie Parker and Malcolm X used it to get high . . . *Good enough for me!*

I took out my electric hand mixer and assaulted the butter and sugar with glee.

Sell me half a story? Sure! I'll buy it!

I added the eggs, one at a time, ferociously beating between each addition.

Yeah, you're one crack interrogator, Cosi. Homeland Security should put you on speed dial!

Stress always did this to me. I had to bake. At times, nostalgia was the reason. Baking brought me back to those early hours with Nonna in her grocery store's kitchen: hot ovens warming the chilly air; sticky white dough coming together beneath flour-dusted hands; battered sheet pans emerging from their transmuting fire baths heavy with the gold of fresh Italian loaves and crunchy, sweet biscotti.

On a morning like this one, however, other things drove me to the beating of the batter: a sense of reassurance for one, a reclaiming of the feeling I had control over *something*.

Measuring the flour calmed me somewhat (a different part of the brain apparently calculated ounces and grams, sifted out lumps). Then I married the wet and dry ingredients.

"I now pronounce you Doughnut Muffin batter . . ."

In flavor and texture, the resulting muffin would indeed taste like an "old-fashioned" doughnut. It wasn't magic, just a culinary trick. (Most quick-bread batters called for a simple stirring of ingredients, but the dump-and-stir muffin failed to yield an optimal product. Creaming sugar into butter whipped air into the batter's foundation, substantially improving its texture. In this batter, the technique would evoke the same airy tenderness as a classic cake doughnut.)

I filled the paper lined cups, opened the heavy oven door, then slid my pans home with the satisfied sigh of a weary body slipping into a warm bath.

I guess what I most appreciated about baking was its transformative qualities, and not simply because the end product was more than the sum of its parts. The entire process served as a much needed reminder of a simple but profound truth: the fundamentals of cooking never changed.

In a world where firebombs went off in your face and your lover held back on you, just knowing that stirring sugar into liquefied shortening would always give a different result than creaming it into softened butter was an honest-to-God comfort.

I still didn't know how I was going to get the whole truth out of Mike, but I would find a way. In my view, family feuds were ticking time bombs. I'd already had one incendiary device go off in my face. I wasn't about to let it happen again.

WHEN I finally headed upstairs, I felt much calmer—less like a rube of an interrogator than a capable woman back in control. Entering the bedroom, however, my momentary illusion of calm was blown away by a brand-new storm.

The steady sound of beeping may have been weak, but its familiar meaning shot adrenaline through my body as effectively as a blaring ambulance siren.

My cell phone!

I rushed to the dresser and saw the blinking light. Someone had left me an urgent message.

Joy? Madame? Mike? Dante?

I played back the recording, and the frantic voice of my ex-husband assaulted my ear.

"Clare! Where the hell are you?"

I checked the time stamp on the message. Matt had phoned me during my lengthy talk with Rossi.

"I get off my plane at JFK, pass a newsstand, and what do I see? My mother on the front page of two tabloids! Why is she on a stretcher for God's sake? And surrounded by firemen? What the hell happened? I can see *you* standing in the background! Why didn't you call me, Clare? Now I can't reach her! Or you! And my battery is dying. Will you please call me back when—"

Click.

A robotic voice followed. "End of messages."

Fourteen

~~~~~~

THIRTY minutes later, my hair still damp from a quick shower, I descended the back staircase to my coffeehouse. Grabbing a Village Blend apron off a pegboard in the pantry, I peered through the open archway into the main shop.

"Good morning," I called to the lanky back of my assistant manager.

Tucker Burton turned around, tossed his floppy brown mop, and flashed a footlights-worthy grin. "Well, hello, sleepy head! How are you?"

I avoided a direct answer, which might have resulted in a primal scream. Instead I firmly tied my apron strings and pointed to our machine.

"How's she running today?"

"Not bad."

I didn't reply. I didn't have to. Tucker already knew what to do next. He turned back to pull me a test shot, so I could judge how bad "not bad" really was.

The machine itself was a beauty, reliably stable when it came to maintaining temperature and pressure. The espresso was what worried me. Like a gifted but temperamental child, my favorite elixir had easy days and difficult days; days of generous glory with lush, oozing *crema,* and days of stingy infamy with thin, diluted sourness.

The process of coaxing every bit of sweetly caramelized flavor from Matt's superlatively sourced beans was truly a kind of java alchemy. Three solid months of flight time had to be logged by my trainee baristas before they could attempt even one perfect shot for a customer.

What my newbie baristas had to fully understand was the array of variables that could devolve the process; how their perfectly dosed and tamped pulls of sultry-sweet nectar, executed in the exact same manner, with the same equipment and coffee beans, could suddenly turn into acidy slipstreams of espresso hell. Only when the untried learned to get comfortable with confusion, friendly with frustration, would the one-true-God shot be within reach . . .

As Tucker worked on pulling my taste test, I peered over the blueberry marble counter. Our tables were half empty, a normal pattern for a late weekday morning. The occupied seats were recognizable regulars—NYU students with open text books, neighborhood freelancers with open laptops, and a few hospital workers on open cell phones.

Tucker's morning backup, Esther Best (shortened from Bestovasky by her grandfather), appeared to be chatting with a small group of fans. (Yes, I said *fans.* Esther may have been one of my strongest latte artists, but her true renown as a local slam poetess had spread through at least two of the five boroughs. New customers, mostly aspiring "urban poets" and rappers, were showing up every day just to talk to her. Lucky for our bottom line they ordered coffee drinks from her, too.)

I finished scanning the room.

No sign of Matt yet.

After hearing his frantic message, I'd speed-dialed the man. All I got was voicemail (no surprise). So after my shower, I pulled on jeans and a Henley the color of toasted coconut and descended the stairs. I wasn't scheduled for another hour, but

Matt would be bursting in here any minute, and I theorized he'd be more likely to stay calm in a public place.

As the high morning sun broke through the low clouds, it made *me* feel calmer. The dazzling rays gleamed in the sparkling glass of our shop's French doors. The restored wood-plank floor was all waxed and shiny; the twenty marble-topped tables stood reliably in place.

With new eyes, I gazed at the wrought-iron spiral staircase, soaring like a modern sculpture up to the second floor seating area where my tiny office waited with its shabby familiarity of battered desk and nonswiveling swivel chair.

Not even the relentlessly temperamental espresso-making process, the loudly squeaking back door, or our dangerously low supply of whole milk could shake my (guilty) feeling of thankfulness that it was Caffè Lucia and not my beloved Blend that had gone up in smoke.

"So, anyway, I didn't know what my agent was thinking . . ."

I glanced back to Tucker, who had spoken again but not to me. He was in the middle of a conversation with Barry.

Like many of our regulars, Barry, a sweet doughboy of a guy with a receding hairline and soft brown eyes, was a freelancer who worked from home and used the Blend as a way to mingle with humanity—or escape from it. Sometimes he brought his laptop, sometimes a paperback; other times, like today, he felt chatty and pulled up a barstool.

"Wait—you mean you don't like the new job?" Barry asked between sips of his latte.

"Well, *now* I like the job. But when she told me about it, I said, 'Honey, the *stage* is the thing for me—'"

"What about that soap you did last year?" Esther interjected from across the room.

"Nobody calls them *soaps*, anymore," Tucker replied. "It's daytime drama."

Esther propped a hand on her ample hip. "Well, whatever you want to call it, that was *not* a 'stage' job!"

Tucker smirked. "You never heard the term *soundstage*?"

"Repeat after me, Broadway Boy: *As the Stomach Turns* ain't *Masterpiece Theatre.*"

"Just ignore the Dark Princess," Tucker told Barry, making an insect-shooing motion with his hand.

Esther finally noticed me standing behind the work counter. She lifted her chin. "Oh, hi, boss."

"Hi, Esther."

Tucker had already preheated the portafilter (a required step for maintaining temperature during slow periods). He dosed and leveled off the proper amount of grinds and expertly packed them down with his personal purple tamper. Once more he tempered the group head with a quick flush of water. Then he locked the handle into the machine, positioned a clean shot glass, and hit the go button.

I closely watched the twenty-five-second extraction process. As I teach all of my employees, a barista does not have to taste a shot to know when it's gone bad. The speed of extraction, visual viscosity of the liquor, even the color, are clear indicators of quality.

A full-flavored extraction, for example, has the texture of dripping honey; the color of a deep reddish-brown ale. An espresso with a thinner body and a light golden color might be prettier to look at in the cup, but it was completely sour on the tongue—*not unlike Lucia Testa.*

Hmmm . . .

Conversely black streaks in the *crema* meant there would be a level of bitterness at midtongue.

More of a Mrs. Quadrelli experience . . .

Okay, so I had Rossi's case on the brain. What can I say? Finding solutions to puzzling problems intrigued me, and the puzzle of bad espresso was something I'd already mastered, to wit—

In case number one (the light golden color), there were two possible culprits: either the grind was too coarse or the brewing water not hot enough. In case number two (the black streaks), the grind was either too fine or the water too hot.

Solving bad espresso was usually a matter of testing new

grinds and new water temperatures. The irony did not escape me. When it came to finding out who had torched Enzo's caffè, Rossi would have to test the waters, too . . .

"Anyway," Tucker went on, "I told my agent: 'I will act the lines, I will write the lines, but I *draw* the line at radio announcing. Then she explained that it wasn't radio announcing. This ad agency was looking for 'character' voices to do a series of PSAs—"

"PSAs?" Barry said.

"You're doing PSAs?" Esther asked.

Tucker deadpanned to Barry. "Didn't I just say that?"

Her interest clearly piqued, Esther moved with all speed to join Tucker behind the work counter. "You have any 'ins' at the radio stations?"

"No."

"Boris has a new YouTube upload ready to go. It's called *Strangers on a Train*. He's looking to get some airplay." (Boris was Boris Bokunin, aka BB Gunn, assistant baker by day, urban rapper by night.)

"What is it?" Tuck asked. "A riff on that old switcheroo Hitchcock movie?"

"No," Esther replied. "More of a hookup thing on the midnight A Train."

"Sorry, sweetie," Tuck said. "I'd help your man if I could, but PSAs are prerecorded in studios. I don't have anything to do with FM program directors or their playlists."

"Excuse me," Barry said, "but what's a PSA exactly?"

"It's a public service announcement," Esther said. "You've probably heard a million of them."

"Like?"

"Like . . ." Tucker shrugged. "'If you see something, say something.'"

"Yeah," Esther said, "especially if it's an abandoned backpack in the subway that's ticking real loud."

"'Teachable moments with children . . .'"

Esther nodded. "If Zombie's attack, aim for the head."

"'Just say no,'" Tucker continued.

"Especially to some foreign guy who promises you an exotic vacation in the Middle East."

Tucker raised an eyebrow. "Speaking from experience, are we?"

"No comment."

"You know what my favorite was?" Barry said. "The one with Smokey the Bear. Now how did that one go?"

"'Only you can prevent wildfires,'" Tucker said.

If only, I thought with a sigh.

"You know what my all-time favorite PSA is?" Esther asked.

Tucker folded his arms. "Do I know or do I care?"

"It's that one where some dude cracks an egg into a sizzling hot pan, and says,'This is your brain on drugs.'"

"I remember that one!" Barry said. "The egg's a visual metaphor. Like when you're *fried*."

I also recalled that PSA, but a half-assed omelet didn't even begin to cover the extent of the nightmares I'd dealt with when my ex-husband's gray matter had been on cocaine.

Tucker finished pulling my shot and handed it over.

Generally speaking, espresso became more temperamental as the day wore on. The reason (in geek-speak) was the coffee's tendency to be *hygroscopic*, which basically meant that it readily sopped up surrounding air moisture, or in cases of excessively dry conditions, released it. So, in the morning, with lower temperatures and higher humidity, the extractions were magnificently thick and slow—not unlike the start of Mike's lovemaking last night. But as the sun came up and the air dried out, the extractions tended to run fast . . .

Boy did that analogy give me pause.

Tucker's test extraction for me looked pretty darn good. The viscosity was there, the color a deep reddish brown. But as I looked closer, I noticed a marked lack of tiger mottle— the deep brown flecking in a truly great pull.

I sipped.

Tuck fell silent, met my eyes. "What's wrong?"

"There's a slight hint of bitterness . . ."

"I didn't taste it."

"It's there."

Tucker sighed. "The humidity again?"

"I'm not sure . . ." I checked the machine's gauges.

Esther came around the counter. "*This* I want to hear."

"It can't be the humidity!" Tucker protested. "I already went to a finer grind."

"You did?" That surprised me. I turned to Esther. "You better get me the Glass."

Esther showed her palms to the tin ceiling and pumped her arms in a victorious hip-hop club gesture she once told me meant *raise the roof*. "I told you, I told you, now the Best Girl she'll scold you!"

"Oh, don't be a ninny!"

As a gleeful Esther rushed into the back pantry to get the infamous Glass, I grabbed a paper towel, put it under the doser, and ran the grinder. A pile of fine black sand now sat on the flat white background like a negative satellite photo of K2.

"Here you *go-oh*!" Esther sang, setting a Holmes-worthy magnifying glass next to my grind sample. She tossed a smirk at Tucker. "I told you *so-oh*!"

"Tucker's right," I said.

"About what?"

"You're being a ninny."

"I am not!"

"*Silenzio!*" I picked up The Glass. Tucker and Esther flanked me, wordlessly watching as I spread out the grounds and closely examined them.

"There it is. You see?" I motioned them closer. "Evidence of irregular lumps."

"Not again!" Tucker cried.

"Yes, again," I said.

Coffee properly ground in a burr grinder displayed uniform particles with beautiful lattice networks (at the microscopic level), which properly maximized the area of coffee exposed during the intense espresso extraction process. But the uneven grains I was now studying had clumpish, oafish shapes. They were *almost* as horrific as what a cheap blade grinder would produce.

(Every so often I'd encounter a customer who regularly paid a higher price for our premium coffee beans but balked at investing in a decent burr grinder. Inexpensive blade grinders were fine for chopping spices, I'd always explain, but far too violent for chopping coffee beans. When those suckers started whirring at 20,000 to 30,000 RPMs, they produced enough frictional heat to scorch the beans they were grinding, which was why the coffee ended up tasting bitter. Blade chopping also produced uneven grains, a disaster for getting consistent quality.)

The final coffee might be drinkable, but it was far from achieving its potential. A sad thought because I knew just how much blood, sweat, and tireless tasting went into cultivating, picking, sorting, processing, sourcing, shipping, and finally roasting our premium beans.

My present problem, however, wasn't with the freshness of our roast, the skill of our baristas, or the quality of our appliances. Like any other serious espresso bar, we used a conical burr grinder. The issue today was maintenance.

"Our baby's blades have gone slightly dull from overuse." I didn't actually need to state this. Tucker had been through this many times before.

"Another teachable moment." Esther smirked at Tucker. "I *told* you it wasn't the weather."

"Don't rub it in. It's bad form."

"I'm just being honest, PSA Boy. You of all people should know the motto I live by."

"Huh?"

"If you see something, say something!"

Tucker's eyes narrowed. "Listen, Clare, I have an idea. Why don't I give the Duchess of High Dudgeon her very own teachable moment, like how to change the blades. Then she can start sharing in the fun."

"Good idea," I said.

"But, boss—" Behind her black-framed glasses, Esther's big brown eyes turned pleading. "My friends are here! And I don't really care about learning how to—"

"Good idea," I repeated, cutting her off. "I'll take over the bar. You two take the machine to the worktable downstairs."

We had a backup grinder for situations like this one. I pulled it out as Tucker unplugged the problem appliance. Then off he went, a pouting Esther in tow.

When I glanced up, I found Barry watching all this with a cross between curiosity and amusement. "Wow. I didn't realize so much scientific rigor went into making my latte."

"You have no idea."

I'd once explained it all to Mike, or tried to. When things went wrong in making espresso, any number of variables could be the offending agent—a good barista had to go through each variable, eliminating suspects one by one, until the true offender was found.

Mike replied with one sentence: "Sounds like my job."

I smiled at Barry. "Would you like another latte?"

"Yes, please! You have the best in the city."

"In that case," I told him, "this one's on the house."

Twenty minutes later, Barry was gone, and Tucker and Esther had returned to the espresso bar to help with a brief flurry of prelunch rush customers. I was just finishing the pour on my last order in line—a Hazelnut-Caramel Latte, which I topped with the flourish of a heart-crowned rosetta—when I heard a familiar door slam. *Don't ask how I can recognize one particular man by his door slam. I just can.*

A minute later, our shop's front bell was ringing and so were my eardrums.

"Clare!"

The customers in my half-filled shop came alert at their tables.

"What the hell is going on with my mother!"

My ex-husband had arrived.

Fifteen

〜〜〜〜〜〜〜〜〜〜〜〜〜〜〜〜〜〜

Matt dropped his suitcase (loudly) next to a barstool
while simultaneously sliding a heavy backpack off his
Nautilus-sculpted shoulders. It hit the ground with an
equally subtle thud.

"I touched down at JFK an hour ago, after a truly hor-
rendous red-eye out of Charles de Gaulle, and what do I see
when I pass the first newsstand?" Matt threw a folded-up *Post*
down on the bar. "A front-page photo of my mother being
hoisted into an ambulance by a passel of firemen with my
ex-wife looking on!" He glared. "What *happened,* Clare?"

I sighed. *So much for my public-place-will-keep-him-calm theory.* "Your mother's fine, Matt. She's perfectly okay."

"She's okay?"

I nodded.

His hard body sagged a moment—until his righteous
anger got a second wind. "Why didn't you call me? I mean,
last night she wasn't okay, was she?"

Before I could answer, Esther snatched up the paper.
"Boss! Front-page news and you didn't mention it! I knew

I should have watched *In the Papers* this morning. I hardly ever miss that segment, but Boris slept over."

"Excuse me," Tucker said, "but why should Boris have anything to do with it?"

"Because he didn't want me to watch New York One first thing in the morning. He wanted to, um . . . I mean, well, he *distracted* me . . ."

"Distracted you?" Tucker folded his arms. "Esther, I'm shocked. A euphemism?"

"A girl has a right to her boudoir privacy."

By now Matt was fairly vibrating with impatience, but he failed to interrupt our baristas, primarily because he was still doing a double-take at Esther. He hadn't seen our most popular employee since she began piling her wild dark hair on top of her head in an ebony half beehive à la torch singer Amy Winehouse.

Tuck, who was familiar with the pop star's unfortunate bouts with alcohol and drugs, had already dubbed it the "Detox Rock look." According to Esther, it was driving her boyfriend mad with desire.

"What's the point of having a news anchor read from the papers, anyway?" Tucker was saying. "Why don't you just read the papers yourself?"

"Because if I watch *In the Papers*, I don't have to read the papers!"

"Okay, Esther. If you don't read the papers, then hand that one over. I'd like to read all about it."

"No!" She clutched the dog-eared tabloid to her Renaissance chest.

"Listen," Tucker said, "I can do New York One's morning anchor in my sleep. I'll read it to you."

"You can do Pat Kiernan?"

"The Clark Kent of local news?" Tucker waved his hand. "He's your basic cross between Mr. Spock and Mr. Rogers."

"Okay." Esther offered up the now substantially wrinkled *Post*. "Do him for me, Tucker!"

"*Clare . . .*"

I glanced over at Matt who was standing stiffer than Oz's Tin Man. His jaw was grinding so visibly, I thought he might actually need the oil can.

"Esther, Tucker," I quickly said before the man blew, "I need to speak with Matt in private. So you two 'read all about it' while you're covering the counter, okay?" I met Tucker's gaze. "Two *doppios*?"

"No problem."

I gestured for my ex to follow me to a corner table. "Like I said, your mother's fine." I kept my voice low as we walked, hoping he'd take the hint.

(He didn't.) "Then why didn't she answer my calls this morning!"

"Please lower you voice. Your mother went to sit with a friend in the Elmhurst ICU. They don't allow cell phones in there. Last night I tried to make a call and I couldn't even get a signal."

"Who's in the ICU, Clare? What friend?"

"Lorenzo Testa."

"Aw, no . . ."

We came to our usual little corner table, which stood next to the line of tall French doors. On days like this I expected a drafty chill, but our old hearth was close by; and even though the fire wasn't what it used to be, the heat was still there for Matt and I, providing just enough warmth to keep us comfortable.

I sat with my back to the smoldering embers and pointed to the chair opposing mine. "Sit. I'll tell you the whole story . . ."

Matt dropped heavily and I talked . . . and talked. Finally, I ran out of words.

"Sorry I blew up," he said.

"It's okay."

Tucker brought over our double espressos. Matt thanked him and bolted his. I sipped mine slowly.

With an agitated hand, he rubbed the back of his short, dark Caesar. Then (at last) my ex relaxed, stretching out his wrinkled khakis until they extended well beyond the table-top's disc of coral-colored marble. His shoes—black high-top sneakers with white laces—were purposefully urban hip. In New York they ran over a hundred dollars. Matt had purchased his in a South American market stall for under two bucks.

Strapped to his right wrist was a glittering Breitling chronometer. Encircling his left was a multicolored tribal bracelet made from braided strips of Ecuadorian leather—and that pretty much summed up the paradox that was Matteo Allegro: one part slick international coffee buyer and one part fearless java trekker, lightly folded together in a larger-than-life concoction that I once couldn't get enough of and now sometimes found hard to swallow.

"How's our daughter?" I asked, still savoring my double. (Replacing the grinder had fixed all issues. Tuck's shots were now spot on, the nutty-earthy sweetness of the *crema* drenching my tongue in the liquefied aroma of my freshly roasted beans.)

"Joy's doing great," Matt said. "I have pictures to show you once I get this piece of crap recharged."

He threw his latest electronic device onto the cold slab of marble between us—PDA, phone, camera, calculator, microwave oven. I'm not sure what tasks it was supposed to multi.

"Why didn't you just use a camera?" I said.

"Joy did. She's going to e-mail you photos of my visit when she can find the time. She's been working extremely hard, but she says she's still loving it."

"Good. I'm glad to hear it. And does she have a new boyfriend?"

"None that she mentioned. But I think she's too busy. Which is more than fine with me." Matt rubbed his eyes. "Frankly, if my baby throws in the towel on this chef thing and decides to join a convent in Lourdes, I'll breathe a whole lot easier."

"Well, I wouldn't. Nothing against the good French sisters, but I want to be a grandmother."

"Bite your tongue!"

"Give it up, Matt. One of these days, Joy is going to settle on a guy, get married, and have kids—and then you'll have to hear it—"

"Don't say it—"

"Grandpa."

Matt visibly cringed.

"Or would you prefer the cheekier 'Gramps'?"

Ribbing the man was just too easy. I'd married him at nineteen. He'd been twenty-two at the time, although in matters sexual he'd been a virtual Methuselah. We'd met one summer in Italy (I'd been staying with relatives while studying art history), and when I'd ended up pregnant, after a blindly blissful summer of love, his mother had pressed him to the altar.

Back then, she was the one who'd wanted a grandchild—a legitimate one. So we never looked back, which is why he was far from the age of your average granddaddy.

Needless to say, our wedding hadn't been the wished-for, dreamed-for event of most young couples, planned down to the last flower petal and Jordan almond. It just happened. And for years I thought that was the reason Matt had gone through such difficulty accepting the ring and the vows and that forsaking-of-all-others-in-short-skirts thing.

I couldn't have been more wrong.

Matt's occupation was partly to blame. I was a needy bride, an uncertain new mother, infatuated with her young handsome groom whose job of sourcing coffee beans took him all over the world, all year long.

Matt had lived for it.

I died a thousand deaths.

Now that we were partners in coffee (instead of matrimony), my feelings about the man's peripatetic gene were completely upended. So go the astonishing ironies of middle age. Live long enough and you come to love the thing you loathed, embrace the thing you dreaded.

These days, I was downright grateful to my ex for trekking the globe, chasing harvest cycles to bring back the world's finest crops. And that's what they were: *crops*. Despite a corner of the industry sealing coffee up in cans with expiration dates implying freshness through a nuclear winter, coffee was seasonal. In Matt's view (and I didn't disagree), it belonged in the produce aisle, right next to the fruits and vegetables.

"How was Ethiopia?"

"Great. Our Amaro Gayo is outstanding, picked at the perfect time and the sorting is good. You should see the first shipment any day."

"I'm looking forward to roasting it."

"And I'm looking forward to tasting your roast." He smiled then, a genuine vote of confidence, which I appreciated.

"Does Breanne know you're back?"

Matt stifled a yawn as he nodded. Annoyed by his own jet lag, he reran a hand over his dark head then waved at Tucker. "Another double!"

"How's Bree been?"

I hadn't seen her since the Blend's holiday party last December. But then Breanne Summour, the ultratrendy, trend-setting editor of *Trend* magazine, traveled in much different circles than *moi*. The woman was a definite trade-up for my ex—in wealth and looks.

Before their marriage last spring, wagging tongues had speculated what a wayward coffee hunter and a socially ambitious fashion maven could possibly share. But I didn't question it.

Despite their wildly different career choices, I knew Matt and Bree weren't so very different under their toned tans. Both enjoyed living large, both craved excitement, and both jetted around the world for their respective careers. Granted, Matt's dusty treks through Nairobi and Bogotá were more exotic than Breanne's glittering tours of Milan and Barcelona, but to someone left behind, globetrotting is globetrotting no matter where your loved one trots. Conveniently, the Allegro-Summour union left no spouse behind while conveniently providing each nomadic partner with the comforting illusion of a rooted marital home.

"We texted each other before I got on the plane," Matt said. "She's on her way to Milan by now—another trade show. I missed her at JFK by ninety minutes."

"That's too bad."

"Not really." Matt shrugged, a little too casually. "Gives me a little space to relax, kick back, enjoy some time alone in the Big Kumquat . . ."

I frowned. After years stranded on Matteo Island, I'd become way too fluent in Matt-speak. Even his eyes were sparking with that regrettable when-the-cat's-away look.

Before I could challenge the man's wet noodle of a moral code, the Blend's front bell jingled. Glancing up, I saw James Noonan's wife coming through the door.

Valerie Noonan wasn't much taller than I, but the dynamic charge of her fast-clicking heels across my woodplank floor appeared to lift her to the stature of her firefighter husband.

"Clare!" she called with the burning energy of a Con Ed plant. "We need to talk!"

Sixteen

~~~~~~~~~~~~~~~~~~~~~~~~~~~~~~~~~~~~~~

"**How** are you?" I asked when Val approached our table.

"Great—now that I know I've caught you!" Val's low, throaty voice belied her bubbly demeanor and freckle-sprinkled nose. What it betrayed was a pack-a-day habit.

I felt for her. I'd smoked a little in high school but quickly kicked it (the kick in the pants from my grandmother had helped). Val said she hated her addiction, had stopped for a few years, but the recent stresses of her job had sent her back.

"You made quite an impression on James last night!"

"Really?" It was the last thing I expected her to say.

"Yes, and let me tell you"—she arched a slender eyebrow—"it's not easy hearing your husband gas on about another woman's heroism before you've even had your coffee!"

"Heroism? Not me. James and his friend Bigsby Brewer were the ones who ran into that burning building. They're the real he—"

"Don't say it." She held up her palm. "James hates the word. He'd say he was just doing his job and that a hero is a sandwich."

Matt coughed—loudly.

Yeah, okay, Matt, keep your pants on. "Val, this is my business partner, Matt Allegro."

As Matt rose to give up his chair, Val cocked her head. *"Allegro?"* She glanced at me then back to Matt. "Clare's daughter's name is Allegro— Oh! You must be Clare's ex—"

"We're still partners," Matt said. "But only in business. Very pleased to meet you, Val. That's a pretty name. Short for Valerie, right?"

Matt took her hand, the simple shake turning into a meaningful squeeze. He moved a little closer, the dilation in his dark pupils as clear a sign of the man's interest as a construction worker's wolf whistle.

If I didn't know Matt better, I might have assumed he was having a simple, Pavlovian reaction to the rich, russet shade of the woman's short, bouncy curls and trim business suit, both of which displayed the exact color of a perfectly pulled shot of espresso *crema.* But I did know Matt, and his reaction had everything to do with woman's curvy figure beneath that stylish suit.

"Val's *husband* is a *firefighter,*" I told him with pointed emphasis. *And he'll break your head with his Halligan tool.* "He's also the very same fireman who pulled your mother out of that burning building last night." *So poach elsewhere, please.*

Matt instantly dropped Val's hand. With a weak little smile, he asked her to thank her husband for him then excused himself to "freshen up" in our restroom.

As he sauntered away, I noticed Val considering his well-built back. I shook my head. Matt's Tabasco-colored tee may have appeared to be an easygoing choice, but I knew he'd purposely selected the tighter size to show off his molded pecs. And while his open denim work shirt looked loose and casual, those sleeves had been rolled with strategic precision, giving full exposure to his tanned, sinewy forearms while tempting the ladies with that first teasing curve of his bulging biceps.

Val lowered herself into Matt's chair and leaned toward me. "You actually divorced that hunk?"

"Yes. With relish."

"Do dish."

"It's a lengthy saga."

"Let me guess. He's a womanizer."

"One of his many issues, yes . . ."

"Too bad you handled it by divorcing him. He looks like a real catch . . ." She gazed after Matt once more to connect with him, but he was gone—a succinct description of my young marriage.

"If James ever cheated on me," Val said, "I wouldn't be divorcing him. I'd be dealing with the female involved."

That view surprised me. "Isn't James the one who made you the promise of fidelity?"

"A married man is already taken. The woman is the one who's doing the poaching. She's the one who needs to be dealt with."

"But don't you think your husband owes you—"

"Hey, that's just my view. To each her own." She laughed, but it sounded a little force. "I'd love to hear your side of the story. You and me, after work, over a couple of microbrews, okay?"

"Beer?"

"Oh yeah. That's *my* drink, don't mess with it."

"To each her own, then." I smiled. "Now how about one of mine?"

She nodded, and we moved to the espresso bar where I fixed her up with our latest special, a Belgian Mochaccino (espresso, foamed whole milk, a pump of coffeehouse vanilla, and a half shot of my homemade special syrup, which consisted of imported bittersweet chocolate, cream, sugar, and a pinch of French gray salt).

I leaned on the bar. "So, Val, what is it that you need me to do for you today?"

Val laughed. "How did you know I needed something?"

"The way you came in here. Most of my customers come for a break. You strode in like a general looking for volunteers."

"That's what my husband calls me at home. The Little General." She sighed. "Well, Clare, you're not wrong. I need your help . . ."

She pulled a colorful ad card out of her tote bag. "Can you display this?"

I scanned the sign: *Bake Sale! Union Square! Be There! Live music, hourly raffles, and the best goodies in the five boroughs. Benefits the NYC Fallen Firefighters Fund.*

"Riveting." I smiled. "You wrote the ad?"

"I'm also the gullible chump who had it printed. Tina Wade was supposed to do both, but she crapped out on me—two kids with the flu and a husband pulling 24/7 mutuals. I took care of it. I've got a stack of these going to businesses all over town. I was hoping you could take a few and spread the love."

"Glad to. I'll post ours right now."

I moved to the front window and set the placard beside our own plaque, the one that simply read: *Fresh Roasted Coffee Served Daily.* With the exception of our standing sidewalk chalkboard, the century-old tin was the only sign the Blend had ever displayed—or ever would as long as Madame had anything to say about it.

The bell jingled just then, and I glanced up to find the silver-haired woman herself breezing through the front door, black pants flowing like silk drapery, magenta and lime jacket displaying expressionistic swirls so vibrant they rivaled the feathers of a peacock.

"Clare, we need to talk."

"You're the second person who's said that to me in the last ten minutes."

I was smiling. She was not. *Oh, no.* The news was there in her red-rimmed eyes, the strain around her mouth.

"Enzo?"

"When I got there . . ." She shook her head. "They said he had a stroke very early this morning. He's in a coma. They don't know if he's going to make it."

I was dreading exactly this. My initial shock gave away to sadness, and then I remembered Rossi.

"You weren't able to speak with Enzo?"

"Child, he's in a *coma*."

I closed my eyes. "Sorry."

When I opened my eyes again, I found hers tearing.

"I'm the one who's sorry," she said. "This is my fault."

"No. It's *not*." I took hold of her shoulders. "The person responsible is the monster who set that fire." In my mind, the connection was automatic. "His daughter," I said. "Enzo asked me not to call Lucia unless things got worse. I have her number upstairs—"

"Lucia's already at the hospital. Mrs. Quadrelli called her last night. The child was very upset, of course."

"Did she say anything to you?"

"Very little. I tried speaking with her, but she brushed me off and not very politely. You saw how she acted last evening."

"Sorry to interrupt . . ." It was Val, she had crossed over from the espresso bar. I hadn't noticed her standing right behind us and wondered how long she'd been listening. (I didn't like anyone eavesdropping on me, although, I had to admit, I'd done it myself enough times in the name of snooping.)

"I should be going," Val told me, "but I did have one other thing to discuss with you."

"No problem," I said, "but first let me introduce you to my employer, Mrs. Dubois. Around the Village, everyone knows her as Madame."

"Very nice to meet you," Val said.

"This is Valerie, Madame. The wife of James Noonan, the firefighter who carried you out of that caffè last night."

A moment of blank surprise passed over the older woman's features; then she opened her arms and hugged Val tight. "If there's anything Clare or I can do to thank James for what he's done."

"Actually," said Val, glancing meaningful at me. "I do have an issue you might be able to help me with."

Madame released her and nodded. "Tell us, dear."

"Well, I had planned to use the same beverage vendor for the bake sale that supplies my catering events at the hotel. Unfortunately, they're letting me down. I just got word. I was wondering if you could hook me up with your coffee distributor. I know it's last minute, but . . ."

"The Blend is its own distributor," Madame said, "and we'll be delighted to help."

Val's nutmeg eyes widened. "That's very good of you—"

"Clare, you can set up a kiosk, can't you?" Madame said.

"Easy."

"And the Blend will supply a free cup of coffee for anyone who makes a bake sale purchase," Madame declared.

Val's mouth gaped. "That's a lot of coffee!"

"Those young firemen saved my life, and they jeopardize their own health and safety every day. It's the least we can do."

"Thank you both!" Val said, then grabbed her bag and headed for the door. "Sorry I've got to dash. Tons to do yet and only my lunch break to do it!"

Outside, I noticed she stopped abruptly, fished in her handbag, and lit a cigarette. For another moment she stood there, inhaling with visible signs of relief. Then she quickly headed up Hudson.

"Mother!"

I turned from the window to find Matt striding across the floor. Before Madame or I could say a word, my ex had swept his mother up in a hug so enthusiastic her heels took flight.

Seventeen

~~~~~~~~~~~~~~~~~~~~~~~~~~~~~~~~~

"Son! Put me down! My goodness!"

Matt complied—after a gentle spin and a peck to her cheek. "I was worried about you!"

She glanced at me. "First a troop of doting firefighters, now a public display by a wayward son. Perhaps I should become trapped in burning buildings more often."

"Please don't," I said. "My heart can't take it."

Madame smiled. "I want to show you both something." She motioned us to the espresso bar where she drew a yellowing snapshot out of her bag. "This came from the photo album Enzo gave me last night. There's your father, Matt . . ."

Her expression softened, one wrinkled but beautifully manicured finger caressing the image. "And that bouncing little *bambino* is you as a toddler! Such big brown eyes and thick black hair, just like your daddy . . ."

Tucker peered over Madame's shoulder. "*Bambino* Matteo. *Très* cute, not unlike the big-boy version." He threw Matt a wink.

Matt smirked. "I'm still straight, too, Tuck."

"I know." Tucker waved his hand. "Such a waste."

The shop bell rang again and a customer rushed in. I barely noticed, too distracted by Matt's (admittedly) adorable baby pic (and my own disturbing nanosecond of yearning for one just like it—the baby, not the picture). Too late my peripheral vision registered the fedora coming at me.

"You are no longer *boss* to me!"

Oh, no. Now what?! Looking up, I realized Dante Silva was looming over me. "What's this all about?" Was he angry? Was he quitting?

"I can't call you *boss* anymore, Clare, because you're my *hero*!"

Before I knew what was happening, Dante put his arms around me and lifted me off the floor.

"Hey! Put me down!"

Instead, my crazy barista spun me around. The flight path was much the same as Air Matteo, but with a much higher altitude.

"Did you hear me, Clare? You're my hero!"

"A hero is a sandwich!"

"A hoagie is a sandwich. A hero is my boss!"

Now I knew how James Noonan felt—embarrassed. "Okay, okay, I get the idea! *Down*, please!"

Dante finally obeyed.

"What's with the hat?" Esther asked, pointing to his fedora.

He removed it to show her. His shaved head was swathed in bandages.

"Look, look, everyone!" Esther cried. "It's the Thief of Baghdad! Tell me, oh, genie of the lamp, if I rub you the right way, will you grant me three wishes?"

"Esther, you don't rub anyone the right way," Dante replied, "except maybe your commie ex-pat boyfriend."

"Boris was never a communist. He believes in freedom of expression."

"Okay then. You won't care if I express myself." Dante reached into his backpack's pocket, pulled out a digital camera, and snapped her photo. "That's going on my Facebook page. Amy Winehouse hair and all."

"Good. Link to my page while you're at it. I'm about to post a new poem about a coworker with brain damage."

Dante took another photo. "For Twitter."

That did it. Esther turned on her heel and marched away.

"Well, my friend," Tucker said, gesturing to his swathed head, "my only advice to you is: Do not grow a goatee. Homeland Security might mistake you for Osama bin Laden."

"Oh, yeah? *As-Salamu Alaykum* to you, too, my brother."

"Hey, you said that pretty well." Tuck tapped his chin. "Maybe you *should* grow a goatee. Fox is filming another one of those thriller franchise movies in New York this summer. I think my agent could get you hired as an extra."

"Stop teasing Dante," I shook my finger. "He's lucky to be alive. So is Madame—"

The camera flash went off. I blinked.

"Good one," Dante said, lowering the camera.

"You did *not* just take my picture!" My scolding finger was still hovering in the air. I instantly dropped it.

Matt laughed. "Hey, Dante, do me a favor. E-mail a copy of that one to Joy. If it doesn't keep our daughter in line, I don't know what will."

"Not funny." I folded my arms. "And that blaze last night was no joke, either. But I'm going to nail whoever set it."

Matt cursed.

"What's the matter?" I asked.

"Don't start, Clare."

"Don't start what?"

"I know that look. You're getting all sleuth-y on me."

"I am not getting sleuth-y," I lied.

Madame tilted her head and smiled. "It's like you're both still married, he knows you so well." Then she glanced at the picture in her hand and sighed. "I would so love another grandchild. A little boy this time." She pinned her son with a formidable look. "Perhaps you and Breanne could work on that. She's not menopausal yet, is she?"

Matt paled.

The man was not having a good morning.

LUNCH rush came and went. Madame departed for a date with Otto, and as the pace of the café wound down again, Matt pulled up a stool at my espresso bar.

"Tell me the truth," he said. "What's going on with this arson thing you mentioned?"

"I'm determined, Matt, enraged and determined. That's what's going on."

"If you care so much about who started the fire at Enzo's place, why didn't you share your theories with the fire marshal?"

"I did. I called the man this morning."

"And?"

"And Marshal Rossi strongly implied that he wouldn't mind my help as an informant—"

"You've got to be kidding!"

"Keep your voice down."

"Are you telling me that snooping around for the NYPD isn't providing enough of the thrills you missed as a stay-at-home mom? Now you want to play with the FDNY?"

"I am not playing. Rossi is going to find the forensic evidence to prove arson, and I don't want him going after Enzo. I'm certain, down to my bones, that others were responsible. You'd feel the same way if you'd been there. Your own mother was almost burned alive."

"Burned alive!" Matt's olive-skinned face went paler than the cream in my espresso con panna. "I thought you said she was never in any real danger!"

Woops. "Okay, maybe I, uh, downplayed things a little, but you were in a state—"

"And I'm getting there again! Did the marshal at least *say* it was arson?"

"I told you, they won't discuss the case with me—"

"Then drop it, Clare. Let the pros handle it."

"Excuse me," Dante said, interrupting us. "But the pros didn't pull me out of the fire last night. It was Clare who saved my life."

Tucker tapped my shoulder. "Now that you bring it up, sweetie, I think you may be onto something with this arson thing." He slapped Matt's *New York Post* back on the bar top and paged quickly through it. "Look at this." Tuck's finger touched a small square of newsprint deep inside the paper: *Blaze Burns Bensonhurst Beanery*.

"According to the story, there was a coffeehouse fire last night on Avenue O in Bensonhurst, Brooklyn. It started around the same time as your Astoria fire. *Très* coincidental if you ask me."

I frowned, scanned the story. "This is odd."

"Why?" Matt said. "Tucker is right. It's a coincidence, that's all."

Was it? Another one of Mike Quinn's pithy pieces of law enforcement philosophy suddenly came to mind: *In a criminal investigation, there are no coincidences.* I couldn't help wondering what Mike's cynical cousin would say to that.

Wᴛʜɪɴ an hour of my thought, the cell in my pocket vibrated. I didn't recognize the number on the screen—a 718 area code, which meant a borough other than Manhattan—so I answered tentatively.

"Hello?"

"Clare Cosi. Guess who it is callin' ya, darlin'?"

Although the man's voice was keyed an octave lower than usual, I would have recognized Captain Michael's roguish lilt even without the played up brogue.

"Don't hang up on me now."

"How did you get this number?"

He didn't tell me. What he said was: "Now I'm *sure* my cousin told you to steer good and clear of me—"

"As a matter of fact he did."

"Well, I can't blame him. But I'm not callin' for my own account. I'm callin' for my guys. They're in trouble."

I bet they are.

I assumed Rossi had started questioning his men, but I couldn't have been more wrong.

"They need help, Clare," the captain went on. "The kind only *you* can provide."

"Me? Why would a crew of New York's Bravest need my help?"

"Simple, dove . . ." I could almost see the man's gold tooth flashing from across the East River. "You know how to make coffee."

Eighteen

~~~~~~

For twenty minutes the Arsonist observed the activity in the slick chain coffeehouse—the customer traffic, the counter service, the café tables—all while nursing the contents of an absurdly large cappuccino . . .

This whole thing should have been over by now. The old man's place was supposed to be empty. It's all because of that *bitch* things got so screwed up . . .

"Excuse me, ma'am."

Across the room, a Latina worker apologized for bumping a female customer and then resumed rolling a stainless steel cart filled with bottles, cleaners, rags, and sponges. She pushed it through the restroom door, and then hung a Closed for Cleaning *sign on the knob.*

There's my ticket . . .

The Arsonist stayed focused on that closed door, listened to sounds of running water, continued taking hits off the twenty-ounce paper cup. But the dregs of steamed milk tasted cold, the last drops of espresso bitter.

If only I could set off the damn bomb right now . . .

All around the Arsonist, young urban professionals were complaining about stalled careers and condo costs, lost benefits and air-

line delays, needy kids and presumptuous parents—a petty list of privileged problems. A few more minutes of listening to whining in quad and the Arsonist wanted to nuke the place, not just torch it.

Impatient, the Arsonist bent over the orange shopping bag. A small alarm clock sat inside, along with a large battery, a giant jar of high-octane spiked petroleum jelly, and a bleach bottle with no bleach inside. The Clorox bottle had been refilled with a mix of gasoline, naphtha, and benzene—all of it rigged to that clock. When the alarm went off, a quiet spark would awaken the sleeping beast. Then the petroleum jelly would ignite and poof, instant napalm.

Highly destructive, hell to put out . . .

The Arsonist reached into the orange bag, attached two wires sprouting from the battery, fixed them to circuits on the converted bleach bottle.

All ready . . .

The young coffeehouse worker finished cleaning the unisex facility. After tucking her cleaning products back onto her stainless steel cart, she rolled it into a closet adjacent to the restroom.

Time now . . .

The Arsonist rose and walked—easily, casually—to that restroom. Pretending to choose the "wrong" door, the Arsonist opened the closet, quickly slipped the bag onto the bottom shelf of the cart, between two giant bottles of cleaning fluids. The closet door was closed and the restroom door opened.

No one took notice of the Arsonist's "mistake"—not one customer or employee.

After leaving the Long Island City shop, the Arsonist turned for one last look at the posted hours of operation. The timer on the bomb was set for 10 PM, well past the seven o'clock closing. Outside, the day was still pleasant, but the chill was coming.

Another package still had to be delivered—to the Village Blend coffeehouse in Greenwich Village. This one would be for that troublemaking bitch who'd tipped off the fire marshals to look beyond Testa for their torcher . . .

Two firebombs started us down this road. Two more will end it. And if that Cosi bitch doesn't get the message after tonight, we'll just have to end her.

Nineteen

Locating the captain's firehouse wasn't a problem. Amid a sea of tiny clapboard row houses, Michael Quinn's sovereign domain towered over the landscape like a redbrick citadel.

I parked my near-vintage Honda on the quiet street just off Northern Boulevard. Despite the temperate twilight air, I slipped on my coat and gloves. March was a tricky time in New York. Days might feel bright and balmy, but nightfall could bring the kind of cruel winds that would kill every plant foolish enough to put out its vulnerable buds.

On the face of it, I'd come back to Queens for one reason: Lucia Testa had donated the still-functioning espresso machine from her father's caffè to this firehouse, and the men needed some lessons in how to use it. With Enzo's comatose condition, Lucia was too busy to teach them, so I agreed.

Of course, this was the least I could do to pay these guys back for their rescuing of Madame. But the truth was my little visit this evening would give me the chance to question these guys, find out who among their ranks might be seeing Lucia.

Along the curb I noticed a line of parked cars. Every one

displayed FDNY-related placards or window clings. One of
the SUVs had a bumper sticker that caught my eye: *Honk If
You're Buffing*.

"Buffing?"

I wondered if it had something to do with weight lifting,
that is, *becoming* buff? Maybe it was something one did in the
buff? Did that make it a sexual reference? I craned my neck
at the towering red challenge in front of me.

The FDNY certainly counted women among its ranks.
They drove ambulances and fought fires right alongside the
men, but this engine and ladder company didn't have a female among them.

This isn't just a firehouse. It's a Temple of Testosterone.

A granite cornerstone announced the original use for the
building as a station for the Queens Company Rail Yard.
But the structure's odd Gothic flourishes—including carved
stone moldings over the doors and a corner turret with a
crenellated roof—gave the impression of a medieval strong-
hold, complete with castle battlements.

A sudden freezing gust tore at my ponytail. I ignored
it, moving with determination into the glowing, cavernous
interior of the firehouse garage, the clanking barista supplies in my backpack making me feel like Cervantes's crazy
knight again, embarking on a quest in rusty armor.

Amid the industrial tangle of ducts, pipes, and hanging
chains, I noticed tire scuffs on the concrete, evidence the fire
trucks had been here.

So where are they now?

One thing I knew: Captain Michael absolutely assured
me that he would not be here this evening, so there was zero
chance of my going back on the promise I'd made to Mike
to stay away from his cousin.

I guess a part of me was still curious about the captain
(not to mention suspicious), and I wouldn't have minded a
crack at interviewing the man. On the other hand, with him
out of the firehouse, I could freely question his men without
the threat of a red devil looking over my shoulder.

"Ms. Cosi?"

I looked up to search the vast echo chamber for the source of the familiar, upbeat voice.

"James?" I called back.

"Yeah, it's me." James Noonan crossed the track-marked floor to greet me, passing under a high metal catwalk that ran along all four windowless walls. "Sorry the guys are gone. A call came in. But they'll be rolling back soon."

Under the banks of hanging florescent lights, the man I liked to think of as my own personal hero looked like a poster boy for All-American football: glowing skin, close-cropped hair, a dazzling smile. He was as warm and friendly as I remembered, and just about as tall as the two Mike Quinns. By the time he reached my side, I was bending my neck just to meet his translucent blue eyes.

He shook my hand with a wide grin, and then jerked one thumb over his shoulder. "Come on back. I'll show you the espresso machine."

I followed him down an industrial green hallway. At the end he opened a stout wooden door, and the taint of diesel exhaust gave way to a much more appetizing array of aromas—fresh, floral herbs and piquant spices intermingled with the pungent-sweet fragrance of roasting garlic and the heavy but alluring scent of sizzling pork fat.

With quick hands James draped a grease-spattered apron over his gray T-shirt and distressed denims, pulled the strings completely around his lean waist, and tied them at his belt buckle. (The front of the apron assured me the wearer was *Also Good in Bed*.)

I pointed. "Gag gift from the guys, right?"

"You must be psychic," he said flatly.

I smiled. "My staff gave me one of those."

"Oh? So you're also good in bed?"

"No. *I Serve It Up Hot*."

He laughed. "Come on . . ."

James led me around a corner, into a sprawling kitchen area

with two huge refrigerators, a pizza oven, a deep fryer, and a grill-and-gas-range combination under a ventilation funnel.

"Whoa, does every firehouse have such great facilities?"

James snorted. "Are you kidding? I put this place together by my lonesome. Over the past two years I've gone to every restaurant closing and bankruptcy in the five boroughs to gather this stuff."

The savory scent of roasting meat distracted me. I pointed to the oven. "Something in there smells amazing."

"Pork shoulder." James opened the door to display his handiwork.

"¡Hola, pernil!" I admired the beautiful bone-in pork shoulders, four in all, slow-roasting on two cooking racks.

"A PR classic," James noted.

"So you've got Puerto Rican guys in the company?"

"Only one, plus a dude from Cuba and one from the Dominican Republic. All the guys love the *pernil,* though. It's economical, feeds a hungry crew, and leaves enough meat for Cuban sandwiches in the morning."

"And what's in the Dutch oven?" I pointed to the stovetop.

James lifted the lid. "A sweet onion and cheddar casserole."

I sniffed. "Mild cheddar, right? And lots of milk and butter?"

"Yeah. The onions give up a lot of moisture so I use bread crumbs to keep it from getting too watery."

I sniffed again. "A little bland, isn't it? Especially for Latino guys. You should try some dry mustard in there. Maybe a dash of cayenne. I think you'll like the result."

James nodded, gave me a little smile. "Color me impressed."

"Fire's your job, *flavor* is mine."

His smile widened. Then he replaced the lid and closed the oven.

"Do you cook like this at home?" I asked. "Val must appreciate it."

At the mention of his wife, James's good cheer fell away. "We hardly eat together these days."

"I'm sorry to hear that."

He shrugged. "If Val's not working late, I'm on a mutual."

"Mutual? Val used that term. What is it exactly?"

"A 'mutual' is when the guys juggle work schedules so we can do back-to-back shifts."

"Why would you want to do that?"

"If you work twenty-four or forty-eight hours straight, you can get three or even four days off in a row. It's a nice arrangement for guys with kids."

James glanced at his bright orange digital watch. "I don't actually start my mutual for another thirty minutes. I came in early to get some dinner up and running before things got hairy."

"So that's why you're still here while the rest of the guys are off on a call?"

He nodded and turned to take another peek at his pork shoulders. He looked so happy to be here on the job—maybe *too* happy?

Twice now I'd seen the man frown at the mention of his wife. *Why?* Were James and Val just having the typical troubles of a busy married couple? Or were their problems more serious? It wouldn't have been my business, except for the fact that Lucia Testa was fooling around with one of the men of this house. Was James's marriage so unhappy that he'd decided to stray with Lucia?

My God . . . I hope James isn't the fireman I've come here looking for . . .

I cleared my throat, brought up the same question in a new way. "So, I'm sure the guys appreciate having a cook like you in the house, but . . . you must prefer dining with your wife, right?"

"Actually, Val never wants me to go to any trouble. That woman's happy with a cold beer and a couple of sliders."

"Yeah, she mentioned her love of microbrews to me the

other day. I was surprised. Considering her party-planning title, I figured her for a wine-and-brie girl."

James folded his arms. "I'm the guy who won't touch beer, not to save my life. Give me a nice glass of Bordeaux with dinner, a few stinky French cheeses at the end of the meal, and I'm a happy boy."

An electronic crackle interrupted us. James stepped over to a shelf and turned down the volume on what looked like a small, boxy radio receiver.

"Sorry," he said, "I was buffing."

"What is that exactly? I saw a bumper sticker outside—*Honk If You're Buffing!*"

"You saw Oat Crowley's car. That guy buffs in his sleep. When he dies, they'll probably put an FDNY radio in Oat's coffin."

"So buffing has something to do with a *radio?*"

"Buffing is when you listen to FDNY chatter while you're off duty. Even civilians do it, hence the title."

"Oh, buffing is for fire *buffs*. Like fans?" *Or potential arsonists?*

"Bingo," James said. "But lots of firefighters do it, too. You don't climb the ranks without putting in the time, staying on top of what's happening—and I'm taking the lieutenant's exam in a few weeks."

As James turned back to his cooking, I began moving down the counter, checking things out (snooping really). Despite all the appliances, most of the floor space was taken up by a single scuffed table. My gaze ran over some job-related notices on one wall, then snagged on a colorful calendar taped to a cupboard door. The calendar was one of those famous FDNY specials—hunks in fire hats.

"Excuse me, James?" I pointed to the bulging muscles of Mr. March. "Is that who I think it is?"

"Yep," he called from the stove, "that's Bigsie in that cargo net. He's still so proud of being named Mr. March he won't let us take it down."

"Take it down?" I absently repeated, my attention focused on the near-naked, shirtless giant, his arms and chest standing out in bold relief as he clung to a net woven of thick hemp.

Right behind me, I suddenly heard James laughing. "Like every red-blooded American woman who passes through here, you failed to notice that you're gaping at *last year's* calendar."

Woops. I tore my gaze away.

"Don't worry about it," James said. "All the ladies love Bigsie. He's the wildest wolf in this lair, with the possible exception of our captain. But you already know that, right? I mean . . ." He lowered his voice. "That's why you're really here, aren't you?"

"What? No! I'm here to help you and the guys with the donated espresso machine, *that's all*. I hope you're not implying—"

"Sorry." James put up his hands. "Not my business."

I changed the subject (fast) and pointed to the thick, wooden dining table. The circumference looked large enough to accommodate King Arthur's crew. "So how many guys do you cook for on a given day?"

"Twenty or so, I guess, depending on who's doing a mutual and who's coming in for a visit."

"You're the only cook?"

"I'm the only one who actually knows what he's doing. A couple of the guys have tried, but when I'm not around, meals come down to microwave reheats or calls for takeout."

That's when it hit me: all this trouble he'd gone to with the set up, all this passion he put into the firehouse meals . . .

"James, it sure looks like you could manage your own restaurant . . ." *Especially if you had the money to back you—like, say, money from a fire insurance payout?*

"No. Not for me."

"You're that certain?"

"Ms. Cosi, I was raised in my family's diner. Managing a restaurant's all about routine—boring, boring, boring routine. And I like to keep things lively. I'll cook for the guys, sure, but that's it. I'd much rather be running into burning buildings than running a restaurant."

Another danger junkie, just like my ex.

But what James and Matt described as boring, I saw as constancy, dependability—maybe even loyalty.

Sure, my trade demanded that you show up every day and perform the same basic tasks. But the customers I served gave up their hard-earned money in exchange for those tasks, and that wasn't an unworthy thing. To me, maintaining high standards was far from tedious. Every morning, I embarked on my own little war, or at least a series of ongoing battles. Managing the Blend was a continuously renewing challenge.

Of course I didn't articulate any of this. I wasn't here to debate James on my view of the food-and-beverage service trade. I was here to fight another kind of battle . . .

"Excuse me, Ms. Cosi," James said when a kitchen clock pinged. "I'll just need a few minutes . . ."

"Take your time," I said, and went back to looking around. I scanned the various posters on the wall, but they were mostly job related: official announcements, charts, and instructions. Then I spotted a worn wooden closet door across the room. It was covered from top to bottom with personal photographs.

I moved closer. The pictures were all taken at what looked like annual firehouse picnics. Each was hand labeled by year.

"Looks like you guys have a lot of picnics," I called to James.

"Guess so," he replied from the sink. "The guys with families do a thing in August at Six Flags, but our biggest event is the bash right after Medal Day. The captain has a great spot in Flushing Meadow Park on permanent reserve for us."

Medal Day . . . I'd heard all about the tradition at the Quinn's St. Patrick's Day bash. Every June, select firefighters of the FDNY were honored with citations for their bravery and heroism.

As James continued working, I examined the picture gallery. The photos were hung year by year in vertical columns that ran from the top of the door to the bottom. One or two group shots of the company were followed by pictures of the men paired with their wives, families, or significant others.

I noticed an older photo of Captain Michael Quinn and got down on one knee for a closer look. The picture was taken during the 2000 picnic. Captain Michael was grinning like a giddy boy. He looked so relaxed, so lighthearted. He had a woman on his arm. She was nearly as tall as the captain with a voluptuous figure and long, straight raven hair. The photographer caught her in the middle of a laughing fit, and her face was partially hidden by her hand. She was in the 2001 pictures, too—or I was fairly sure it was the same woman. In this photo her beautiful windswept hair was off her face and I got a good look—oval face, long nose, slightly pointy chin, wide, perfect, carefree smile.

In the photos after 2002, the woman was gone. Captain Quinn appeared alone, dateless, and far less lighthearted. In some of these later photos he hadn't even mustered a smile.

My gaze continued moving up through the years of picnic photos—and then it stopped moving. As I stared at one particular photo, taken just three years ago, the tight, forced smile of Lucia Testa stared back at me.

Just then, I heard heavy footsteps walking up behind me.

My gaze still focused on Lucia's face, I tapped the photo.

"James," I said. "Did you know that Lucia Testa is in one of these pictures? She's standing among a group of men. Was she seeing one of these five guys, do you know? I see Oat Crowley is in the group—"

And about fifty pounds lighter . . .

I also recognized Ronny Shaw, the fireman who'd ended up in the ER next to Madame. There were a few other faces I didn't know. One was a Latino man wearing a *Puerto Rican*

Pride T-shirt, and another had a gray flattop—the kind of 'do my Mike called cop hair.

"I see Captain Michael is in this photo. You mentioned what a wolf the man is. Was your captain ever involved with Lucia?"

James didn't answer, but I knew he was there. I could feel the presence of his large body right behind me.

"And while we're on the subject of Michael Quinn's love life, who is that very pretty brunette he's obviously with in the earlier photos? And why isn't she in any of the later ones?"

Again, no answer. A little annoyed by now, I turned around and found myself facing the last man I expected to see this evening.

Michael Quinn's big arms were folded across his white uniform shirt. Beneath his scarlet *Lonesome Dove* mustache, his jaw was working, and the tendons in his neck were stretched as taut as the cables on the GW Bridge. Even the man's burn scar was flushing with fury.

We stared at one another so long I could feel my own cheeks getting warmer than the hot plate of a Mr. Coffee.

Finally James returned, drying wet hands with a towel. "There. All done— Oh, hi, Cap. How's it going?"

"You should be workin' boyo, not gossiping," the captain practically spat, still pinning me with his eyes.

James blinked, obviously confused by his superior's sudden anger. "We were just talking, Cap—"

"Show the lady the espresso machine. That's why she's here, isn't it?"

"Uh . . . yeah, sure," James said. "Right, over here, Ms. Cosi."

I followed James back to the newly installed machine. Captain Michael Quinn remained beside the photo gallery, scowling silently.

Twenty

THE espresso maker from Caffè Lucia was a shiny, Italian-made Gaggia with two group heads.

"It's a beauty," I said, stealing uneasy glimpses at the Captain.

"Lucia delivered it . . . uh, not *personally*." Now James was shooting glances at the man. "It was delivered the day after the fire. The Gaggia didn't come with instructions so I downloaded the manual from the manufacturer's Web site and installed it. Oat helped."

"Oat?" I tensed, remembering my unpleasant run-in with the man. "How did he help?"

"He put together the cabinet it's sitting on."

I nodded, trying to concentrate. It wasn't easy. I was too upset by Michael Quinn's unexpected appearance. *Why is he here? Is there an explanation? Or did the man just outright lie to me?*

"So, did I hook this thing up right?" James was asking, face expectant. "Ms. Cosi?"

"Oh . . . right, sorry . . ."

"I've installed a lot of the stuff around here myself, so I'm pretty sure I hooked it up correctly. The metal parts weren't really damaged. I only had to replace some rubber tubes and gaskets that were effected by the heat of the fire."

The fire. Yes, the fire. That hellish inferno came back to me fast, and so did the image of Enzo, fighting for his life in the ICU. I took a breath, refocused.

"I'll check it out," I told James. "Can you hand me my backpack?"

I noticed a commercial burr grinder sitting nearby. It bore the marks of heavy use, but the espresso machine appeared to be relatively new—

Enzo had invested in this thing, I realized. *He wasn't expecting to retire anytime soon. And Lucia had to know that . . .*

Of course I also noted the woman had "donated" this machine to the firehouse in record time. Sure, Enzo had admitted the choice was hers to rebuild or not, but the speed at which she gave up the Gaggia suggested to me that Lucia didn't exactly wrestle with the question. More evidence of motive.

My focus went back to the machine itself. The Gaggia's filtration system and nickel-lined tank were already connected to the water main. According to the gauge, the tank was properly filled. The gas jets appeared to be working, too.

When James returned with my backpack, I fished out one of the Blend's thermometers to check the temperature at the water spout. It was a little high at 205 degrees, and the pressure at the pump was also high. I adjusted both and bled off the excess heat.

Finally I checked the portafilters and the heads. They were spotlessly clean—so clean the heads still needed "seasoning" before a perfect espresso could be pulled. (Like a new pan needing a layer of cooking oil, the heads of an espresso machine required a patina of coffee oil to eliminate the sharp taste of raw metal. A test pull or two at the beginning of each day always solved that problem for me.)

"Good job setting it up," I said at last.

"Thanks."

"The temperature and pressure levels are close to perfect.

You want the temperature at the head around 203.5 degrees, and"—I tapped the pressure meter—"at 8.2 bars for the pressure at the pump. With those settings and the proper grind, you should be able to pull a perfect espresso every time."

"Perfect is good," James said. "In my book if it ain't perfection, it's broke—"

Another ping from the kitchen timer interrupted us.

"I'll be right back," James said with another unhappy glance at his captain, who was still silently standing and staring.

When James was gone, I stuffed the thermometer into my pack and crossed the room. "I want to talk to you," I quietly told the man. "I need to ask you some questions and I want honest answers."

"About my love life?"

"No." I gritted my teeth. "Not about your love life. I don't care about your stupid love life."

He raised a skeptical eyebrow.

What was that? A Quinn family trait? "Okay, *maybe* I'll ask some questions about your love life, but it's not why you *think* I'm asking—"

"You're a terrible liar, darlin'."

"Me! You're the one who said you wouldn't be here!"

The captain smirked. "Now why would I have said a thing like that? This is my firehouse, isn't it?"

I was about to reply (with a string of less-than-ladylike verbiage) when the blare of a truck horn made me jump. A second later I heard rumbling engines, so powerful they reverberated the floor along with the hanging pots and pans.

Captain Michael looked down at me. "Looks like your burnin' questions will have to wait." He unfolded his thickly muscled arms. "My boys are back and you've got some teachin' to do."

A few minutes later, a masculine monsoon swept into the kitchen. For an unnerving second I feared I'd have to teach almost twenty outsized men the art of espresso making—an undertaking I feared would take all night. But after wolfing down plates of James's dinner, the horde vanished into a nearby community room. The entire evening meal took seventeen minutes flat.

Only eight firemen remained in the kitchen, counting James Noonan and his friend Bigsby Brewer (and not counting the unnamed probie who was put to work cleaning the dishes and pans).

While Captain Michael continued his silent watching from the sidelines, the eight arranged folding chairs in a semicircle around the espresso machine.

"So this is everyone?" I asked James.

He nodded. "Yeah, from every shift, too. Some of the guys came in just to learn how to use the Gaggia."

"Great," I said. And I meant it. If these were the core espresso drinkers of this firehouse, they were the most likely to have frequented Caffè Lucia and had continual contact with Enzo's daughter. Scanning the faces, I recognized Oat Crowley and Ronny Shaw. The final three I'd never met. Well, now was the time . . .

"My name is Clare Cosi and—"

A hand shot up. I recognized the lined face under the gray flattop as one of the men in the photos with Lucia.

"No offense, Miss, but I don't know why I'm here. I can't stand coffee. It smells real nice, but most of the time it tastes like brown water."

The speaker leaned back and folded his arms. The kitchen was so quiet I could hear the metal folding chair creak under his weight. Suddenly the group laughed, and I realized I'd missed out on a private joke.

"Dino's just yanking your chain, Ms. Cosi," James informed me from the front row. "Elfante lives on coffee. Like ten or twelve cups a shift."

"Yeah," said Bigs. "We make him kick in extra for beans, the weasel drinks so much—"

"*And* it tastes like brown water. Around here, anyways,"

Dino insisted, and then he continued to rant about their typical firehouse brew until Ronny Shaw beaned him with a balled-up paper napkin.

"Let the lady talk!"

The last time I saw Shaw, he was lying on a stretcher in the ER, Oat Crowley hovering near. Both had eavesdropped on my conversation with Madame, and I still wondered why they seemed so interested. When he raised his left hand to throw the paper ball, I noticed it lacked a wedding band. Then it occurred to me that getting injured in a fire you started yourself is a good way to deflect attention away from your guilt.

"Thank you," I told Ronny. "But Mr. Elfante actually makes a good point—"

"Call me Dino, honey . . ."

"The delicate flavor oils in the bean are volatile," I said, ignoring Dino's wink. "The reason is because if they're released too soon during the brewing process, they go up in steam and you experience them through your nose instead of your palate."

"Told ya," Dino cracked smugly—and got beaned again.

"The purpose of an espresso is to extract the essence of those oils in such a way that the flavor goes into the cup. A perfectly pulled espresso should taste as good as great coffee smells."

As I walked the men through the anatomy of the Gaggia machine, the heads, the control functions, the proper readings for the temperature and pressure, I got to know them a little better.

"Pressure and heat. Like brewing illegal hooch, eh, ma'am?"

This was Ed Schott, the senior member of our class. A pink-skinned man with a bald pate, pug nose, jutting chin, and perpetually clenched fists, he spoke in short, staccato bursts, like a military drill instructor (which he may very well have been, given the Marine Corps' eagle and fouled anchor was tattooed on his meaty forearm).

"Let's move on to the coffee itself. A good espresso starts with a good bean, so—"

"You mean espresso bean, right, ma'am?" said Ronny Shaw. "I've seen them in the grocery store. Is that what we should use?"

"There's no such thing as an espresso *bean*," I explained. "What you saw was an espresso *roast*. Any type of good Arabica bean that's roasted dark can be called an espresso roast."

"What about caffeine, Ms. Cosi?" Bigs said. I noticed he got up to stand beside his chair like a kid in Catholic school called on by his teacher. "Will I get a bigger jolt from espresso than, say, a regular cup of joe?"

"What's the matter, Brewer? Worried you won't be *up* for that hot date after your mutual?" Dino Elfante asked.

Bigsie's smile was lopsided. "It's just that I need a lot of energy. Pep, you know. My lady friends expect it. I got a reputation to uphold."

Bigsby Brewer seemed so guileless it was difficult to see him as a cold-blooded fire bomber. But I had to consider that one of his many "lady friends" could be Lucia Testa. Sweet as he was, Bigs would be an easy mark to manipulate, especially if someone convinced him the fire would end up helping Enzo instead of hurting him.

Alberto Ortiz spoke up just then—I recognized him as Mr. "Puerto Rican Pride" in the Lucia photo.

"If you need pep, Big Boy, try a Red Bull. Or maybe that little blue pill if the situation is code red. But, dude, if you're having *real* trouble with one of those Manhattan fillies, just send her over to me—"

A silver cross hung from Ortiz's neck, and a thin gold band circled his ring finger, but outward symbols aside, Ortiz seemed as randy as the rest of this pack.

"Mr. Ortiz is right," I cut in. "About gulping espressos, I mean. It's not a very efficient way to perk up."

Bigs frowned. "But I thought espressos *had* caffeine."

"Of course there's caffeine in an espresso. But espresso's high-pressure, high-heat extraction process removes more caffeine than regular drip brewing."

"In other words," James said, "if you want a jolt, stick to drip, *drip*."

Bigs poked his friends so hard James tumbled from his folding chair. "Ahhhh!"

"Snots don't know how to behave," muttered Ed Schott.

When things settled down again, I demonstrated the best way to grind the beans for espresso. "If you grind too finely, friction and oxidation from the grinder will ruin your dream of a perfect cup. Grind too coarsely and some of the flavor stays in the portafilter."

I ground enough beans for a few shots and dosed a single into the basket. Then I showed them how to even out the grinds before tamping.

"Grip the portafilter handle with one hand. Using the other, gently sweep the excess grinds away with the edge of your finger. By moving forward, then back, you're evenly distributing the grinds in the basket while you level them. Now it's time to pack."

I rummaged through my bag and produced the brand-new scale from my duplex closet. (Unfortunately, it was pastel blue with pink sea horses—Joy had picked it out a few years ago, and I'd never taken it out of its plastic until now.)

"We don't have to weigh in to make coffee, do we?" Bigs asked.

"I'm not gettin' on that girly scale," Dino said, pointing at the pink seahorses. "It'll make me look fat."

The man laughed.

"What we're going to measure is the amount of pressure applied as we pack coffee into a portafilter. This is the most important step in the espresso pulling process, and the one you're all going to have the most difficulty mastering—"

"Why is that?" asked James.

"The grinds in this filter basket have to be perfectly packed and level when the hot pressurized water streams from the spout, or you're facing disaster."

"Because?"

"Because like all things under pressure, water can turn insidious . . ."

I heard someone shifting uneasily in his chair at that. I looked up to see who, but all the men appeared settled again, gazes expectant.

I cleared my throat. "It's the barista's job to create an even, consistent resistance to that streaming force. If there's even one tiny crack or irregularity in your pack, the pressurized water will find that weakness and exploit it, gush right through, missing the rest of the grinds and completely ruining any chance you had at success."

I handed the tamper to Al Ortiz and placed the full portafilter in the center of my bathroom scale. "I want you to press straight down on the coffee with that, giving the tamper a twist at the end to dislodge any coffee grinds that are sticking to the metal."

"Sure." Ortiz raised his shoulder.

"One more thing," I said. "Watch the scale as you press down, I want you to use about forty pounds of pressure."

"Okay," he said, a little less sure of himself.

It took Ortiz several tries before he got the pressure right, and even his final result was anything but level.

"My turn," Bigs declared. Avoiding the scale, he set the portafilter down on the edge of the espresso cabinet. Gripping the tamper, he pressed until the veins bulged on his sculpted arms.

A tremendous crack boomed as the edge of the particle-board surface broke away. Following a moment of stunned silence, the room exploded with laughter. Even Oat and the captain looked amused.

"Ya stupid mook!" James cried. "Oat just built that!"

Bigsie's cheeks blushed redder than an Anjou pear. "Guess I don't know my own strength."

Ed Schott rubbed his chin. "Maybe you better warn your dates, Hercules."

"My girls work in Manhattan office buildings," Bigs replied with a cocky grin. "Believe me, after ten hours with smooth dudes in penny loafers, most of them are downright desperate for a guy who'll pop their buttons—"

"O-kay," I cut in. "Mr. Brewer, let's give it another try—and this time use the scale."

"Sure, Ms. Cosi, but where's your tampie thing?" Bigs asked.

"It flew off somewhere," Ortiz said.

"Can somebody look for it?" I asked.

"Why don't we improvise?" Bigs suggested. "We can use my roof spike. It's got a flat head like your tampie."

"Tamp*er*, and I don't think your tool—"

But Bigs was already rushing off, retrieving a foot-long piece of stainless steel. "See, Ms. Cosi," he proudly announced upon returning. "This is my roof spike . . ."

I stared at the thing. "Okay, I'll give. What's a roof spike?"

"When we vent the fire, you know, like you saw us do at the caffè the other night?"

I nodded. "You go up to the roof and saw holes in it?"

"Right, well, in case of an emergency, we all carry PSS—personal safety systems. It's a rope with an anchor hook."

"We didn't always carry them." The voice was Oat Crowley's. It was the first time he'd spoken.

I glanced at the man. "Why not?"

"Ask the damn brass," he said. "Back in '05 two good men died because they weren't carrying ropes."

"Well, *now* we carry them," James pointed out.

"And we got these roof spikes, too," Bigsie said. "They're new. We trained on them for two months, but none of us have actually used them in a fire yet."

"Yeah, Big Boy, and you can thank your lucky stars about that," Dino said.

I frowned. "What's it for, exactly?"

"If you're on the roof, venting the fire, and you can't get off again by the fire escape or the building stairs, then you need to attach your escape rope to something to rappel down. But if you end up trapped and there's nothing around to hook onto, then you use the roof spike. Here, Ms. Cosi . . ." Like a student eager to impress his teacher, he grinned with pride. "You want to hold it?"

"Uh . . ."

"It's okay, honey," Dino said. "You don't have to be afraid of handling Bigsie's spike. I hear the ladies all enjoy the experience."

Oh, brother. I took the thing—at the very least to prevent more ribbing. It was heavy in the hand, like an espresso tamper, with a flat head (also like a tamper). Its girth was also the perfect thickness to hold comfortably. But that's where the similarity ended. The spike was a foot long and, well, a *spike*, just as the name suggested.

"So this can save your life?"

Bigs nodded. "See if you were stuck on the roof, you'd drive you ax into the roof itself, then you'd put the spike end into the cut, hammer it down with the back of your ax. It's spring-loaded, like a switchblade, so you can trip these prongs to anchor it." He hit a button and the spring-loaded tool snapped open. "Then you clip your rope to this ring and jump."

"Well . . ." I touched the flat end of the tool. "I'm sorry to tell you. For what I need, this head's too big."

Dino snorted. "That's a first."

"What I mean is we'll need that *tamper* to continue. So why don't we all look for it?" I glanced at the men who just sat staring. "I mean it, guys. Let's get down on our hands and knees and get it done.

"Okay, Ms. Cosi," Ortiz said with a wicked grin. "You go down first and we'll be right behind you."

Now the men glanced at one another with smirks.

"Come on, guys! Give me a break!"

The men burst out laughing—and finally did what I asked. They found the tamper, I washed it, and we began again.

Thirty minutes later, two out of three attempts by each firemen resulted in a decent (if far from perfect) shot. Another half hour and the guys were producing passable espressos—far from Village Blend quality but a start.

"I feel like I've mastered something," Ortiz said.

"You know the basics now," I told him. "But you need to keep practicing. You still have a lot to learn. We've hardly touched on humidity levels, barometric pressure, heat or cold weather, the characteristics of different beans and blends, and the effect these things have on extraction."

Ed Schott laughed. "She sounds like a fire-academy instructor."

"Espressos, gentlemen, are a lot like life, the more you learn the less you know—and the quicker you surrender to not knowing, the faster you will progress."

"*Zen and the Art of Espresso Machine Maintenance* by Clare Cosi," James said with a wink.

"I'll take that as a compliment."

With class dismissed, the men crowded around to thank me, a few of them asking more questions. I pulled out a copy of an Espresso-making guide, one I gave to all of my rookies.

"Damn, even *she's* got a manual!"

The men laughed.

"What's so funny?"

"Are you kidding?" Ortiz gestured to a board filled with official notices on procedures and new equipment. "Welcome to the FDNY. Manuals 'R' Us!"

I smiled, nodded, then quickly broke away and approached Captain Michael.

"Nice job handling the men," he said softly.

I could tell he meant it. His expression was more relaxed now. Whatever I'd done tonight, it had impressed (or amused) him. His earlier anger at finding me snooping around his firehouse was obviously gone.

"Can we talk now?" I whispered. *"Privately."*

"Can't wait to get me alone, eh, darlin'?"

"Cut the crap, will you?"

"What crap?"

"You know what."

"Ah, well, maybe I do . . ." His voice went lower and now his gaze was moving over me. "It's just that when I see a lady such as yourself with so many *feminine charms* . . ." He flashed a grin, his gold tooth winking. "I can't help myself."

"Baloney, Captain, and let me tell you something. I don't like baloney. It's cheap and indigestible."

"You're reading me all wrong, dove. My nature compels me to reveal the truth of my heart. It's just the way the Lord made me."

"The Lord made trees. I sincerely doubt divine inspiration had anything to do with your cheesy pickup lines."

Beneath the crimson trim of his Victorian mustache, the man's patronizing smirk finally vanished. He chucked his thumb toward the heavens. "Upstairs."

Twenty-one

≈≈≈≈≈≈≈≈≈≈≈≈≈≈≈≈≈≈≈≈≈≈≈≈≈≈

STRUGGLING to keep up with the man's long strides, I followed Captain Michael across the kitchen, down a hallway, and into a narrow stairwell. We traveled north a level then moved along another industrial green hallway, passing an office door with a plastic plaque that read *Lieutenant Crowley*. The door was ajar and I heard papers rattling, but I couldn't see the occupant.

The captain's office was no fancier than mine although it was a great deal larger. A battered wooden desk dominated the room. There were two chairs, banks of metal filing cabinets, and an old leather couch. The dark, heavy office felt warm to me. I attributed this not to my hormones (or the captain's, for that matter) but to the clanking, hissing radiator in the corner.

Michael felt the heat, too. He opened the room's only window and gestured to his office door. "Close it if you want privacy."

I did. Then I settled onto a chair opposite his desk. He leaned back on his creaky office throne and cradled his fingers.

"So, I'm guessing you want to know what the fire marshals are sayin', right?"

"That's an ongoing investigation," I said with a straight face. "I'm a civilian, remember? It's none of my business until it's a part of the public record."

Captain Michael blinked, obviously surprised by my answer.

"I have another matter on my mind."

He smirked. "My love life?"

"No. The other fire. The one that happened on the very same night as the fire at Caffè Lucia."

His eyes narrowed. "I wasn't aware there *was* a second fire."

You're lying again. "It made the papers. A privately owned coffee shop in Bensonhurst, Brooklyn. Doesn't that strike you as suspicious? Two coffeehouse fires the same night, at almost the exact same time?"

Captain Michael opened the top button of his pristine white uniform shirt, and then, almost impatiently, he waved the question aside. "This firehouse caught two bakery delivery van fires this morning. Does that strike you as suspicious?"

"No, but—"

"There are just about as many coffee shops in this town as bakery delivery vans. Two vans, two coffee joints. I'd call it a coincidence either way."

"What if both fires turn out to be arson?" I asked. "What then?"

"Then the crimes will be investigated and it's not your business, right? Isn't that what you just said?"

I folded my arms. "Yes. I'm a civilian. But I have a coffeehouse, too. I want to know what you think is causing these fires if it's not arson? I mean, considering the two fires, I'd like your opinion on fire prevention. As a civilian, I think that's a fair question."

We stared at one another for a few silent seconds. He was obviously considering how to handle me.

Your move, chum.

He finally made one—a dodge. "You may be a civilian, Clare, but I'll give you this, you're a big-hearted one. Coming out here tonight after a long day of work, helping out my guys. It was very kind of you."

"I was glad to help." I was, too. Even if I hadn't come to gather information for Fire Marshal Rossi, I would have come to help these men.

A phone trilled just then. It wasn't the land line on the captain's desk. It was a cell phone.

"Excuse me." Michael didn't bother checking the caller ID. He answered quickly, and when the other party spoke, his expression chilled, his lively eyes went dead. With an abrupt lurch, he swung the chair around until all I could see was the starched cotton shirt stretched across his hunching shoulders.

"What do you want?" he said.

He listened for another few seconds, then replied, "No, Josie, and this is the third time you've asked. Three strikes you're out."

Josie? I tucked that name away. I couldn't glean much more from the conversation—just grunts and one word replies. It was also obvious Josie was a woman.

With the captain's back to me, I decided to take advantage of the moment. Rising, I glanced around, looking for any sign the man might be seeing Lucia—a photo of her maybe? Whoever Josie was, she was clearly on the outs, and I found myself curious about the raven-haired woman who'd made the captain so happy in those photos from years ago.

One of the office walls was peppered with framed diplomas, citations, and awards. An "I love me" wall was what they called it in the military because every officer above a lieutenant has one at home or in the office (according to a former U.S. Navy SEAL I'd crossed paths with one summer). But in Captain Michael's case, it was an "I love my little brother" wall. As I moved closer, I realized every single item posted had something to do with Kevin Quinn: from a faded high school newspaper picture in his varsity football uniform to more recent images of Michael bowling with Kevin at Sunnyside Lanes, shooting hoops on a Queens outdoor court, and fishing on the rocky banks of the East River. It was the kind of devotion and pride one usually reserved for a child, not a brother.

I'd heard someone mention Kevin at the Quinn St. Patrick's Day bash. He'd just relocated to Boston this past fall. The most recent photos attested to this, showing Kevin with his family on Boston Commons, at a Yankees–Red Sox game at Fenway Park, hanging out near Plymouth Rock.

The final picture showed Captain Michael standing between Kevin and the man's wife, two smiling preteen daughters on either side. All were bundled in sweaters and coats, and snow dusted the suburban lawn behind them. The handwritten inscription read: "Hey, bro . . . Your visit made our first Thanksgiving in Boston feel like home. Love, Kev, Melody, Melinda, and Megan."

"Look, Josie, I'm on duty. I'm hanging up now."

Michael ended the call. He swung around, noticed me by the Kevin wall and immediately strode across the room.

"Where were we, Clare?"

"I'm a civilian."

"With a big heart, that's right . . ." He relaxed himself, shedding the uneasy business of that call with the ease of a practiced chef crumbling old skin from an onion. "I'd like to thank you for what you've done. I mean it. *Personally* thank you." He smiled down at me, it actually appeared genuine.

"No thanks necessary."

"No baloney now, Clare. It's not every day I meet someone like you. You're something special. All those guts and brains inside that alluring little package—"

"I have some serious questions for you."

"Okay, all right." He showed me his palms. "If that's what it takes. You can go ahead and question my past. I've had my share of women, it's true. At my age, what do you expect? I wasn't exactly a monsignor in my youth."

"Were you ever in a relationship with Lucia Testa?"

The captain's eyebrow arched again. "A gentleman never kisses and tells."

"Tell me anyway."

"Why do you need to know?"

"Were you?"

He took a breath, exhaled it. "No."

I didn't believe him. "Then why is she in a photo on the wall downstairs? Was she seeing one of your men at any time? Maybe a few over a period of years?"

"There are no Firehouse Annies here, and I won't be spreading any gossip. But weren't we talking about you and me, Clare—"

"You're delusional. There is no 'you and me.'"

"But I'd like there to be. You're different. I can see that . . . special."

"I'm involved with your cousin. Is that what you mean?"

"Just give me a chance." He snapped his fingers. "How about a weekend getaway? Maybe Cape May, the Jersey Shore. How about Atlantic City? Dinner. A show. A little Texas Hold 'Em—" His gold tooth flashed.

"Don't hold your breath—"

"I know my cousin, Clare. The guy lives for his job. When was the last time you two went out and had some fun, eh?"

He paused, waiting for my reaction. I didn't offer one.

"Then consider the invitation open-ended. Some weekend when my cop cousin lets you down or ticks you off and you need a nice strong, sympathetic shoulder to lean on, ring me up. Mikey never has to know about it—"

This is a waste of my time.

I wasn't going to get anything more out of this guy. That was obvious. My decision was clear. I would give Rossi all eight names of the men who'd attended my espresso-making lessons this evening: Captain Michael Quinn, Lieutenant Oat Crowley, and firefighters Dino Elfante, Ronny Shaw, Ed Schott, and Alberto Ortiz. Bigsby Brewer and James Noonan would be on that list, too. I hated adding their names. To me, they were heroes who'd risked their safety to carry

Madame and Enzo out of that collapsing caffè—but if there was a chance they were guilty, then I had to tell Rossi, let him investigate, decide for himself.

"Good night, Captain," I said, cutting him off midpass.

"Wait." Michael moved with me, blocking my way. "One more thing, Clare . . ."

"What?"

"I want you to know: Whatever Mikey told you about Kevin"—he lifted his chin toward the I-love-my-brother wall—"it's *his* version of events. Remember that . . ."

Confused for a moment, I turned back to the Kevin Quinn shrine, looked over the photos again. "Your *brother* is the reason you and Mike have been feuding all these years—is that what you're saying? Because that's not what Mike told me . . ."

"What did he tell you?"

I conveyed the story about Mike's old girlfriend Leta, about her dad being shot in cold blood during a bodega robbery, about his classmate Pete Hogarth's father being the killer and Mike's being labeled a narc at the academy because of Hogarth's two relatives being in the same class. "Mike chose to be a cop instead of a firefighter," I finished, "so you felt betrayed, like he let you down and you never got over it."

"My cousin's very good at twisting the truth."

"So are you."

"That's not why we want to take each other's heads off, Clare."

"Okay then. What is it your brother did to Mike?"

"Other way 'round."

I narrowed my eyes at that one. "I'm listening."

"Good. Because you ought to hear this. And once you do, you'll know why he never told you the truth about our feud . . ."

I exhaled. "Never told me *what* exactly?"

"My little brother, Kev, was all set to start at the fire academy. Some of his buddies took him out for a few rounds to help him celebrate. On his way back home, a couple of ex-jarheads in blue pull him over. You know why? Because his SUV had FDNY stickers plastered all over it."

"Why should that matter?"

"The annual FDNY–NYPD football game had just gone down in favor of the fire boys. These cops lost a very juicy bet. So they took it out on Kev. He told them about Mike, said 'Listen, I got a cousin who's a detective, cut me a break.' So they let Kevin call Mike on his cell, and you know what your asshole boyfriend told those cops?"

I stared.

"Mike told those mutts to *arrest* Kevin for DUI. The kid's future was destroyed, Clare. The FDNY wouldn't take him after that. He did jail time. Imagine if it were your little brother—or your child—*for a few beers . . .*"

The man's eyes were flashing. He moved closer, invading my space. "Kevin and I were supposed to be FDNY brothers together. We had wanted that since we were kids, since our dad died. Now Kevin's had to relocate for his civilian job— all the way up to Boston. I hardly see him anymore—my only brother, gone from my life because of my pigheaded cousin's NYPD advancement dreams."

"But . . . aren't you blaming Mike for something that Kevin got himself into . . ."

"Aw, darlin' . . ." He shook his head, looking more heart-broken than angry. "Don't you get it? Mike didn't want to look bad. He didn't want to risk someone finding out that he got the rules bent for a relative. Your precious boyfriend put his police career before helping his own flesh and blood."

My mouth went dry. I wanted to chalk this up to the captain's twisted version of events, but there was such sincerity in his tone, in his eyes . . . I couldn't chalk this one up to baloney. Still, I had to tell him . . .

"That doesn't sound like the man I know."

"You haven't known him long enough, then." His voice went low and soft, like he was doing me a serious favor, warning me of a coming earthquake. "I'm tellin' you, Clare, you should move yourself good and clear of my cousin, for your own well-being . . ."

My reply came, but it was hardly audible. "I don't agree."

"You will, darlin'. Like I told you, my invitation is open-ended. One weekend when you see the jerkoff for what he is and you're cryin' you eyes out, you give me a call . . ."

A loud, throbbing electronic tone interrupted us. A second later, knuckles rapped on the door. The captain held my eyes a long moment then tore himself away, stepped into the hall.

"We got a hot one, Michael . . ."

It was Oat Crowley's muffled voice. On the floor below there were shouts and pounding feet.

"One second, Oat . . ."

The captain ducked back into his office. "Stay here, Clare. I have more to tell you. *Wait* for me to come back."

When he left again, I went to the doorway, watched his broad back moving quickly away.

"What's the job?" the captain asked.

"Long Island City," Oat replied, hurrying to catch up. "It's a two-alarm, going to three . . ."

The heavy bang of the stairwell door cut off their voices. In less than a minute, I felt the massive trucks rumbling under my feet, heard the sirens screaming as the ladder and engine companies raced into the night. When the building was still and quiet again, I headed down to the kitchen to retrieve my backpack. I bundled up tightly—coat, scarf, hat, gloves.

A part of me was curious to hear what else the captain had to say, but I wasn't stupid. Whatever he wanted to tell me was going to come with those increasingly aggressive advances that had nothing to do with my "feminine charms" and everything to do with his vendetta against Mike.

The walk back to my car came with bitterly cold wind gusts. I had expected them, prepared for them, but I shivered just the same. This whole evening had ended badly, and I suddenly knew how those men felt at the end of my espresso lesson. Getting a few answers seldom settled anything, it only confirmed the need to ask more questions.

I didn't want to admit it, but the captain's story had shaken me. I'd always had so much faith in Mike Quinn. We'd been through so much together. But the same had been true with me and Matt—until I'd learned the truth of his behavior during our marriage . . .

When my cell phone vibrated in my front pocket, I was shivering so hard I almost didn't feel it. I tugged off one glove, checked the screen. Who was calling from the Blend?

"It's Tucker. Someone left a package for you."

"What do you mean *someone?*"

"There's no return address."

"Well, didn't you *see* who left it?"

"No, sweetie. Some NYU students noticed a backpack under an empty table. They looked inside and all they found was this brown paper package addressed to you so they brought it to the counter."

It took me a second to add up two and two: abandoned package, nothing else in the backpack, addressed to me, left in our coffeehouse.

Oh my God. "Tucker, clear everyone out of the building! Call 911! Tell them to send the bomb squad! Now!"

Twenty-two

~~~~~~

It was the longest drive of my life—with the possible exception of that predawn cab ride to the ICU all those years ago, when my young, stupid husband had nearly killed himself partying too hard.

Northern Boulevard led straight to the Queensboro, and I ascended the bridge ramp in record time. Just one day ago, shades of magic hour light had gilded this span. Tonight's lonely crossing felt blacker than outer space.

Twice I smacked the button on my car's heater, but the unit was hardly working. It failed to lessen my bone-cold chill, and the dark void between bridge and river only made me shiver harder.

As I hurled my old car toward Manhattan's wall of flickering windows, a distant memory flashed through my mind—the image of a luna moth, throwing herself against the glass of our porch lantern.

"Why is she doing that, Daddy!"

"Just her nature, honey. It's how God made her . . ."

"But she'll burn up!"

"She's not worrying about that part, muffin. She's just trying to get to the light . . ."

Now I knew how that little moth felt. A part of me wanted to soar away, fly off somewhere to get some peace, think everything through. But that's not how I was made. As long as I cared, there was no flying away.

Traffic thickened at the bridge's end and my impatience rose. Spotting an opening, I sped up. Angry horns bleated as I cut off slow-moving bumpers, swung in a careening arc onto the wide, multilaned spectacle of Second Avenue.

Now I was racing south from Fifty-ninth, a straight shot downtown. Green lights tasted sweet, like seedless grapes; red lights were bitter. Yellow felt longer than midsummer days, my excuse to squash down the pedal.

At Fourteenth I turned west, zoomed across the island to Manhattan's West Side, traveled south again and looped around to Hudson. I parked in front of the Blend, cut the engine. The shop's front door was locked but the lights were on. Tucker, Dante, and Matt were standing inside. I rapped on the glass.

"Where is it!" I cried when Tucker threw the bolt.

"Calm down, sweetie." He held up his palms. "Like I told you before you hung up on me, there's no bomb in the package."

"Where!"

"Take it easy, Clare . . ." Matt's face was in front of me now, gaze steady. "I looked the whole package over myself. It's like Tucker told you. There was no need to call the bomb squad. There's no firebomb . . ."

My ex-husband's hands felt firm on my shoulders, but worry lines were creasing his forehead.

"*Show* me," I said.

Matt led me to the marble counter. Dante stood silently behind it, head still bandaged under his fedora, ropey arms folded. I met his eyes.

"That arsonist's ass is mine," he said quietly.

I'd never heard this tone from Dante before. I mean, sure,

he was serious about his painting, but as a barista at the Blend, he was always a carefree dude, as mellow as his ambient playlists.

Not at the moment. The burning demons in Dante's retinas now rivaled Captain Michael's.

"Whenever you nail this asshole, you give him to me."

"She's not nailing anyone," Matt snapped. "Whatever lunatic quest she's been on stops *tonight*."

I still didn't understand what they were talking about—until I moved closer to the counter. A charcoal gray backpack was sitting there with every pocket unzipped and turned out. A small, brown box sat beside it, already opened. Inside was a plain piece of paper displaying three typewritten words.

FOR CLARE COSI

"What's for me?" I whispered.

"A warning," Matt said. He reached in, lifted up the paper.

Beneath it was a box of wooden matches. A single match had been taken out of its box. The slender charred stick had been struck, then blown out, half burned.

FIFTEEN minutes later I was standing amid a sea of banged up desks in the Sixth Precinct's detective squad room.

"Mike, I'm sorry to bother you," I said above the raised voices and ringing phones.

"It's okay . . ."

Mike Quinn was jacketless, his weapon holstered under his left arm, leather straps making their usual indelible creases in his starched white shirt. Under the harsh fluorescence, his features looked just about as starched. Then his gaze moved over me and his expression softened, his voice melting with it.

"What do you need, sweetheart?"

For you to put your arms around me, that's what I need. For you to explain your cousin's ugly accusations. I need you to make love to me . . .

"Can we talk? Privately."

"Yeah, Quinn." Matt stepped out from behind me. "Make it as soon as possible."

A dunking in liquid nitrogen would have been warmer than the look Quinn gave my ex. His eyes found mine again, as if searching for an explanation. Then he looked back to Matt.

"Give me a second."

"Why's your flatfoot working so late?" Matt loudly asked after Quinn departed.

"Lower your voice," I whispered when a female detective glanced our way. "Mike's launching an undercover investigation. It starts tonight."

My gaze followed Quinn as he strode back over to a cluster of desks in the corner. He spoke for a minute to the tight group of detectives he oversaw, one of whom I recognized immediately by his ruddy face and carrot-colored cop hair: Finbar "Sully" Sullivan.

Sully was wiring up another man for surveillance. (I knew this because when I was helping Quinn on a case a short time ago, Sully had wired *me*.) This second man was also familiar—Sergeant Emmanuel Franco.

Because Sully was still prepping him, Franco's flannel shirt was open, revealing a weight lifter's six-pack and part of a tattoo. A hard hat covered his shaved head and one hand gripped a bright orange vest. The construction-guy costume made sense for his new undercover assignment.

After the trendy Manhattan club near the Williamsburg Bridge was cleared of dealing ecstasy and Liquid E to its clientele, the nearby construction site's workers became the squad's new target.

Matt nudged me, pointed across the room. "That younger guy your flatfoot's talking to, the one in the hard hat with his shirt open, he looks familiar."

"No," I lied, "he doesn't."

"Sure he does. That's the cop who interrogated us last December. Franco was his name. I remember now. Sergeant Emmanuel Franco," Matt spat. "I'll never forget that mook."

I gritted my teeth. Our daughter had failed to inform her father that she'd had several "hot dates" with Sergeant "Mook" after our Christmas party. With Joy back in France, I figured their relationship was over and it didn't matter, anyway. So why bring it up?

Quinn returned and motioned for us to follow him. "I don't have a private office," he said as we crossed the busy floor. "We'll have to talk in an interview room."

"That's fine," I said, expecting as much.

Like the NYPD Bomb Squad, which was also based at the Sixth, the jurisdiction of Mike's OD Squad spanned all five boroughs. With his work mostly in the field, there were no proper offices for his small crew, just that tight cluster of desks in the open squad room.

"I'm not too keen on interview rooms," Matt said as he dodged two suits and a uniformed officer. "You're not planning to chain me to anything, are you, Quinn?"

"I don't know, Allegro. That's entirely up to you."

Mike shut the door and we sat down at a metal table with four equally uncomfortable metal chairs. The interview room's walls were concrete block and the only window had one-way glass.

The space had all the warmth of a closet at the city morgue. But the stifling feeling was exactly the point. Detectives didn't bring suspects in here for tea parties. They brought them here to extract confessions, and the only differences I could see between this airless space and the dimly lit confessional where I'd recited my girlish sins was the kneeler—and the lighting. In Father Pentanni's box, I could hardly see a thing. Here in Quinn's confessional the glare was even harsher than in the squad room.

After we sat, I began to explain the situation.

"Just *show* him," Matt said, cutting me off.

I chafed at my ex's tone, but I didn't say a word. Matt distrusted cops (and all authority figures)—partly because of his run-ins with the NYPD and partly because of his bad experiences with corrupt officials in banana republics. I knew how difficult it was for my ex-husband to come here with me. The last thing I wanted to do was get into an argument.

I set the backpack on the table, pulled out the package.

Quinn almost never showed emotion on the job. But as he studied the box of matches, the single charred stick, and the arsonist's note to me, his features twisted openly with fury, worry, and frustration. When he finally spoke, it was a single, quiet curse.

"That son of a bitch . . ."

Matt folded his arms. "Is that all you've got to say?"

"No . . . I'm going to get this to our people in the Crime Scene Unit, but . . ." Quinn exhaled.

"I know," I said, reading him. "It's been handled to death."

"Who opened it?" Quinn asked.

I turned to Matt. "You explain . . ."

"One of our customers, Barry, first noticed the backpack—"

"Barry?" I interrupted. "Tucker said it was a group of NYU students."

Matt shrugged. "Barry found it first. He went to the students next, asked if it was one of theirs. They all passed it around."

I still didn't like the sound of that. "What was Barry doing in the Blend so late?" For months now, the man had been coming in mornings or early afternoons, never in the evenings.

"Tucker said something about his having a fight with this new boyfriend. The guy's on some anticaffeine or anticoffee kick. I don't know. One of those political food movements. He wanted Barry to give up coffee. Barry said no. They had a fight, and Barry came to the Blend to spite him . . ."

"Excuse me," Quinn said. "But how *many* people handled this thing? An estimate?"

"Ten, maybe twelve," Matt said.

Quinn went silent. The cop curtain finally came down on his emotional show.

"I'm sorry," I said softly. "I know that makes it impossible for your people to find forensic evidence."

"Not impossible. Just harder . . . We'll have detectives from this precinct assigned to your case. After we're done in here, you tell them everything, okay? They can work with the fire marshals investigating the Caffè Lucia fire. You'll also have to get me the names and addresses of everyone who touched this thing. Any fibers, fingerprints, or other DNA evidence we find, we'll have to match against your customers and baristas, and eliminate them one by one."

Matt folded his arms. "How long with *that* take?"

"A while. It's not attached to a homicide—"

"Not yet," I said. "But Enzo is in a coma. He's not expected to live. And if he doesn't, the person or persons who set that fire are going to be—"

"Murderers." Quinn said. "I know."

"What happens in the meantime?" Matt snapped. "While we're waiting for some technician to lift a fiber from the asshole who threatened Clare. We go up in flames?"

Quinn focused on me. "When we're through here, I'll speak to my captain. We'll get you protection."

"It's not me who needs it," I said, meeting his eyes. "I have you, don't I?"

Quinn gave me the sweetest look. I returned it.

"Excuse me!" Matt cried. "What about the *Blend?*"

"I'll take care of it," Quinn said, still holding my gaze.

"Good," Matt grunted.

Quinn reached out then, opening his hand as he moved it across the table. He waited, keeping it there until I put mine in his. Then he gently but firmly closed his fingers.

Matt blew out air. "Are we *done* now?"

"I need to talk to Mike about something else," I said softly. "Privately, if you don't mine."

"Fine. I'll wait for you downstairs." Matt rose, left the room, and shut the door—more of a slam really.

"You okay?" Quinn asked.

I nodded, swallowed the sand in my throat. I wanted to tell him everything then, what I'd learned at the firehouse and not just about possible suspects in the Caffè Lucia fire. I wanted to speak to him about the disturbing story that Captain Michael had told me. But this arid, airless room was so awful—and it was Quinn's turf. If I were going to question the man about his past again, I wanted it to be on mine.

"I need to see you tonight, Mike. My place, okay?"

He arched an eyebrow. "You want me to wake you up at four in the morning?"

"Yes."

The corners of his lips lifted. "Okay then. I will."

I rose. "I'm sorry it isn't easier."

He stood, too, picking up the contaminated evidence. "I'll take this to my captain, explain what you've been up to. We'll get sector cars doing routine checks of the Blend all night, and when you open tomorrow, you'll have at least one plainclothes officer undercover inside throughout the day."

"Thank you, Mike." It was far from the first time I'd said it, but I meant it as much as ever.

"One more thing, Clare."

"Yes?"

"Would you please send Allegro back in here? I'd like a private word with him."

Twenty-three

~~~~~~

"Don't move . . ."

The male voice at my ear was no more than a whisper. I'd been sleeping the sleep of exhaustion, so soundly, so sweetly under a heap of bedcovers. Then came the voice, dragging me back to the land of the conscious, the anxious, the miserably alert.

"Mike?"

"You heard me. Don't move . . ."

I was lying on my side, still groggy and disoriented, when I felt the mattress sinking behind me. Under the blankets, large hands caressed my curves.

"What time is it?"

"All the clocks have stopped, sweetheart. There is no time. Right now there's nothing but you and me . . ."

Soft tugs coaxed off my nightshirt. The touch of slightly calloused fingers were cool at first, but quickly warmed on my naked skin. Tender kisses came next, to the back of my shoulder, along my neck, around my jawline . . .

I smiled in the dark.

A few minutes later, Quinn's long, heavy body was covering mine, and I found my way back to sweet oblivion.

An hour later, we were lying together, still under the covers, my head on his shoulder, his durable arm around me.

"Mike . . . ?"

My voice sounded shamefully hesitant in the shadowy chill of the pre-dawn room. "There's something I didn't tell you earlier . . ."

"That makes two of us."

"Oh?"

"Yes. But you go first."

"No," I said, far from eager to spill. "You."

"All right, well . . . Remember that private word I had with your ex-husband?"

"Yeah, what was that about? Matt wouldn't tell me . . ."

"I asked him to stay here with you."

"You're *kidding* . . ."

Not so long ago, Mike nearly broke up with me because Matt was still making use of this duplex. "I can't believe it," I said. "You asked Matt to stay *here* with me?"

"I didn't want you to be in the building alone. That's all. Matt agreed with me."

"Oh, no, he didn't. I was up here all night alone—until you came."

"You were alone in the duplex, Clare, but not in the building. Allegro spent the night downstairs in the Blend, doing business with Europe and Japan on his PDA. I spoke to him before I came upstairs to you, told him to get home, try to get some rest . . ."

Once again, I was surprised, but only a little. Matteo Allegro's long list of petty vices continued to be trumped by one major virtue: the man had a ferocious protective streak. Whether it was his daughter, his mother, his new wife, or old, my ex-husband refused to accept someone he loved being in harm's way.

"Okay, sweetheart, your turn," Mike said, his voice almost teasing. I felt a soft kiss on my hair. "What didn't you tell me earlier?"

"I went to your cousin's firehouse last night."

Mike's big, warm body froze against mine.

"I'm sorry," I said. "Your cousin swore to me on the phone that he wouldn't be there—"

"But he was anyway."

"Yes."

"I asked you to stay away from him, Clare."

"I thought I was staying away from him. I swear. He lied to me—"

"You *promised* me."

"You're not listening, Mike. Try to understand . . ."

I did my best to explain my side of it. "I needed to do it. I needed to find answers. The problem is . . . I found more questions . . ."

Mike let my final statement hang for a moment. "Okay," he said. "You want to explain what that's supposed to mean?"

"It means your cousin told me about the history between you and his younger brother, Kevin . . ."

Mike exhaled, loud and long. "Let's get this out of the way, all right? I want to know every single thing that son-of-a-bitch cousin of mine told you."

"Fine." I threw off the covers and got up.

"Clare! Where are you going?!"

"I'm not going to discuss your cousin in this bed," I said, grabbing my robe, wrapping it tight. "Are you hungry? I need to cook."

"Oh?" Mike blinked, his tone suddenly more pliable. "What did you have in mind?"

CRAB cakes. That's what I had in mind. Mike loved them, and I'd already picked up two pounds of fresh lump crabmeat from the Lobster Place on Bleecker. (Blue, of course. For Maryland-style cakes, the crabs really should be blue.)

So, okay, seafood wasn't your typical breakfast fare. But Mike had been up all night and this was going to be dinner for him.

Now, as the coral glow of dawn lightened the darkness beyond my window, I made a pot of coffee and poured two mugs. Quinn sat at my kitchen table in sweat pants and a faded Rangers T-shirt, his feet bare, his dark blond hair mussed. The man had a strong presence, even when he didn't say a word. With his twilight blue eyes watching my every move over the rim of his coffee mug, I found it difficult to focus on the cooking, but I did my level best.

Back around midnight, I'd already mixed the crabmeat with binders and herbs and formed the small patties. Now I pulled the wax paper covered plates from the fridge, brushed them lightly with an egg wash, and carefully rolled each in a crisp breading of Japanese panko.

The clammy texture of the chilly patties against my fingers and palms reminded me of another dish—my *nonna*'s spinach and ricotta *malfatti*, just one of the daily take-out specialties we made for her grocery.

Malfatti, which translates to "badly formed," were essentially dumplings of ravioli filling (hold the pasta). But the idea I found useful at this very moment was bigger than that. Italian culinary philosophy dictated that you never apologized for your mistake. You just made up a little name for it and moved along.

My malfatti *look lumpy? Hey, don't blame me! They're called badly formed, aren't they? Those little meringue-hazelnut cookies of mine resemble toadstool tops? So what! They're called* brutti ma buoni*, right? Ugly but good!*

It was exactly the tack I took with Mike, explaining (but never apologizing) for my encounter with his cousin the previous evening.

Laughable, wasn't it? I mean, it wasn't my fault your cousin was there. Don't blame me!

(Of course, I was careful to leave out the part about his flame-haired twin inviting me to play Texas Hold 'Em in

Atlantic City.) But then I got to the story of how Mike had put his career ahead of his younger cousin Kevin . . .

When I finished, Mike appeared to come down with a prolonged case of lockjaw. Finally, he let out a harsh laugh.

"He's such a piece of work . . ."

"Kevin?"

"*Michael*. He gave you selected highlights, Clare, a carefully redacted tale of Quinn ancient history . . ."

"You'll have to explain."

"Kevin Quinn was supposed to follow in his late father's footsteps, just like his older brother. But Kevin's partying got out of hand. Underage drinking became a major problem. And then he began to drive drunk."

"So it wasn't just a one time thing?"

"No. When Kevin was pulled over in Manhattan one night, he used my name to get the officers to give him another chance. The pair contacted me themselves—I was on duty so I showed up inside of ten minutes to take my idiot younger cousin off their hands. I drove Kevin straight home, warned the kid to sober the hell up and straighten out. But Kevin blew it."

"What do you mean? He drove drunk again?"

"A few months later, just before he was supposed to start training at the fire academy, the kid was back behind the wheel, loaded up on boilermakers. This time it wasn't just a pull over, it was a traffic accident. He went right through a red light, banged up another vehicle. No one was badly hurt, but a few seconds' difference in that crash and Kevin could have injured or even killed two young women."

"Oh my God . . ."

"The story's not over: this time Michael came to me, hat in hand, asking me to help out his little brother, just like I'd done before. *Make it go away.* Those were his words. But things were different this time. Kevin was falling down drunk when the arresting officers took him in. By the time I heard about it, he was already in the system. I made sure the kid got a good lawyer. I stood up for him in court, vouched for his character. It was all I could do."

"It didn't help?"

"The judge didn't care in the least that Kevin had a relative on the job. She believed he needed a hard lesson. I didn't say so at the time, but so did I. Kevin pleaded guilty and went to jail for a brief time. It killed his chances of becoming a New York City firefighter, and Michael never forgave me for not doing more to help his brother. But, Clare, I swear I did all I could."

I turned back to the stove, considering Mike's words as I slipped six panko-breaded crab cakes into the hot peanut oil. The patties sizzled, the fresh herbs inside giving a hint of floral fragrance to the kitchen, but the primary sensation in the air was heavy and cloying, the kind of feeling you get when you know something is being fried.

"I don't understand why you and your cousin have to be at war over this," I said. "Your actions were obviously reasonable and Kevin was in the wrong. How could anyone trust a kid like that to be a responsible firefighter, for God's sake?"

"Most of the family is on my side, Clare. Kevin even forgave me for not doing more to get him off the hook. But Michael never did."

"Why not? If what you say is true—"

"It is. But my cousin's told his version of that story for so many years now he actually believes it. And that's the tragedy."

I turned back to the burner. Mixing and forming crab cakes was simple enough, but cooking them was not. For one thing, there wasn't much keeping the patties together (not if you wanted to taste crabmeat instead of bread crumbs and binders), so poking them was a bad idea. Flipping should be done only once. And turning them was tricky. Anything held together this precariously had to be handled with finesse.

I glanced over my shoulder at Mike, tried to keep my voice light and casual. "How many years ago did all of that happen, anyway?"

"I don't know. Twelve or so, I guess . . ."

"Is Kevin okay now?"

"Kevin's doing just fine for himself, Clare. He's an engineer, married with two kids, and makes a perfectly good living. Until last summer, he had a great job at a firm in the city."

"But he had to move to Boston, right?"

"That's right . . ."

Mike's voice trailed off, and I let it go, focusing on the completion of his meal. Using a spatula I slipped four of the hot crab cakes onto a large dinner plate, placed three colorful mounds of my homemade condiments around them: lemon-garlic mayo; dill-laced mustard sauce; and avocado, gherkin, and roasted pepper relish. Finally, I piled a generous side of my Thai-style coleslaw into a small salad bowl. (In my opinion, the sweet heat and bright astringency of my Thai slaw was the perfect accompaniment to the unctuous richness of the pan-fried seafood.)

Mike picked up his fork and dug in. "Oh, man, this is good . . ."

I made up my own plate and sat down.

"So . . ." I carefully poked. "Boston?"

"Yeah," Mike said, pausing to chew and swallow. "Kevin was downsized recently—just last year—and he had to relocate for a new job, but I hear he's happy in Massachusetts. And the last time I checked, he no longer touches alcohol."

As Mike inhaled his dinner, I ate my two warm cakes in silence, trying my best to enjoy the freshly fried flavor of lightly breaded seafood, the complementary notes in the tricolored accompaniments. But I still wasn't satisfied.

"Are you sure there isn't anything else between you and your cousin? Just the incident with Kevin?"

Mike looked down, suddenly focusing his attention on the last little bits on his plate. "The thing with Kevin, Clare . . . that's what Michael won't forgive."

"You know, it sounds to me like your choosing your words carefully again. There's more to this story, isn't there?"

"That's all I can tell you . . ."

"You mean that's all you want to tell me."

Mike looked up then, finally met my eyes. "Sweetheart, I'm going to ask you one more time to stay away from my cousin. Will you do that?"

"Yes."

"Promise me, Clare."

"Mike—"

"Promise me."

I sighed. "I promise you, Mike."

"Good, let's change the subject, okay? Mind if I watch the headlines?"

"No . . . I'd like to see them, too."

Mike flipped on the small television in the corner of the counter, turned it to NY1, our local twenty-four-hour news channel.

"I'll make more coffee," I said.

Obviously, Mike was done talking about his cousin, but I couldn't stand having secrets between us, and I was determined to get this one out of him.

As I measured out our Breakfast Blend, I considered how to reopen the subject. For about twenty seconds, the noisy gears of my burr grinder drowned out the dulcet tones of NY1's morning anchor. Then the grinder stopped and Pat Kiernan's voice came back.

". . . a three-alarm fire in Long Island City. The coffeehouse was part of a popular international chain . . ."

"Coffeehouse!"

I turned quickly, just in time to see last night's recorded footage. I recognized several members of the fire station I'd just laughed with the night before. Then I recalled what Oat had said to Captain Michael as they strode away from his office—*"Long Island City . . . a two-alarm, going to three . . ."*

". . . and the mayor will make a statement later today about this sad turn of events," Kiernan continued. "The coffeehouse was closed at the time of the blaze and no customers or employees were injured. But one of New York's Bravest lost his life . . ."

I glanced at Mike. We both tensed, waiting. Finally, the still, color photograph came up on the TV screen—a picture of the dead man.

I stumbled backward, fell into a chair.

". . . best known for his appearance as Mr. March in last year's famous FDNY calendar, Bigsby Brewer died instantly after jumping from the building's roof. The cause of the fire is deemed suspicious and is under investigation."

Twenty-Four

〰〰〰〰〰〰〰〰〰〰〰〰〰〰〰〰

THREE days later, a public funeral was held in Queens. Dante, Madame, and I attended. The mayor was there and the city commissioners. The cardinal came, the FDNY Emerald Society Pipes and Drums, the local press, and every member of Bigsby Brewer's beloved firehouse.

The pomp and turnout were overwhelming, the grieving genuine. Thousands of firefighters from every borough showed up in dress blues. The small army couldn't fit inside the church so they lined up in formation on the streets outside, where cops redirected traffic for hours, all the way to the burial ceremony in Calvary Cemetery on Laurel Hill Boulevard.

The younger firefighters looked steely, the older ones visibly haunted, unshed tears glazing their eyes, tense expressions barely masking rekindled memories. Back in fall 2001, this city had seen hundreds of funerals just like this one, final farewells to those who'd answered their last alarms.

Now it was Bigsby's turn. And on the morning of his funeral, that's when it hit me. I'd *heard* his last alarm.

*   *   *

THE cluster of days that followed blew by like fast-moving storms. Time felt compressed, and so did I. Tensions were so high that most mornings I woke up feeling as though I'd slept with my head inside a panini maker.

The Blend's business went on as usual—morning crush, lunchtime takeouts, evening regulars—but just as Mike promised, detectives from the Sixth took shifts in plain clothes while sector cars drove by so often I was starting to feel like I managed a gangland hangout.

There were no more threats, however, and no more coffee-house fires. My two follow-up calls to Rossi and the precinct detectives handling my case yielded polite but completely fruitless conversations.

Madame continued to spend part of every day at the ICU, reading the newspapers aloud to Enzo. He was still coma-tose, but his condition was stable, at least. Until he woke up—if he ever did—the doctors wouldn't be sure of the ex-tent of his stroke damage.

I met with Valerie Noonan twice (in microbrew bars, her choice) to finalize details for the bake sale. Mike and I man-aged to meet a few times for dinner, too—Cornish hens with coffee glaze and Cumberland sauce; an outstanding recipe for Triple-Threat Firehouse Penne Mac 'n' Cheese (that James shared with me); steak with a Jim Beam reduction; and Korean-style fried wings (my first attempt to identify the ingredients and technique behind those delectable Un-identified Flying Chickens).

As usual, Mike swooned for my cooking, but his under-cover operation near the Williamsburg Bridge sapped so much of his time and energy that we failed to connect be-yond the dinner table.

No more spicy-sweet 4 AM wake up calls. In the wee hours before dawn, Mike would come back to the Blend and relieve Matt from his night vigil of global coffee trading. Then Mike would come up to my bedroom, collapse onto the mattress, and by the time he stirred again I was already at work, pulling espressos . . .

FINALLY, the day of the big bake sale arrived.

Val had chosen the location and it was perfect—Union Square Park, an island of green space ringed by skyscrapers. The park was three city blocks long and the northern perimeter was frequently used to stage open-air farmers' markets. That was the real genius of the location. New Yorkers were already used to stopping by the area for food purchases so the turnout was practically guaranteed.

Early that morning, volunteers from the NYC Fallen Firefighters Fund began setting up their tents and tables. Matt and I spent two hours transporting supplies and erecting our little blue Village Blend stand. Now he was gone—off to catch some sleep since he'd been doing business with Europe and Japan most of the night—while I stayed to man the booth, test our espresso machine, and marshal the troops.

Behind our portable counter, Dante and Esther began unpacking columns of plastic lids and cardboard cups.

Then Tucker arrived, waving the *New York Post* at us like a signal flag. "People, people, did you see this!"

"See what?" Dante asked.

Esther and I stared blankly.

"Oh my *gawd*!" Tucker was close to apoplectic. "There's something in this paper you all *need* to hear!"

"Lottery numbers?" Esther asked.

"Listen!" Tucker cleared his throat and his best PSA announcer voice began to read: "Coffee is a drug. Coffee is toxic to the human body. Coffee is a capitalist tool and should be eradicated from the earth—"

"What is that?" Esther cried.

She reached for the paper, but Tucker pulled it out of reach. "It's a letter from the 'Coffee Shop Arsonist'—according to the headline, that's what the police are calling this Looney Tune. Last week, this letter was sent directly to the *New York Post*. Apparently, they just got the okay from the authorities to publish it."

"*Keep reading*, Tucker," I said quietly.

"Farmers in developing countries should be growing crops, not coffee. Coffee is a threat, a *weapon*! But I have a weapon, too, and I will use it. Close your coffeehouses or suffer the consequences—"

"Toxic?" Esther said. "On what planet? Try reading a Harvard study once in a while, why don't you? And did he say coffee is a *weapon*? That's lunacy. Coffee is the most traded commodity on earth next to oil. And they make *napalm* out of oil. So you tell me—which one is the weapon?"

"Blame it on the writer, Esther. I'm just doing a dramatic read of the lines."

"You'd expect an actual arsonist to know the difference between a thousand-year-old beverage enjoyed around the world and a combustible fluid used to make firebombs. Isn't that his *job*?"

"All I can tell you is that the arsonist's 'job' has got me goosey. And I'm sure I'm not alone. I signed up for mixing espresso drinks, not fielding Molotov cocktails."

Esther shook her head. "Well, I'm not sweating it. This nut job has only burned three coffeehouses. Do you know how many cafés there are in this city? Statistics are on our side."

"Listen, Missy!" Tucker snapped his fingers. "When somebody's out to turn me into a human torch, having the 'odds on my side' is not a comfort! And in case you've forgotten, this firebug already left a warning package in *our* coffeehouse."

"Where's your dramatic spirit? Think *Method*. Can't you see yourself playing Joan of Arc?"

Tuck went quiet a moment. "I realize you're joking, Esther, but that's actually not a bad idea for a black box production—I mean, given that Peter Pan is usually played by an adult woman, I don't see why I couldn't do Joan, although . . ." He flipped his signature floppy 'do. "I'd never want to cut my hair *that* short."

"Either way, you're not in a coffeehouse at the moment," Esther pointed out. "You're outdoors. In a park. And you're surrounded by highly trained members of the New York Fire Department. I really do think you're safe from a fiery death."

Just then a tremendous *whooshing* sound made Tuck and Esther yelp, and me jump. A wave of hot air wafted toward us and we quickly turned our heads. The stand beside ours had erected a banner: *Crème Brûlée! Torched to Order!*

To the enthusiastic applause of a growing group of spectators, two burly firefighters in bunker suits and safety visors proceeded to caramelize the sugar on top of several servings of the classic French egg-custard dessert.

Neither of these guys was using a kitchen salamander; dainty, handheld chef's torch; or even a standard oven broiler (an option I gave my Jersey readers when I was writing my In the Kitchen with Clare column). No, these guys were finishing their crème brûlée with an industrial-sized acetylene torch mounted on a wheeled gurney.

"You're right, Esther," Tucker said, staring. "I feel so much safer with a tank of explosive compressed gas next door!"

"Let's keep it down, guys," Dante told Esther and Tucker. "Remember, these firefighters lost one of their own to this psycho bastard."

"Oh God, you're right," Tuck said, glancing around. "I wasn't thinking."

"Well, I think this letter is absurd," Esther muttered, smacking the newspaper. "And probably a hoax, too."

Tuck clutched his head like the kid in *Home Alone.* "A hoax!"

"Okay, enough," I said in a stern managerial voice. But I shared Tuck's apprehension. Blowtorch aside, this development was a bombshell. *No wonder Rossi and his colleagues were so tight-lipped with me.* If Homeland Security wasn't on board before, they certainly were now.

"Let's get back to work," I said. "Customers are starting to line up."

"Fine with me," Esther said, then she pointed toward the crème brûlée stand. "You know, I've tried making that stuff, but I can never get my custard tops to come out smooth."

"Full of pockmarks?" I assumed.

Esther nodded. "Pothole central."

"You didn't follow the recipe," I stated flatly. "You upped the temperature."

"The lower temperature takes forever!"

"When you turn up the heat, you boil the custard," I said. "Cooking is like a lot of things in life, Esther. Rushing the process only gets you burned . . ."

And speaking of getting burned . . .

I asked Tuck if I could borrow his *New York Post*. Then, letting my capable baristas handle the drink orders, I took the paper to a nearby bench and began reading every story I could find on the Coffee Shop Arsonist. Apparently, the *Post* had received the letter from the alleged bomber the day after Bigsby's death. The *Post's* editors promptly handed it over to the authorities—after copying the text verbatim for today's edition.

Prior to the letter appearing, no one had announced anything connecting the three seemingly separate coffeehouse fires: Enzo's caffè, the shop in Brooklyn that had burned the same night, and this chain store that ended up costing Bigsby's life.

Thus far, the only speculation I'd heard was on the chain store's fire. That particular coffeehouse chain was currently at the center of an ongoing labor dispute over wages and benefits. People assumed the fire was set deliberately by an angry employee.

But this letter changed everything. Now all three fires looked like terrorism, or at the very least a serial arsonist. Its appearance also wreaked havoc on my own suspect list. While I could imagine Lucia Testa or Mrs. Quadrelli torching Enzo's shop for their own selfish reasons, I doubted either woman was capable of burning *two* additional coffeehouses to cover their tracks.

A gust of morning chill swept suddenly across the park, crinkling the tabloid in my hand and stirring the canvas of our nearby Blend tent. In line at our stand, pedestrians shivered inside their light jackets and sweaters. I shivered, too, thinking of the threat I'd received.

But what if the letter isn't real? What if it's a decoy?

Even Esther used the word *hoax*, and the idea stuck with me. The more I thought about it, the more I realized that the pattern of fires made no sense for a political activist. *The authorities have to see that, don't they?*

I glanced up to see our line had gotten even longer. And it appeared there was a problem with the espresso machine. Great.

Break's over . . .

As the sun climbed higher in the cloudless sky, the weather warmed into a perfect day for an outdoor event. The bake sale was soon packed with customers.

"Hey, boss," Esther called after a sudden rush. "The way I'm calculating it, we're going to run out of cups in another two hours."

I glanced at my watch. "Don't worry. Matt wanted a nap and a shower, but he'll be back this afternoon with a van full of supplies—"

My words were drowned out by a sudden cacophony. Pigeons took flight and squirrels escaped into the trees as amplified bagpipes howled from a temporary stage in the middle of Union Square. Over the heads of a hundred off-duty firemen and their families, six men in kilts launched into what would best be described as a *unique* rendition of the Doors' "Light My Fire."

Tucker moaned, his musical aesthetics clearly assaulted. "I hoped to avoid this."

Dante snorted. "Avoid the magnificent sound of the bagpipes? At a fireman's *anything*? What planet are you from?"

"One without men in kilts, apparently," Tuck replied. "Although they do have good legs."

"Look! It's Roger Clark from New York One!" Esther was so excited by the media presence we could actually hear her voice over the racket. "And there's the eleven o'clock news team from WPIX. Looks like the Firefighters Fund will get good publicity."

"Good publicity is an oxymoron," Dante said. "Bad news trumps good news in this town."

"Huh?"

"They're not here for charity. The press came because of Brewer's death and the arsonist's letter." Dante jerked his thumb in the direction of the stage. "See that Asian guy Channel Four is talking to? The dude's name is Jason Wren. He was the owner of Avenue O Joe, that coffeehouse in Brooklyn. The one that burned the same night as the Queens café where I almost became human kindling."

Esther shrugged. "So?"

"So the Channel Four news team brought him down here *specifically* so they could interview Wren about the arsonist's letter, using this fireman's event for a backdrop. Tragedy is opportunity to the media." He touched his bandaged head. "They better not stick a mike under my nose and ask for a statement or . . ."

My barista proceeded to describe a use for a handheld microphone that no sound technician would ever consider— not sober, anyway.

While the bagpipers segued into a rendition of Johnny Cash's "Ring of Fire" (I was catching a theme here), my eyes were drawn to a familiar male strut.

The cocky guy approaching us wore a sunny yellow hard-hat over his more typical red, white, and blue 'do-rag, and a dusty flannel shirt over his muscular shoulders, but I instantly recognized the distinctive swagger of Sergeant Emmanuel Franco. Under one arm, he toted a number of pastry boxes and his free hand held a large sandwich cookie.

"I'm still working undercover, Coffee Lady," Franco warned me as he munched the cookie. "So pretend you don't know me."

"My pleasure."

Franco laughed. "You're funny."

"Yeah, I'm a laugh riot. Well, anyway, *stranger*, you look pretty stocked up already, but feel free to peruse our baked good offerings . . ."

I pointed to the table next to our espresso counter. The last few days, I'd been in a lousy mood. Now, amid the sunny sky and cheerful crowds of the charity bake sale, I realized the nicknames I'd given my home-baked treats *might* have been a little dark.

"*Killer* Caramelized Banana Bread?" Franco read, moving down the table. "*Murder by* Mini-Coffeehouse Cake?"

Franco glanced back at me. I shrugged.

"O-kay. What else have we got? *Death by* Double-Sized Double-Chocolate Chip Cookies. Hey, those look tasty, give me six. *Sinful* Salt-Peanut Caramel Shortbread Bars. Oh, yeah, sinful's definitely up my alley, I'll take a dozen of those . . ."

He continued down the table and glanced back at me once more. "*Chokehold* Chocolate Brownies? What are you on, Cosi Lady?"

In my defense, I'd made a half-dozen *normally* named things, too: Blueberries 'n' Cream Coffee Cake Pies (which were—surprise, surprise—a cross between a cake and a pie); Fresh Glazed Strawberry Tarts; Almond-Roca Scones; Star Fruit Upside-Down Cake; and my old standby Cinnamon-Sugar Doughnut Muffins, with a surprise twist this time, a raspberry-flavored heart. I pointed out the muffins to Franco.

"We have jelly doughnut muffins."

Franco just shook his head. "It's a mystery what you have against selling me a good, old-fashioned American jelly doughnut!"

Esther leaned over the counter. "So what are *you* eating, Bob the Builder?"

He held up the cookie. "According to the guys I bought it from, it's a 'Stuck on You' Linzer Heart." Franco winked as he offered her a taste. "Yummy, huh?"

"Peanut butter and marshmallow. Not bad . . ."

"Ladder 219 has a thing for Elvis," Franco said. "All their stuff has the King's theme: Chocolate Hound Dogs, Love Me Tender Blueberry Corn Muffins, Jailhouse Rocky Road Bars, Big Hunk O' Burnin' Fudge. They even dubbed their firehouse 'Graceland.'"

Esther licked some marshmallow off the corner of her darkly glossed lip. "Sticky, but good."

"I wonder if Joy could bake this?" Franco said.

I was about to inform the sergeant that my daughter's interest in Fluffernutters ended when she quit the Girl Scouts. But I bit my tongue. I'd learned a thing or two during Joy's teen years. *Better not encourage their relationship by* discouraging *it.*

"So, Coffee Lady, I heard something about a free cuppa joe with a purchase."

I nodded. "That's right. And for a purchase *that* big he deserves a large."

Esther presented Franco with his coffee—black, no sugar.

"*Mmmm,* hot stuff," he said after a sip. "Kind of like that new batch of digital goodies Joy sent me from France."

When he waggled his eyebrows, I nearly lost it. "Just what kind of photos is my daughter sending you?!"

"Calm down, Momma Hen." Franco laughed over his coffee cup. "They're pictures of some of the dishes Joy's been making. A sweet roasted chicken, some pretty vegetable medleys, a glistening glazed duck, and a *very* sexy puff pastry."

"Oh, thank God," I said, relieved—until I noticed Tucker exchanging a look with Esther.

"Did you know Frenchies eat pigeons?" Franco asked, completely serious.

Esther folded her arms. "You mean *squab*?"

"Squab? Is that what—" Franco suddenly stopped. He seemed to be listening to something that we couldn't—like a micro radio receiver in his ear. "Sorry. I'd love to continue this discussion about what Frenchies call rats with wings, but I gotta go."

"What a relief," I said to Esther when Franco was out of earshot. "I thought my daughter was sending him . . . Well, never mind what I thought."

"Oh, boss . . ." Esther gaped at me with pity. "You are so naïve."

"What do you mean?"

"Franco may come off as a mook, but Joy's really into him. She says he's got these *way* wicked magic hands, and when they're alone together—"

"Stop! I don't want to know!" Now I was the one holding my head like the kid from *Home Alone*.

Tuck put his hand on my shoulder. "Add it up, Clare. Joy's a professional cook. It's her passion. And she's sending Franco pictures of her dishes."

"So?" I said, still feeling clueless.

"Hello!" Esther's eyes bugged. "You never heard of *food porn?*"

The thought of my daughter sending that cocky sergeant *any* form of porn left me sufficiently horrified. For a moment, I was so distracted, I didn't notice what Dante already had.

"Boss . . ." He said, gently tapping me. "James Noonan is here . . ."

Dante lifted his chin and I looked in the direction he'd subtly indicated. The crowd was breaking up after the bagpipers turned the stage over to a local politician. James stood only a few feet away from our tent. He was surrounded by firefighters. I didn't recognize the other men, but it was clear they knew James and were offering their condolences.

"He looks like a freakin' zombie," Dante whispered. "Even worse than at the funeral."

It was true, James seemed to have recovered little since

that heartbreaking day. He'd been inconsolable at the church—so overwhelmed by grief that he'd left the mass early. He never showed up at the wake, either, though his wife made a brief appearance. I'd hoped to see Captain Michael step in and help, but he had his hands full comforting Bigsby's mother and two sisters.

I waited until the other firemen drifted away, and then I brought James a double espresso.

Twenty-Five

❧❧❧❧❧❧❧❧❧❧❧❧❧❧❧❧❧❧

"**Hey**, Ms. Cosi."

"Hey to you," I replied, giving him a smile.

He brightened a little when he saw me, but his smile was barely there. In the strong morning sun, James' complexion looked like stale bread dough, his bloodshot eyes were dulled and shadowed, the crimson webs as pronounced as wild mace growing over nutmeg seeds.

I pointed to a bench just vacated by a pair of EMS workers, and we sat down. "So, what do you think of the sale?" I asked, starting with what I hoped was a neutral question.

"It's nice. Real nice. And thank you for the espresso." James sipped once then stared across the park. "Bigs was looking forward to today. All the 'tempting offerings' as he put it."

"He enjoyed home-baked goodies?"

"Yeah . . ." James glanced at me. "Those, too."

He tipped his head and I followed his gaze to a trio of young women—chic, fashionable, and thin as celery stalks—flirting with two young firefighters. The Manhattan girls were shopping for something warm, sweet, and comforting, and it didn't appear to involve chocolate, sugar, or pastry flour . . .

"This town's raining estrogen, you know?" James said. "Ladies in hose and heels. Bigs loved them."

"I noticed. So did Dante. The number of single white roses at Bigsie's funeral was hard to miss . . ." (Not to mention the number of single, well-dressed women.)

"Yeah, Bigs liked to send a white rose to a girl after he had a nice, uh . . . *evening* with her."

James paused and his frown deepened. "You know the worst part of it, Ms. Cosi? My best friend died for nothing. It shouldn't have happened. He did everything right. It was someone else who screwed up . . ."

"I don't want to cause you any more pain," I said as gently as I could, "but I'd like to know more about what happened that night. I'd like to know exactly how your friend died."

James rubbed his neck for a moment then finally spoke. "Two companies were fighting the flames when we got there. It had already spread to the ground floor of the building next door. Oat ordered us up the fire escape to vent the second structure—me, Bigs, Dino Elfante, and Ronny Shaw."

A cloud crossed James's pallid features. "Everything was going okay, by the book. The roof was flat with no apparent hot spots, not much smoke, either. Bigs kind of moved away from the rest of us, poking the roof with his Halligan tool. Then all hell broke loose. There was a blast, and a chunk of the roof flew into the air. It was like a volcano of fire that suddenly just blew."

James paused, gulped at his double.

"The fire marshals said the basement had an illegal conversion. That's what funneled the fire so fast from the coffeehouse to the office building next door. And the second floor of that office structure was undergoing some kind of unlicensed renovation. There were combustibles all over the place. So when the first floor started cooking the second, everything went up without warning."

James drained his cup dry. "We hit the same fire escape

we came up on. Dino and Ronny were long gone when I realized Bigs wasn't behind me."

He crushed the paper cup in his fist.

"I went back up. The roof was still partially intact. There wasn't much smoke, but the heat and fire were unreal. I could see Bigs on the other side of that burning hole. There was no way he could make it back to the fire escape, but he was ready."

"Ready?"

"Bigs had already found a heavy rafter and pounded down his roof spike. He'd hooked the safety line to the spindle, and he was about to jump over the side—"

"Roof spike?" I interrupted. "That's the same tool Bigs had me holding the night I came by the firehouse, right?"

"Yeah," James said.

"So what happened next?"

"Bigs saw me through the flames and he kind of waved. He was even laughing, looking forward to testing out the spike, I think. Then he jumped over the side. That's when the secondary hit—"

"Sorry. What's a secondary?"

"A second explosion. Almost as big as the first. Flames shot up from the lower floors and knocked me on my ass. I hit the fire escape and didn't stop until I kissed the ground."

"Was it the second blast that caused Bigs to fall?"

James stared straight ahead. "That's what Oat said. But that's not the way I see it. I think Bigs was murdered, Ms. Cosi, just like someone shot him with a gun."

I thought I understood. "Don't worry, James. The authorities will catch this arsonist—"

"It wasn't the arsonist." His whisper sounded more like a hiss. "It's worse than that—"

He suddenly stopped talking and his entire body tensed. I followed his stare and realized for the first time that we had an audience. Not far away, Lieutenant Oat Crowley was watching us.

Now I was tensing, too. I noticed Oat take a cigar out of his jacket and light it. Every smoker I knew used lighters. Not Oat. He'd just lit his cigar with a *wooden match*.

Oat wasn't standing alone. Another man was conversing with him—and doing most of the talking. With Oat's gaze still on James and me, he slipped the box of matches back into his hip pocket.

My mind was racing now, but I refocused on James and something significant he'd said: "What did you mean when you said Bigs was murdered? If not by the arsonist, then by whom?"

James had been staring at his lieutenant. With my question, he lowered his eyes. "Forget it, Ms. Cosi. I didn't say a thing, all right?"

"I can't forget it, James. You helped me once, now I want to—"

"Forget it," he repeated.

Oat and the other man were now approaching us. The stranger had a friendly, lopsided smile under shaggy, wheat-colored hair. A crooked line of freckles sprinkled his pug nose and his ears seemed comically large for his head. The awkward boyishness was not without charm, however, and the addition of small round glasses and laugh lines had him coming off more as an absentminded professor than a stand-in for Alfred E. Newman.

Cigar clenched between his teeth, Lieutenant Crowley wore his usual scowl. Blue smoke floated almost satanically around his head. The aroma washed over us. Not the crisp, woody scent of fine tobacco, but the sharp, rank stench of cheap stogies like the ones my bookie father used to hand out to winners, along with their pay out.

I stifled a cough as I rose to greet them.

"What are you two gossiping about?" Oat said around his cigar. The hostility radiating from the lieutenant was nothing new, but there was also *suspicion*.

The boyish bespectacled stranger picked up on the tension and stepped in fast to pump James's hand. "You're Noo-nan, right? We've met, haven't we? I'm Ryan Lane," he said, flashing a warm smile.

"Hello."

"Oat told me about your loss. I'm really sorry. Brewer was a real hero."

James nodded. "Thanks for that."

"No thanks necessary," Lane replied. "The sacrifice of men like Brewer is what the Fallen Firefighters Fund is all about."

Lane's practiced pitch came as no surprise. I'd noticed the name tag on his camel hair sport coat identifying him as a board member of the firefighters' charity.

"You're the woman responsible for this superb coffee, right?" Lane asked, looking at me now.

"I'm Clare Cosi. Thank you for the compliment."

"The Village Blend is a landmark. I've been there several times," he said.

I forced a smile, trying harder to remember if I'd ever waited on him.

"Excellent coffees, and a nice variety, too. Your espressos are as good as anything I've tasted in Italy. I do a cycling tour every five years." He grinned, adjusted his glasses. "Un-fortunately I live and work in North Jersey right now, too far away to be a regular customer. But I buy your whole-bean coffee whenever I'm in town."

"That's nice of you to say."

"Well, I just love coffee, Ms. Cosi! I'd love to tell you about the time I visited a coffee farm—"

This Lane guy was a real talker, but I tuned out on his story the second I noticed Oat speaking to James: "So, kid, you got a shift coming up, right? You heading out soon?"

"Not yet," James replied. "Got stuff to do first."

Oat stared at James for a moment, and then his gaze shifted to me. He took the cigar out of his mouth and flicked the ashes off.

"Like what?" Oat said with a sneer, loudly enough to

make Ryan Lane pause and listen, too. "Like hitting on divorced broads ten years your senior?"

I can't believe he just said that. "Excuse me, Lieutenant?" I said. "But just what are you implying?"

Oat opened his mouth to respond when Mr. Lane (who appeared equally horrified by the man's insult) interceded. "Hey, come on, we should go," he said, touching Oat's arm. "I've got to meet and greet the organizers, you know? And the mayor's entourage is due any second."

"Right," Oat said, still openly glaring at me. Finally he stuck the cigar back in his mouth and walked off, puffing up a cloud like a two-legged dragon.

Ryan hurried to catch up, calling over his shoulder: "A pleasure to meet you, Ms. Cosi."

I waited until James and I were alone before I spoke. "How does that nice guy know Oat?"

"Ryan Lane? He works for Fairfield Equipment."

"What does Fairfield Equipment do?"

"They make rescue gear for firefighters."

"And where does Oat fit into that?"

"Well, as I understand it, Oat's father was a rookie firefighter with Ernest Fairfield back in the 1970s. Fairfield had a nose for business, and Oat's old man was a do-it-yourself type. Together they made a bundle."

"A bundle? How? Gambling?" (Given my father's bookie business, I rarely saw any other way for a working-class man to make real money.)

"Not gambling, Ms. Cosi. Patents."

"Patents?"

"A lot of the old-timers would make their own tools on the job—anything they could think of to make their lives easier. Kind of what I did with our house's kitchen, cobbled together a bunch of appliances."

"Oh, I see . . ."

"So Crowley Senior invented a lot of useful stuff, and Ernest Fairfield quit the department and started a company to manufacture it."

"And Ryan Lane works for Fairfield."

"Yeah. He showed up at our seminar a few months ago when we started training with the roof spikes."

James was shifting impatiently now. It was obvious he didn't like my new line of questioning.

"James, I'm sorry to bring this up again, but when you were talking about your friend's death earlier, you used the word *murdered*—"

"Excuse me, Ms. Cosi. I see my wife heading our way."

A moment later, I heard the fast-clicking heels of Valerie Noonan.

Twenty-six

~~~~~~~~~~~~~~~~~~~~~~~~~~~~

"JAMES, I've been looking for you all over!" Val cried, close to breathless. "*Where* did you park our car? I went to the vendors parking area on Sixteenth and—"

"Couldn't find a spot on Sixteenth," James said tightly. "The designated parking area was full."

"Oh, damn." Valerie's shoulders sunk. Her auburn French twist looked a little ragged from the March wind gusts. Her cucumber green linen suit was still crisp, but the name tag on its lapel sat askew.

"So where's the car?" she asked.

"I parked it at the St. James garage on—"

"You paid for parking?" One arm rose and fell, taking her thick clipboard with it. "That's like fifty bucks or more! You know my job situation, James. You know how tight things are going to get for us soon—"

"The fund has an expense account, doesn't it? Take the money from there. You worked hard enough for it. Why do you need the car, anyway?"

"I don't need the car. I left something in the trunk."

James exhaled hard. He took her arm. "Fine. Let's go."

"Oh, forget it now," Val said, pulling away. "I've got a crisis with the sound system on my hands. I've just got to hope that—"

"Sorry," James said, glancing at his watch. "But I ought to get back to the house."

"Oh? Okay. Well, since you're taking the car, could you stop at the store first?" Val said. "I wanted a bowl of cereal this morning and we're out of milk. Paper towels, too, and pick up—"

"I meant the *firehouse*," James said.

Val's mouth closed. Then she reached into her pocket. "You're coming to the party tonight, aren't you?" she asked, fumbling with a pack of cigarettes.

Val was referring to the post–bake sale party. Every borough was having its own for the volunteers, and I'd been invited to the one being held at a Queens pub. Mike was supposed to meet me around eight.

"I'll be there at nine, maybe sooner," James replied, his gaze was unhappily focused on Val's cigarette.

"It's at Saints and Sinners. That's in Woodside—"

"I know where it is," James said. Then he nodded in my direction. "See you tonight, Clare."

Val frowned as she watched her husband's back. I stood and touched her arm. "Are you okay? Would you like to sit down for a few minutes?"

Cigarette between her lips, Val shook her head as she flicked a disposable lighter a half-dozen times in rapid succession without coaxing a flame. She groaned and—in a broad gesture of disgust—tossed the lighter and cigarette into a Parks Department trash can.

"It's been hell since Bigsie died," she said. "James is shutting down. I can't tell his family, his friends. They don't want to hear it."

"What do you mean 'James is shutting down'?"

"He's short with me when I ask questions, he's miserable and pouting all the time, and he won't discuss what's on his mind. Not with me, anyway. He's talking to someone, though, because he disappears once in a while, goes to the garage where he has these long conversations on his cell phone."

Three in the long and tragic list of warning signs your husband is having an affair. Pretty soon he'll be going out with the guys or spending time with a client, or he just won't come home one night.

"Listen, Val, your husband is going through a really bad time, but I think—"

A loud ring tone interrupted us. I'd heard Val's cell go off many times, but I'd never heard it play this set of notes before.

"Sorry, Clare! I have to take this!"

"Sure, of course."

The tinny tune sounded like one of those club hits of the 1980s: "You Spin Me Round (Like a Record)." Val answered the cell without bothering to check the caller ID.

"Dean! I can't believe you called back . . . What? . . . You're *here*? Really?" With her free hand, Val felt the condition of her hair, adjusted her lopsided name tag. "I'm on the north side of the park, across the street from that big Barnes & Noble— Huh? Turn around?"

She did and laughed when she saw a man with sun-bronzed skin in a black leather jacket, standing right behind us, cell phone at his ear.

Val closed her phone and air-kissed the newcomer. "Thank you so much, Dean."

"My guys are at the podium right now, setting things up." Dean's voice was deep, with a slight foreign accent. *Greek?*

"You have a band?" I interrupted.

Val turned to me. "He has a sound system—and that's what I desperately needed. The one I leased for the day cut out, and their so-called technician couldn't fix it. The mayor's coming, so is the fire commissioner and a whole bunch of celebrities. I was in a total panic, so I put in a call to my old friend here . . ." She turned back to the man. "I didn't think you'd get here in time."

"My darling, you sounded so distressed on the phone that I rushed it here from Brooklyn. The nightclub's main system is permanent, you know, so I brought the portable stuff. We use it for live acts, but you're welcome to it for as long as you need it."

"I *so* appreciate this," Val said, again patting her wind-ravaged twist. "Make sure I send you a charitable giving form to fill out. You can declare you labor as a tax deduction."

Dean waved away the thought. "I did this for my dear friend, not for a tax break."

"Clare, I want you to meet the man who saved my life. Clare Cosi. This is Constantine Tassos—Dean for short."

"Nice to meet you," I said. "So you run a club?"

"Oh, yes." Dean nodded, handing over a business card in a smooth, practiced gesture. "The Blue Mirage in Bensonhurst. Actually I own several catering halls in Brooklyn and Queens, and I have two other Mirage clubs. The Purple Mirage in North Jersey—"

"And the Red Mirage in Astoria?" (It was right there on his card.)

Dean nodded. "That's correct."

He was a compact man, a little shorter than Val, with not an ounce of spare weight on his slight form. His eyes were dark and intense under unruly ebony curls. I guessed the man's age around forty, but it was only a guess. His smile looked whiter than bleached sheets, contrasting strikingly with his tanned face. *Florida golf courses or a day spa's tanning booth?* My guess was the latter, given the manicured state of his fingernails when he'd handed over his card.

"Are you a patron of my Queens establishment, Ms. Cosi?"

"I've seen the place," I replied, recalling the garish neon reflected in the wet black pavement the night Caffè Lucia went up in flames. "I met one of your managers." (The jerk who called my car a junk heap.) "And he was kind of . . . pushy."

"Ah, well, the business can do that to you. There's rough

trade around every nightclub and tavern. I'm compelled to operate with managers who know how to handle many situations, some of them ugly." His Clorox smile returned. "I hope the experience wasn't too unpleasant."

"Not at all."

"Listen, Dean," Val said, squeezing his arm. "I need to know how soon we'll have sound."

"It's probably ready," he replied. "Let's go check."

Val turned to me. "Sorry, Clare, I've got to get back to work—"

"I understand. It was a pleasure to meet you, Mr. Tassos."

"The pleasure was mine," he replied, politely shaking my hand.

I watched Val and Dean walk toward the podium. They paused for a moment, while Dean lit a cigarette for Val with a silver Ronson lighter. Then he lit one for himself. Smoking together, they strolled in the direction of the stage. I noticed Dean's hand rest familiarly on Val's waist. She did nothing to shrug him off.

After Val's tirade, I assumed James was having the affair. Now I wondered if my assumptions were misguided. Or maybe it was both partners finding sympathetic ears and arms outside of their unhappy marriage.

How sad it all seemed . . .

On my way back to the Blend's kiosk, prerecorded music blared, signaling the sound system was working again. A moment later the master of ceremonies took to the podium. Corey Parker, action-hero star of *Six Alarm!* a show about the trials and travails of the hunky men on the FDNY, was greeted by applause and whistles from the women—and a few gay men.

Finally I moved on and spied Matt standing at the door of a dingy white rental van that had seen better days.

Dante was just walking away from the truck's open side doors with an arm full of paper products. Matt doublechecked the interior to make sure it was empty.

My ex had changed out of his morning sweats, into blue jeans, retro sneakers, and a black crew-neck sweater. He'd shaved and worked on his hair, too, and as I approached, I detected the musky citrus scent of the latest French cologne—compliments of his new wife, no doubt.

"Thanks for the delivery. I'm sure Esther was frantic," I said.

I think my eyes bugged just then, because Matt stared at me with alarm.

"Clare? What's the matter?"

My attention was fixed on a sleek gold car across the street, and the two people chatting beside it. One was Oat Crowley, still puffing up a storm. The other was a woman with short, slicked-back, salon-blond hair. I felt chilly just looking at her thin capri pants and four-inch metallic gladiator sandals—such was the woman's chosen attire for this blustery March day, along with a silk scarf over a tight blouse with the kind of plunging neckline more appropriate for a night of clubbing than a day in the park. She was laughing, too, which is why it took me a moment to recognize her. The last time I saw this piece of work, she looked like she'd been sucking sour pickles.

"Matt! That's Lucia!"

"Who?"

"Lucia *Testa*, Enzo's daughter, and she's laughing it up with Oat Crowley—oh God, they're getting into her car—"

I opened the door of our rental van and shoved Matt into the driver's seat. I didn't waste time running to the passenger side and going through the door, either. I just climbed right over my ex.

"Clare, what the hell are you—"

"Quick, they're leaving!"

"But—"

"Matt, shut up and drive!"

"Drive where?"

I pointed, my finger tapping the windshield like a mad woodpecker. "Just follow that car!"

Twenty-seven

~~~~~~~~~~~~~~~~~~~~~~~~~~~~~~~~~

Our lumbering, weather-beaten rental van didn't have a lot of pick up—and neither did Matt's reaction time—so Lucia and Oat got a good head start. By the time we pulled away from the curb, their gilded coupe was five vehicles away, all ready to swing onto Fourteenth when the light turned green.

"Who exactly are we following?"

"The people in that car!" I pointed again. "The one with its stupid rear end sticking up!"

"Don't you know anything about cars, Clare? It's shaped that way to reduce resistance to air—"

Not that tone again! "We're too far away."

"It's a *Corvette*, by the way. Looks like a 2009 C6 model. Breanne rented one when we were in Los Angeles. Handles nicely but—"

"Enough with the *Motor Trend* review! You need to get us closer! I want to spy on them!"

"Why?"

I leveled my gaze on the man. "Because these two might be the people who threatened to torch the Village Blend."

Matt's eyes went cold and his smirk vanished. He reached into the sun visor, brought down a pair of Ray-Bans, and slipped them on.

"Buckle your seat belt."

I did. The green light flashed and Lucia's Corvette took off like a Formula One car at the Grand Prix.

"You have to make this light. Pretend you're driving in Zimbabwe."

Matt gunned the engine then slammed the brakes, throwing my torso forward then back.

What the——? In front of us, a yellow taxi stopped moving!

"Do something!" I shouted.

Matt laid on the horn. The cabbie ignored us. Completely. He was picking up a fare.

"Go around! Go around!"

Matt jerked the steering wheel. Our van abruptly nosed into the other lane, rudely cutting off an SUV. The driver blew her horn so loudly I was sure I'd go deaf, but we made it. Matt veered around the taxi and slammed the gas pedal. We sped into the intersection, swinging into the turn so violently that we tipped onto two wheels.

"Holy cats!"

My rear left the seat and my head bounced off the foam ceiling. I dropped down, along with the van, and felt another jolt as Matt hit the brakes, then wrenched the wheel to get around a slow-moving delivery truck. He plowed right through a set of construction cones, bumped us onto a closed sidewalk then off again.

"What are you doing?!"

"Zimbabwe, Clare! Remember?"

Matt made another turn, onto Third Avenue. Now we were heading uptown, our rumbling white antique weaving through traffic at twice the speed of the cars around us. Finally, he slammed the brake for another traffic light.

"And that's how it's done!"

A cocky smile appeared below his Ray-Bans, and I took

my first breath since we'd tipped onto two wheels. A single car now sat between us and Lucia.

"Thank you—"

"You're welcome."

"—for not killing us."

"Have you ever been to Zimbabwe, Clare?"

"Not lately."

"The airport minibus drivers don't like to leave until all of their seats are filled. It can take hours before they depart, then they make up for lost time by racing along lousy roads, shaky bridges, and clogged villages in excess of ninety miles an hour."

"Well, here in New York, we have a little thing called the NYPD. The last thing we need is a pull-over from a sergeant having a bad-cop hair day." I checked the mirror. No sector cars, wailing sirens, or nickel-plated badges—yet.

"Okay, start explaining," Matt said. "Why does Enzo's daughter want to burn down our Village Blend? Something you did, no doubt."

"I'm *this* close to snapping."

The light turned green, and we started uptown again, at a normal speed, thank goodness.

"Clare?" Matt said. *"Explain."*

"This Coffee Shop Arsonist is bogus. I'm sure of it."

"You're sure a terrorist threat is bogus. Right. Uh-huh. And have you told Homeland Security?"

"Matt—"

"The CIA will want to know, too. And don't forget the FBI. They get very testy when they're kept out of the loop."

"Shut up and listen! The pattern of fires makes no sense. Not for a political activist. Terrorists choose targets that have high visibility, targets that will make an impact. Enzo's place is just a small, independently owned caffè. Why would someone with an agenda target it?"

"Because the agenda's crazy—and so is the someone. Maybe this mad bomber lives near Enzo's caffè and found it a convenient target. Come on, Clare, you know very well the chain coffeehouse that burned last week has outspoken detractors all over the world. A few years ago, someone tried to bomb one in Manhattan, don't you remember?"

"Yes, I remember. And I'm sure Oat Crowley did, too."

"I don't follow."

"I think Oat set that third fire to take the heat off the investigation of the arson at Enzo's place. I think he and Lucia sent that letter to the newspaper to mislead the authorities, too."

"What about the other fire, the one in Bensonhurst, Brooklyn?" Matt challenged. "It was set the same night and practically the same time as the fire that almost killed my mother in Queens."

"I don't know about that fire. Oat may have set it as well."

"Why? How could that fire help him?"

"I don't know . . . unless they were planning this coffee shop arson thing from the start to throw off the fire marshals."

"That's a stretch."

I thought it over, glanced out the side window. "It could have been a coincidence."

"Coincidence?" Matt laughed, short and sharp. "Aren't you always quoting your flatfoot back to me when I say that?"

I slumped backward, unable to argue, and reluctant to admit (out loud, anyway) that Matt was right. Mike Quinn would never accept such a lame explanation from a fellow investigating detective. He would probably move forward by reviewing the facts related to that fire, which I didn't have. Still . . .

"I want to start with what's in front of me, okay? Oat has been acting hostile ever since he overheard me vow to find the person who set the Caffè Lucia fire. He used a *wooden match* to light his cigar in the park, a match just like the one I received as a threat. I want to see for myself where exactly Lucia and Oat are going together, what they're up to . . ."

Matt frowned, the quipless quiet an indication the man was at least considering that I might be right. "Maybe I should have brought a weapon."

"I think you've had enough run-ins with the police in this town. And don't get too close to them! They might see us."

"They don't know me, Clare, and I'm wearing shades. As usual, you're the problem. Scrunch down a little and they won't see you."

"Fine. I just don't want to miss anything."

"There's nothing to miss because these two are not lovers."

"How do you know?"

"Watch them," Matt said. "There's no evidence of intimacy that I can see . . ."

"Suddenly you're a relationship expert?" I sat up again and looked for myself. The van was high, the Corvette low, so I could easily peer through its rear window. I watched the pair as Matt eased us into the left lane at Fifty-seventh, then climbed the Queensboro bridge on ramp.

"She's laughing," I said. "She must be having fun with him—"

"She's being polite. See how stiff she is."

"Look there! She's reaching out her hand—"

"To adjust the radio. We're on the bridge now; some stations won't come in."

I folded my arms. "So why are they in a car together?"

"I didn't say there was *nothing* going on between them. The guy's clearly interested. Look at the way he's talking to her, waving his arms. He's fully engaged and really trying to connect. But she ain't buying."

"You're misinterpreting. She's stiff because driving in this city is stressful!"

Through yet another game of urban bumper cars, Matt managed to fend off vehicular interlopers and hang close to Lucia's Corvette from the lower level of the bridge all the way to a tree-lined block in Astoria.

About halfway down the sleepy side street, Lucia swung

into a driveway beside a modest, two-family home. Matt had been hanging back and now stopped the van half a block away. Together Lucia and Oat emerged from the golden coupe and climbed the porch steps. She unlocked the front door, and he followed her inside, still puffing his cigar.

"Look! Lucia let Oat smoke that cheap cigar in her Corvette, and now she's letting him stink up her apartment, too! That's *proof* she's hooking up with him."

"Or she's being polite," Matt said.

"Trust me. Lucia Testa is *not* polite."

Matt bet the pair would be out in minutes. They were in that house for well over an hour. Finally they emerged, strolling casually back onto the porch.

While they were inside, Matt and I had spent the time making up several scenarios for what they might be doing. When Lucia paused to lock her front door, however, the answer was clearer than bottled spring water. Oat stepped close behind Lucia, snaked an arm around her waist, and kissed her neck.

"Matt, look!"

Lucia let the man fondle her for a few seconds then she turned to shake a naughty-boy finger at him. Oat laughed again and lit a new cigar. Then they descended the porch steps and climbed back into her Corvette.

"Where are they going now?" Matt griped as we turned off the side street and onto the main drag of Steinway.

"Admit it, Matt. You were wrong."

He shot me a frown, admitted nothing.

A few minutes later, we were back on Northern Boulevard, then turning onto another shady block.

"I know this street," I said. "They're going to Michael Quinn's firehouse."

Lucia pulled up in front of the redbrick fortress, and Oat emerged from the car, still puffing up a noxious cloud. He walked through the open garage doors, between the two fire trucks, and vanished.

We sat, fifty feet away, waiting for Lucia to leave. But

she remained sitting in her parked vehicle. A few minutes later, Oat appeared again, carrying a bright orange shopping bag.

I sat up straighter. "Matt! Do you see that bag?"

"Yeah."

"It's the same kind of bag that Sully and Franco brought for me and Mike the night of Caffè Lucia's fire."

"What's in it?"

"Well, it's supposed to hold UFC Korean fried chicken. But I doubt very much *that* bag has chicken in it."

"Okay, I'll bite. What does it have inside, Clare?"

"Some kind of bomb-making material."

"And you think that because . . . ?"

"Oat's cigar," I pointed. "It's gone. I'm sure he was afraid to smoke while he was carrying combustible materials."

Matt didn't reply, but he didn't argue, either. He started the van's engine and rolled up behind Lucia as she left the curb.

"So where is she going now?" I said. "Where do you hide a bomb?"

"Drop down in your seat," Matt snapped. "We're right on top of her now."

I scrunched down, staying just high enough to peek over the dashboard. We followed Lucia all the way back to her place again. But she didn't park this time. As soon as we swung onto her quiet street, she suddenly braked her Corvette. We were still a half block away from her place and Matt slowed the van almost to a stop.

"What's she doing?" I whispered.

Lucia's rear lights went on, and her Corvette began backing up until it nearly struck the front of our van. The door opened and Lucia climbed out.

I sank down even farther. "What's happening? I can't see!"

"We're made, Clare. Lucia figured out I was following her."

"Is she angry?"

"No, the opposite. She's coming to my side of the car, shaking her finger and grinning."

"Grinning! Why is she grinning?"

"Because she thinks I'm trying to hit on her. She's got that flirty naughty-boy expression she had on her face with Oat." Matt smirked. "I guess she likes what she sees."

"Can you handle this?"

"Of course."

"*Without* sleeping with her?"

"I'll give it a shot."

But Matt didn't have a chance. As Lucia's metallic sandals teetered closer to our van, she spotted me. Her face flushed and she immediately shifted direction.

"Where is she going now?"

"Your side of the van," Matt said. "I hope you're ready for a cat fight."

Twenty-Eight

〰〰〰〰〰〰〰〰〰〰〰〰〰〰

My door was yanked open before Matt finished his sentence. Lucia stood glaring. "What the hell are you doing following me?"

I sat up. "We know everything, Lucia. You might as well admit it."

"Admit what?"

"You torched your father's caffè."

"You little bitch! Come down here and say that!"

"My pleasure!"

"Oh crap," Matt muttered as I unbuckled my seat belt. I heard his door opening and closing, but I didn't look back. I jumped right down from the high vehicle, letting my low heeled boots hit the cracked concrete with a satisfying slap.

I'd forgotten how tall Lucia was. For a moment, those four-inch gladiators made me feel like a mud hen next to a flamingo. But I stood firm, leveling my sights on her heavily lined eyes. I was glad it came to this, relieved to confront her at last.

"You and Oat Crowley have been seeing each other secretly," I charged. "You persuaded him to help you set the fire in you father's caffè. I'm sure neither of you expected anyone to get hurt, but people *were* hurt. The investigation got so hot that you tried to cover up the arson by setting another fire—"

"What!"

"This time you and Oat conspired to set the blaze in a chain coffeehouse—one that's been targeted in the past by political activists. Then you sent a fake letter to the newspapers in a pathetic effort to mislead the authorities."

Lucia stood gaping at me. "You've got some imagination."

"I'm not going to let you get away with this! You father's in the hospital, Bigsby Brewer is dead—and someone is going to have to answer for that. So you might as well make it easy on yourself and confess everything to Fire Marshal Rossi. I'm sure he can cut you a deal if you're willing to testify against the man who set the bombs for you."

Lucia's eyes widened. She didn't look outraged anymore. Now she looked scared. "You're crazy!"

"Oh, yeah? Then what's in that orange shopping bag?"

"Shopping bag! What are you talking about?"

"I'll show you!" I pushed past her, went right to her car, and jerked open the passenger side door.

Lucia shouted, waved her hands. "What are you doing?"

"Proving that you were getting rid of evidence!"

"Evidence of what?"

"Of a firebomb!"

"How?"

"With this!" I opened the bag, looked inside.

Matt caught up to me, peered in, too. "Oh, brother."

"I promise you, Ms. Cosi, no one is making a firebomb out of *that*!"

Inside the bag was a smaller bag: silver with pink stripes, the name of an upscale lingerie store splashed across in script. Oat had just given Lucia a white silk-and-lace teddy, white stockings, and two garter belts—clearly a gift that would keep on giving, especially for his next booty call. The fast-food bag had been some kind of foil, probably a way to hide the gift from the guys at the firehouse.

Lucia glared down at me. "What makes you think I'd want to set fire to my father's caffè?"

"Your own father told me that you want nothing to do with it."

"I don't. I'm sorry my father was hurt in that fire—truly sorry. But I don't care a fig about the caffè going up."

"How can you say that! Your father worked his entire lifetime in that caffè. And his wall mural was astonishing!"

"Shows what you know. It was worthless."

"Worthless!"

I couldn't hold back any longer. I launched myself at the woman, ready to shake some sense into her, but a pair of strong arms hooked my waist and yanked me backward.

"Let me go, Matt!"

"Calm down! Both of you!"

Lucia pointed. "Tell *her* to calm down!"

"How can you say that your father's art was worthless?"

"It's not me who said it! I called up an art critic, had the guy come down and check it out. He said it was executed well enough, but he didn't see anything unique about it."

"How long ago was that?"

"I don't know! Five, six years."

"Your father has worked on it since then, Lucia. The new sections were groundbreaking! Don't you have any sense of aesthetics, any appreciation for his use of line, of color!"

"No!"

"No?"

"No!" Lucia shouted. "I'm color-blind!"

I stopped struggling. "What?"

Matt released me. He looked surprised, too. In the awkward silence that followed, Lucia expelled a long, weary breath. All of her fight appeared to go with it.

"My father wanted me to be a painter, Ms. Cosi, an artist like he was." She closed her eyes. "I tried. I *did*. I took the damn classes for him: beginning painting, still life, figure drawing, anatomy—I sucked at it all!"

She threw up her hands. "After that, nothing could make me care about swirls on a wall. *Nothing*. Finally, my father accepted that I wasn't going to be the next Mary Cassatt, but then he started pushing me to try all these other things: dancing, singing, acting. I had no talent for any of it. I just didn't care about that crap! I still don't!"

I exchanged a glance with Matt. This interview wasn't going at all the way I'd imagined. On the other hand, the woman's answers weren't exactly exculpatory.

"Lucia, what you've just said makes you look even more guilty. Like you had a grudge against your father and the caffè . . ."

"You still don't understand! I'm glad the caffè went up in flames because my father hasn't been happy there—not for years, not since my mother died. If it weren't for his obsessive work on that stupid mural, he would have retired, gone back to Italy to be with his sisters. He could have found some peace instead of lying in that hospital bed. God knows if he'll ever wake up again."

The woman's eyes were glistening now, tears spilling down her cheeks. Her charcoal liner began to run. I glanced at Matt again. He stepped up to offer her a handkerchief.

"Thanks."

Lucia sniffled. As she wiped her eyes, her makeup smudged. She looked like a sad raccoon, and I felt like a heel. Still, I had to ask . . .

"How am I supposed to believe anything you say? You lied about Glenn, didn't you? You claimed you were engaged to him."

"Glenn and I *are* engaged."

"Then why are you sleeping with Oat?"

"Not that it's any of your business, but Glenn hasn't given me a ring yet. He keeps saying he wants to find the right one, but I think he's stalling . . . not so sure about me yet."

Lucia shook her head, glanced in the direction of the fire-house. "Oat and I were hot and heavy once. When he started hanging around Dad's caffè again, I decided to have a little fun with him, a last little fling. I needed a break from the hospital today, and Oat's the kind of guy who can make a girl forget her troubles . . ."

"So you have no interest in Oat? You're just leading him on?"

"Oat doesn't want to get married." She waved her French tips. "He's a confirmed bachelor, just like his captain. He knows I'm just playing around, waiting for my stupid boy-friend to get off his ass and marry me. I'm actually hop-ing Glenn will get wind of what's going on. Nothing like a little jealousy to get a man off his behind and make him commit."

A match made in heaven. "Here." I handed the bag back to her. "If you didn't set the fire, then who do you think did?"

"Some *nut* obviously. Haven't you read the papers?"

Matt tugged my arm. "Let's go, Clare."

"Wait," I said. "One more thing, Lucia."

"What?"

"The arsonist threatened to burn down my coffeehouse. An unmarked package was left for me with a box of wooden matches inside."

I closely watched Lucia's reaction. Her raccoon eyes widened; her glossed lips parted. She looked genuinely surprised.

"I don't know whether you're telling me the truth or not," I said. "But I want you to know: I'm going to *get* this arson-ist. I'm going to nail him—or her—right to the wall."

"I hope you do, Ms. Cosi," she said. "As long as you leave *me* alone and stay out of my business. Or I'll nail you to the wall with *real* nails."

"Oh, yeah?"

"Yeah!"

Matt tugged my arm again, harder this time. "Let's *go*, Clare."

As he pulled me away, Lucia returned to her Corvette and slammed the door. I watched her drive away, then I faced my ex.

"I'm not giving up."

I half expected a lecture or at the very least a smirk. Instead, Matt put his hands on my shoulders and said—

"I know you won't."

The guy always did come through when I least expected it.

Twenty-nine

HOURS later, the bake sale over, the Village Blend kiosk packed up and put away, I found myself back in Queens, sitting across from Val Noonan in the shamrock green booth of Saints and Sinners.

The Irish pub had all the traditional trappings: darkly paneled walls, a long bar, authentic Gallic hops on tap, and shiny brass fittings everywhere you looked. (I would have given half my New York lottery winnings for a *doppio* espresso—if I had lottery winnings—but the only coffee this pub served was Irish, so I'd ordered up a Harp.)

Val, who preferred a darker brew, was now nursing a pint of Guinness, eyes riveted on the front door, while I finished up my cell phone conversation.

"Say that again? You're going to be late because of . . . ?"

"A pizza delivery," Mike replied. "We got a last-minute tip. A delivery is scheduled for tonight. The *stuff's* coming in a pizza-delivery car, but it's *not* pizza. You follow me, sweetheart?"

"I do."

I was happy for Mike. I was. Sergeant Franco had ferreted

out a solid lead in their current case. A pizza car was the method of delivering the buffet of club drugs to key players on the construction site—at least Mike thought so. His squad still had to prove it.

"I'm sorry, Clare. I wanted to be there with you tonight, but this is the break we've been waiting for . . ."

I heard the regret in Mike's tone, followed by the barely suppressed excitement. I didn't mind. I knew how he felt— and in more ways than one.

My confrontation with Lucia left me feeling like Don Quixote again, although I wasn't kicking myself for charging a pair of stiletto heels instead of a fire-breathing beast because I'd seen Mike make the same kind of run. He and his squad would spend days, even weeks, racing after some lead only to find their well-meaning lances lodged in a windmill.

"So I won't be seeing you at all tonight?" I said, banishing any timber of disappointment.

"If this turns out to be bogus, I'll be there in an hour or two. But if we make an arrest—"

"I won't see you until morning, I know. Okay, well . . . good luck, Mike. I hope you nail them . . ." I cringed, remembering Lucia's threat to use *actual* nails on me. *Time for a new go-to catch phrase.*

"I'll miss you," I added, "but I understand."

"Thanks, Clare." Mike paused. "You know how much I appreciate what you just said, right?"

"I know . . ."

The man's ex-wife never would have been so understanding (that's what he meant). Every time Mike had to cancel, delay, or let me down because of his job, I always heard the same tension in his voice, as if he were bracing for a Leila-like tongue lashing. But he never got one. Not from me. I wasn't Leila.

"Be careful, okay?" I whispered.

"I always am."

I sighed as I hung up, not because I was left dateless for

this post–bake sale shindig. I'd hoped Mike's skills would help me loosen up James Noonan, get him to explain what he'd meant earlier today when he'd declared Bigsby Brewer was murdered. Now it was up to me alone—if James ever showed.

I glanced around the pub. The place was jammed with firemen and their wives or significant others. I'd already said my hellos to everyone I knew. Many of the faces still packing the place included guys from Michael Quinn's house: Manny Ortiz and the flirtatious Mr. Elfante. The veteran of the company, Ed Schott, was here, too . . . but no James, no Oat. Not even Captain Michael had shown—although for that I was profoundly relieved.

In the corner, an acoustic band played: singer, fiddle, frame drum, tin whistle. The scent of beer saturated the air, the cacophony of laughter and lyrics making it hard to concentrate, which was, of course, the point.

This isn't the time for thinking, Clare. This is the time for drinking . . . (Matt's words from years ago . . .)

We were young then, having a night out downtown, but I couldn't relax. I was too worried about our daughter, our bills, our books, our marriage. Matt couldn't stand that about me, and I'd spent half my life feeling bad about my nature, trying to pretend my mind wasn't working. But that time was good and over: The beverage I pushed was sobering, and I preferred to think . . .

I still suspected Oat Crowley of something here. And the more I considered it, the more I decided I wasn't totally off base with targeting Lucia as the center of the arson spree.

Oh, I believed her claim today—that she was innocent. What I didn't believe was that Oat was a confirmed bachelor. I'd seen the way he looked at her, the way he touched her. And his intimate gift of lingerie looked more romantic than risqué: He'd chosen *white*, hadn't he? Bridal white.

If Mike was sitting across from me instead of Val, he'd probably ask me for a theory on motive. Well . . .

What if Oat wants Lucia for his own, but the young car mechanic Glenn Duffy stands in the way?

Maybe Oat was trying to do Lucia a favor—without her knowledge. Fire was his business, wasn't it? Burning down the caffè would force Lucia's father to retire and return to Italy, leaving Lucia free. And wouldn't a shocking event like a fire make Lucia see how much she needed a man in her life, a *real* man (as Enzo had referred to Oat) and not a boy like Glenn?

Getting Enzo out of the way—one way or another—already appeared to be working in Oat's favor. Lucia was clearly distressed today, but she hadn't sought out Glenn for comfort, she'd sought out Oat . . .

"What's up?" Val asked when she saw me spacing out. "You okay?"

"Sorry, yeah . . . Looks like I'm on my own."

"You and me both, sister." Val tapped her watch. "James was supposed to be here an hour ago." She pulled an even longer face and drank deeply. Then she put down her Guinness and clawed inside her bag for a pack of cigarettes.

"Are you going outside?" I asked. Given my position, I knew chapter and verse of the no-smoking codes of New York's Health Department.

Val closed her eyes, shoved away the pack. "I forgot. I'll go out back later . . ."

I nodded, sipped my Harp, and heard a sudden eruption of voices—

"Hey! There he is!"

"How ya, doin', Cap?"

"Glad you came!"

"Let me buy you one . . ."

The commotion was behind me, near the front door. I turned in the booth but couldn't see—too many giant male bodies.

"What's going on?" I asked Val.

"Michael Quinn is here . . ."

Crap. "Where is he exactly? Can you see?"

She silently tilted her chin. The man was striding past our booth that moment, a crowd of men around him. I couldn't see the guy, but I could almost feel his energy as he passed.

"I'm surprised he came . . ." Val said.

So was I. And I wasn't happy about it. My gaze tracked the mob across the room to the far end of the long bar. A few guys made way so Michael could have a stool. The men shook his hand, pounded his back. The bartender began to pour.

He wore jeans and a knobby fisherman's sweater, both black; *mourning* black, I realized. Behind his flame red handlebar, his complexion looked colorless. A charcoal grayness seemed to surround him now, like the creeping smoke that hissed off the caffè blaze as the engine company doused the life out of the roaring fire.

Michael abruptly glanced up from the bar. I didn't expect it. His eyes locked onto mine. He was surprised to see me here, too. I broke the connection, focused back on Val.

"He looks worn down," I said. "Worse than the last time I saw him."

"When was that?" she asked.

"At Bigsby Brewer's funeral. He's taking Bigs's death hard, isn't he? As hard as James . . ."

Val took a long sip of her dark beer. As she set the glass back down, her hand appeared to be shaking. The Irish band finished its set, and the pub suddenly got quieter, loud voices falling to murmurs and laughter becoming muted. I leaned into the table to hear Valerie's next words—

"Bigs is the first man the captain lost since 9/11. Did you know that?"

"No. I don't know all that much about Michael Quinn."

"He lost every member of his company when the first tower fell. Did you know *that*?"

"No." I risked a second glance at the man. He was knocking back a shot with one of his men. As the bartender refilled their glasses, his eyes found mine again.

"Well, Michael Quinn can be a class A jerk at times, I'll

admit. But I always cut him some slack because of what he lost."

"It must have been hard for him . . ."

"It messed him up. That's what James told me—not that he knew from personal experience. James only joined the FDNY seven years ago. But older guys like Ed Schott and Oat Crowley—they know Michael's whole story—passed it along to the younger guys on the down low."

Val glanced at her watch again, checked the door. "Where *is* James . . ."

"Why don't you try calling him again?" I suggested.

"I left *two* voice mail messages, Clare. He hasn't bothered to return either. What good will a third one do?"

"I'm sorry. I didn't mean to upset you."

She studied the table. "I think he's having an affair."

I tried to sound surprised. "What makes you say that?"

"I just think so."

"With whom?"

Val took another hit of hops, lifted her head, and stared hard at me. "Exactly how long have you known my husband?"

"Not long. The night of the Caffè Lucia fire—that's when we met."

"He talks about you a lot."

"Oh?"

"I heard you went to the firehouse, helped the guys with something?"

"Espresso making. I gave them lessons."

Her eyes narrowed. "And did my husband enjoy it?"

"Excuse me?"

"Forget it . . ." She glanced away.

"Val, look at me." I waited until she did. "I am not having an affair with your husband. I am in a very happy relationship at the moment, and I intend to keep it that way."

"I'm sorry . . ." Despite Val's words, her expression remained stony. "It's just that . . . like I told you at the bake sale, James has been acting so odd since Bigs died. I mean, I expected grief. Those two guys were really tight. But this is something else. He doesn't want comfort from me. He's just snappish and then distant . . . but mostly so angry . . ."

A portrait of James came to me then, a quixotic image of the way he'd looked in the park. A gray fog surrounded him, just like the captain, shrouding his energy. His expression was haggard yet his eyes were wary, continually glancing at Oat Crowley . . . Oat with the wooden matches . . . Oat with his scowls and insults for me . . .

What if James Noonan suspects Oat of setting that second fire to cover up the first one at Caffè Lucia? Is that what James meant when he said Bigsby Brewer was murdered? Does James suspect— or even know for a fact—that Oat is responsible?

I cleared my throat. "Val, I think I might know what's bothering your husband."

"You do?"

"He mentioned something to me at the bake sale. Something that's weighing on his mind. I'd like to talk to him about it. I'd like your help with that. Maybe if we can get him to open up—"

"Ladies! Good evening! How are you doing?"

The overly cheerful greeting was jarring, like a rodeo clown skidding into a morgue. I looked up to find a man standing there—shaggy wheat-colored hair, small round glasses.

"Hello," Val said, obviously forcing her replying smile.

"Just doing the usual rounds," the man told Val. "Two boroughs down, three to go . . ."

She shook the newcomer's hand. "Glad you could make it, Ryan."

Ryan—that's right, Ryan Lane.

I remembered the man now. He served on the board of the Fallen Firefighters Fund, the charity benefiting from today's bake sale.

Lane's camel hair jacket was gone this evening. His simple white dress shirt and sweater vest made him seem more relaxed. He still had those slightly goggle eyes beneath the glasses and ears that were too large for his head, but his wide, lopsided grin appeared to lacquer over his uneven features with a boyish charm. I'd noticed the same effect in the park today when he'd been talking with Oat Crowley. My body stiffened as I realized—

Oat! This man knows Oat!

Thirty

⊙⌒⊙⌒⊙⌒⊙⌒⊙⌒⊙⌒⊙⌒⊙⌒⊙⌒⊙⌒⊙⌒⊙⌒⊙

My mind racing, I vaguely registered Ryan Lane introducing the unsmiling man at his left.

"This is the battalion chief for the entire borough of Queens, Donald O'Shea."

"Good evening, ladies," the chief said, voice gruff, an impatient hand jingling change in his pocket.

O'Shea sported a salt-and-pepper flattop and an expression that appeared equally flat. His outfit reminded me of Fire Marshal Rossi's—pressed dark slacks, nylon jacket, and what looked like a white uniform shirt beneath—which meant he'd just come off duty or was just going on.

Val and I greeted him, and he immediately excused himself. "Some business," he said to Ryan and moved off.

Ryan then gestured to the woman at his right. "And this is my lovely boss, Mrs. Josephine Fairfield. Valerie, you know Josie."

Josie? Now why did that name sound familiar? She was tall and well formed with elegant almond eyes and a long, patrician nose sloped to a wide mouth of glossed cranberry. I'd seen her before. I was sure of it. *Is she a Blend customer?*

Her outfit carried that conflict of classes not uncommon among Manhattan's urban wealthy. The denims appeared stressed and worn, but the sweater was cashmere; her matching scarf—the dazzling color of a dragon fruit cactus—was patterned with front-and-backward *F*s, trumpeting the House of Fen; and her shoulder bag of polished black leather was a cool thousand if it was a penny.

"Good job overall, Valerie," Mrs. Fairfield said, her words clipped. "But the mayor had to wait *fifteen minutes* for the sound system to come online. What was *that* about?"

Val tensed. I felt for her. Over the years, I'd waited on thousands of Mrs. Fairfields, their auras vibrating like crashing cymbals as they worked overtime to advertise how very important they were. Valerie answered the woman with the same tone of pained patience I used on this perpetually displeased Clan of Narcissus.

"The city provided the public address equipment, Mrs. Fairfield. Once I realized the problem, I called my close friend Dean Tassos—he owns the Mirage clubs? Anyway, Dean drove portable equipment all the way from Brooklyn to help us out and that took time."

"Well, *next* time you should test the system out *first*, don't you think?"

Val's fingers tightened around her dark pint. "I assure you, we did test it first. Why don't *you*—"

"Josie," Ryan Lane firmly interrupted, "I'm sure we want to *congratulate* Valerie, too, don't we?"

I had to give it to Lane. He was one good executive. He'd defused Oat the very same way when the guy had been rude to me.

"All of the numbers aren't in yet," said Ryan, "but I can already tell, we had a record take with the bake sale this year."

"It must have been the coffee," Val said.

Ryan nodded. "It was outstanding, wasn't it?"

Val pointed across the booth. "Thanks to Clare."

Ryan looked confused for a second. "Oh, yes! You're the coffee lady. Sorry, I've met so many new people today . . ."

He extended his hand. I shook it.

"No problem," I said. "I'm glad it all worked out."

"Did it ever. You know—"

"I'm moving *on*, Ryan," Mrs. Fairfield announced. She turned and headed straight for the end of the bar where Michael Quinn was perched—and that's when it hit me.

I had seen Josephine Fairfield before, just not in the flesh. She was the mystery woman in those firehouse picnic photos, the ones taped to the door in Michael Quinn's company kitchen.

Mrs. Fairfield was older now, of course, her figure fuller, her free-flowing hair bobbed like a Jazz Age flapper's, but she was just as attractive as her younger self. I could still see her frozen in time with Michael's arm around her. Of course, she hadn't been dressed in designer duds in those old picnic photos, just a simple white cotton sundress. But I remembered Michael's expression—a different man, so buoyant, so carefree . . .

"I'm sorry about Josie." Ryan's voice was low. He had leaned down close to us. "She's easy to misunderstand."

Val shot me a look: *The woman is a be-yotch. How hard is that to understand?*

Ryan straightened. "Anyway, it was good seeing you ladies. Have a nice—"

"Wait!" I lunged for the man's sleeve. "Don't go!"

Ryan was taken aback, but I couldn't let him escape. I needed to question him about Oat!

"Won't you join us, Mr. Lane? For one beer, at least?"

"Uh . . ." Ryan looked worried as he glanced back toward his boss. I didn't blame him: given the level of drinking going on in this working man's bar, if Josie Fairfield treated anyone else like she'd just treated Val, she'd be getting a black shiner to go with that shiny black handbag.

"One drink," he said.

"Great!" I scooted over.

He pointed to our glasses. "But you two need a refill. Allow me—what are you drinking?"

"Let me," Val said. "I have a tab open already. Do you drink beer?"

"Sure do. I'll have what Ms. Cosi's having. Harp, right?"

I nodded. Val got up, and Ryan sat down across from me, fiddled with his cuffs. "Your coffee is quite good, Ms. Cosi, exceptional. Who's your roaster?"

"You're looking at her."

"Is that so?" He considered me with new interest. "I'd enjoy seeing your facilities one day."

"Come by anytime. I do small-batch roasting in our basement."

"You know, I fell in love with coffee years ago . . . on a trip to Nicaragua."

"Oh? I'd really enjoy hearing about it."

Okay, so I wouldn't, but as Mike often said (in a piece of advice that sounded almost culinary), grilling an informant met with much more success if you tenderized him first. So while I half listened to Ryan, I turned my peripheral eye to his boss.

Given Josephine Fairfield's past relationship with Michael Quinn, I was curious to see how he'd react at her approach. But Donald O'Shea had gotten to Michael first. The still unsmiling Queens battalion chief didn't shake Michael's hand or pat his back. They weren't sharing drinks, either. The close conversation looked official—and it didn't look pleasant.

". . . and I ended up in the Samulali region, a rather untamed area," Ryan was saying. "On that first morning, just as dawn was breaking, I drank fresh black coffee in a battered tin cup."

I nodded politely.

"The beans had been dried in the sun and roasted inside a converted oil drum, which was turned by hand over an open fire. It was almost a spiritual experience . . ."

It took me a second to register that Ryan had stopped talking.

"How interesting!" I finally said. "You know, you should

meet my partner, Matt. He's our coffee buyer and travels frequently to South and Central America."

Ryan sighed, his eyes glazing a bit. "Ever since that time, my dream was to buy my own coffee farm."

"It's not an uncommon dream," I conceded. "One of the farms we buy from is run by a former California banker who followed his passion and purchased an estate in Panama after retiring."

"I'm retiring from my job. Very soon."

Finally, an opening. "Speaking of your job, Mr. Lane, you introduced Mrs. Fairfield as your boss?"

"That's right. She is."

"That's unusual, isn't it? For a woman to be in charge of a company that makes rescue gear for firefighters?"

"It was her husband's company. He passed away last year and she took over. But it's just an interim thing. She has no real interest in the business . . ."

"Is that right?"

"Yes, a larger corporation is in the process of evaluating us. In another month or so the purchase of Fairfield Equipment should go through without a hitch."

"Is that a good thing? The company being bought?"

"Oh, yes. It's really just a big infusion of cash and resources. We'll have the opportunity to expand worldwide."

"That's good news, then, but I'm also wondering, Mr. Lane—"

"Ryan."

"Ryan, how well do you know Oat Crowley?"

"Well enough, I guess." He shifted uneasily, scratched the back of his head. "I'm really sorry about the things he said to you today in the park. That was uncalled for. I mean, look at you here. You're obviously friends with James's wife."

"Oat and I aren't exactly on the best of terms, but there's a reason for that and it's not James."

"Oh?"

"I have a female friend named Lucia. She's involved with Oat. Has he ever mentioned Lucia to you?"

Ryan laughed. "Oat and I aren't *that* close."

"I see. Well, Lucia is convinced that Oat's not the marrying kind. That he has no interest in settling down. Would you say that's true?"

"Odd you should ask."

"Why?"

"Any other time, I'd probably say I have no idea. But just today, in the park, when I mentioned retiring, Oat asked after my position. I don't blame him—my job's a lot less hazardous than his." He smiled. "Anyway, I agreed he'd be a good candidate for it, and he confided that he was planning to retire from the department soon. He said he was finally ready to settle down, buy a big house, maybe even start a family."

I knew it.

Crowley was after Lucia for more than the occasional booty call. He wanted to marry her. But with Enzo and Glenn standing in his way, Oat had to find a way to upset the balance in Lucia's life. The caffè fire did that—and if the authorities determined the blaze was random arson (à la some mad coffee shop bomber), then Lucia would also net a portion of a big fire-insurance pay out, a convenient nest egg for a newly married couple to put a down payment for a "nice, big house."

"Here you go, kids!"

Val was back, and in a much brighter mood. She set our topped-off pints in front of us and we toasted the successful bake sale. I was about to question Ryan further when Val waved us closer, hunching down, as if she were going to reveal who stole Salvador Dalí's *Two Balconies* out of Rio's Mansion in the Sky museum.

"So did you notice what's happening at the bar?"

"What?" Ryan and I asked together.

She pointed. "See for yourselves."

We all turned our heads to find Mrs. Josephine Fairfield, affluent owner of Fairfield Equipment, friend of New York City's illustrious mayor, putting her manicured hands all over Michael Quinn. And he did not appear happy about it. Every time she laid a paw on him, he firmly removed it.

"Now that's what I call chutzpah!" Val declared, taking a delighted swig of Guinness.

"Are they a couple again?" I asked.

"No," said Val, eyes bright. "James told me she's been calling him repeatedly, trying to get him back. It's common knowledge at the firehouse. Ever since she dumped him, he can't stand the sight of her!"

My mind flashed back to that night in the captain's office, the same evening I'd discovered his "Kevin wall." Michael had been annoyed by a personal cell call—a call from a woman named *Josie*.

"Look," Val pointed, even more amused, "she's throwing herself at the man!"

Lined up on the bar were a half-dozen shot glasses, sparkling like newly cut diamonds. Standing at the ready was a freshly opened bottle of well-aged, single-malt Irish whiskey (which probably cost as much as your average gemstone).

Josephine knocked back a shot, clearly not her first, and gave up on the patty-cake game. She began wrapping her dragon-flower designer scarf around Michael's neck. She laughed, pretending she was choking him. Then she pulled him forward, expecting a kiss. He pushed her away.

"Son of a *gun*," Ryan Lane spat. "I better get up there . . ."

Val looked surprised by Ryan's disgusted reaction, probably assuming (as I did) that the man would take a *little* delight from his haughty boss's comedown. Then again, if Fairfield Equipment was being evaluated for purchase by a worldwide corporation, seeing your half-drunken boss throw herself at an off-duty member of the FDNY wasn't exactly the optimum public relations moment.

"I'm sorry, Ryan," Val said, quickly sliding across the booth to let him out.

"Don't worry about it," he said, picking up his pint. "Thanks for the beer."

As Ryan moved toward the bar, Val sat back down and leaned across the table. "Josie Fairfield and the captain were supposed to be married. Did you know that?"

I arched an eyebrow. "The leader of the wolf pack was ready to tie the knot? When was this exactly?"

"Oh, like ten years ago," Val said. "Josie broke it off with the captain just a few months after 9/11. According to Ed Schott, she just didn't want to deal with the captain's grief. Six months later she was hooked up with a much older guy who had *a lot* more money and a lot less baggage, the head of Fairfield Equipment—"

"And now that her husband is dead, she has her freedom and her money, so—"

"She wants her first love back. It's a very old song." Val tipped her head toward the bar. "Only it looks like Michael Quinn's not in the mood to be played."

"NO! *YOU'RE* NOT LISTENING!"

Val and I froze, along with every other patron in the pub. Josie Fairfield finally lost it. She was now shouting at the top of her lungs.

Oh God, poor Michael—and poor Ryan. He stood right behind his boss, trying to talk sense into her ear, but she'd belted back too much booze. Her arm windmilled crazily, trying to wave him away.

"NO! I WANT TO KNOW—WHAT DO I HAVE TO DO? START *ANOTHER* FIRE?"

I blanched, looked to Val. *What did that mean?*

Val mouthed something, but I didn't understand her. Then we watched Michael rise from the bar, take Josie by the elbow, and calmly escort her to the pub's front door. He caught my eye as he past our booth, but I couldn't read him.

Ryan trailed behind the two. He also made fleeting eye contact with us and, brother, did he look miserable.

"What a job that guy has," Val said when they were gone. "Now I really need a smoke. You want to come?"

"Sure."

We crossed the crowded room and stepped out the back door, leaving the warm, golden light for the dark, quiet patio. The hulking outline of a large Dumpster sat a few yards away, but the prevailing smell on this dim square of concrete was stale tar. A carpet of butts had been crushed into the ground below my low-heeled boots, and I considered for a moment the hundreds of conversations (drunken and sober) that must have preceded those ends.

A laughing couple rose from a weathered, wrought iron bench, nodding a greeting as they headed inside.

Now Val and I were alone.

She dug into her bag, put a cig between her lips, and snapped her disposable lighter three times. When the tricolored flame kissed the cylinder's tip, she glanced my way.

"Want one?"

I was running on a serious caffeine deficit, so I was sorely tempted. But I'd given up nicotine once in my life, and (like my addiction to a certain ex-husband) I had no intention of fighting that battle again. I thanked her for the offer then said, "So tell me. What did Mrs. Fairfield mean when she shouted that stuff about—"

"Starting *another* fire?"

I nodded.

Val moved to the wrought iron bench and sat down, took long silent drags. "Oh, man, I needed that."

I pulled up a battered garden chair, checked for beer spills, and sat down opposite her. The metal was freezing and the cold seeped through my blue jeans to the backs of my thighs. I ignored it, along with an increasingly edgy feeling that I simply attributed to a creeping jonesing for my own drug of choice.

"So?" I pressed. "Josie Fairfield is an *arsonist*?"

"I always thought that story was just a story. Guess we know the truth—I mean, given her little drunken confession in there. But it's not unheard of, right?"

"What?"

"Come on, Clare, haven't you heard of that game the occasional *whacked-out* New York female plays? Setting a fire to meet a fireman?"

"You've got to be kidding."

Val released a delicate but toxic plume of white into the black night. "James says it probably happens a few times a year."

"And that's how Mrs. Fairfield met Michael?"

"They met when her apartment's kitchen caught fire. That's all I knew . . . before tonight, I mean—"

A muffled ring tone sounded in Val's bag: *You spin me right round, baby, right round . . .*

Val instantly brightened. She hastily dug into her handbag again then silenced the tinny eighties tune as she brought the phone to her ear.

"Hey, what's up?"

As Val chatted, I noticed she was careful not to say the name of the caller. It didn't matter. I already knew she'd set that ring tone for one very special friend.

"Hold on a second," she told Dean Tassos and turned to me. "I'm going to take this in the ladies'. Then I'm heading home. Would you give me a ride, Clare? James obviously isn't showing."

"Of course."

With unexpected relief I watched the shapely outline of Valerie's suit move into the glow of the open doorway. My wool sweater wasn't thick enough for the March night, but I liked the solitude of this smokers' patio so I folded my arms close, leaned back in the battered metal chair, and closed my eyes.

Inside the crowded pub, the band was starting up again. I had no desire to join the party. So much had happened tonight, let alone in the past ten days, that I just wanted a few minutes peace. Too bad I never got it.

"Hello, Clare."

My eyes immediately opened. A wide-shouldered silhouette loomed in the doorway, blocking most of the pub's golden light. Shifting shadows veiled the giant's face but not his identity.

"Hello, Michael."

Thirty-one

∂◎◎◎◎◎◎◎◎◎◎◎◎◎◎◎◎◎◎◎◎

"I hadn't pegged you for a smoker."

"I'm not. I was just leaving." I rose from the chair.

"Don't go. I want to talk to you."

"I don't think that's such a great idea."

"Why not? Is my cousin around? I didn't see him."

"He had to work."

"When doesn't he?"

"Like I said, I should go—"

Michael folded his arms, leaned against the doorframe, effectively blocking my exit.

The closer I stepped toward the man, the more he came out of shadow. His pasty complexion appeared to have more color now, flushed from drink or that little drama queen act with Josie or both.

"That was quite a scene in there," I said.

Michael shrugged. "Josie can't take no for answer. She never could."

"You have zero interest in her, I take it?"

"Let's just say the woman's well-cushioned life hasn't brought out the best in her character."

"I see. Well, I should go back inside . . ." I tried to step around him.

"I saw you at Bigsie's funeral," he said. "It was nice, you comin'. I'm sorry I didn't have a chance to say hello to you at the church."

"You were comforting the man's family. I'm the one who's sorry. I'm sorry for you loss . . ."

He gestured to the empty bench. "Won't you sit down with me? Just for a minute?"

I glanced over his shoulder into the crowded pub. "Val's coming back."

I folded my arms. "What's the matter, dove?" His crow's feet crinkled. "You think I'd stoop to ravishin' you in a bar's back alley?"

"When anything involves you, Michael, I don't know what to think."

"You can trust me." He crossed his heart with two fingers—the good Boy Scout. "Promise."

"I don't know. Seems to me your promises leave something to be desired."

"Maybe they do. But I need to talk to you about something important . . . About the way Bigs died."

Okay, that I didn't expect. "What can you tell me?"

He leaned down, his breath heavy with the smell of alcohol. "He was murdered."

"That's what James said."

Michael straightened. "James shouldn't have shot off his mouth."

"Please," I whispered, "talk to me. Who's responsible?"

"It's complicated . . ."

Somewhere over our heads, an unsettling thunder began. The Number 7 line was just a block away from where we stood. In midtown Manhattan the tracks were buried deep underground, but here in Queens, the subway train was elevated, periodically roaring over neighborhood streets, making quiet talk impossible. (Then again, in my experience, whenever *any* previously buried thing was brought out into the open, polite talk became impossible.)

The captain untangled his arms as he moved around me. With unsteady steps, he went to the bench, sunk heavily down. When the deafening noise finally died out, he spoke again.

"I got the evidence today, put it in a package addressed to you."

"Me?" I sat down next to him on the bench.

"I would have sent the thing to Mike, but one look at the return address and he'd surely toss it in the bin. I want you to give the package to my cousin, explain why it's important. You'll know once you look it over. Mike will listen to you. And after you're done convincin' him, you two call me and we can get this whole thing handled right."

"You want Mike's help?"

"Mikey and I have had our differences. But I know he's a good cop. To a *fault* maybe, but he's still my blood—and he's the only government official in this town I trust."

"What's that supposed to mean?"

"Never let the fire get behind you, darlin', that's what it means."

"English?"

"I can't give the evidence to any of the brass above me. Someone may have been paid off. There's no way I can know . . ."

"What's in the package? Can't you tell me?"

"Not here. Not now." He glanced at the doorway again. Shadows moved past, but none materialized. "I shouldn't even be talkin' to you. But I noticed you came here alone tonight. And you were lookin' my way an awful lot this evening . . . and I thought maybe . . ."

His eyes held mine. As I waited for him to complete his sentence, an icy breeze touched my hair. I tried not to shiver. "Well?"

"I thought maybe you were havin' second thoughts about my offer."

"You mean Atlantic City?"

"I mean me, Clare. You and me."

Oh brother. "There is no you and me. Is there even a package? Or are you playing me again?"

"What I told you in my office, Clare, that was true. I've never met a woman quite like you."

"Stop it. You're still trying to get back at Mike."

"Not this time."

"Listen to me: I've got your number. Mike told me the truth about what happened with your little brother, Kevin. The *whole* truth. You left out enough of the story to make Mike look like a cold-hearted monster. You told me that story to make me doubt him."

"Can you blame me?"

"Yes! I know you've been through terrible things in your life, Michael, terrible things . . . and I'm sorry for that. But it doesn't excuse your treatment of your cousin."

"My little brother would have been my brother in the FDNY if it wasn't for my cousin—"

"Mike had nothing to do with what happened to Kevin! Don't you get it?"

"Get what?"

"Your little brother self-destructed right before he was supposed to enter the fire academy because he was afraid."

"Afraid? Of who?"

"Of you, Michael. I'm a mother! I know!"

He just gawked at me, looking confused.

I sighed. To me it was clear as sunlit glass. Kevin and Lucia had been on the very same unhappy ride, driven by father figures who wanted them to be something they just didn't want to be.

"Kevin didn't want to join the FDNY, but he didn't want to risk your disappointment. He was terrified you'd turn your back on him. So he screwed up royally by driving drunk. He blamed the police, Mike, anyone but himself—and you bought right into it."

"If my little brother had come to me, told me how he felt,

I would have understood. I'd never turn my back on my own flesh and blood."

"You turned on your own cousin, didn't you? You've been treating Mike like the enemy, but he isn't. All you did for all these years was twist the real story until it fit into a bogus 'truth' you could live with."

Michael blinked. He suddenly looked less sure of himself. I could only hope it was because a thin wedge of insight was finally penetrating his thick cranium.

"Come on. Don't you think it's time that you two buried the hatchet?"

"Aw, darlin' . . ." He exhaled hard, rubbed the back of his neck. "There's too much bad blood between us. Years of it. Too much we did to each other. I'd like to be on level ground with my cousin again . . . I would. But Mike won't want to bury the hatchet with me—not unless it's in my skull."

"How can you say that?"

"You don't know everything." He parted his lips, pointed. "You see this gold tooth? That was Mike's right hook . . ."

"What don't I know? Tell me."

"No . . ." He held my eyes. "You tell me. Tell me why you're still sitting here now, talking to me . . . You must feel what's between us, Clare, because I can feel it . . ."

I began to answer, but somewhere above, the Number 7 train was approaching again, the insistent machinery growing louder, drowning out my words.

Michael leaned closer, his breath so saturated with whiskey I could almost feel the burn of the shot. Before I knew what was happening, the man's iron band of an arm was behind my back, crushing me close.

"Michael, no!"

He was half drunk and fumbling, more sad than dangerous. The rough brush of his handlebar mustache moved over my mouth first then down my cheek. I felt his lips at my jaw line, my neck, a hand groping my breast. I squirmed and struggled.

"Stop it right now! Stop!"

The captain froze, finally hearing me above the subway's deafening thunder. His lips moved off of my neck, his hand was no longer groping. He lifted his head and was just beginning to release me when—

"You son of a bitch!"

It was Mike—*my* Mike—standing at the pub's back door. He'd come to Saints and Sinners after all, his shout of outrage half swallowed by the unrelenting movement of the elevated subway. Before I could say a word, he launched, hauling back and punching his cousin in the side of the head.

"Mike, *don't*!"

The fire captain reeled, and Mike punched him again, this time in the gut. The captain's arms remained at his sides. He took the blows, like he knew he had it coming. Michael wasn't even trying to defend himself!

"Stop!" I shouted. "Your cousin's drunk! He didn't mean it!"

Another punch to the face.

"You'll *kill* him! Stop!"

But Mike just kept pummeling his cousin.

I ran to the pub's doorway. "HELP! SOMEONE HELP ME!"

A mob of firefighters rushed out and pulled the cousins apart. A few swings landed on Mike for payback.

"Leave him be," Michael shouted, wiping blood from his nose.

The men complied.

Mike stood there, scowling with fury. The mechanized storm had finally subsided, and the night went deadly quiet as his gaze found mine. We locked eyes—a split second in hell.

"This isn't what it looks like." My voice was raspy and far too weak. "You have to let me explain . . ."

Mike exhaled, glanced at the defensive line of firefighters, most of them his cousin's men. It was the last place he'd want to hear an explanation, and I couldn't blame him. Without a word, he turned and strode down the alley, toward the street.

"Don't leave, Mike. Come back!"

I moved to run after him, but someone caught my arm, held it firm. I turned. It was Val.

"Let him go, Clare. Let him cool off . . ."

I wheeled again, back toward Mike, but he was gone, swallowed up by the city's darkness.

Thirty-two

⟨decorative border⟩

"Ever heard of a fire triangle, Clare?"

"Fire triangle?" I said, turning up the car's heater—to little effect.

Val waved her lit cigarette in the air. She'd opened her window to keep the interior from filling up, but the night had gotten colder and my clunker hadn't gotten any newer.

"Fire needs three elements to exist: fuel for it to consume; oxygen for it to breath; and heat to ignite the other two in a chain reaction—"

"Oh, right, I do know this," I said, recalling Captain Michael's little lecture the night Caffè Lucia went up.

"Well, *you*, my friend are in a fire triangle."

"Excuse me?"

"Fuel and oxygen in a room together don't do squat. But introduce heat and . . . *whammo*."

"I am *not* heat. And that wasn't supposed to happen back there. Michael and I were just talking."

Val took a drag. "Timing's like that. You can't always control it. Just like fire . . . or men."

Tell me about it. I'd already tried reaching Mike by cell

phone—*ten* tries in a row. I'd gotten voice mail every time (and I'd left multiple messages). He hadn't bothered to return even one, and my sympathy for the man was slowly turning to impatience. In another hour, it would be full-fledged anger.

"I could understand Mike being upset," I told Val, "but he should have trusted me better than that. He should have waited for an explanation instead of charging in and busting up his cousin!" I struck the steering wheel. "At least Michael didn't fight back. I have to give the man credit for that . . ."

After that one-way boxing match, the captain's men had helped him back inside the pub, where they began to clean him up. That's when Val hustled me outside, saying it was better if I got clear of the place. I didn't argue, and I knew Val's husband would be in much better shape than Michael to discuss Bigsby Brewer's death.

Now I was driving east on Roosevelt, toward the nearby neighborhood of Jackson Heights where Val shared a home with James.

The trip from Saints and Sinners wasn't long, only a few miles. When we turned onto Val's street, she pointed out her address, a redbrick row house three stories high. At the first open spot along the curb, I swerved and parked.

"You have the whole house?" I asked, impressed with the size.

"Just the first two floors," she said. "It's a rental, but we've got a lot of square footage for the money, which is good because I'm probably about four weeks away from losing my job."

"You are?"

"We have a separate garage in back, too. Come on . . ."

As I locked up the car, Val went to the front door. There was still half a cigarette left, but she snuffed it out in the base of a dying potted plant.

"James!" Val called as she strode across the tiled foyer and into the carpeted living room. The lights were blazing all over the house and somewhere a radio was barking the play-by-play of a basketball game.

"James!"

No answer.

"Sit down, Clare, relax. He's probably in the upstairs bathroom. The one down here isn't working."

As Val climbed the stairs, I considered sitting down, then reconsidered. I really needed a caffeine hit now, and if I knew James, he had a decent supply of Arabica beans in his cupboards.

The Noonan kitchen was neat and well appointed. No surprise, considering the way James had manned his firehouse post. Every pot and pan hung efficiently on its pegboard hook. A sparkling clean coffeemaker stood at attention on the counter, its companion grinder on duty beside it. Flour and sugar canisters were lined up by descending height and a four-foot tall wine rack stood in the corner, fully stocked—again, not a surprise given James's preferences.

I half smiled when my eye caught the bright orange of a shopping bag on the floor near the trash can. *Yet another fan of UFC Korean Fried Chicken. Val, no doubt . . .*

I was about to check the cupboards for whole bean Arabica when I noticed something on the kitchen table (other than the lazy Susan of condiments): a single bottle of beer. A pilsner glass sat next to it. The glass was nearly full, *nearly* because there was no head, the frothy white bubbles had died long ago.

But James doesn't like beer . . .

I glanced up and noticed something curious beyond the back door window. A soft yellow light was glowing between the cracks in a small wooden shed—the garage Val mentioned. The structure was separated from the main house by a narrow concrete drive.

I moved to the kitchen's back door and turned the handle. It was unlocked. I exited the house, feeling the chill of the night once more.

As I crossed the narrow drive, I became aware of a low

rumbling. But this wasn't the Number 7 train. This was the sound of an idling car engine. With every step closer to the shed, the rumbling grew louder. But why would someone want to run a car motor *inside* a garage?

Oh my God!

I lunged the last few feet to the door, tore it open, and gagged on the toxic white fog. A man's body was slumped over the steering wheel.

I stumbled back outside, choking and coughing. Taking a deep breath of fresh air, I charged back in, yanked open the car door, and used every molecule of strength to drag the big, inert body out to the cold concrete.

My heart was pumping, my adrenaline racing. Gasping violently, I turned over the unconscious man, desperate to help.

It was James Noonan, and there was no helping him. He was already dead.

Thirty-Three

~~~~~~

METAL clinked against the windshield. I started at the sound. Disoriented, I licked my lips, tasted salt, and realized I'd cried myself to sleep. Then I remembered the reason and my eyes welled up all over again.

My ex-husband rapped the rain-flecked window a second time. To spur me to action, he pointed to the stainless steel thermos in his hand.

Coffee. Oh, thank goodness . . .

I sat up and popped the door lock. Matt climbed into the front passenger seat. His half-porcupine head looked like the before-and-after picture of a men's hair gel commercial; his eyes were bloodshot; and twin emotions warred on his face, an epic struggle between concern and annoyance.

Without a word he unscrewed the thermos lid and poured. I grabbed the metal cup, bolted it, held it out for more, and gulped a second. Now I knew how Val felt, taking those first drags on the smokers' patio.

"Okay, Clare," Matt said, "I'm here. What the hell is going on? You were crying so hard I couldn't understand half of what you were blubbering over the phone."

I spilled the whole awful story: the drunken pass by Mike's cousin, the unholy timing of Mike's seeing it, the ugly bar fight, then my going home with Valerie and discovering her husband's asphyxiated body in their small garage.

My hero firefighter was dead. As I described the baby pink color of James's corpse, I broke down again. Matt handed me a handkerchief then put his arm around me. When I finished getting his leather jacket good and wet, I began telling him what happened after the police arrived.

"An army of them tramped all through the Noonans' home," I said. "Detectives interviewed Val and me in separate rooms, and I told them that I believed James was murdered."

"Murdered? Why?"

"That's what the detectives wanted to know."

"And?"

"James was killed because of what he knew about Bigsby Brewer's death. I'm sure of it."

"What did he know?"

"James wouldn't tell me. That's why I went to see him. He was supposed to be at the pub, but he never showed. So I asked Val to help me try to coax the truth out of him . . . and I *know* there's a truth. Michael Quinn even confirmed it."

Matt looked about as convinced as those guys with the gold shields.

"I told the detectives to speak with the captain. They wrote his name down in their notebooks, assured me they'd follow up in the morning, but I don't know . . ." I shook my head.

"What's the matter, Clare? The cops will follow up."

"It's just that . . . despite my assuring them that James was murdered, they began looking hard for a suicide note, and unfortunately they found one—in Val's e-mail box."

"What did it say?"

"Five words. 'I am so sorry. Good-bye.' It was a text message sent from James's phone earlier in the evening."

"That's it?"

"Anyone could have written it! Especially if James had texted Val in the past. The addresses would be right there, stored inside his phone!"

"Did you tell the cops?"

"Yes," I said, "but I don't think they believed me. Val broke down at the sight of the message, sobbed openly about her husband's depression; his erratic behavior and mood swings; how James was mourning the death of his best friend, Bigsby Brewer; how hard he'd taken the loss . . ."

I met Matt's eyes. "Bigsby was a hero to me, too. He went with James into that collapsing caffè, helped save your mom and Enzo."

I paused to gulp more coffee (and cry a little more).

"Here." Matt pressed a second handkerchief into my hands (the first one he'd given me was already soaked).

With frustration I swiped at my uncontrollable waterfall. "Sorry," I said.

"Don't be. After your call, I laid in a supply." He pulled open the right side of his jacket, the inside pocket was bulging with folded handkerchiefs.

I would have burst out laughing. But it struck me as touching and I started crying all over again.

"Oh, boy . . ." Matt held on to me.

"I don't believe that lame text message," I said against his jacket. "The killer sent it. I'm sure of it."

"I don't know, Clare . . . How can you be?"

"The beer on the kitchen table." I leaned back, finally dried my eyes. "James *hated* beer. If he wanted to get drunk one last time, he had a four-foot rack of good wine he could have guzzled instead."

"People who decide to off themselves do irrational things."

"Right. So if you were going to end it all, you would add arsenic to an espresso made from freshly roasted Yirgacheffe peaberries? Or a cup of green tea brewed from a grocery store box?"

Matt scratched the back of his head. "I see your point."

"And . . . there's something else . . . As I was sitting here, waiting for you, before I nodded off?"

"What?"

"I remembered: At the bake sale in Union Square Park, I met this club guy, Dean Tassos, a 'friend' of Val's, only he was acting like more than a friend: fawning words, lingering touches, sweet looks—"

"Where are you going with this?"

"Just listen: Dean called Val while she and I were at the pub. She didn't want me to hear their conversation so she took the call in the ladies' room."

"And how do you know it was Tassos?" Matt asked.

"The ring tone—'You Spin Me Right Round' . . . Val had it set especially for him, and immediately after Dean calls her, she decides her husband isn't going to show and asks me to give her a ride home."

"So?"

"So what if Dean called Val to tell her the deed was done?"

"Come on, Clare. You're starting to suspect conspiracies 24/7."

"It makes perfect sense: Dean calls Val to tell her that James is dead. She now knows it's safe to come home, and she brings a witness, *me*. One more thing: Dean is part owner of the Mirage clubs." I dug into my bag for the business card the man gave me, handed it to Matt. "Look at the locations."

"North Jersey, Brooklyn, and—"

"Astoria! The Red Mirage club sits right next to Caffè Lucia, and their business has slowed. Before this whole thing started, I even had a run-in with one of Dean's shady managers, an argument over a parking space in front of his club. Yet when this same club was threatened by the caffè fire, this jerk was suddenly nowhere to be seen. Why? Because he knew about—or was involved in—setting the fire and was afraid of being questioned at the scene!"

I took a breath. "I think Dean's dirty. Given Val's *close*

friendship with him and her marriage to a firefighter, she may have been the one to give him the idea to torch the business next to his club so he wouldn't be accused of arson. Then the marshals would pin it on Enzo, and Red Mirage clubs would walk away scot-free with a big fire-insurance paycheck."

"Well, it didn't work out that way," Matt said.

"Yeah, because James's fire company was too good. They stopped the blaze before it spread to the nightclub, and I turned out to be a fly in the ointment, too. I witnessed the start of that fire, gave Marshal Rossi reasons to look beyond Enzo for motive. That's why they threatened me! To get me to butt out. That was the reason they set the second fire, too, the one that killed Bigsby, then sent a fake letter to the newspaper—they needed to throw off the scent."

"So why kill James?"

"Maybe James figured it all out—maybe Val slipped and James overheard a phone call with Dean. Maybe James threatened to go to the authorities unless Dean turned himself in. He and Val could have plotted to kill him to keep him quiet."

Matt rubbed his bloodshot eyes. The midnight rain had stopped by now, but the combination of chilly outside air and steamy coffee had fogged the wet car windows. The effect was far from intimate. It felt almost threatening, as if a gray curtain were closing around us.

"Okay, Clare. If you still feel that strongly in the morning, you can call the police, right? Give them your new theory? So, can we go now? I'm parked behind you. I'll drive you back to the Blend, and we'll come back here tomorrow to get your car."

"I didn't bring you here to be my chauffeur, Matt. I need you to watch my back."

"Excuse me?"

"I'm paying a visit to Mike's cousin—right now."

Matt blinked and stared. "You mean the *drunken* fire captain who felt you up and had a fistfight with your boyfriend?"

"Yes. You don't think I'd be stupid enough to confront him alone?"

"So I'm your muscle again?"

"You don't mind, do you?"

"Me? Why should I mind taking on a giant, inebriated firefighter awakened from a stupor in his own home? Presuming he isn't armed, of course. You do know how to drive to Elmhurst Hospital, right? Because I don't want to bleed to death waiting for an ambulance."

"Things won't go down like that."

"He's a Neanderthal, Clare. And your boyfriend let himself get dragged right down to his level. I see enough of this crap on my buying trips: Family feuds. Tribal wars. Old grudges flaring up into new violence. Why should I let myself get dragged in, too?"

"Because I asked you . . ." I sighed, weary of playing this card again, but . . . "I was always there for you, Matt. Remember? Your addiction, your rehab, your relapses—"

"I know you were. And for *you*, Clare, I would do anything. But this isn't for you. It's for Dudley Do-Right and his hose-wielding cousin."

"Have a heart, okay?" I said. "Someone has to tell the captain he just lost another man in his company. And I need to find out exactly what he knows about Bigsby's death."

"What makes you think he knows anything?"

"Back at the pub, when we were alone together, Michael confided that he put important evidence in a package for me."

"You've got to be kidding."

"What?"

"A minute before the randy fire captain goes octopus on you, he whispers that he has a special *package* for you."

"He didn't mean it like *that*!"

"Clare, you're so gullible. Some guys will spin anything to get you in their bed. I promise you, there's no package."

"And I promise you there is. He even confided he wanted me to show it to Mike—and I was glad to hear it. I thought it might be a way for those two to finally reconcile. I thought Mike would want that, too."

"Who cares what the flatfoot wants?" Matt threw up his hands. "Why do you want to stick your neck out for Mike Quinn anyway?"

"Because I *love* him, that's why!"

My voice sounded almost amplified in the confined space. I'd never said those words out loud before, not even to Mike, and after all I'd been through in my life, I knew Matt understood what it took for me to make that declaration. For a long moment, he fell silent.

"Okay, Clare . . ." he finally said. Lifting his arm, he used his coat sleeve to wipe away the smothering curtain. "Where does Captain O'Lunkhead live?"

"See that redbrick row house three doors down? Val told me he just moved here from Astoria about three weeks ago. He wanted to live closer to work." I pointed farther down the rain-swept street. The captain's fortresslike firehouse was just half a block away.

"And you're sure he's not on duty?" Matt asked.

"Not the way he was drinking."

Matt popped the car door. "Let's hope we can wake this guy up."

"I'll make the man some coffee," I said. "It'll be fine."

I climbed out from behind the wheel and fell into step behind my ex. As he moved to dodge a wide puddle, I caught a striking image in the blue-tinged pool: a perfect reflection of the captain's redbrick row house, only in reverse.

It was exactly how I'd paint the two cousins, I realized, as mirror images; back-to-back monochrome profiles, like Warhol's prints, cool blue and raging red. I'd always seen those men as primary colors. I understood why now. Each was singular in his own characteristics; neither able to change the other . . . *And when they mix, the shade is violence* . . .

"Clare? Are you coming?"

"There's something here . . ."

An object was floating in the puddle. *A ball of cloth?* I

bent down. No, it was a glove. In the uncertain light, it looked black, but when I picked it up, I saw it was cranberry colored. A mirrored *F* pattern was embedded in it . . . *Just like Mrs. Fairfield's House of Fen scarf.*

"What is it?" Matt asked.

"A woman's glove."

"And I care because . . . ?"

"Because"—I tilted my chin toward the second-floor windows—"it may mean we won't find Michael alone in his bed."

"Great," Matt muttered. "Another reason for the guy to be just *thrilled* with our visit."

I tucked the designer glove into the outer pocket of my handbag and followed Matt to the building's front porch. Unlike Val's row house, the three floors had been divided into three separate apartments. New tape over the bell confirmed that Michael Quinn lived on the second floor. Matt touched the button. *Nothing.* We waited and buzzed again.

"He's passed out." Matt glanced at his Breitling. "It's almost three AM and he probably won't wake up until noon."

Matt was ready to leave when I noticed the interior door hadn't closed properly. The last person to leave had left it ajar. I pushed through, entering a narrow hall. "Come on." I hit the carpeted staircase. But when I got to the top, I stopped so abruptly that Matt's nose jammed into the small of my back.

"Clare—"

"The door's open," I whispered.

Matt gripped my arm, holding me back as he stepped around me. He crossed the narrow landing, used one foot to nudge open the door a little wider. I leaned around him, peered inside.

Captain Quinn was lying facedown on the bare hardwood floor. His arms were splayed wide, legs folded over one another. His face was unrecognizable under a scarlet mask of blood. Blood pooled on the floor, too.

"No!"

Matt tried to hold me back again; I broke away hard, rushed to the captain, dropped to my knees. I touched his bloody cheek. It was still warm—and he was breathing!

"He's alive! Call for help!"

Matt pulled out his cell, dialed 911, gave the address. I yanked open Matt's leather jacket, pulled out his stack of handkerchiefs, pressed them against the bleeding wound on Michael's head.

"Your boyfriend's lucky," Matt said as he closed the phone.

"What? What did you say?" Blood was seeping through the thick wad of cloth, staining my fingertips like my oils used to.

"I said your boyfriend didn't kill his cousin. So he's lucky."

"What are you talking about? You can't *think* Mike had anything to do with this!"

Matt didn't reply. He stepped away, found some clean towels, and returned to help me staunch the bleeding.

"Neanderthals . . ." he murmured.

Thirty-Four

~~~~~~

Detective Sergeant Hoyt caught Matt's 911 call. He arrived with a younger, shorter detective named Ramirez and a slew of uniforms, just minutes after the paramedics. The moment the medical team carted the still-unresponsive Michael Quinn off to the ambulance, the two investigators sealed the apartment.

The detectives separated Matt and me for questioning. I remained with Detective Hoyt in the apartment while Ramirez escorted Matt downstairs.

Hoyt was a tall man, about my age with a ruddy complexion and a dramatically receding hairline that made him appear bald (from my angle below him, anyway). His ill-fitting suit was bread-crust brown, and the only design on his pineapple gold tie was a fresh coffee stain. He was thick through the middle yet his craggy face was lean. Given the hour, I half expected him to be as worn out as I was, but Hoyt was wide awake; his eyes giving off an aggressive vitality, like twin flames trapped inside a shrunken pumpkin.

His first question (beyond my name, address, and relationship to Matt) was my connection to Michael Quinn.

"He's my boyfriend's cousin," I said. "We're on friendly terms."

"And why did you pay him a visit so late?"

"One of the men in the captain's firehouse died a few hours ago, under mysterious circumstances. We came here to tell Michael about it."

I told Hoyt everything that happened regarding James Noonan, along with my theory that James's death and the captain's assault were related.

"Come again, Ms. Cosi? The Noonan case sounds like a suicide."

"I think Michael Quinn was attacked because of something he knew or something the attacker thought he might have. He spoke to me earlier this evening about a package—"

"A package? Are you talking about drugs?"

"No, the captain said he had evidence in this package, information about the death of one of the men in his firehouse." I explained about Bigsby Brewer's death, about the Coffee Shop Arsonist. "I'm sure that's why this place was ransacked."

Hoyt glanced around, scratched the back of his head with a pen tip. "Not much to ransack, you have to admit . . ."

That was true. A single recliner, a standing lamp, and a barstool subbing for a table were the extent of Michael Quinn's living room furniture. He'd set a small television on top of a stack of cardboard boxes, but the shattered unit had been knocked down and the contents of those boxes— mostly clothing—were scattered all over the parquet floor.

"Does anything appear missing?" I asked.

"We generally learn that kind of thing from the victim," Hoyt replied in a tone that indicated I'd just asked the stupidest question in the world.

"Okay, well . . . here. You better take this . . ." I dug into my handbag pocket, held out the damp glove.

"And what's this, Ms. Cosi?"

"I found it in the puddle in front of this building. I'm

betting it belongs to Mrs. Josephine Fairfield. She and the captain used to be engaged. There was a scene at the pub. He rejected her pass. I think you should question her."

The detective waved over a uniform officer who bagged the glove for the detective. "Okay, Ms. Cosi, spell that name for me. Fairfield, you said?"

"I *said*: Get the hell out of my way! I want to see my captain!"

The roaring male voice echoed up the staircase, an audio assault on my tired brain. The Bad Lieutenant was here— Oat Crowley. He'd either heard the 911 call while buffing, seen the emergency vehicles down the street, or both.

A few seconds later, Detective Ramirez appeared. He stood on the landing, just beyond the open front door. Oat Crowley loomed behind him—at more than a head taller than the detective, Crowley could easily see into the apartment.

"What the hell is *she* doing here?!" the lieutenant bellowed.

Ramirez jerked a thumb in Oat's direction, announced his name. "This guy claims to know the victim."

"Victim?" Oat said, now looking alarmed. "Where the hell is Michael Quinn?"

Hoyt narrowed his eyes on the blustering firefighter. "By now I'd say he was in the intensive care unit at Elmhurst. Unless he graduated to the morgue."

"It's her fault!" Oat rushed toward me. Hoyt blocked him, the cop in uniform stepped up to help. "I don't know what story she's telling you, but she started this thing, and her cop boyfriend obviously tried to end it—"

"You're crazy!" I shouted.

"Ask her!" he shouted right back, stabbing the air with his finger. "Ask her how she played two men against each other: my captain and Mike Quinn."

"I didn't play anybody!"

Hoyt exchanged a glance with his partner.

"You want them separated, Sarge?" Detective Ramirez asked.

"Not yet. Let's see where this goes . . ." Hoyt turned to Oat. "You clear this up, okay? Mike Quinn is the name of the *victim*."

"It's a family name," Oat said. "Michael Quinn is my captain, Mike Quinn is an NYPD detective with some hotshot squad in Manhattan. The two are first cousins—and *she's* the reason it came down to fists earlier this evening."

"How do you know about that?" I challenged. "You weren't even there."

"Half the firehouse was there, lady! It's all the shift's talking about tonight!"

"Then you haven't heard yet?" I said, hardly able to believe it. "None of you have heard about James?"

"James?" Oat said. "What about James?"

"Quiet! Both of you!" Hoyt said. Now he turned to me. "What was this fistfight about earlier in the evening, Ms. Cosi? You didn't mention it to me."

"It was nothing," I said. "A misunderstanding, that's all."

"That's what you call it?" Oat barked a laugh. "Listen to me, *Sarge*, earlier this evening, in front of a dozen witnesses, her boyfriend—Detective Mike Quinn of the NYPD— worked over his cousin at Saints and Sinners pub in Woodside after he caught her making out with him—"

"I was doing no such thing!"

"Call it what you want, honey, your lousy cop boyfriend obviously came here to *finish* the job he started on his cousin."

"Well, it didn't go down like a fistfight here," Hoyt said. "It appeared the victim was struck from behind with a blunt instrument. The attacker shook down the premises, stole the victim's watch, wallet, rifled his pockets, and then fled with the weapon."

"To make it *look* like a robbery," Oat said. "Quinn's been on the job all his life! He knows how to cover up his own crime!"

"You're wrong!" I said. "Mike might have thrown a punch

in a bar, but he would *never* ambush a man with a club, beat him into a coma."

"Calm down, Ms. Cosi," Hoyt said. "I'm just looking at all the angles, and it sounds like this fight was a heat of the moment thing, except that *you* never mentioned it, which makes it clear to me that you're far from an objective party."

"But that fight has nothing to do with what happened here," I said.

"Bull!" Oat bellowed. "There's been bad blood between the pair of them for years. A real history. Listen to me, Hoyt, you better not try to protect Detective Quinn just because he's another cop, or I'll—"

"You don't want to *threaten* me," Hoyt said, his own threat clear under the tight reply. "Just tell me about the history."

I expected Oat to spill that old Kevin Quinn story or tell Hoyt how betrayed Michael felt about his cousin quitting the fire academy. Instead, he said a name that I never expected to hear.

"Leila Quinn."

"Mike's ex-wife?" I whispered, feeling a creeping sense of dread. "What about her?"

"So your boyfriend never told you?" Surprised by my ignorance, Oat turned disgustingly smug. He played to Hoyt. "About ten years ago, my captain nailed her boyfriend's wife, Leila—a real hot broad, too, former lingerie model. The captain invited Leila down to Atlantic City for a weekend. She took him up on it. Who knows what lie she told her dumb-ass cop husband to get away for the weekend, but off she scampered making herself very available."

I felt cold inside, so cold I shivered. Matt was up the stairs by now, lingering on the landing beside a uniformed officer. Needing a friend, I met his eyes.

"Was there any violence back then?" Hoyt asked.

"Oh yeah," Oat replied. "Detective Quinn didn't find out for months. The wife finally brought it up when they were having some fight, just to stick it to Mikey, and when she

told him the truth"—Oat looked skyward and made a fist—
"*whammo*."

"Define 'whammo' please," Hoyt said.

"Your fellow detective went *nuts*, how's that? The captain's got a gold tooth in his mouth for a reason. Mike Quinn knocked out the real one."

Hoyt exchanged a long glance with Ramirez—and the sight made my stomach turn. *They're making Mike for this.*

Oat folded his arms. "That guy is no damn good. What he did to my cousin Pete, I'll never forget."

"Pete," I said. "Pete who?"

"Pete *Hogarth*," Oat replied. "My mother's family knows all about Mike Quinn. The prick framed Pete's old man on some trumped-up murder charge, planted evidence in his bird coop on the roof of his building."

"That's not true," I said, struggling now to hold my temper. Matt stepped up behind me, put a hand on my shoulder.

"What do you know about it?" Oat spat. "Quinn wasn't even a cop back then, just some rat kid with a Hardy Boys complex. He even got some phony civilian award from the mayor. The jerk was working the angles before he even set foot in the police academy, laying the groundwork to move right up the ladder."

"Pete Hogarth's father was a *killer*!" I shouted, moving fast toward Oat. The man actually took a step back. "He murdered a Dominican bodega owner in cold blood while he was robbing him—"

"Shut your mouth—"

"That's enough," Hoyt said. He turned back to me. "Ms. Cosi, can you account for Detective Quinn's whereabouts after the incident at the pub?"

"Not exactly . . . I mean, Mike left and then . . ." I swallowed. "I called him several times. He hasn't returned my calls yet, but—"

"Then you can't vouch for his whereabouts?"

"No, but I'm sure—"

"Thank you, Ms. Cosi." Hoyt turned to his partner. "Get Detective Quinn's shield number from One Police Plaza and bring him in."

"Wait!" I cried.

"He had motive and opportunity, Ms. Cosi. Unless he can come up with a credible alibi for the last couple of hours, he's going to be a person of interest in this case—"

"What about him!" I pointed at Oat. "He may have had a motive to do this. Let me tell you why—"

"I was *on duty* at the firehouse *all night*," Oat replied levelly. "We had three runs, and every man I worked with is a witness. Go ahead, check me out. Have fun wasting your time."

Oh God. I turned back to Hoyt. "You have to listen to me. Mike didn't do this. The captain had evidence in this apartment—"

"Yes, I already have your statement about that. We'll keep that in mind. Thank you for your help," Hoyt said, waving over a uniformed officer. "You and your business associate are free to go now—"

"But—"

"Now."

The uniform stepped up, hand on the butt of his night stick.

"Come on, Clare," Matt said, tugging my arm. He deliberately moved his body between me and the smirking Oat Crowley. Good thing, too. I was close to ripping the lieutenant's face off.

Outside, several police cars surrounded the apartment building. It was 4 AM, still pitch-dark, but the spectacle had drawn a cluster of gossiping neighbors, coats thrown over robes and pajamas. We stepped clear of it all and headed back to the Honda.

"Now I know why . . ." I said, voice hoarse.

"Why what?"

"I was angry with Mike for reacting so violently behind the pub, but I didn't know about Leila . . . I didn't know what his wife did to him behind his back."

I stopped walking, faced Matt. "I can understand why the captain didn't tell me. He wanted to play me. But why didn't Mike tell me the truth?"

"I'll tell you why. He was ashamed."

"Of what?"

Matt tilted his head back, as if he were going to read me the answer in the stars. "You women talk endlessly about your problems. With your girlfriends, your sisters, your mothers. Talk, talk, talk. But men aren't like that. Mike didn't tell you about his wife going to bed with his cousin because he was ashamed and embarrassed."

"If he had told me, I would have understood."

"Clare . . ." Now Matt was rubbing his neck, as if he were struggling to translate Portuguese into Mandarin. "If I know Dudley Do-Right—and I think I do—whatever he kept from you . . . he did it because he wanted your love, not your pity."

I nodded then whispered, "So now what do I do?"

"Well, Clare, if I know you—and I think I do—you don't give up."

Then my ex-husband, business partner, and oldest friend put his hand against my back and pressed me into forward motion again.

THIRTY-FIVE

An hour later, dawn broke—although it was hard to tell. Beyond the French doors of my Village Blend, gray buildings met gray clouds in an unending urban haze. Even the sun was too weary to shine.

"How bad is it?" I asked the men sitting across from me. I wasn't due to open for another hour, but I already had two customers: Detective Finbar "Sully" Sullivan, Mike's right-hand man on his OD Squad; and Emmanuel Franco, his younger, street-wise protégé.

"How bad is it?" Franco echoed. "On a scale of one to ten: I'd say a ten."

"The man's not dead," Sully countered. "He's just in custody."

Franco shook his shaved head. "He's charged, which means he's dead to the department, and for a guy like Mike Quinn, when they take away your shield, they might as well put you in the ground."

I closed my eyes, from anguish as much as exhaustion. Matteo was sacked out upstairs. But I couldn't rest, not with Mike in hell. *What awful thoughts must be going through his mind and heart? Is he cursing me now? Sorry he ever met me, ever walked into my coffeehouse?*

"Guys . . ." I said, unable to stop a few tears from spilling out, "isn't there *any* way for me to see Mike? Talk to him?"

Sully reached across the café table, squeezed my hand. "I'm sorry, Clare. We can't even talk to him."

"Or work his case," Franco noted.

"But you can," Sully said.

"His case?" I opened my eyes, wiped my wet cheeks.

Beyond the Blend's windows, a ray of gold had broken through the morning fog, giving Sully's carrot-colored cop hair an almost rousing vibrancy. The man's shared glance with Franco, however, remained darkly pensive.

"You're a civilian," Sully reminded me. "IAB and the Department of Investigations can't sack you for turning up some leads to exonerate him."

"But I already have," I said. "That's why I called you two."

The detectives exchanged glances again, but their expressions were no longer pensive. Now they looked hopeful.

"What have you got?" Sully asked, leaning forward.

"I have three theories," I said.

"Good, let's hear them."

"Okay, but first . . . I need some coffee." I rose from the table. "You guys want some?"

"Are you kidding?" said Franco.

"Please," said Sully.

"A bite to eat would be nice, too," added Franco.

Sully whacked the back of his billiard-ball head. "Don't be an ass."

"Hey, it's not my fault the Coffee Lady makes excellent baked goods! I can see where her daughter gets her, uh"—he waggled his eyebrows—"talent."

I stared at the man. "Detective, you *are* talking about my daughter's *cooking* right?"

"Of course," Franco said, although the wink he threw to Sully gave me pause.

"Well, you're in luck," I called, moving behind the counter. "The pastry delivery just came, and I have some warm pistachio muffins back here. I gave the recipe to my baker for St. Patrick's Day, but the customers liked them so much they asked me to keep them on the menu."

"I'll have three!" Franco said.

"I actually wouldn't mind a couple," Sully added.

Franco snorted. "And I get a head whack? For what?"

"Just for being you."

Ten minutes later, we were sipping hot mugs of my freshly roasted Breakfast Blend, devouring a half-dozen of my warm, green pistachio muffins, and going over my theories on Mike's case.

"Theory number one," I began. "The Crazy Girlfriend. Josephine Fairfield's glove outside the captain's house truly gives me the creeps. The woman already admitted to being an arsonist—in a bar full of firefighters, no less. And she was acting lovesick at the pub. I could easily see her waiting for Michael Quinn at his apartment. Maybe he was harsher with her in his own place, maybe he even slapped her or pushed her, and she retaliated by grabbing an object and braining him with it before running off. What do you think?"

"I think it doesn't answer why the captain's apartment was ransacked," said Sully.

"Yeah," said Franco. "Whoever put down Captain Quinn did it with a cool head."

"And a ruthless one," Sully noted.

Franco agreed. "While the man's lying there, presumably bleeding to death, this scumbag preps the scene to look like a break-in robbery."

"Well, if you want ruthless, I have the perfect candidate," I said. "Theory number two: the Bad Lieutenant."

I told them all about Lucia Testa's secret love affair with Lieutenant Oat Crowley and his possible motive for setting fire to her father's caffè (winning Lucia as his wife along with a fat fire-insurance inheritance that would help feather his retirement nest).

"But why would he attack the captain?" Sully asked.

"Because Michael Quinn had evidence against him," I said. "When James's best friend died during that chain coffeehouse fire, I think James got suspicious of Oat. So he went to the captain with some kind of evidence. Oat got wind of it and eliminated both men. The only problem is Oat's alibi. He claims he was on duty all night and his crew will verify it."

"So how could he have killed James and attacked Michael Quinn?" Sully asked.

"He might have slipped away," I suggested (weakly).

Sully and Franco glanced at each other. *Doubtful.*

"What else have you got?" Sully asked.

"Theory number three: the Fireman's Wife and the Arsonist . . ."

The stars of my third scenario were Valerie Noonan and Dean Tassos. I laid out Dean's motives for arson and Val's desire to see her husband gone. As I talked, Sully and Franco both leaned farther forward in their chairs. The glances they shared felt increasingly energized.

". . . and I think those two set the chain coffeehouse fire and sent a fake letter to the papers to throw off the authorities," I said. "If James Noonan knew about Dean's arson and gave evidence to the captain, Val could have tipped off Dean. She may not have killed her husband with her own hands, but she could have agreed to look the other way while Dean murdered James and made it look like a suicide, then beat down Michael Quinn and made it look like a robbery."

"I think she's got something here," said Sully.

"So do I," said Franco, "and it makes a *helluvalot* more sense than Homeland Security's current theory."

"Is that who's in charge of the arson investigation now?" I asked.

Sully nodded. "They're all over the threat you got here at

the Blend. Word is they're making a case against some anti-caffeine fanatic connected to one of your customers."

"Which customer?"

"Barry something or other."

"You've got to be kidding," I said. "Barry wouldn't hurt a fly. And it's hard for me to believe he'd hook up with a bomb-setting terrorist."

"That's the rumor," said Sully. "This friend of Barry's supposedly has a checkered history and some memberships in activist groups that have gone nuclear in the past. He lives in an apartment near the chain coffeehouse that burned, was seen near Caffè Lucia the day of that fire, and has friends near the coffeehouse in Brooklyn that went up—that's where the backpack was purchased that held the package that threatened you. I'm not supposed to know any of this, of course, and neither are you, Clare."

I blinked. "Who am I going to tell?"

"Your friend Barry for starters," Sully said flatly. "So tell him to get a good lawyer for his boyfriend."

Off my shocked look, Sully simply shrugged. "I'm ready to hang with Mike."

"No!" I said. "I don't want anybody to hang!"

"*Ladies!*" Franco sang. "Before you two get your panties in a twist over Barry and his buddy, can we come up with a strike plan?"

"Yeah . . ." Sully shot him a sour look. "And let's make sure it's better than our last one."

"Hey, Sully, my intel was golden. Last night's op failed because those dealers are smarter than the badges who conducted the stop-and-search. The drugs are *in* that pizza delivery car. I *know* it."

"You know it, but you're the only one," said Sully. "Try, try, again, Detective . . ."

It took me a moment to catch up: These two were talking about their squad's operation last night, the one that went down badly or else Mike would never have shown up at

Saints and Sinners. Val had called it "bad timing." I closed my eyes again, wondering what else it was.

"Clare, you okay?" Sully asked.

"No," I whispered. "I'm thinking about Mike again and what happened last night in Queens . . ."

"Well, don't beat yourself up. After our op went down in flames, Franco was almost made, which meant his life was endangered not just his cover. Believe me, Clare, by the end of it all, Mike was ready to punch out a choirboy, never mind the cousin who pawed you up."

I opened my eyes. "Do you think Mike knows I never meant for it to happen? Does he know I'm not Leila?"

Sully put a hand on my shoulder. "Of course he does. Mike knows who you are, Clare. And he knows who his cousin is."

"Mike trusts me?"

"Not just trusts, Clare. The man loves you. When he lost it last night at that pub, the reason was his cousin, not you."

"Yeah . . ." Franco shifted, scratched the side of his head. "What he said."

"So have you got anything more on this guy, Tassos?" Sully asked.

"Just his business card." I went to my bag, brought it over.

Franco nodded as soon as he saw it. "I know this club. The Blue Mirage? It's in Bensonhurst, Brooklyn, on the *same block* as the coffeehouse that burned down."

"That's two connections," Sully looked to me. "Right, Clare?"

"That's right." The pieces were falling into place. "Lorenzo Testa was hassled by guys from the Red Mirage club. The neighborhood busybody confirmed that to me the night of the fire."

"How about the coffeehouse owner in Brooklyn?" Franco asked. "Was he hassled by Mirage club goons, too? That'll seal the deal."

"I don't know," I said.

"You have to find out," Sully said. "Do you know the owner's name?"

"Jason Wren. He was at the bake sale yesterday. One of my baristas even pointed him out to me. I could kick myself for not speaking to the man then, finding out more about his fire . . ."

"Take it easy," Sully said. "You didn't have these other leads then. Now you do. Just don't let this guy Wren clam up on you."

Easier said than done. "I don't know anything about this man. I mean, I could confide that my own coffeehouse was threatened, but if he's been threatened in the past, he might ask me why I'm not getting answers from the police, then start to wonder if I'm working for Dean Tassos . . ."

"She's right," said Franco. "We need an angle for her."

"I've seen Wren give interviews on television," I said, thinking it through. "If I could get him to believe I'm a reporter, I could actually get his statements about any threats from Tassos or his people on tape."

"Do you need a video camera?" Franco asked.

"My barista Dante Silva is a serious painter. He has a lot of friends in the art world. He could probably borrow something convincing, act like my cameraman. I just need a credible way to set it up . . ."

We drank more coffee, discussed some options. None seemed very strong. Finally, the shop's front bell jangled.

"Well, hello, gang!" Tucker called, his actor's basso booming through the quiet shop. "What's up? Will I read about it . . . *in the papers?*"

As my assistant manager waved his favorite New York tabloid, he continued talking about the headlines in a perfect Pat Kiernan accent. *Pat Kiernan, the famous local anchorman. Pat Kiernan the well-known voice of NY1.*

Sully and I exchanged glances. Franco smiled.

"Oh, Tucker . . ." I sang. "I need a little favor."

Thirty-Six

∞∞∞∞∞∞∞∞∞∞∞∞∞∞∞∞∞∞∞

"Mr. Wren?" I called. "I'm Clare . . . Clare Stanwyck."

(The alias wasn't my idea. The name came to Tucker as a last minute improvisation. "It's a lock, Clare. I think intrigue and I channel Barbara's performance in *Double Indemnity*." At least Tuck didn't ask me to wear an ankle bracelet—although he did suggest the business suit and stacked heels. I also agreed to the blond wig. A drag queen customer was nice enough to drop it off. It did make me look more "TV polished," and if Dean Tassos saw me on the street, it would cloud immediate recognition.)

"Hey, there!" Jason Wren rose from the floor. He had been using an acetylene torch on the base of a booth in his restored shop. Now he turned off the blue-white flame, yanked off his safety googles, and dropped them next to a box of matches. "You're the people from New York One, right? I spoke with Pat Kiernan this morning about your coming."

Even in my stacked heels, Wren was much taller than I. He pumped my hand, then pulled off his flameproof apron and took his time rolling up the sleeves of a scarlet University of Phoenix tee. His eyes were smoky brown, his hair cut into a spiky mop, and a barbed-wire tattoo ringed one leanly muscled arm.

I placed his biological age at thirty—but when I realized he was watching me for a reaction to his working man's strip tease, I placed his mental age as much younger.

"Hang on a second," Wren said.

Four flat screens adorned the shop walls. Each was broadcasting the same drag racing sequence from *The Fast and the Furious*. Wren fiddled with a remote control. The screens went blank. He ejected the DVD and tossed it on a pile of films, all of which involved car racing, with the odd exception of the Alfred Hitchcock classic *Strangers on a Train*.

"So, what do you think of Speedway Pizza?" Wren asked as he popped in a new DVD. Now the screens lit up with an animated loop of his logo revving up and driving away.

I glanced around the unfinished interior. The walls were white with red racing stripes, the tiled floor looked like a black-and-white checkerboard flag. In the window, a neon sign welcomed customers: *Speedway Pizza: Home of the Cone.*

I wasn't all that surprised the man's coffeehouse was now a pizzeria. Before Dante and I had driven to Brooklyn, I'd dug up every article I could find on Jason Wren. He never mentioned threats, but he did say that his shop was so badly damaged by the fire he decided to make a "big change."

"You're smart, Mr. Wren," said Dante, who was acting the part of my cameraman. "With the Blue Mirage next door, you should do well. Boozing and raving make people *real* hungry. I worked a pizzeria on club row. We spun dough until five AM."

Wren happily nodded at the comment.

I was glad Dante said something positive. This neighborhood had changed so much since I'd last visited that I had no idea what businesses would work here anymore. Years ago, a little Italian bistro sat on the corner of Avenue P. That bistro was now an Asian karaoke bar. The old-time movie palace was now a Dim Sum Palace Buffet, and the Italian pork store now hawked Chinese herbs.

"So what are you working on today, Mr. Wren?" I asked, warming him up with an easy one.

"Installing booths for my customers," Wren said. "I'm using partial shells of restored classics. That's a Trans Am over there, that's a 'Vette, and over there's a Pontiac Firebird."

"I'm seeing a theme here."

"You're seeing a franchise, Ms. Stanwyck. These booths, this décor, it's all going to be trademarked. This is only the first Speedway Pizza. The first of many."

"Impressive," I said.

He preened. "After I hooked into the cone pizza idea, the rest was easy."

"Cone pizza?" I said. "I assumed you were doing a combo pizza/ice-cream shop thing. You aren't actually going to serve pizza—"

"In a cone?" Dante finished.

"You got it!" Wren fired twin finger guns at us. "The crust is a cone. The cheese, sauce, and toppings are melted inside. I'm putting cone holders in the booths for convenience. They're trademarked, too."

"Cool," Dante said unconvincingly.

"Best of all, no ovens!" Wren grinned.

I blinked. "No—"

"Ovens?" Dante finished.

"All done in a microwave," Wren said with a nod. "In Europe they make cone crust from scratch, but Americans only care about the filling, right? So *my* cones are really more like a cracker than a crust. They come prepackaged, too. No more training baristas for weeks on an espresso machine. A one-armed monkey can learn to make my cone pizza in five minutes!"

Dante and I exchanged looks. *Now there's an inspiring motto.*

Wren paused. "Hey, is this the interview?"

"No, but . . ." I glanced at Dante. "We can get started now."

Dante looked around the shop. "Why don't you stand here, beside your porcelain Godzillas?"

"Dude!" Wren said. "Godzilla is Japanese. Those are Chinese dragons. Nine of them. For luck. My cousin's traditional, says they'll bring fortune to my new business . . ." He waved a dismissive hand. "I'm going to replace them before I open." Wren pointed to a burnt orange chassis. "Shoot me by the Firebird. I'll sit on the hood."

"Sure, okay," Dante said, shouldering the camera again.

"So, Mr. Jason Wren," I said into the microphone, "it looks like you're off to a great start rebuilding after the fire. You must have had lots of help. Did the insurance company jump in for a rescue?"

"Rescue?" Wren laughed. "Dealing with the insurance company involves miles of red tape, but with the arsonist coming forward in the papers, my situation should be resolved pretty quickly now."

"But without an insurance settlement, how could you afford all of this? Were you maybe . . . *forced* to take on business partners?"

"I had some cash saved. Enough to get started."

"What about the other business leaders in the community? Has the owner of the Dim Sum Palace offered to help? How about Mr. Dean Tassos from the Blue Mirage next door? Has he helped you? Or has Mr. Tassos and his club presented a problem for you? Now or in the past?"

"Well . . ." Wren's brows knitted. "I don't know Mr. Tassos, only by name. And the club guys are pretty good neighbors . . ."

Great . . . Now what?

"Mostly I'm doing the work myself," Wren went on. "I used to work in a junkyard and later at an auto-body shop. And some of my friends have helped. One of them was here earlier. He ducked out for lunch."

"I see . . ." *Come on, Clare, another question.* "I, uh, I guess you're eating cone pizza for lunch, then?"

"Soon!" He laughed, pointed to a bright orange shopping bag. "I grabbed some Korean fried chicken on my way to work. That's the way it is when you're trying to get your business started. You work all the time!"

"Let's talk about the arsonist who torched your coffee business." *Okay, here we go . . .* "Any thoughts about who that person might be?"

"None at all. I just hope they get caught. I don't want anyone else hurt."

"Do you think the arsonist was one of your customers, Mr. Wren? Did you get a warning letter or a threatening message? A *package* in a *backpack*, maybe? Another coffeehouse received a threat like that. Did you know?"

Wren's demeanor immediately changed. His open, friendly face went rigid; his smoky brown eyes went cold. "I didn't read about any packages in backpacks or see anything like that on TV. How do you know about it?"

"Surely you read the arsonist's letter. It was published. Do you—"

Wren abruptly stood. "I don't want to talk about the arsonist. I've talked enough about that—with the fire marshals, the insurance people, a whole army of officials. I thought you were here to talk about my *new* business."

"Well, I just wanted to clarify—"

"You know what? I have major work to do today so maybe you better go."

I glanced at Dante. "I think we have enough."

We couldn't gather our stuff together fast enough for Mr. Wren, who looked at his watch three times before he hustled us back onto the sidewalk.

"He made us, right?" Dante said.

"Are you kidding? The guy didn't even ask when his piece would air."

The wind kicked up and I shivered. Dawn's heavy gray clouds had ripened into an afternoon storm front. Holding down my wig, I glanced back through the pizzeria's plate glass window. Jason Wren was making a cell call. *Now who is he contacting so quickly after our interview?*

"There must be some real motor heads around here," Dante said, nudging me. "Check out that sweet number across the street."

The restored Mustang hadn't been parked there when we'd arrived. I would have noticed. The coupe gleamed redder than strawberries in a newly glazed tart. The convertible top and leather interior were white as castor sugar. Racing stripes ran from bumper to fender, and rising on the hood was a classic bonnet scoop.

"Are you okay, boss?" Dante asked. "You look a little pale, or maybe it's the makeup. I'm not used to you wearing any."

"That car," I whispered. "I've seen it before . . ."

"Really?"

"That's Glenn Duffy's car. I'm sure of it."

"That's an odd coincidence—"

"It's not a coincidence." I faced Dante. "I had the right triangle all along—but the wrong guy!"

"What?"

"Listen," I said, excited now. "Wren was using matches to light his torch; Glenn Duffy's car is parked across the street; and that old Hitchcock film that I saw inside? It was completely out of place with those car racing movies."

Dante stared down at me. "Okay. I think you officially lost it."

"No, I found it. I found our arsonists." A chilly drop of rain splashed on the end of my nose. I ignored it. "Have you ever seen *Strangers on a Train?*"

"I'm into David Lynch."

"It's the story of two men who meet during a rail trip. One wants to marry his lover, but he can't get a divorce. The other wants somebody dead so he can inherit a fortune. One suggests they swap murders."

"Boss, maybe I'm slow, but—"

"Jason Wren is friends with Glenn Duffy. Glenn is the

man who stepped out for lunch! Don't you see? The two swapped arson jobs. Jason burned Caffè Lucia. Glenn burned Wren's business."

"How does swapping jobs help them?"

"Alibis, Dante. The day the firebomb was set in Queens, Glenn could have set up an all-day alibi in *Brooklyn*. Then he picks up Lucia in plain sight at the Queens caffè and is off to Jersey. If there's no sign of the guy anywhere near Caffè Lucia that day—even that week—how could he have set the firebomb?"

"And Jason Wren?"

"Same thing, only he sets up an alibi in Queens. Makes it impossible for a Brooklyn fire marshal to pin the firebomb on him."

"What about the threat for you?"

"One of these guys must have set me up with that package the same night the other one set the bomb in the chain coffeehouse. Then they sent a fake letter to the papers to make it all look like some crazed fanatic . . ."

The wind was blowing harder now, the big drops falling faster.

"Okay, boss, you convinced me. So can we go back to the car now?" Dante eyed the violet sky. A white-hot slash seared the dark canvas. "I can't let this camera get drenched. I borrowed it from a friend—"

"Here, take my keys," I said. "Put the camera in the trunk and come right back. I have to see Glenn Duffy for myself. Once I confirm his association with Wren, I can go to Fire Marshal Rossi with it."

Dante took off at a run, shielding the camera with his coat. Unfortunately, we'd parked over three blocks away— so Wren wouldn't see that we'd arrived in my clunker instead of a news van.

I went back to the corner and crossed the street. The water was really coming down now, and I was getting very wet, but I had to get a closer look.

Thunder rumbled a warning. I stepped up to the Mustang anyway, peered into the side window, hoping to spy some identifying item, solve my problems faster. That's when I felt it, hard and cold, pressing into my back.

"It's a nine-millimeter, Ms. Cosi," the man's voice informed me. "That's a gun, in case you didn't know."

"What do you want?"

Glenn Duffy reached around fast, opened the car door. "Get in. Move." I could see the gun in his hand now. He held it low, aimed at my belly. "I said *move!*"

I moved.

"Crawl across. Get behind the wheel."

Oh God. Isn't anyone seeing what's happening to me? I looked up and down the street, but the storm had cleared the sidewalks.

"Buckle up," Glenn insisted, ignoring his own belt.

Everything felt hyper-real. I could smell the dampness of the raindrops, the sharp peppermint scent of the gum Glenn must have discarded before he ambushed me. I forced myself to stop staring at his weapon, lifted my gaze to meet his eyes. The boyish, blond Elvis was gone; the younger man's bland, amiable expression was replaced with a mask of frustrated rage.

"How did you know?" I asked.

"Jason called me. When I saw you staring at my ride across the street, I knew I was made . . . Christ, Jason thinks he's the brains, but he was duped by a reporter act and a bad wig. What a publicity hog."

"Don't do this. You're just making things worse for yourself. Why don't you—"

"Why don't you *shut up?*" He reached over, shoved a key into the ignition and turned it. "Drive. We're going somewhere to talk things over. *Maybe* we can reach an understanding."

I pulled away from the curb, frantically glancing in the rear view mirror, praying I'd see Dante. But there was no sign of him. Was Jason Wren going to take care of my barista while Glenn kidnapped me? *Oh God . . .*

I swallowed hard. "Where to?"

"Stay on Bay Parkway."

I tried again to engage him: "So whose idea was it to copy *Strangers on a Train*?"

Glenn snorted. "That boring movie? That was Jason's idea."

"That's right," I said. "You said *he* was the brains."

"Shut up and drive!"

I counted to three. "It's obvious you burned Jason's business, and he burned Enzo's place. Wren gets to start a cone pizza franchise with his insurance money. What do you get out of it?"

"I get Lucia and her insurance money."

"Lucia Testa? You've got to be kidding. She's Oat Crowley's sex toy. Do you know Crowley? He's a fireman."

Glenn's face flushed. "You think you're telling me something I don't know? I smelled that cheap cigar smoke in Lucy's 'Vette. But that'll change once I get her over to Jersey, away from her sneering old man, away from this city and that fat fireman!"

The low rise buildings were gone now. We were driving through a lonely stretch of two-lane road bordered on either side by rusty chain-link fencing.

Oh God, I know where's he's taking me . . .

The flat, featureless acreage of Washington Cemetery was so isolated it seemed almost rural. The only indication we were driving through one of the world's most populated cities was the elevated subway ahead of us and the Art Deco towers of the Veranzano Narrows looming like pale headstones on the hazy horizon. A lone vehicle rolled maybe five hundred feet in front of us—a city garbage truck.

"Make the next left," Glenn said. "It'll take you right through the cemetery gate. Nice private place for us to have our little talk."

We weren't going to talk and I knew it. Once I pulled into that graveyard, I was never coming out—a sacrifice to the fast-food franchise dreams of Jason Wren and the twisted love of Glenn Duffy.

Do something, Clare . . .

Ahead, the huge garbage truck pulled over to the side of the road. Two men jumped out and flanked a large metal Dumpster. The driver stayed in the cab, began lowering the lift.

"Pass them nice and slow," Glenn warned.

"Slow, okay . . ." At the edge of my vision, I saw Glenn shifting. He was moving the gun from one hand to the other!

NOW, Clare! Do it NOW!

I slammed my foot so hard on the gas pedal I broke my stacked heel. The Mustang shot forward, tires spinning on the wet pavement. We fishtailed into the other lane, then back again.

Duffy shouted obscenities but he didn't shoot (or couldn't). Instead, he threw himself at me, tried to punch the brake. I impaled his foot with my other heel while I pressed the horn and held it.

The impact came in seconds, but at least I was wearing my seat belt. Glenn wasn't so lucky. Like fragile candy the Mustang's front end crumpled against the mammoth truck. The windshield shattered as a large object flew through space—Glenn Duffy's body.

God knows where the gun landed.

The sanitation crew was shouting at me or each other; I couldn't tell. They were speaking English, but nothing registered, just my own hard breathing, the hiss of the shattered radiator, and the occasional moan from Duffy.

I unbuckled my seat belt, stumbled out, and pointed at the groaning hood hanging off the ruined hood.

"Lady, are you okay?" one of the men asked.

"Call the police," I said. "That man is a killer."

Thirty-Seven

～～～～～～～～～～～～～～～～～

"Clare . . ."

My eyes were happily closed, my body stretched out beneath the warm, soft bedcovers. A man's voice was calling my name. I felt his strong hand on my shoulder. I smiled, waiting to feel more.

"Mmmm . . . Mike?"

"Clare! Wake up!"

I opened my eyes. My ex-husband was shaking my shoulder. He stood beside the bed, holding out my cell. "It's that detective, the one you mentioned before you hit the sack. Sullivan something . . ."

"Sully!" I sat up, grabbed the phone. "What's going on? Is Mike free? Tell me this is over."

"I've got good news and bad news."

"Good news. Please. I could use some."

"You bagged your firebugs, Clare. Much to the dismay of a few smug suits and a whole team of Feds, the case of the Coffee Shop Arsonist is now closed."

"Duffy and Wren confessed?"

"Yeah, those two geniuses broke when the boys in Brooklyn played one against the other. The shields told Jason Wren that Glenn Duffy confessed on his 'deathbed'—that's what they called it, even though the little punk is going to be just fine. Then they turned around and told Duffy that Wren blamed everything on him. Both went for plea deals and signed confessions . . . ."

When Sully's positive patter stopped, so did my breathing. "A *but* is coming, right?"

"I'm sorry, Clare. What you accomplished doesn't clear Mike. Neither Wren nor Duffy had anything to do with that midnight assault on Mike's cousin. They both had solid alibis and claimed they had never heard of Captain Michael Quinn—or James Noonan, for that matter."

I glanced at Matt.

"What's wrong?" he whispered and sat down on the edge of the bed.

"What happens now?" I asked Sully.

"My hands are tied. Mike's case is with the Manhattan DA and the Department of Investigations, which means Franco and I still can't go near it. We were hoping you had another theory."

I closed my eyes, took a deep breath. "I'm going to need a little time—" *And a lot of coffee.* "I'll call you back, okay?"

"That's fine," Sully said, "but listen . . . I've been put in temporary charge of the squad. We're heading over to the construction site for another all-night tour. Franco's still undercover. If you need anything, call *him*, okay? You have the number. I'll be in the surveillance truck and can't use my cell. I'll check in with you again when I get the chance."

"Wait. One more thing . . . what's next for Mike?"

"He's downtown, Clare. They're holding him in the Tombs. And unless something changes, he's going to be arraigned in the morning. The charge is attempted murder."

I think I said good-bye. When Matt called my name again, I was staring at the bedcovers, the phone still in my hand.

"Clare, are you okay? What did the guy say?"

I told him, feeling so numb I hardly even cried. My tear ducts finally went as dry as the Dead Sea.

"Come on," he said. "Get up. You'll want an espresso, right?"

"A double . . ."

An hour later, I was showered, dressed, and sitting at the Blend's bar. In an atypical switch, Matt was behind the espresso machine, pulling shots for me and our last lingering customers.

As Esther ended her shift, she gave me an unexpected hug ("You looked like you needed it, boss.") Then she told me about a roast list Tucker left on the basement work table, wrapped her mile-long black scarf around her neck, and headed into the night with her boyfriend Boris.

By now, Matt and I had gone over my theories twice, but I still couldn't be sure who'd attacked Michael Quinn or why. I considered Oat Crowley again, and I couldn't stop thinking about that House of Fen cranberry glove I found lying in the puddle.

Was it Josephine Fairfield who assaulted the captain? If she didn't, did she see something? Hear something? Know something?

"Tomorrow morning, I'll talk with Mrs. Fairfield," I decided.

"What about that mysterious package," Matt reminded me. "The one Captain Octopus claimed he had for you? Did it ever arrive?"

"No. I rifled the mail before I sacked out. Junk, bills, tax forms from the NYC Fallen Firefighters Fund, and a few invoices addressed to you. Maybe it will come tomorrow."

"Well, don't count on it," said Matt, sliding over another espresso. "Like I said, the whole thing was probably just another ploy to get you into bed—"

"Stop! Please. Let's not speak ill of the comatose, okay?"

I'd called Elmhurst earlier, but the word on Michael

Quinn wasn't good. Just like Enzo, he was in the ICU, his condition touch-and-go.

With a sigh I picked up Matt's demitasse and sipped the burnished *crema,* hoping another golden shot of warmth would revive my weary mind.

"You mentioned invoices for me?" Matt said.

"They're upstairs—check the desk in my office."

"I'll look them over after we close up." He stared at me. "You should move around a little. It'll help you think. Why don't you bake something?"

"I'd rather roast something."

"Okay," Matt said, glancing up at the sound of the front door's bell. A few final customers were just walking in. "I'm giving these orders wings. Then I'm closing up. You go on downstairs."

O̶U̶R̶ back stairs were narrow but the basement was expansive—and the ambient smells incredible. Generations of coffee roasting permeated these stone walls and thick rafters, and under the overhead lights, my crimson cast-iron Probat gleamed shinier than a ladder truck.

I hit the starter button and turned up the gas, then watched the digital numbers on the infinite temperature control tick upward. A muted roar from the fans filled the enclosed space, and the chilly basement began to warm. Soon the drum would be hot enough to add the first batch of green beans.

But what to roast first?

Tucker had left me a list of the coffees we needed: our signature Espresso Blend, the smooth yet sparkling Tanzanian Peaberry, and the amazing Amaro Gayo from Ethiopia with those exotic berry overtones.

I looked over the line of drums, which held superb Arabicas from around the globe. The right kiss of heat would bring out the absolute best flavors in these green beans—and the wrong would destroy them forever.

Matt was right. The act of roasting (like cooking) held a singular magic for me. Simply warming up the roaster gave me a renewed sense of head-clearing comfort.

I was just reaching for my roasting diary when—

"Clare! Clare!" Matt's voice was so loud I could actually hear him over the roasters' lively hum. Turning, I saw him waving a sheaf of papers.

"What is that?"

"Captain Octopus wasn't playing you! That package came!"

"When? Where?"

"It was upstairs with the mail. That Fallen Firefighters Fund envelope you mentioned? The man used it as a cover. When I looked inside, I didn't find tax forms . . ."

Matt moved over to our wooden work table—the one Tucker and I used to sharpen burr grinder blades. He spread out the pages and we looked them over.

"They're schematics for some kind of tool," Matt said. "But I don't get why the guy sent these to you? Do you even know what this is?"

"It's a roof spike," I said. "I saw one at the captain's firehouse. And look what it says there: 'Property of Fairfield Equipment, Inc.'"

"There's a cover letter from someone named Kevin Quinn."

"That's Michael's brother."

Matt scanned the letter. "Kevin says he hacked into the computers of his old employer and got this evidence of product fraud."

"Old employer? Michael never mentioned his brother worked at Fairfield!" But then I remembered. He didn't— not anymore. Kevin lost his job in New York and was forced to relocate to Boston.

I read the rest of Kevin's long letter side by side with Matt.

"Jesus," Matt said. "Someone at that company replaced

the central titanium core with metal that has all the durability of a cheap furniture rod."

"It was done for profit." I pointed to the end of the letter. "The move cut production costs in half but left the roof spike with a fatal flaw. It couldn't stand up to the high levels of heat the original prototype had been tested under."

"Why would the FDNY approve it?"

"They wouldn't," I said. "I'm sure all the testing and training was done on roof spikes that had been manufactured correctly . . . Oh, Matt, that's what James meant when he said Bigsby Brewer was murdered. When Glenn Duffy and Jason Wren set that final coffeehouse fire, Bigsby was forced to use the roof spike to escape the flames. But the tool failed because someone at Fairfield changed the manufacturing specs."

"Yeah, but who?" Matt asked.

We looked over the papers again. Kevin didn't give any names.

I thought it over. "Do you remember when I found that House of Fen glove in the puddle outside of Captain Michael's apartment?"

Matt nodded.

"I think it was Josephine Fairfield's glove. When her husband died last year, she took over the company. I'll bet she changed the specs on the roof spike and found out the captain was investigating the fraud. Then she paid him a private little visit."

"Yeah." Matt nodded. "Sounds like a strong possibility."

"There's only one problem," I said, pointing to Kevin's documents. "Would a society wife be smart enough to do all this on her own?"

"None that I've ever met," Matt said. "Someone must have helped her."

I considered Oat Crowley or some other member of the FDNY. But it seemed to me the man most likely to help Josephine Fairfield execute this awful scheme was—

"Ryan Lane."

"Who?" Matt asked.

"Ryan works for Mrs. Fairfield," I explained. "He hustled her out of the pub last night when she got drunk and loud. Ryan also talked to me about retiring soon, about giving Oat Crowley his job. And he said Fairfield Equipment was on the verge of a big corporate buyout."

Matt rubbed his chin. "Cutting costs on the roof spike would definitely up the company's profits, make the operation look more valuable to a prospective buyer."

"I'll bet Lane's an officer of the company, in a position to make big money from the sale—except time ran out for him and Josie."

"What do you mean?"

"That buyout isn't final yet," I said. "So I'm guessing he and Josie simply played the odds. The roof spike worked in most situations. They took a chance there wouldn't be any catastrophic failures before they sold the company. But there was—Bigsby Brewer lost his life."

"They must know there's going to be an investigation, right?"

"Yes, but typically something like that will take weeks, maybe even months. James Noonan got suspicious right away and started making waves. He went to the captain, and they bypassed the usual time-consuming bureaucratic process. Michael Quinn used his little brother Kevin to cut to the truth. Ryan and Josie must have found out about it, assaulted Michael, and murdered James—that would buy them enough time to make a clean getaway before the truth comes out."

"But, Clare, does Josephine Fairfield even *know* James Noonan?"

"Ryan Lane does. He spoke to James at the bake sale, and I saw Lane talking to Oat Crowley, too. I'll bet Oat blabbed the whole thing about James's suspicions and the captain's investigation. Lane could have approached James after that, told him he wanted to talk. He could have gone to James's house last night under the pretense of coming clean about the roof spike—but instead Lane killed him."

"Killed him how? You said the police believe Noonan's death was a suicide."

I considered the possibilities, thought again about that glass of untouched beer on James's kitchen table, the Harp that Ryan had enjoyed at the pub. That's when I knew: "James didn't pour that beer for himself! He poured it for his killer!"

"What?"

"James hated beer. I'm sure he poured it for Ryan Lane— and Lane must have found a way to slip a drug into James's wineglass, which he would have taken with him to eliminate any evidence. That would explain the single beer on the table. If Lane was careful not to touch the glass, it would only have James's fingerprints on it. Then James passes out, Ryan hauls him to the garage and stages his suicide. Afterward, he meets up with Josie on her post–bake sale rounds and makes an appearance at Saints and Sinners to establish an alibi."

Matt frowned. "I don't know, Clare, that scenario's a little out there, don't you think? And it's not very smart. Wouldn't a drug be detected in Noonan's autopsy?"

"So what if it was? As long as the cause of death matches the manner of suicide, what difference does it make if James had a drug in his system? The case for murder is pretty thin with Val confirming her husband's depression—not to mention that suicide note." I shook my head. "The scenario I described isn't out there. It's ingenious."

"But what if Ryan Lane isn't the one who helped this Fairfield woman?"

"Well, if he didn't, then I'm sure he won't have any trouble telling a grand jury who did."

Matt thought it over. "Okay, let's do something about this. Get on the phone. Call—"

I heard a meaty smack. Matt's body went limp and fell against me. I stumbled, caught myself, but couldn't stop my ex's heavy form from sagging to the floor.

"Matt!"

"Shut up or I'll hit you, too."

One end of a Halligan tool now loomed in front of my face. I saw dried blood on it, pieces of hair. The other end of that gruesome object was in Ryan Lane's right hand. His left was pointing a gun at me.

I lifted my gaze, met his stare.

Ryan tossed the fireman's tool on the table and threw a bundle of rope at me. "Tie him up."

Thirty-Eight

≈≈≈≈≈≈≈≈≈≈≈≈≈≈≈≈≈≈≈

"**He's** bleeding," I said. "He needs a doctor!"

Ryan aimed the gun at Matt's head. "He'll be dead if you don't tie him up. Anyway, I didn't whack him nearly as hard as I hit the captain."

I bit back a curse and began to tie the rope—*loosely*. Ryan caught me. "Tighter, honey. If he gets free before I leave, he's dead. And so are you."

"You're going to kill us anyway."

"Not at all!" Ryan's deceptively boyish face lit up with a grin. "I just want you indisposed while Josie and I get out of the country. After we're gone, I don't care what happens to you."

Ryan sniffed the air. "Mmm . . . coffee. The aroma is magnificent down here"—he took a deep breath—"gives me a jones, you know?"

"Let's go upstairs. I'll pull you a fresh espresso."

Ryan wiggled his gun like a naughty finger. "Nice try, Ms. Cosi, but I'm going to have to wait until I get to Williamsburg. There's a great little all night spot off the bridge. Then I'll pick up Josephine, who thinks we're going on a short business trip, and we're off on a private jet to . . . well, as long as Josie's with me, it'll be paradise . . ."

That's when I knew. "Josephine Fairfield isn't involved in any of this, is she?"

"No. She isn't."

"Then why did I find her glove outside of Michael Quinn's apartment? Did she go there last night to throw herself at him?"

"No. After we left the pub and Josie passed out in her limo, I grabbed her glove and planted it there."

"Why?"

"In case the lady gets homesick. You see, Josie didn't embezzle millions of dollars from her company. That's on me. But if the police suspect she attacked her old lover, well, that's one more nail in her coffin. And once she understands that nothing but prison time awaits her here, she'll be all too happy to keep the bed warm in my new hacienda."

Oh my God . . . This guy is Glenn Duffy in a buttoned-down shirt. Deluded, lovesick, willing to do anything to obtain a woman . . . one who obviously wants someone else.

When I finished tying Matt, Ryan checked the ropes. "Okay, your turn."

I resisted, but Ryan didn't threaten me, he *hit* me with the gun. I bounced off the floor, and he flipped me over like a steer at a rodeo. He placed his foot on the small of my back while he bound my wrists tightly, then roped my ankles together. When he was done, I struggled against the bonds.

"I like to be thorough, Ms. Cosi."

"Were you being thorough when you killed James Noonan?" I spat.

"I thought so."

"What about the captain?"

Lane sighed. "He was my biggest problem. When James told me the captain obtained evidence of my little switch on the production line, I knew I had to pay the man a visit."

"So you broke into his apartment and ambushed Michael with his own Halligan tool."

"The captain didn't have all the documents in his apartment, but—lucky for me—I found a copy of his brother's cover letter stapled to this—"

Ryan leaned over me, displayed a United States Post Office tracking slip.

"I knew the captain sent the package to this address, but I had to wait for it to arrive." He stood up straight again. "You know, a lot of people give the post office a hard time, but their tracking system is really very efficient. I knew it was delivered today, so I stopped in to retrieve it."

Ryan gathered up the letter and schematics, and stuffed them into a backpack. Then he pulled out a strange device. A large battery was connected to an alarm clock and a pair of plastic bottles filled with clear liquid. The whole thing sat on a piece of plywood the size of a small serving tray. He placed the device on the table and set the alarm clock.

"All done," Ryan said, slipping the bag over his shoulders. "In a few minutes the Coffee Shop Arsonist will strike again."

Ryan doesn't know that crime is solved. It hasn't made the news yet! "You won't get away with this! The arsonists have already been caught."

"So?" Ryan smirked. "The police will conclude this is a copycat. Bye, bye, Ms. Cosi."

With the roar of the roaster hammering my ears, I couldn't even hear the jerk's feet on the stairs—but with that bomb ticking away, I didn't bother waiting to make sure he was gone before I began to yell.

"MATT! MATT!" I nudged him with my bound up feet. "WAKE UP!"

Not even a groan. Now I was starting to sweat, from fear as much as the heat radiating from the thrumming Probat. I looked around, searching for something to cut the ropes. A rough edge, a knife, or—

A coffee grinder blade!

Tucker had been giving Esther lessons on how to use a metal file to sharpen our burr grinder blades. One of those blades was sticking out of a vice on the edge of the wooden work table. Was the thing sharp enough to cut through the rope around my arms? Could I even get to it?

One way to find out . . .

I rolled my body across the basement floor. When I felt my torso bump the table, I folded and turned, pressing my back against the leg. When I got my feet under me, I slid up the table leg and moved toward the vice. Balancing on my bound-together feet, I pressed the ropes against the sharp edge of the blade and started rubbing.

It took a few minutes—and lots of abrasions to my hands and wrists—but I felt the hemp snap! When it did, I tumbled, falling across Matt's body. He moaned as I worked on my ankles. By the time I got the ropes off my ex, he was awake.

"What hit me?"

"A Halligan tool."

"A *what*?"

"Never mind. There's a bomb down here and it's about to go off."

Matt was on his feet like a shot. He stared at the device. "I don't know what to do to stop it."

"You don't have to! The city's bomb squad is right up the street!" I dug for my cell phone as I ran for the stairs. "Matt, come on!"

"Unlock the front door!" Matt cried.

"What are you going to—"

"Just do it!"

I raced up the steps and across the Blend's main floor. Ryan had left the door unlocked when he fled, and I yanked it open. Matt emerged from the stairway a second later, the bomb cradled in both hands like a harmless tray of cookies.

"Matt, you're crazy!"

"I'm not letting the Blend burn."

He bolted across the street, where a clothing store had gone bankrupt two months before. The space was being gutted and an enormous construction container sat in front of the building. That's where Matt tossed the bomb. Then he turned and ran.

The device exploded, sending an orange and red fireball into the sky, but the core of the blaze (thank goodness) was contained inside the metal box.

In the firebomb's glare, I spotted a black BMW parked down the block. Ryan Lane stood beside it. He'd been waiting to make sure his device went off! Now he was jumping into his car.

"Matt, look!" I pointed. "That guy's the bomber."

My Honda was parked in front of the Blend. I unlocked the door, slid behind the wheel, and started the engine. Matt got in beside me.

"I'm driving," he said.

"No time to switch!" I replied, hitting the gas hard.

"Fine. I'll call the cops." But patting his pockets, Matt realized he'd left his cell in my Blend office.

"Reach into my pocket and take mine," I said.

Ryan was speeding north on Hudson. He hooked a right on Clarkson Street just as the light turned red. I ignored the signal and followed, horns blaring behind me. He made another sharp right, but Matt managed to grab my cell despite the turns.

"Press six three times," I told him.

"Not 911?"

"It's my speed-dial code for Sergeant Franco."

"That jackass!"

"Tell him you're Joy's father."

"Joy? What does our daughter have to do with—"

"Remember last year's Christmas party? Remember when you told Joy to *stay away* from Franco? Bad idea!"

"Franco?" Matt said over the phone. "I'm Joy's father—"

"Tell him we're chasing the guy who assaulted Captain Quinn and murdered James Noonan! Tell him the scumbag tried to kill us and now he's fleeing the country!"

"He heard you," Matt said, and held the phone to my ear.

"He's on Delancey Street and coming your way!" I yelled. "He's heading for the Williamsburg Bridge. Watch for a black BMW!"

"This is Manhattan, Clare," Franco replied. "All the BMWs are black."

"He has a big white NYC Fallen Firefighters Fund sticker on his bumper, and I'll be right behind him in my red clunker. Where are you?"

"I just hijacked a pickup from the construction site. If your perp makes the bridge, we could lose him."

"You have to stop him, Franco! Any way you can!"

I saw the bridge lights ahead. I was closing in on Ryan's BMW, too, until a little green pizza delivery car cut in front of me. I braked to avoid a collision, and Ryan raced toward the ramp.

The delivery car sped up, too. It was hard to see Lane's BMW past the big *Jackrabbit Pizza* sign on top of the little green car, and I looked for a way around him. That's when Franco's dirty yellow pickup shot out from between two other vehicles and T-boned Ryan's BMW!

The delivery car was so close it slammed into the BMW, too. And I ran into both of them. Time crawled as I watched my hood flip open and the safety glass shatter. The shoulder strap bit into my chest, my nose flirted with the steering wheel, and my cell phone flew out of Matt's hand and right through the windshield.

Then everything got very quiet. Matt and I exchanged stunned glances. Finally, we popped our doors.

Franco, in construction clothes, stood next to the BMW, a handgun aimed at a moaning Ryan Lane.

"Are you okay?" he asked, glancing our way.

"I'm fine," I said.

"I *was* fine," Matt replied, "until I found out you're dating our daughter."

"Come again?" Franco said without shifting aim. Suddenly, the door on the pizza car opened and the driver took off at a run.

"Hey, you!" Franco shouted, but didn't try to follow, his aim stayed true.

I pointed to the wrecked pickup. "I'm sorry, Detective. Did I just blow your cover?"

"Yeah," Franco replied. "But you also solved my case."

I didn't understand what the man meant until more police arrived, Sully among them. The older detective eyed my totaled Honda and turned to me. "You have insurance, Clare?"

"Not enough to buy a new car . . ." But Mike was cleared. The cost was more than worth it.

Then Sully joined Franco, who tucked his gun away and pointed to that little pizza delivery car, a green Nissan. The vehicle was shattered in the front and rear. But Franco was more interested in the illuminated *Jackrabbit Pizza* sign on the roof, now broken loose from the car and lying on its side.

"Check it out!" Franco whacked Sully in the arm. "I told you the drugs were in the pizza car!"

A tidy hole had been cut into the Nissan's roof, a cover for the hole now swung loose on its hinges—and stuffed inside that hollow, lighted sign were dozens of plastic bags. Franco began yanking them out and opening them up. They were filled with club drugs.

Sully nodded, looking pretty pleased. "That delivery driver left the construction site when you grabbed the pickup. I think he thought you were chasing *him*."

Franco shrugged. "Hey, man. Whatever works."

Under other circumstances, that kind of slapdash philosophy might have given me pause. But considering the events of the past few days, I had to admit—

"I couldn't agree more."

Thirty-nine

"**Boy**, oh boy . . ." Michael Quinn lifted a shaky hand and touched his bandaged head. "That expensive whiskey really packs a wallop."

"It wasn't Josie's aged Irish that hit you, Michael. It was her boyfriend. A guy named Ryan Lane."

"Well, can't say as I blame him for it," he said. "Not after the way Josie was goin' on at the pub." He paused. "And I can't say as I blame my cousin for what happened the other night, either."

One of the captain's eyes was covered (the socket required reconstructive surgery), but the other appeared alert behind his bruised flesh. He gazed up at me now through that one good eye, blinking slightly at the bright morning sunlight that washed over the hospital room.

As he stirred and tried to sit up, the IV hose became tangled, and I rose from my chair to help him. "Let me adjust your bed for you," I said. As the head of the mattress elevated, he turned whiter than coconut cake.

"Ouch."

"You okay?

"Yeah, but I think I'll be payin' a little visit to that Ryan fella when I'm out of here."

"If you do, it'll be behind a sheet of Plexiglas." I adjusted his pillows. "The man's in custody—for assaulting you . . . and for killing James Noonan."

Under his scarlet moustache, Michael's lips tightened. "I still can't believe Jimmy's gone."

"I'm so sorry . . . he was a real hero, and his killer will pay. The charges against Lane are piling up. The DA's nailing him on Bigsby Brewer's death, and they're exhuming the body of Josie Fairfield's husband."

"Old man Fairfield?" The captain's one good eye squinted.

"Turns out Lane was originally trained as a pharmaceutical engineer. He whipped up some concoction that knocked James out long enough to fake the suicide, brought it to him in a bottle of wine. Apparently he used a higher dose of the stuff to murder Josie's husband. According to Josie, she and Ryan Lane had been sleeping together behind her husband's back. That's when Lane became obsessed with her. He wanted her for his own, so he killed her husband."

"The poor bastard . . ."

"But then Josie began losing interest in Lane and looking around for a new conquest—you were an oldie but goodie, Michael, and she decided she wanted to rekindle the old passion."

Michael grunted. "She was the only one . . ."

"Unfortunately, Ryan Lane had already decided to force Josie into 'retiring' with him. Given the roof spike fraud and embezzled millions, she looked as guilty as he did. Lane expected an even bigger payday in a few months when the sale of the company went through. He'd planned out his and Josie's getaway, their change of identities, their new life in South America. He'd even purchased an estate with a coffee farm."

"He must have known the roof spike would eventually fail . . ."

"I think he was counting on that. Just one more reason Josie could never return to her old life. But when Bigsby died, Lane knew his time was up. He probably could have gotten away with it—if the wheels of bureaucracy had ground as slowly as usual. But you and James messed that up, jeopardized everything. He killed James and tried to kill you to buy himself enough time to escape with Josie—and the millions he'd already stolen . . ."

I stopped talking when I realized Michael's attention had drifted.

"Noonan . . ." he whispered. "That lad's my last . . ."

"What do you mean?"

"Forget it." He shifted again. "Anyway, Clare, I want you to know . . . I'm not proud of the way I acted the other night. I owe you an apology."

"No, you don't."

"Yes, I do. And you're not the only one—"

The sound of a throat clearing stopped Michael's words. I turned to find a broad-shouldered detective leaning against the doorframe. It appeared he'd been listening a while.

Mike Quinn glanced briefly at his cousin. Then his arctic blue gaze locked onto me.

"Hi, Clare."

I couldn't find my voice.

"Sully gave me a ride over," Mike said. "Filled me in pretty good. Sorry about your car."

"I'm not."

Mike opened his arms and I went into them. When we were through embracing, I noticed Michael on the bed. Despite his pain—and for the first time since I'd arrived—the man was smiling.

Mike released me and approached his cousin. I held my breath, watching the two stare at each other.

Finally, Michael lifted his hand and held it there.

With a silent nod, Mike shook it.

ℰPILOGUE

ⓐⓞⓐⓞⓐⓞⓐⓞⓐⓞⓐⓞⓐⓞⓐⓞⓐⓞⓐⓞ

SIX weeks later, Madame and I were heading back over the Queensboro Bridge. This time, I'm happy to say, her art-dealer boyfriend, Otto Visser, was driving.

We were attending the opening of Osso Buco *Pronto!*—a nouvelle Italian restaurant. The location was Long Island City, but the event looked more like a gallery show in SoHo than the launch of an outer-borough eatery (even one with a Manhattan-esque ironic name). Oh, sure, there were trays of samples from the restaurant menu, and a brigade of food writers (online and print) were in attendance, but there were just as many members of the art world here, and for very good reason.

From our corner booth, Madame and I joined the applause when Lorenzo Testa appeared in a wheelchair pushed by his daughter. Grinning tearfully, he joined Dante Silva and the other young artists who had diligently worked to re-create his original mural. (For reference, they'd used blowups of the digital photos that Dante had shot just before Caffè Lucia burned.)

As Enzo rolled by to pose for the press, I caught sight of Lucia's impressive engagement ring, courtesy of Oat Crowley.

According to Madame, Enzo couldn't be happier that his daughter at last had chosen a man over a boy. (Of course, I didn't see that she had much choice, given the third point of that particular fire triangle—Glenn Duffy—was now facing twenty-five years to life.)

"What happened to your man Otto?" I asked Madame, after the restaurant's young chef-owner proposed a toast to Enzo. "I lost track of him . . ."

Madame pointed across the large, crowded space to a tall, dapper fellow, leanly built with thinning but still-golden hair. "He's over there, dear, explaining to that *New York Times* reporter how it took Dante and *six* of his friends an entire month to recreate what my old friend envisioned and painted by himself."

Madame drained her champagne flute and shot me a sly smile. "Of course, what Otto is really doing is laying the foundation for Enzo's public show this summer at his Chelsea gallery."

"Whatever works," I said (my new go-to catch phrase).

The paintings to be shown at the Otto Visser Gallery weren't new. Enzo was still weak and recovering from his stroke; it would take lots of time and therapy before he could paint again. What the world was going to see, for the first time, were the canvases Enzo had painted of his wife—a subject to which he'd lovingly devoted himself for decades. And though the artist himself remained reluctant to part with any of his creations, Enzo at least agreed to a public show, which wasn't bad publicity for Otto, either.

After a few rounds of Prosecco and trays of delightfully seasoned morsels, Madame found me again.

"So where is your noble knight this evening?"

"Another undercover operation," I said. "He phoned to tell me he's running late."

"The wheels of justice perpetually grind, don't they, dear? Well, if he doesn't make it, Otto and I will be happy to give you a lift home."

"Thanks. Matt made the same offer a little while ago—

in front of Breanne, unfortunately. I told them I'd take the subway."

"Well, he knows you don't have that little Honda anymore—"

"Yes and that's fine. I've decided to live without a car for a while. After crashing two of them in one day, I probably couldn't get affordable auto insurance, anyway."

As I sipped my sparkling wine, I noticed Tucker and Esther bantering (or bickering—who could tell?). They shared a booth with Kiki and Bahni, Dante's fawning apartment mates. The girls looked thrilled that their boy was finally getting some critical attention from the press. I was happy for Dante, too, but worried I was about to lose one of my best baristas to the fickle arms of the art world.

"Did you notice that sign across the street when we came in?" Madame asked. "It says the Pink Mirage is coming to Long Island City."

I nodded. "Dean Tassos isn't stupid. He closed the Red Mirage to relocate in this hotter area. Did I tell you that Valerie Noonan is working for him now?"

"That lovely girl from the bake sale?"

"Yes, she's overseeing the activities at all of Dean's catering halls . . ." My eye wandered back to another section of the astounding mural, one of Enzo's later editions to the sprawling piece. Madame noticed my interest.

"That particular image intrigues you, I see."

"Self-portraits always intrigue me." Enzo had painted himself into his mural, a stylized figure peering into a mirror. "But I suppose it's really two self-portraits, if you consider the mirror . . ."

"That's right . . ."

"And the face in the mirror has a different expression than the one looking in—impish, slightly mischievous. More like a dark doppelganger than a reflection."

"Yes, I see that . . . now that you mention it," Madame said, slipping on a delicate pair of glasses. She glanced at me. "So how is that fire captain?"

"The former captain, you mean. I hear he's very happy as a civilian now, up in Boston . . ."

At the urging of his little brother, Michael Quinn resigned from the FDNY and took a job consulting for the company where Kevin Quinn worked. (Now I knew what Michael meant when he'd told me James Noonan was his last. James was the last man he intended to lose under his command.)

Madame nodded. "Best for everyone, I think, that the man's not going to be tempted to drop by the Blend for your espressos . . ."

"I agree," I said. "And I'm sure Mike would, too."

A short time later, the party wound down and the dining room emptied. I was still alone. No call from Mike, no sign of him, either.

As the lights dimmed, Madame and Otto moved to the back of the restaurant to give their final farewells—and I spotted a familiar trench coat coming through the front.

"Hi, Clare."

"Hi, Mike."

"I'm sorry, sweetheart, I wanted to get here sooner, but . . ."

"That's all right," I said. "You're here now."

Mike sniffed the air, still aromatic with butter and lemon, rosemary and thyme, sizzling seafood and caramelized garlic.

"The party's over, right?" he said.

"Why?" I asked. "You hungry?"

"Starving." He held my eyes. "Feels like I haven't eaten all day."

"I can fix that."

He smiled. "I know you can."

Then Mike reached out his hand, fingers open. I placed mine in his and we found our way home.

AFTERWORD

∾ ୧ ᧗ ୧ ᧗ ୧ ᧗ ୧ ᧗ ୧ ᧗ ୧ ᧗ ୧ ᧗ ୧ ᧗ ୧ ᧗ ୧ ᧗ ୧ ᧗ ୧ ᧗ ୧

ALTHOUGH the firefighters of New York City use plenty of specialized equipment in the course of their hazardous and heroic work, including personal escape ropes, the spike device in this novel is not one of them. As mentioned in the acknowledgments, however, a very real incident did inspire the creation of this plotline.

On January 23, 2005 (a day known in the FDNY as "Black Sunday"), two members of the department lost their lives in the line of duty—and four more were very badly injured—because they did not have escape ropes. After that terrible day, the FDNY changed its policies and now provides high-heat resistant ropes to their firefighters.

This true, tragic incident left a lasting impression on me and my husband as we began to consider how the life and death of any firefighter may hinge on something as simple as possessing a single piece of reliable equipment.

Like the spike device we invented, the charity in this book is a fictional creation, but there is a very real firefighters' charity that I'm pleased to tell you about right now.

The Terry Farrell Firefighters Fund is a nonprofit organization dedicated to providing firefighters and their families with financial assistance for their educational, medical, and equipment needs. This charity was formed in honor of Terry Farrell, a decorated firefighter with FDNY Rescue 4 who perished on September 11, 2001, while fighting fires and rescuing victims at the World Trade Center.

Originally based in New York, this charity is currently expanding with chapters in other areas of the country. To find out more about the Terry Farrell Firefighters Fund, including how you can help simply by buying a specially labeled bottle of Jim Beam bourbon or purchasing a *California Firehouse Cookbook*, visit the fund's Web site at www .terryfarrellfund.org

RECIPES & TIPS
FROM THE VILLAGE BLEND

Visit Cleo Coyle's virtual Village Blend at
www.CoffeehouseMystery.com
for coffee tips, coffee talk, and the following *bonus* recipes:
* Crunchy-Sweet Italian Bow Tie Cookies
* St. Joseph's Day Zeppoles
* *Brutti Ma Buoni* ("Ugly but Good") Italian Cookies
* "Malfatti" (ravioli filling without the dough)
* Dutch Baby Pancake (Bismark)
* Honey-Glazed Peach Crostata with Ginger-Infused
Whipped Cream
* Mini Italian-Style Coffeehouse Cakes
(with Coffeehouse-Inspired Glazes)
* Pistachio Muffins
* "Stuck on You" Linzer Hearts
* Three-Alarm Buffalo Wings with
Extinguisher Gorgonzola Dip
* Puerto Rican-Style *Pernil* (Pork Shoulder)
And more . . .

GUIDE TO ROASTING COFFEE

∼◉◡◉◡◉◡◉◡◉◡◉◡◉◡◉◡◉◡◉◡◉◡◉◡◉∼

COFFEE roasting is the culinary art of applying heat to green coffee beans in order to develop their flavor before grinding and brewing. The entire process is highly complex, but this brief guide should give you a helpful overview—as well as something to consider the next time you sit down to enjoy a cup of joe.

Factors of flavor: According to food chemists, roasted coffee has one of the most complicated flavor profiles of all foods and beverages with over eight hundred substances contributing. Many factors influence the taste of the coffee you drink. Coffee beans grown in different microclimates of the world, for example, will display vastly different characteristics with flavors that may range from deep notes of chocolate to bright overtones of lemon.

Botany also plays a role. Coffee comes from a plant (genus *Coffea*) with ninety different species. Only two of those species (*Coffea arabica* and *Coffea robusta*) are primarily grown as cash crops, but different varietals (or cultivars) within those species are cultivated all over the world. Kona, Geisha, Blue Mountain, and Bourbon are just four examples of the many Arabica varietals.

Finally, the journey coffee takes from the seed to your cup will also influence its flavor. Let's begin our coffee trek with . . .

The coffee cherry: Your cup of joe begins its life as a seed or pit within the fruit or "cherry" on a coffee plant. (The coffee plant is often called a tree but is really a shrub.) The cherries on the coffee plant will ripen from green to yellow to red. They are then picked, either by hand or machine.

The coffee bean: Each coffee cherry contains two green coffee beans, which grow with their flat sides facing each other. The exception is the coffee cherry that contains a "peaberry," which is a single, rounded seed. (The peaberry is rarer and for a variety or reasons considered to be of better quality than regular coffee beans.) Once coffee is picked, it must be "processed" as soon as possible to prevent spoilage.

Processing: Most coffee drinkers never consider this unglamorous step in the seed-to-cup journey, but how coffee is processed can greatly affect its final flavor. Before the hard green coffee beans can be roasted (which will turn them brown), they must be extracted from the skin and pulp (or flesh) of the fruit surrounding them. This is usually done by a dry, wet, or semidry processing method.

Dry, natural, or unwashed processing: This method of processing coffee is the oldest and is still used in many countries where water resources are limited. After the cherries are picked, they are spread out to dry in the sun for several weeks. The outer layer of dried skin and pulp is then stripped away, usually by machine. This method is used in Ethiopia, Brazil, Haiti, Paraguay, India, and Ecuador. Because these beans are dried while still in contact with the coffee fruit, they tend to have more exotic flavor profiles than wet processed coffee. They often display more fruity or floral characteristics, for example, and are heavier in body.

Wet or washed processing: Special equipment and large quantities of water are needed to execute this processing method, which gradually strips away the layers of soft fruit that surround the hard coffee beans. The beans are then dried in the sun or machine dried in large tumblers. This processing method, used in major Latin American coffee-growing countries (except Brazil), produces more consistent, cleaner, and brighter flavored coffees than the dry method.

Semidry or pulped processing: This method is a kind of combo of both. Water is used to remove the skin of the fruit but not the pulp (or flesh), which is left on and allowed to dry on the bean. After it is dried, the pulp is removed by machine. This method, which is used in Brazil and (a variation of it) in Indonesia, produces coffee that has the fruity and floral notes of dry processing with the clarity of wet processing.

Home roasting: After green coffee is fully processed, it is ready for roasting. Until the early twentieth century, coffee was primarily roasted in the home, over fires or on stoves, using pans or a hand-turned drum appliance. In the eighteenth, nineteenth, and early twentieth centuries, stores and cafés also used small "shop roasters" (also called microroasters) to roast fresh coffee for their customers.

As the twentieth century progressed, however, coffee roasting became a major commercial endeavor. Preground, packaged coffee roasted in factories overwhelmed the market. Home roasting disappeared along with most small shop roasters until late in the twentieth century when coffee drinkers rediscovered the superior quality of freshly roasted coffee. Now the United States and other industrialized countries are enjoying a Renaissance of "small batch" or "boutique" roasting.

These days, a variety of small appliances are available that allow you to roast your own green coffee at home. To learn more, visit the Sweet Maria Web site, which sells home roasting equipment, green beans, and includes information for the home roasting enthusiast: www.sweetmarias.com. Kenneth Davids's excellent book *Home Coffee Roasting* is another great resource.

Roasting Stages

Given all of the factors that can influence a coffee's flavor, roasting has the greatest impact. As Clare well knew from her Village Blend roasting room, "The right kiss of heat would bring out the absolute best flavors in these green beans—and the wrong would destroy them forever."

The roasting itself goes relatively quickly, 11 to 18 minutes. Here is a short list of very basic steps that should give you a general overview of a typical *small-batch* roasting process.

Stage 1—Raw Green Coffee: The green, grassy-smelling beans are released from the roaster's hopper into its large drum. The drum continually turns the beans to keep them from scorching. As the beans dry and cook, they start to turn yellow to yellow-orange in color and give off aromas like toasted bread, popcorn, or buttery vegetables.

Stage 2—Light, Cinnamon, New England–Style: As they continue to roast, sugars start to caramelize and the beans begin to smell more like roasting coffee. At around 400°F, the small, hard green bean doubles in size, becomes a light brown color, and gives off a popping or cracking sound, which is why this stage is called "the first crack" stage. What the master roaster is seeing now is the change in the chemical composition of the bean. (The process is called *pyrolysis* and it includes a release of carbon dioxide.) The acidity or "bright" notes in this coffee will be powerful, and its unique characteristics (based on the origin and processing of the beans) will be pronounced, but the body will be pretty thin. The surface of the light brown bean will be dry because the flavor oils are still inside.

Stage 3—Light-Medium, American Style: The temperature rises to about 415°F and the color of the bean changes from light brown to medium brown. The acidity or "bright" notes are still there but not as strong. The characteristics of the varietals will still be pronounced but the body will be fuller. For residents of the East Coast of America, this is the traditional roasting style.

Stage 4—Medium, City: The temperature rises from 415° to 435°F and the color of the bean is a slightly darker medium brown. The subtle flavor notes in the varietals are not as strong but still quite clear, the acidity or "brightness" is still present, and the body is even fuller. This is the traditional style for the American West.

Stage 5—Dark-Medium, Full City, Viennese Style: Now we are moving toward "the second crack" stage (this stage sounds less like corn popping and more like paper crinkling). This second *pyrolysis* usually happens between 435° and 445° F, the roast color is dark medium brown, and the beans begin to take on a slick sheen as the roasting "sweats out" the oils. The smell in the air is sweeter, the body of this coffee is heavier, the acidity or "brightness" more subdued. Coffees with more pronounced characteristics (such as Kenyan) will retain their strong flavor notes, but those with subtler notes will be lost to the increasing caramelized "dark roast" flavor of the process. Coffee drinkers in the Pacific Northwest, including northern California, traditionally enjoy this style of roast.

Stage 6—Dark, Darker, Darkest: Continuing to roast from this point will yield increasingly darker styles of roasted coffee. (See the basic styles and temperatures below.) Sugars continue to caramelize and more oils will be forced to the surface. The roasting smells turn from sweeter to more pungent and finally smoky. Pushed to the limit, beans will turn very dark and shiny, taking on intense flavors before they become completely black, charred, and worthless.

  * Espresso, European Style: (445° to 455°F) This style of roast displays a moderately dark-roast flavor.

* French, Italian: (455° to 465°F) This style has more of a bittersweet dark-roast taste. While too pungent for some coffee drinkers, these roasts will stand up to mixing with milk and other flavorings to create coffee drinks.

* Dark French, Spanish: (465° to 475°F) The more bitter side of the "bittersweet" flavor is displayed here. A smoky taste may also be present. As the beans continue to roast, charred notes will begin to appear, and regardless of their origin all beans will begin to taste about the same.

Stage 7—Cooling: The master roaster will monitor this process by temperature gauges but also by sound (crack or pop), smell, and sight (bean color). When the desired roast style is achieved, the process is stopped by the release of the beans from the heated drum. The still-crackling beans fall into a cooling tray where fans and stirring paddles quickly bring down their temperature. When completely cooled, they are ready for grinding, brewing, and (finally!) drinking.

Recipes

∞∞∞∞∞∞∞∞∞∞∞∞∞∞∞∞∞∞∞∞∞∞∞

With a contented stomach, your heart is forgiving;
with an empty stomach, you forgive nothing.
—Italian proverb

Eat with joy!
—Cleo Coyle

Madame's Osso Buco

See photos of this recipe at www.CoffeehouseMystery.com

Osso Buco (or ossobuco*) is an elegant and beloved Italian dish of veal shank braised in wine and herbs. The shank is cut across the bone to a thickness of roughly 3 inches, browned, and then braised. Braising is a very slow cooking process, but preparing the dish itself is relatively simple, and the results pay off with rich, borderline orgasmic flavor. This is the recipe Madame shared with Diggy-Dog Dare in the Elmhurst ER. It was taught to her by Antonio Allegro, her first husband and Matt's late father.*

Makes 3–4 servings

3–4 veal shank crosscuts, about 3 inches thick (see your butcher)
½ teaspoon sea salt
½ teaspoon freshly ground black pepper
½ cup all-purpose flour
3 tablespoons olive oil
1 large yellow onion, diced
1 large carrot, diced
4 celery stalks (hearts), sliced
4 garlic cloves, minced
1 cup dry white wine (such as Pinot Grigio)
1–2 cups chicken or veal stock (see note)
1 tablespoon minced fresh rosemary
1 teaspoon minced fresh thyme
Gremolata (a simple garnish; recipe follows)

Step 1—Brown the shanks: Preheat oven to 350° F. Season shanks with salt and pepper, then dredge in flour and set aside. Heat the olive oil in a Dutch oven over medium-high heat until the oil is rippling but not smoking. Place the veal in the hot oil and sear the shanks on both sides, turning once (about 4–5 minutes per side). Remove veal from oil and set aside.

Step 2—Prepare the aromatics: Drain most of the fat and oil from the Dutch oven, leaving just enough to cover the bottom. Add the onion and cook for 6 minutes, until brown. Add the carrot, stirring occasionally, about 3 minutes. Add the celery and garlic, stirring frequently, until they release their flavor and become aromatic, about 2 minutes. (Do not dump everything in at once, the order is important for the best flavor results.)

Step 3—Deglaze and prep the broth: Add the wine to the pan, stirring to incorporate all the ingredients. Simmer for 4–5 minutes, until the wine is reduced by half. Return the veal shanks to the pan, along with all the juice it may have released while sitting. Add enough chicken or veal stock (about 1 to 2 cups) to cover the shanks about two thirds of the way.

Step 4—Simmer and braise the meat: Over a low heat, bring the pot to a gentle simmer, then cover and transfer to hot oven. Braise for 2 hours, turning occasionally. Then add rosemary and thyme, and braise for one more hour, removing the lid during the last 15–20 minutes to cook off excess liquid.

Step 5—Make gravy and garnish: Remove veal shanks. Keep warm and moist before serving by placing in a covered serving dish. Meanwhile, place the Dutch oven on the stovetop again and simmer the cooking liquid over high heat for 5–8 minutes, adding salt and pepper to taste. Now you're ready to serve! Plate your veal shanks, pour a bit of the hot gravy over each shank, and garnish with Gremolata. Eat immediately—you've waited long enough!

GREMOLATA:

Combine 2 tablespoons of finely chopped fresh Italian (flat-leaf) parsley, 1 minced garlic clove, and 1 teaspoon lemon zest (grated lemon peel).

Madame's Note on Veal Stock: If purchasing your veal shanks from a butcher, ask for the top of the shank, which is mostly bone (this is usually discarded) and use it to make your own veal stock. Making stock is a snap. Simply simmer these extra bones in 4 cups of water. Throw in any of your favorite aromatics (1 tablespoon of fresh thyme, rosemary, and parsley, for example), add a bay leaf, a chopped onion, a celery stalk or two, salt and pepper. Simmer for an hour, strain out the liquid, and there is your stock!

Clare Cosi's Jim Beam Bourbon Steak

This outrageous blend of earthy beef with "spirited" brightness makes for a superb gastronomic experience. To help firefighters, Clare happily recommends purchasing a bottle of Jim Beam bourbon with the Terry Farrell Firefighters Fund label. To see what this inspiring label looks like, visit the following Web site, where you can also learn more about the fund, named after one of the fallen heroes of 9/11: www.jimbeam.com/partnerships/terry-farrell-fund

Makes 2 servings

⅓ cup aged bourbon (Jim Beam in the Terry Farrell bottle!)
¼ cup cold strong coffee or espresso
4 tablespoons sesame oil
3 tablespoons Worcestershire sauce
1 teaspoon freshly ground black pepper
2 T-bone, rib-eye, or shell steaks (2–3 pounds total)

Whisk together the bourbon, coffee, oil, Worcestershire sauce, and pepper and pour into a shallow dish or pan that is large enough to hold 2 steaks flat (single layer, no overlapping). Cover the dish, pan, or container with plastic wrap, and marinate the meat for 1 hour in the refrigerator, then flip and marinate for a second hour. Sauté the steaks in a large cast-iron skillet over medium-high heat, about 5 minutes per side for medium rare, or 7–8 minutes per side for medium well. You can also broil or grill them. Eat with joy!

Clare Cosi's Crab Cakes

There are two keys to good crab cakes: (1) keep the binders to a minimum so you can taste the meat, and (2) form the cakes a few hours before cooking so they can be chilled in the fridge, which will help them stay together during the cooking process. As for the meat, fresh lump crab meat from blue crabs will give you an authentic Maryland-style cake. But if you can't get fresh, a good quality canned will certainly work, too. Clare likes to brush the chilled cakes with a beaten egg just before final breading and frying. This is certainly more of an Italian-style method of frying seafood than a traditional Maryland-style, but Clare believes this step adds a delicate layer of flavor while helping to keep the cakes together during cooking. For an accompaniment to this dish, try Clare's Thai-Style Seafood Sauce (page 330) and her Sweet and Tangy Thai-Style Coleslaw (page 331).

Makes 8 crab cakes

5 eggs
1 cup unseasoned bread crumbs (not panko)
½ cup freshly squeezed lemon juice (from about 2 lemons)
½ cup scallions, chopped (white and green parts)
1 teaspoon dry, ground, or powdered mustard (all are the same!)
½ teaspoon Worcestershire sauce
½ teaspoon sea salt
½ teaspoon freshly ground white or black pepper
1 pound Maryland blue crabmeat
(or canned backfin or jumbo lump)
1 cup peanut or canola oil
½ cup panko (Japanese bread crumbs for coating)

Step 1—Mix the crabmeat: Lightly beat 4 of the eggs in a mixing bowl, add the unseasoned bread crumbs, lemon juice, scallions, dry mustard, Worcestershire sauce, salt, and pepper. Mix thoroughly. Separate and flake the crabmeat. If the meat is fresh, make sure you pick through it carefully and remove any shell fragments. Add the crabmeat to your egg mixture and blend thoroughly.

Step 2—Shape into cakes: Shape the crab mixture into 8 equal-sized balls, pat into cakes. Refrigerate uncooked crab cakes between two loose sheets of waxed paper for about 2 hours or up to 8. (The longer they chill, the easier they will be to handle.)

Step 3—Finish with egg wash and breading: Heat the oil in a large frying pan over medium heat. Lightly beat the remaining egg in a small bowl. Remove the crabcakes from the fridge and lightly brush each one with the egg wash. Gently roll each cake lightly in the panko bread crumbs. Do this quickly so they do not lose their chill, and do it carefully so they do not fall apart.

Step 4—Fry the cakes: Gently set each crabcake into the hot oil and cook until golden brown on both sides, about 4 to 5 minutes per side. Turn with care, only once or twice during cooking. Serve with Clare's Thai-Style Seafood Sauce on the side (recipe follows) or your favorite condiments or relishes.

Clare's Thai-Style Seafood Sauce

Makes about 1 cup

1 cup mayonnaise
2 tablespoons Clare's Thai Dipping Sauce (recipe on page 331)

In a small bowl, combine mayonnaise and Clare's Thai Dipping Sauce. Chill and serve with seafood. This is an especially good sauce to serve with boiled shrimp (in place of cocktail sauce). It's also delicious with Clare's Crab Cakes (see previous recipe).

Clare's Sweet and Tangy Thai-Style Coleslaw

Makes about 1 cup

½ medium to large head green cabbage, shredded (about 10 cups)
1 large carrot, peeled into strips (about ½ cup)
½ cup mayonnaise
3 tablespoons Clare's Thai Dipping Sauce, or to taste (recipe follows)
Salt, to taste (optional)

Place shredded cabbage and carrot peels in a large mixing bowl. In a separate bowl, mix the mayonnaise and dipping sauce. Fold the mayonnaise mixture into the bowl of shredded cabbage and blend well. Season with salt to taste. Chill and serve.

Clare's Thai-Style Dipping Sauce

This is the traditional recipe used as a dipping sauce for Thai spring rolls, but this tangy, sweet, and hot sauce is also great on salads, barbecued meats, or vegetable tempura.

Makes about 1 cup

1 cup confectioners' sugar
½ cup water
½ cup white vinegar
3 tablespoons finely chopped garlic (about 9 or 10 cloves)

2 tablespoons Thai fish sauce (or one mashed anchovy fillet or
¼ teaspoon anchovy paste)
2 teaspoons sambal oelek—Indonesian hot chile sauce
(or add more to increase heat)
2 tablespoons lime juice
2 tablespoons finely grated or shredded carrots

Step 1—Combine the sugar, water, and vinegar in a small saucepan. Bring to boil and continue boiling for 5 minutes.

Step 2—Reduce the heat to simmer and stir in the garlic, fish sauce, and *sambal oelek*. Simmer for 2–3 more minutes, remove from heat, and cool.

Step 3—When room temperature, stir in the lime juice and carrots. Store by refrigerating in a plastic container.

Clare Cosi's Korean-Style Sweet and Sticky Soy-Garlic Chicken Wings

An emerging foodie trend these days in New York City is the enjoyment of Korean fried chicken (Yangnyeom Dak), *which landed on the U.S. East Coast circa 2007 and began to spread. In Korea, this dish is prepared from whole chickens cut up into bite-sized bits, which are then fried for crispy consumption in karaoke bars and pubs with beer or* soju. *Here in America, Korean fried chicken is prepared with wings or drumsticks, seldom the whole chicken.*

Clare has created a very simple version of Korean fried chicken for the American kitchen, using a technique she honed making Buffalo chicken wings. (You can find Clare's recipe for Buffalo wings at www.coffeehousemysteries.com.) The creation of the glaze came out of Clare's long experience of making homemade syrups for her coffeehouse drinks. (See the Recipes & Tips section of my eighth

Coffeehouse Mystery, Holiday Grind, *for an array of homemade coffeehouse syrup recipes.)*

If you're feeling adventurous (gastronomically speaking) and would like to seek out the authentic Korean ingredients for which Clare has created substitutions, then follow the instructions at the end of the recipe. But remember, the secret to Korean fried chicken is its crunchy crispness, created by the double-frying process. For delicious complements to this dish, try Sweet and Tangy Thai-Style Coleslaw, page 331, or a pile of sweet potato fries.

Makes 24 pieces

10–12 chicken wings, cut into thirds, discarding tips
½ cup all-purpose flour
⅔ cup cornstarch
Salt and pepper, to taste
2 cups water
1 ⅓ cups dark brown sugar, packed
½ cup ketchup
½ cup soy sauce
1 tablespoon Worcestershire sauce
4–6 garlic cloves, minced
Oil, for frying (peanut, canola, or vegetable)

Step 1—Prepare the chicken: Cut the wings into three pieces at the joints and discard the tips (or save and use for making chicken stock). Combine the flour, cornstarch, and salt and pepper in a bowl. Dredge chicken pieces through the mix, coating thoroughly.

Step 2—Make the glaze: Place the water and sugar in a medium saucepan and bring to a boil over medium-high heat. Add ketchup and whisk until the ingredients are blended. Simmer for 15–20 minutes. Mixture should thicken. Finally, add soy sauce, Worcestershire sauce, and garlic and simmer for another 3–5 minutes.

Step 3—Double fry the chicken: In a large skillet, heat the oil until rippling (or until a droplet of water bounces along the surface. In an electric skillet, the oil should be about 350° F). Gently add the wing pieces and cook for 7–9 minutes, turning once. Remove chicken from oil and let cool on a rack for 10 minutes. (Make sure the chicken dries in a single layer—using the rack lets the air circulate around each wing.) Fry a second time for an additional 7–9 minutes, until golden brown and very crisp.

Step 4—Coat the chicken: Drain the refried chicken on a rack over paper towels for a few minutes. Place the prepared glaze in a clean skillet and warm over a low heat. When the glaze begins to bubble, roll the chicken pieces in the mixture until the chicken wings are thoroughly coated.

Note: Right after cooking, the chicken will be delightfully sticky. If you prefer a drier glaze, simply place the wings in a single layer on a foil-covered sheet pan and warm in a preheated 350° F oven for 8–10 minutes.

Authentic Korean Flavor: This recipe is a good copycat of the soy-garlic wings served at the UFC Korean fried chicken stores in New York City. If you're after an even more authentic Korean flavor, substitute 1 tablespoon *myulchi aecjeot* (Korean anchovy sauce) for the tablespoon of Worcestershire sauce. And use Korean brand dark soy sauce.

James Noonan's Firehouse Sweet Onion and Cheddar Bake

This is the recipe that Clare noticed James Noonan cooking in his firehouse kitchen. (She suggested he add a bit of cayenne to kick up the flavor, which you certainly can, too, if you like.)

While Georgia's trademark Vidalia onions are the classic onion to use in this recipe, any sweet onion will work just fine. A sweet onion contains less sulfur and more sugar and water than other onions so it's milder and gentler on the palate. Sweet onions are grown in many places other than the state of Georgia, including Texas (Texas Sweets), California (Imperial), Washington/ Oregon (Walla Walla, by way of seeds from Italy), and Chile/ South America (OsoSweet). One last note from James's recipe file: Caramelized Bacon Bits (page 336) make an outrageously good added topping for this dish, as well as for his Triple-Threat Firehouse Penne Mac 'n' Cheese (page 337).

Makes 6 servings (fills a 2-quart casserole dish)

6 tablespoons butter
5 large sweet onions, thinly sliced
2 tablespoons Wondra flour (see note)
1 tablespoon ground, dry, or powdered mustard
(all three are the same!)
1 cup whole milk
1 cup mild cheddar cheese, grated, plus extra for topping
⅔ cup bread crumbs, plus extra for topping
1 cup Caramelized Bacon Bits (page 336), optional

Step 1—Sauté the onions: Preheat oven to 375° F. Melt 3 tablespoons of the butter in a large shallow pan. Toss in the onions and sauté. When they appear soft and translucent (but not brown), remove the onions from the heat. (This will take roughly 8–10 minutes.)

Step 2—Make an easy cheese sauce: In a small saucepan, melt the remaining 3 tablespoons of butter. Stir in the Wondra flour and mustard. Slowly stir in the milk, *then* add the cheese. (Note: Do not add these two ingredients together—first the milk, then the cheese!). Simmer for 1–2 minutes. When the sauce thickens, it's ready to use. Remove from heat.

Step 3—Assemble and bake: In a 2- or 3-quart casserole or baking dish, layer the onions, cheese sauce, and bread crumbs. (The bread crumbs will help absorb excess moisture released from the onions during baking.) After the final layer of cheese sauce, sprinkle some extra cheese and bread crumbs on top. Bake 30–45 minutes. If using Caramelized Bacon Bits, sprinkle over the top of the casserole before serving.

Clare's Onion Storage Tip: Sweet onions will keep for 4–6 weeks. Because sweet onions will absorb water, don't store them next to potatoes. Store whole, uncut sweet onions in the refrigerator. Place them in a single layer on paper towels in your vegetable bin. For longer storage, wrap them in foil before placing in fridge. To store a cut onion, wrap tightly in plastic and place in fridge.

Clare's Note on Wondra Flour: If you've never used Wondra flour, look for its blue cardboard canister in the same grocery store aisle that shelves all-purpose flour. It's a handy little helper for thickening gravies and making quick sauces. You can make an easy white sauce with it, too. The recipe is right on the side of its cardboard container.

Caramelized Bacon Bits

These bits of carmelized bacon make a delicious salty-sweet topping for cheesy casseroles. (No kidding. They're a perfect complement for mac 'n' cheese.) Just spread them across the top of the warm casserole before serving or present them on the side to your guests for do-it-yourself sprinkling.

Makes about 1 cup

1 pound bacon (regular cut, not thick), cut into small bite-size pieces
½ cup dark brown sugar, packed

Step 1—Slice and sauté: On medium-high heat, sauté the bacon bits in a large skillet, stirring often, until half cooked (still soft and flexible with fat just beginning to change color). Drain the rendered fat from pan.

Step 2—Caramelize: Reduce the heat to medium. Add the brown sugar to the pan and stir until dissolved. Continue cooking and stirring until the bacon crisps up. Remove from heat. Drain and cool in a single layer on a sheet pan or another clean, flat surface. (Do not dry bacon bits on paper towels or they will stick! Use paper towels only to dab away the excess grease.) The longer you allow the bacon to cool and dry, the crisper it will become.

James Noonan's Triple-Threat Firehouse Penne Mac 'n' Cheese

This is the best recipe for macaroni and cheese I've ever tasted. It's a "triple threat" of cheeses that work together in delectable harmony to serenade your palate. And forget the typical elbow macaroni, which simply does not hold a candle to the penne macaroni. When cooked to an al dente texture, the larger penne pasta allows this chewy, cheesy casserole to linger on your taste buds that much longer. This one's an absolute joy to eat.

Makes 8 servings (fills a 3-quart casserole dish)

1 pound dry penne macaroni
2 cups grated sharp cheddar cheese
1 cup grated Monterey Jack cheese
1 cup grated queso blanco or mild cheddar, grated
5⅓ tablespoons butter
1 teaspoon salt
1 teaspoon black pepper

¼ cup all purpose flour
1 teaspoon Worcestershire sauce
2 cups whole milk
Caramelized Bacon Bits (page 336), optional

Step 1—Cook the penne pasta: First, preheat the oven to 375° F. Coat a 3-quart, ovenproof casserole dish (or Dutch oven) with cooking spray. Cook the penne according to directions on the pasta package; do not overcook. You want the penne al dente (still chewy, not soft). Drain the penne well, removing all water, and pour into the casserole dish.

Step 2—Make the cheese sauce: Mix the three cheeses together in a large bowl and set aside. Melt the butter over low heat, in a large saucepan. When butter is completely melted, remove the pan from heat. (Note: To prevent the cheese sauce from breaking on you, make absolutely sure you *remove* the pan from heat before adding these next ingredients!) Stir in the salt, pepper, flour, and the Worcestershire sauce until smooth. Gradually add in the milk. Now return the pan to the stove. Stir constantly over medium heat until the mixture comes to a boil, then reduce heat and simmer until thickened. Add in half of the cheese a little at a time, stirring with each addition.

Step 3—Assemble and bake: After the cheese sauce is warm and well blended, pour it over the macaroni. (Note: Do not mix in the cheese sauce! Just pour it over the top. The sauce will slowly ooze down during cooking. If you mix it in at this stage, too much of the cheese sauce will end up on the bottom of the dish instead of throughout.) Cover with the remaining half of the cheese. Bake for 20–25 minutes. If using Caramelized Bacon Bits, sprinkle them across the top of the casserole just before serving.

James Noonan's Firehouse
Non–Beer Batter Onion Rings

Beer is often added to onion ring batter for flavor, lightness, and crispness. But if you're not a fan of beer (like James Noonan) and still want your rings light and crisp, there are two things you can do: (1) use cake flour because it has a lower gluten content, which makes for a crispier fry batter, and (2) substitute cold carbonated water for beer. You'll get all the lightness of the bubbles without the taste of hops.

Makes 4 servings

2 large Vidalia onions (or another sweet onion),
cut into ¼-inch-thick rings
1 ¼ cups cake flour
(¼ cup for dusting; 1 for the batter—be sure it's cake flour!)
¼ teaspoon cayenne pepper
½ teaspoon baking powder
½ teaspoon garlic salt
Vegetable, peanut, or canola oil (enough for deep frying)
6–8 ounces cold seltzer, club soda, or carbonated water
(be sure it's cold!)

Step 1—Prepare onions: Toss the raw onion rings in ¼ cup of the cake flour and set aside.

Step 2—Mix dry batter ingredients: Note: For best results, do not make the batter in advance. Finish the batter just before you are ready to fry the onion rings. In a large bowl, mix 1 cup of the cake flour, cayenne pepper, baking powder, and garlic salt. Heat the oil to 350° F. Only when the oil is hot and ready for frying should you move to the next step and finish the batter.

Step 3—Finish the batter and fry: Add enough *cold* carbonated water to the dry ingredients to make a loose batter. Coat your onion rings and cook at once. Fry until golden brown, 2–3 minutes. Serve hot!

Clare Cosi's Doughnut Muffins

Tender and sweet, these muffins taste like an old-fashioned cake doughnut, the kind you'd order at a diner counter with a hot, fresh cuppa joe.

Makes 12 muffins

For the batter:

> 12 tablespoons unsalted butter
> 1 cup granulated sugar
> 2 large eggs, lightly beaten with fork
> 1 cup whole milk
> 2½ cups all-purpose flour
> 2½ teaspoons baking powder
> ¼ teaspoon baking soda
> ¼ teaspoon salt
> ½ teaspoon ground nutmeg

For the cinnamon topping:

> ½ cup granulated sugar
> 1 teaspoon ground cinnamon
> 2 tablespoons butter, melted

Step 1—Prepare the batter: Preheat the oven to 350° F. Using an electric mixer, cream the butter and sugar until fluffy. Add in the eggs and milk and continue mixing. Stop the mixer. Sift in the flour, baking powder, baking soda, salt, and nutmeg, and mix only enough to combine ingredients. Do not overmix at this stage or you will produce gluten in the batter and toughen the muffins.

Step 2—Bake: Line cups in muffin pan with paper holders. Fill each up to the top (you can even mound it a little higher). Bake for 15–25 minutes, or until the muffins are lightly brown and a toothpick inserted comes out clean. Remove muffins quickly from pan and cool on a wire rack. (Muffins that remain in a hot pan may end up steaming, and the bottoms may become tough.)

Step 3—Prepare the topping: Mix together the sugar and cinnamon to create the cinnamon topping. Brush the tops of the warm muffins with the melted butter and dust with the cinnamon topping.

Clare Cosi's Jelly Doughnut Muffins

Clare brought this "jelly doughnut" version of her famous muffins to the Five-Borough Bake Sale. Detective Franco is still waiting for her to make him a plain old American jelly doughnut. He'll have to wait a little longer.

Makes 12 muffins

> 1 recipe Doughnut Muffin batter (page 340)
> ¼ cup raspberry jelly or jam
> 2 tablespoons butter, melted
> ½ cup confectioners' sugar, for dusting

Step 1—Line cups in a muffin pan with paper holders. Fill each cup halfway with the Doughnut Muffin batter. Poke a hole into the thick batter and spoon in 1 teaspoon of raspberry jelly. Top with remaining batter (filling cup about two-thirds full).

Step 2—Bake for 15–25 minutes, or until the muffins are lightly brown. Remove muffins quickly from pan and cool on a wire rack. (Muffins that remain in a hot pan may end up steaming, and the bottoms may become tough.)

Step 3—Brush the tops of the muffins with the melted butter and dust with the sugar.

Clare Cosi's Magnificent Melt-in-Your-Mouth Mocha Brownies

When Clare needs a quick chocolate fix, this is her go-to recipe. She whipped up a pan of these babies after she realized Mike Quinn had played her the previous night by keeping his secrets. On the subject of pastry chef secrets: one way to deepen the rich flavor of chocolate in any recipe is to add coffee. And the trick to keeping these brownies magnificent is (1) allow melted chocolate to cool before adding to the batter, (2) do not over bake. With this recipe, undercooking is better than overcooking. And (3) allow pan of brownies to cool completely before cutting. These moist and tender brownies will drench your taste buds with chocolate flavor, but they need time to cool and harden before they can be cut into bar cookies. (While still warm, these brownies do make an amazing dessert and can be served on a plate with ice cream or whipped cream. Otherwise, give them at least 1 hour out of the oven before cutting.)

Makes one 9-inch square pan of brownies (about 16 bars)

Cooking spray
1 cup good quality semi-sweet chocolate, chopped (or chips)

16 tablespoons (2 sticks) unsalted butter
¾ cup light brown sugar
¾ cup granulated white sugar
2 teaspoons pure vanilla extract
2 teaspoons instant coffee crystals (or 1½ teaspoons instant espresso powder) dissolved into 1 tablespoon hot tap water
3 large eggs
1¼ cups all-purpose flour (measure after sifting)
¼ cup unsweetened cocoa powder, sifted
1 teaspoon baking powder
½ teaspoon salt

Step 1—Melt chocolate and butter: Preheat your oven to 350° F and prepare a 9-inch square pan by spraying bottom and sides with cooking spray (or buttering and lightly dusting with cocoa powder). Melt the chocolate and 4 tablespoons of the butter in a microwave safe bowl. (See note at end of recipe on melting chocolate.) Allow to cool as you make the batter.

Step 2—Create batter: Using an electric mixer, cream the two sugars with your remaining 12 tablespoons of butter until light and fluffy. Blend in vanilla extract, coffee, eggs, and cooled melted chocolate from Step 1. After wet ingredients are blended, add in flour, cocoa powder, baking powder, and salt. (Blend well but do not overmix or you will produce gluten in the flour and toughen the batter.)

Step 3—Bake and cool: Spread the batter into your prepared 9-inch square pan. Bake at 350° F for 30 minutes. Do not over bake these beauties. When are they done? As the batter cooks, you will see the top form a crust and begin to show traditional cracking. Gently shake the pan. If the center appears to jiggle a bit, the brownies are still underdone. Continue cooking five minutes at a time until baked batter feels solid when pan is gently shaken. You can also insert a toothpick into the very center of pan. If batter appears on toothpick, continue cooking and checking. Cool pan on a rack to allow air to properly circulate beneath the hot pan bottom. Do not cut brownies before they are completely cool or they may break apart on you. You can always enjoy still-warm brownie squares on a plate with ice cream or whipped cream. Otherwise, simply wait until cool to the touch (about 1 hour), then cut into bars and eat with joy!

Clare's Note on Melting Chocolate: (1) Make sure bowl and stirring utensils are completely dry. Even a few drops of water can make chocolate seize up. (2) Chocolate burns easily so never heat chocolate until you see it turn completely liquid. Heat in microwave only 15 to 20 seconds to soften. Then remove and stir. Reheat if necessary for 10 seconds at a time and stir again until completely melted. (3) If you do not have a microwave, use a double boiler or create one by placing a dry, heatproof bowl over a saucepan of simmering water. Place chocolate in the bowl or top of double boiler and stir until melted.

Poor Girl's Crème Brûlée

What makes this a "poor girl's" crème brûlée? The lack of a pricey kitchen torch to caramelize the sugar. Clare suggests you do what French housewives have done for years: use the oven broiler. The caramelized crust that forms on top of the dessert will not have the hard shell-like texture that comes from using a professional kitchen torch (or even an industrial model à la the firefighter's bake sale), but the taste of the crunchy, warm sugar atop the creamy silk of the egg custard will be sinfully satisfying. This recipe calls for 6 egg yolks, but do not discard the whites: you can use them to make Nonna's Brutti Ma Buoni *("Ugly but Good") Italian Cookies. (See the recipe at www.CoffeehouseMystery.com.)*

Makes 4 to 8 servings (depending on ramekin size)

6 large egg yolks
⅔ cup confectioners' sugar
1⅓ cups whole milk
1⅓ cups light cream
2 teaspoons pure vanilla extract
For topping: ⅓ cup turbinado sugar or "sugar in the raw" (Do not
substitute granulated white sugar. If you can't find raw sugar, use light
brown sugar.)

Step 1—Make the custard: Preheat oven to 300° F. Using an electric mixer, beat the egg yolks with the sugar until smooth. Mix in the milk, cream, and vanilla. Pour the mixture evenly into four individual 7–8-ounce size ramekins (or eight 4-ounce size ramekins). Set ramekins in a shallow roasting or baking pan and create a water bath by pouring water into the pan until it reaches halfway up the outside of the ramekins.

Step 2—Bake the custard: Bake until set, about 1 hour. Cooking time may be longer or shorter based on your oven and the size of your ramekins. So when is it done? You are looking for the top to set. The custard may still jiggle slightly, but the top should no longer be liquid. It should feel firm (spongy but set) when lightly touched, and when a toothpick or skewer is inserted down into the custard at the edge of the cup, it should come out clean. Otherwise, keep baking and checking.

Step 3—Chill it, baby: Remove from oven and cool to room temperature. Cover each ramekin tightly with plastic wrap and chill completely in fridge for 4 hours or overnight. (Note: Covering with plastic will keep a skin from forming, but be sure to allow the custard to cool completely before covering.)

Step 4—Caramelize the top: Okay, here's the "poor girl" part. If you do not have a kitchen torch to caramelize the sugar, then take Clare's advice. Before serving, sprinkle turbinado sugar over the top, set ramekins in a shallow pan filled with ice (to keep custard cool), and place under your oven broiler for a few minutes to caramelize. Check often. Do not let sugar burn. Serve immediately. (Note: If substituting light brown sugar, re-chill in fridge to harden top.)

Clare Cosi's Blueberries 'N' Cream Coffee Cake Pie

See photos of this recipe at www.CoffeehouseMystery.com

Mix, pour, bake, eat. Given the flour and eggs on the ingredient list, this supremely easy batter filling gives you a unique cross between a dense coffee cake and a fruit pie. Blueberries are truly the star of this confection, and their fresh, sweet, slightly tart flavor bursts brightly in your mouth with every delicious bite (and it's just as good, if not better, right out of the refrigerator the next day).

Makes one 8- or 9-inch pie

2 pints fresh blueberries
1 ¼ cups all-purpose flour
1 cup granulated sugar
⅛ teaspoon salt
⅔ cup half-and-half
2 large eggs
1 teaspoon cinnamon
1 Clare's Cinnamon Graham Cracker Crust (recipe follows) or
prebaked 8- or 9-inch graham cracker or shortbread crust

Step 1—Toss blueberries with flour: Rinse and dry your blueberries. Toss with 2 tablespoons of the flour. (You are coating the berries with flour to soak up excess liquid during baking.)

Step 2—Make batter: Preheat oven to 375° F. Using a simple hand whisk, gently blend the flour, sugar, salt, half-and-half, eggs, and cinnamon. Do not overmix or you'll toughen the batter. Carefully fold in the flour-tossed blueberries. (You are not crushing the berries, just gently folding.)

Step 3–Bake: Pour the batter into your pie shell. If using an 8-inch crust, there may be a bit too much batter, that's okay, just hold it back. (See my crust tips below.) Bake about 1 hour. When is it done? The trick here is not to undercook the pie. You want the batter to firm up completely. The pie is done when a knife or skewer inserted down into the pie at the center comes up with little to no loose *batter* sticking to it. (You will always see some blueberry juice smeared on the knife or skewer when you insert it.) After 1 hour, check your pie. If not done, keep returning to the oven for 5-minute intervals until the pie is fully baked. (Depending on your oven, it may take 5–15 extra minutes beyond the initial hour.) Remove from oven and cool on a rack for at least 30 minutes before cutting. Enjoy plain or with sweetened whipped cream or ice cream.

Pie Crust Tip #1—Store-Bought: When I have no time to make a homemade crust, I simply purchase a prebaked graham cracker pie shell from my local grocery. I know that sounds odd. Premade crusts are primarily used for unbaked cream or pudding pies, but they work very well in this recipe! As the blueberry batter bakes, it caramelizes the graham cracker crumbs in the prebaked shell, giving a wonderfully sweet, satisfyingly al dente texture to your final pie crust, a nice contrast with the soft, slightly tart filling. An important point to remember if you do this: before pouring the batter into your store-bought pie shell, set the shell, aluminum pan and all, into a standard, empty metal pie pan. This added sturdiness will make the pie much easier to handle as you transfer it to the oven and finally cut and serve the pie. Final note: the store-bought crusts come with the aluminum pan's edges folded down. Before baking the pie, be sure to *unfold* these edges, opening them up completely. This will make cutting the pie and removing the slices much easier!

Pie Crust Tip #2—Homemade: Press-in graham cracker (or cookie) crusts are very easy to make. If you have time for this extra step, see Clare's Cinnamon Graham Cracker Crust below.

CLARE'S CINNAMON GRAHAM CRACKER CRUST

Makes one 8- or 9-inch press-in pie crust

Nine 2½ × 5-inch square cinnamon-flavored graham crackers
½ cup butter, melted

Pulverize the graham crackers into crumbs using a food processor, blender, rolling pin, or another fun smashing device. This should give you about 1¼ cups of crumbs. Mix the crumbs with the melted butter. Press into an 8- or 9-inch pie pan.

For Clare's Blueberries 'N' Cream Coffee Cake Pie: Chill for 20 minutes before filling and baking. There's no need to pre-bake for my blueberry pie recipe—just chill and fill.

For no-bake pie recipes: If you'd like to use this crust recipe for a cream, pudding, or other no-bake pie recipe, then you will need to bake this crust before filling. Preheat oven to 350° F and bake for 8 to 10 minutes, depending on your oven. Do not over bake or it may turn out too hard!

Final Note: If you prefer regular graham crackers to the cinnamon-flavored variety, be sure to add 2 tablespoons of sugar to this recipe.

Joy's Mini Cake-Mix Biscotti

"Hey, Mom, I just added butter and eggs to a cake mix and made a kind of biscotti dough out of it. What do you think?" Joy came up

*with this one when she was twelve. Clare used it for one of her In
the Kitchen with Clare columns—and began to get a clue that her
daughter might have a future in the world of food.*

Makes 24 to 28 cookies

For Chocolate-Hazelnut Biscotti:

> *1 package chocolate cake mix*
> *3 large eggs, 1 separated*
> *8 tablespoons butter, melted*
> *1 cup all-purpose flour*
> *⅔ cup hazlenuts, toasted and chopped (see note)*
> *White or semisweet chocolate chips (for dipping), optional*

For Vanilla-Almond Biscotti:

> *1 package yellow cake mix*
> *3 large eggs, 1 separated*
> *8 tablespoons butter, melted*
> *1 cup all-purpose flour*
> *1 cup slivered almonds, toasted (see note)*
> *White or semisweet chocolate chips (for dipping), optional*

Step 1—Form the dough: Preheat the oven to 350° F. Line
a large baking sheet with parchment paper. Using an electric
mixer, blend the cake mix, 2 eggs and 1 egg yolk, butter, flour,
and nuts. When a dough forms, turn off the mixer. Using
your hands, form a dough ball in the bowl. Turn the ball onto
the lined baking sheet.Work the dough until smooth and
shape into two cylinders of about 1½ inches in diameter and
10-inches long. There should be a few inches of space on the
baking sheet between the two logs. (They will expand during
baking.) Now generously brush the top, sides, and ends of
each log with the egg white (no need to brush the bottom and
no need to use all of the egg white). This brushing will help
keep the baked log together when you slice it later.

Step 2—Bake and slice the logs: Bake for about 25–30 minutes. The dough logs are finished when they are cracking on the surface, fairly firm to the touch, and a toothpick inserted in the centers comes up clean. Remove the hot pan from the oven. The logs are very fragile at this point so do not move them or they will break apart. Simply cool them on the pan for 2 to 3 hours. The pan should be placed on a rack to allow air to circulate beneath the pan bottom. Note: If you try to cut the logs while they are still the least bit warm, you will see the cookies crumbling as you cut. This is heartbreaking! Let the logs cool completely before cutting. Using a sharp, serrated knife, cut the log into slices on the diagonal. Slices should be about ¾- to 1-inch thick.

Step 3—Biscotti means baked again: Lay the biscotti slices flat on a sheet pan and bake for 8–10 minutes on one side. Then turn them over carefully. Don't burn your fingers and don't allow cookies to break apart! Bake on the flip side for 6–8 minutes. (You are literally toasting the cookies to give them more flavor and make them harder.) Remove from the oven and allow to cool completely before handling or storing.

Step 4—Optional chocolate dip: If desired, melt a cup or two of white or semisweet chocolate chips. Dip the top edges of the cooled biscotti slices into the warm chocolate and set on wax paper. (Or dip half the cookie into the chocolate— your call.) Serve after chocolate has hardened. (For tips on melting chocolate, see Clare's Magnificent Melt-in-Your-Mouth Mocha Brownies recipe on page 342.)

How to Toast Nuts: Spread nuts in a single later on a cookie sheet and bake in a preheated 350° F for 8–10 minutes. Stir once or twice during toasting to prevent scorching.

Don't Miss the Next
Coffeehouse Mystery by Cleo Coyle

*Join Clare Cosi for a double shot of danger
in her next coffeehouse mystery!*

For more information about the
Coffeehouse Mysteries,
and what's next for Clare Cosi
and her baristas at the Village Blend,
visit Cleo Coyle's Web site at
www.CoffeehouseMystery.com